Lizzie's Surprise

Crossroads, Book 1

Lily Dobb

DEDICATION

For my Aunt Dot,
who taught me to love books and reading

ACKNOWLEDGMENTS

Thank you to the many writers and readers who nurtured me along the way. I would not be here without you. Special thanks go to my dear, inspiring friends Sandra Wright and Nicole Dean, who have been there since the beginning, and to my wonderful friend Theresa Gavin for her encouragement and support.

To my friends, I'm so thankful to have you in my life! The world needs more encouragers like Alison Davis, Donna Prettyman, and Renee LaVancha.

To my soul sisters, Lorraine Cohen, Terry Bruno, Sandra Lavini, and Brenda Anglin, thank you for nurturing me through this process! I am blessed to have you in my life. And to Jesse An Nichols George, thank you for helping me find Lily.

To my nieces, Nicole, Rebecca, and Sam, thank you for inspiring me to follow my dream!

And to my extraordinary creativity coach, Julie Belmont, I am deeply grateful for your guidance, support, and kindness. My book baby is ready to share because of you!

CHAPTER 1

Anna Elizabeth Kincaid's Ford squealed into the parking lot, and she quickly scanned the rows for an unoccupied space. As usual, she was running late and, as usual, the only available spot was at the far end of the lot. With a frustrated sigh, Lizzie pulled her ancient car into the spot and turned off the engine. The car let out an unhappy chug-chug-groan, but she didn't give it a second thought. She just grabbed her scuffed hobo bag from the passenger seat and half-jogged into the building.

Between roadwork and a minor fender-bender blocking traffic, her six-mile drive had taken a whopping forty-five minutes, so she found herself rushing into the building at eight-twenty-nine. She sighed heavily as the door whooshed shut behind her, waved at the receptionist, and hurried into the small kitchen off of the lobby. Late or not, she needed her morning dose of caffeine, and she hadn't had a drop yet.

"Sorry," she said, whispering an apology to Mother Nature as she grabbed a Styrofoam cup from the stack beside the coffee maker and filled it with fresh, steaming black coffee. She allowed herself just one brief, invigorating sniff and, head down, rushed out the door.

Lizzie saw the man's feet too late to alter her pace. She slammed into him full force, so hard it propelled her backward a step. Coffee splashed over the rim of the cup, scalding her hand and splattering on the crisp whiteness of the stranger's shirt.

"Damn," she mumbled. "Er … sorry about your shirt." She looked up at him, sheepishly smiling an apology for her clumsiness and found herself staring into one of the most arrestingly handsome faces she'd ever seen.

He was tall, about six-foot-two, lean and broad-shouldered. Thick, curly dark brown hair flopped boyishly on his forehead, framing his intense, deep brown eyes. "Sorry," she muttered again. She was uncomfortable around men she didn't know in general. This one, who bore a striking resemblance to her Hollywood crush, had her quaking in her red Converse sneakers.

He shrugged absently and glanced down at her rapidly reddening hand with concern. "It's only a bit of coffee," he said kindly. His voice was rich and sonorous and bore a delightful, sexy British accent. It was also achingly familiar.

She struggled to conceal her surprise as he dropped his briefcase on the floor with a thud and placed his fingers under her elbow, propelling her to the sink. "Let's have a look at that hand," he said as he took it gently in his own and turned on the faucet.

"I'm sure it's nothing." She let the cool water rain over her hand, grateful for the slight relief it was providing.

"It may smart for a bit," he said. "May I help you to your office?"

"No, thanks. I'll be okay. I'm sorry about your shirt. I'll pay to have it cleaned," Lizzie offered.

"Don't give it another thought." He tilted his head toward his briefcase. "When you travel as much as I, you learn to be prepared. I always have a spare shirt and tie at the ready." His phone beeped, and he frowned. "I'm late to a meeting. Good day, miss." He nodded his head and offered a dimpled smile as he turned to leave.

When he had gone, Lizzie steadied herself against the counter for a second, sucking in her breath. "Damn. Wrong again," she mused as she refilled her coffee cup and took the back way to her office.

Once inside, she turned on her computer and muttered an apology to her co-workers for being late. "Sorry. Traffic was awful. And then I spilled hot coffee all over my hand."

"Gonna be one of those days." Joanie shook her head, her bleached blond curls bobbing against her tanned cheeks. "Typical Friday."

Lizzie nodded, not listening, drumming her fingers as she booted her computer. She nibbled on an unpolished fingernail as she thought about the man in the kitchen.

The voice she had recognized instantly. She'd spoken with Colin D. Blake almost daily for the last month, and she *never* forgot a voice. Lizzie sighed softly as she remembered the very first time she'd heard 'the voice'.

It had been another typical Friday in the travel office, overwhelmingly busy, one phone call after another, with barely a few moments to catch her breath.

By four-fifty-five, she was stressed out and longing for the day to be over. She closed her eyes for a moment and rubbed her forehead, just between her eyes. As she finished up the last of her work, she stared at the phone, willing it, for once, not to ring for the next five minutes.

At four-fifty-seven, the phones were still silent. For once, it seemed, they would all get out on time.

Four-fifty-nine. Everyone started packing up for the weekend. Lizzie let out a deep sigh and waited impatiently for the clock to change to five o'clock.

And then it rang. Cursing quietly to herself, Lizzie touched her finger to the button. "Thank you for calling Corporate Travel, Anna speaking. How may I help you?" She hoped she sounded more enthusiastic and friendly than she felt.

"Colin Blake here. I've come on board in an advisory role and I've just learnt I've a meeting in Singapore first thing Monday morning, which means I must take the morning flight out of Heathrow …"

Lizzie sighed, sucking in her breath in frustration. International reservations were always more complex and more time-consuming than a simple domestic trip. With a frown, she waved sadly as her friends left for the weekend, leaving her alone in the office. 'Great … and I had to pick up the damn call,' she thought to herself. "And when will you be returning?" she asked, trying her best to sound cheerful.

"I shan't, at least not for several weeks. It's quite an involved itinerary," he said. She could hear the tap-tap-tap of his fingers on the desk beside the phone.

'Great,' Lizzie thought. 'And he can't even apologize for calling so late in the day?'

She forced a smile through her annoyance. "Let's get you as far as Singapore, and then we can figure out the rest next week."

"I really must get *everything* settled now," he insisted.

Lizzie took another deep breath. "Fine," she mumbled, trying desperately to stop herself from saying something that would only bite her in the ass. In the end, he'd kept her on the phone until well after seven. She'd been furious by the time she got home, calling him all sorts of names and wishing him only bumpy flights, center seats, and lumpy mattresses on his travels.

Over the next week he called every day to make some

change to his itinerary, his voice always insistent and more than a little impatient. And he always called at the end of the day. And, somehow, Lizzie always got the call.

At four-forty-five on Monday, Lizzie groaned when she recognized the international phone number on her phone. "I need to make some changes."

Lizzie winced, knowing it would be another late night. "Certainly, Mr. Blake," she said, careful to keep her annoyance out of her voice. "Just when you thought you had it all worked out, eh? I suppose change is inevitable."

"Always." His voice was gruff and devoid of even a hint of humor.

Lizzie rolled her eyes and shook her head slowly. Obviously, he wasn't interested in even the most basic conversation. "How can I help?" Once again, Lizzie waved goodbye as her co-workers deserted her and returned to her call. "Where do you need to go?"

"Bangkok on Wednesday, Perth on Friday, then back to Singapore for this bloody conference on Saturday."

It took every ounce of patience Lizzie possessed to make the changes. Colin Blake was terse, answering her questions with monosyllabic responses and, judging by the click of the keyboard in the background, he wasn't paying attention. She finished up the changes without her usual friendly chatter, pausing before ending the transaction to recap the entire itinerary. Twice, just to be sure he was listening. "Are we good to go?"

"Pardon?" he said absently as he yawned in her ear.

"Is everything correct before I complete the changes?"

"Er ... would you mind going through it again?"

Lizzie sucked in her breath, glancing at the clock on her screen. It was already five-thirty, and she had a lot to do before she was free to leave for the day. Without a word, she recapped the new schedule for the *third* time, slowly, to make sure he heard every syllable. "Is that correct?"

"Perfect."

"Alrighty, then. I'll finish it up and email it off to you. Have a good ..." She paused, too tired to mentally calculate the current time in Singapore.

"Day," he supplied.

"Right. Have a good day, Mr. Blake."

"Colin."

"Fine. Have a good day, Colin."

On Tuesday, he called at four-fifty to change three hotels and add another. An hour and four overseas phone calls later, Lizzie was just about to hang up when he mumbled, "bloody hell" under his breath.

"Everything okay?" Lizzie asked.

"More changes," he said, sighing heavily.

"Crap," Lizzie muttered without thinking. "Um ... what do we need to change now?"

"At the moment, I'm not inclined to change anything until these bloody morons get it sorted," he grumbled. He sounded so frustrated that Lizzie almost felt sorry for him. "Go ahead with the changes we've made. Most of what's come up now concerns the end of the trip. For the moment, I'm disposed to leave it as is."

"You could always email me when they get their act together," she said breezily. "For now, the hotels are good to go."

"Thank you, Anna." He sounded tired and more than a little irritated, but since it was the first time he'd thanked her, Lizzie couldn't help smiling. It almost made up for three straight days of overtime.

Almost. She wasn't quite ready to let him off the hook.

He called late again on Wednesday, blaming a weak Internet connection for not sending the promised email.

Thursday's call was even later, just a minute before five but Lizzie hadn't expected him to give her a break. Thankfully, it was quick and almost painless, and she left the office just twenty-five minutes past quitting time.

But by Friday, she'd had it. She watched as her friends all deserted her yet again. When they had gone, she took a deep, steadying breath, took the call off of hold, and said calmly and quietly, "can I make one small request, Colin?"

"What's that, Anna?" he sighed.

"Could you, maybe, *please*, not call so late in the day? I mean, I might not have *much* of a life, but I do enjoy my free time … and, well, I've been here an hour or more past quitting time almost every day for the last week." She bit her lip and held her breath, waiting for the inevitable blow-up.

"Oh God, I'm so sorry! I think I must have got the time zones confused. Please accept my apologies."

She smiled then. He sounded sincere and contrite, and she couldn't help suddenly liking the man, at least a little. "It's okay," she teased. "I'll give you the benefit of the doubt this time. But if it happens again, I'll have to hurt you. You have been kind of a pain in the ass, you know," she teased, hoping for the best.

He laughed softly. "God I needed that!"

"Needed what?" Lizzie asked, puzzled. She'd just told the man that he was a pain in the ass, and he was laughing at it. After everything he'd put her through in the last week, it was surprising, to say the least. She'd been almost positive that he had no sense of humor at all.

"Needed someone to put me in my place, I suppose. I'm so used to people letting me trample all over them that I've forgotten I'm not supposed to. Thank you, Anna!"

"Hey, no problem! Anytime you need putting in your

place you just give me a call."

He laughed again. "It's a deal. And … thanks for making me laugh. The past week has been quite insane. All business, no fun."

"Uh, oh … all work and no play makes Colin a *very* dull boy!" Lizzie shook her head, biting her lower lip as she said it. She never flirted, especially not with clients. "Crap," she muttered.

"Pardon me?" Colin asked, his tone suggesting that he was smiling into the phone.

"Sorry. I was just chastising myself for not behaving."

"Please don't behave on my account," he teased.

Lizzie grinned as she realized he was flirting back. "Are you giving me license to misbehave?"

"A little misbehavior isn't a bad thing," he assured her. "Or so I've been told."

"Tell that to my three uncles and cousin who are police officers!" she laughed. "That's not to say that I'm always a perfect angel, though. I just try my best not to get caught!"

Colin hooted, a deep belly laugh that made Lizzie giggle just as hard. "You truly are something, Anna," he said once he could speak again.

"Oh? And what's that?" she asked, still breathless from laughing. "What am I, Colin?"

"Wonderful," he murmured. "I think you're quite wonderful."

Over the next three weeks, they talked daily on the phone and by email. He had a dry sense of humor, and they developed a rapid-fire, playful banter that was, at times, silly, sarcastic and, surprisingly flirtatious. Lizzie knew that she'd found a dear friend in Colin Blake, but there were times when she allowed herself to wonder if, perhaps, they might be much more than friends.

She rarely allowed herself to daydream about her love life. Though she was a true romantic, she'd long given up on finding her soul mate. Romance had disappointed her, more than once, so she contented herself with romance novels and living vicariously through others.

Until now. Until Colin Blake.

His final stop before returning to London was two weeks in the Pennsylvania office. As his arrival neared, she became more and more nervous. She convinced herself that Colin was probably paunchy and balding. Previous experience had taught her that the voice and the face *never* matched.

Obviously, this time, she was wrong. A bit sadly, she turned back to her computer and lost herself in a barrage of phone calls, barely looking up until a soft voice behind her sent shivers up her spine.

"Pardon me, I …" He paused as Lizzie turned to face him. "Oh. How's your hand then?"

"Much better, thank you." She held it up; although it still stung, the redness had faded to a rosy pink.

"Could you tell me where Anna sits?" he asked.

She took a deep breath and glanced up at the nameplate on her desk, an apologetic smile on her face.

He grinned and took her hand in his. "*You're* Anna?"

"Guilty as charged," she nodded. "Anna Kincaid. It's nice to finally meet you, Colin."

"You knew? Back in the kitchen? You knew it was me?"

She nodded again. "I spend my entire day on the phone. I'm terrible with faces, but I never forget a voice."

"Why didn't you say something?"

"I guess I was nervous and a little … surprised."

"It's lovely to meet you, at last. We've spent a great deal of time together, you and I. The only other person I talk to so often is Tori."

"Tori?" Lizzie asked, trying to hide her disappointment, sure that Tori had to be either his wife or his girlfriend.

"My daughter."

"Oh." Too good to be true as usual. This one's married. "Your wife must hate how much you travel."

"My *ex*-wife was quite happy about it, I believe. It gave her more time to pursue her … er … other interests."

"Oh." Damn, she needed to stop with the monosyllabic responses. "So are you glad to be grounded for a couple of weeks?"

"God, yes. I've never been to this part of the States before. If only I could find some lovely, friendly person to show me around a bit." He smiled charmingly, dimples dancing in his cheeks.

Despite herself, Lizzie laughed. "I could hire you a car and driver," she offered. "I'm sure I can request a cute chauffeur although I'm not sure I've ever actually seen one."

"Er … that's not *quite* what I had in mind. Perhaps we could discuss it over lunch?" He'd promised her lunch weeks ago to make amends for his earlier behavior.

"I can't today; I'm completely swamped. Besides, I only get a half-hour." In truth, Lizzie was just a huge coward, afraid to be alone with him.

"Dinner, then?"

"Tonight?" she squeaked. "I … um … have plans," she lied. "Rain check?"

"I suppose that will have to do," he said sadly. "Any suggestions for what a weary, *friendless* traveler can do on a Friday night, all alone?"

Great, now he was playing on her sympathies. "It's supposed to rain tonight. There's a charming bar in your hotel …"

He grimaced. "God, the very thought is beyond depressing."

"Maybe a movie? There's a multiplex just down the road from your hotel." The phones started ringing incessantly again. Lizzie picked up a line and put the call on hold. "Duty calls. Talk to you later?" she asked with a smile.

He smiled back. "Of course."

When Lizzie finally got a break, she darted to the ladies room and locked herself in a stall. She desperately needed a few minutes of quiet to think about all that had happened and it was the only spot that offered peace and solitude.

Colin D. Blake was simply too good to be true. Handsome, funny, charming and, judging from the perfectly tailored suit and genuine Rolex on his wrist, filthy rich. What could he possibly have in common with a simple, middle-class American like her?

She left the stall and stood in front of the full-length mirror, critically assessing what she saw. She was a petite woman twenty pounds heavier than she should be. Her face was heart-shaped, with chubby cheeks, chocolate brown eyes and a determined chin. A tangle of shoulder-length light golden brown hair framed her face. She was … nothing special.

She was just an average-looking, working woman in her mid-thirties who had, so far, failed to find her Mr. Right. She worked at a mundane job that she frequently detested, and longed for the type of romance and adventure that she loved to read about. Lizzie to close friends and family, but known as Anna at work, she still hoped that, like her heroine Elizabeth Bennet, her Mr. Darcy was out there, somewhere.

Lizzie sighed at her stubborn romantic streak. Colin Blake could have any woman in the world, so what on earth could he possibly see in cute-but-dumpy Anna Elizabeth Kincaid. "And what would he think of that bunch of lunatics that you call your family? Face it. It's hopeless. He's champagne and caviar; you're pretzels and beer. Just let him take you to lunch one day next week and forget about him. Besides, there's no way on earth a man like that could ever be interested in you."

Three floors above, Colin pored through the stack of paperwork on his desk, unable to concentrate as his thoughts returned to the woman downstairs in the travel office.

He'd imagined her a hundred times in the last month, each rendering different than the last. Not that it had mattered. He'd been drawn to her from the first phone call, inventing reasons to call, hoping that she would be the one to answer, berating himself for developing a crush on a voice. It was completely out of character for a man who'd dated rarely and unenthusiastically since his marriage ended many years before.

She was pretty, with her shy smile, big brown eyes, and lush, womanly curves. Shyer in person than the funny, slightly sassy woman he'd met on the phone. It was an intriguing combination. He intended to get to know her better, no matter how many times she tried to wriggle away.

He was attracted to her. He hadn't been so powerfully attracted to a woman in years.

He had two weeks to figure out what that meant. Two weeks to discover if, perhaps, she felt the same way.

Colin sighed, idly twisting the signet ring that he wore on his pinky, tempted to call her and press for dinner. He picked up the phone and started to dial, but quickly cradled it. It wouldn't do to push.

He sighed again, forcing his mind back to the papers in his hand. "Work," he muttered to himself. "For now."

CHAPTER 2

Somehow, Lizzie made it through the rest of the day. She found time to update her two best friends, Meg and Jess, via email, but since they were out of town at a conference, she would have to wait for an evening of chocolate, wine, and sympathy.

For once, the phones died down early and, at five o'clock, she all but sprinted out the door and jumped in her car, intent on avoiding another chance meeting with Colin Blake.

Even so, on a whim she turned left at the traffic light instead of right, heading, God help her, in the direction of Colin's hotel. "Fool."

She forced herself to turn into the parking lot of the multiplex that she'd mentioned to Colin. 'What the heck,' she thought. 'He's not likely to come here anyway.'

Before she could change her mind, she purchased a ticket for a new romantic comedy, paid a small fortune for popcorn and a Coke and settled into the chilly, dark theater, choosing a seat in the middle of the row towards the back.

She glanced at her watch. It was still fifteen minutes to show time. She closed her eyes for a moment, trying to blink away some of the stress of the day. Her thoughts turned once again to the impossibility that was Colin Blake.

"Well, well. May I join you?" It was a voice Lizzie knew all too well.

She looked up, stunned to see the object of her thoughts towering above her, a warm, dimpled smile on his face. "Colin?"

"You did suggest a movie, did you not?"

"But this is a chick flick!" she protested.

"Ah, so I'm supposed to go next door to see how many cars James Bond can blow up this week?"

"Yes, something like that."

"So you object?"

"No, not exactly. It's just, well, most guys I know will barely let themselves be dragged kicking and screaming to a rom-com. And you're here voluntarily and … alone."

"I'm not gay if that's what you're implying." His tone was teasing, reassuring Lizzie that she hadn't offended him.

"Phew! That's a relief! I mean … I don't have a problem if you are but … yeah … " She glanced down at her feet, well aware that she'd all but admitted that she was attracted to him. "Er …"

His smile broadened. "May I join you?"

"Of course." As he settled himself into the seat beside hers, Lizzie noticed a box of Sno-caps peeking out of his jacket pocket. "Wanna make a deal?"

He grinned again, his dimples dancing as he chuckled. "What sort of deal?"

"Trade you some popcorn for some Sno-caps?"

"I don't know about that … I take my Sno-caps very seriously."

"Please?" she pleaded. "I *need* chocolate."

He rolled his eyes. "Fine," he huffed. He opened the box and shook several pieces of candy out into her palm.

She popped one into her mouth, savoring the taste of the semi-sweet chocolate and the crunch of the nonpareils. "I love chocolate," Lizzie sighed. "I just refuse to pay those ridiculous prices!"

He leaned over and whispered conspiratorially in her ear, "these are contraband Sno-caps. Smuggled 'em in. I nipped into one of your convenience stores on my way here."

Lizzie giggled and leaned back in her seat as the lights went down. They watched in companionable silence, laughing in most of the same spots. Their hands kept brushing as they reached for popcorn, sending shivers of excitement throughout Lizzie's body. She struggled to keep things in perspective, as her attraction for Colin Blake became more and more undeniable.

When the movie ended, Lizzie rubbed her eyes and cast a sideways glance at her companion. She expected he'd say a polite but hasty goodbye.

Once again, she was wrong.

"Have you eaten?" he asked, well aware that she hadn't.

She shook her head. "Nope. I came straight from work though I think you already knew that."

"Join me for dinner? Please? It's been so long since I've had dinner with someone … I mean … with a friend and I hate eating alone." He twisted his signet ring, his dark eyes filled with hope.

She should say no. Anything else was only setting herself up for heartache and pain. But she couldn't bring herself to say the word. "Okay," she agreed.

They settled on pizza, walking through the cold drizzle a little way down the strip mall to a tiny pizzeria.

Once they were seated, Lizzie toyed with the idea of ordering a salad to give the impression that she was dieting. But in the end, she decided that since there was no way in *hell* that Colin was interested in her as anything but a friend she could relax and be herself ... and eat pizza.

Colin was watching her as she took a bite. The cheese stretched and broke, slapping her gently on the chin. He laughed. "You're a bit of a mess, you know."

Lizzie nodded, laughing at herself as she dabbed her chin with a paper napkin. "Always. You can dress me up, but you can't take me out. I know I tried to put you off earlier, but ... Colin ... I'm glad we bumped into each other tonight ..."

He continued to stare at her, a slightly guilty grin on his face. "*What?*"

"I ... er ... have a confession to make," he said sheepishly.

"Confession?"

"Since you *refused* to keep me company, I decided I'd take your suggestion and see a film. Do you know I can't remember the last time I went to the cinema? When I arrived you were, I think, three people ahead of me in line. I ..." he grinned. "I overheard you say what movie you were going to see. I was aiming for the James Bond one, but when I got to the window, I asked for a ticket to your movie."

"Why?" she asked suspiciously.

Colin shrugged. "I wanted to spend some time with you."

"Why me? I'm not your type."

He cocked his head to one side, staring at her intently again. "My *type*? And what exactly would that be?"

"I'm guessing here, but I'd say tall, thin and sophisticated. Never a hair out of place. Wouldn't *dream* of having pizza and beer for dinner."

"You must think me quite shallow then," he murmured. "Or a dreadful snob."

"No, no, that's not it at all. I just … I picture you with someone well … more like you. I'm … pretty much the opposite of that."

"I *like* you."

"We have nothing in common."

"How the *hell* can you know that?"

"What kind of car do you drive?" Lizzie asked, her voice serious. She needed him to understand how different their worlds were.

He paused, looking as if he didn't want to answer. "A Jaguar," he admitted.

"I drive a Ford that's missing two hubcaps and has over a hundred thousand miles on her."

"So?"

"We're from different universes. I'm sure you'd find my life quaint and even amusing. But …" Even as she said it, Lizzie hated the way it sounded, but in her heart, she believed it was true.

"But you still think I'd eventually slink back to my kind?"

"Something like that."

"Why is it so difficult for you to believe that I like you. That I'm *attracted* to you. Over the last month, you've become my dearest friend in the world. You're sweet and funny and irreverent, and you make me laugh at myself. I've been looking forward to meeting you for weeks and now that I finally have I find you to be even more charming and lovely than I allowed myself to imagine."

Lizzie blushed hotly and melted completely. Fighting whatever it was between them suddenly seemed like an incredibly stupid idea. "I … I … so … so what happens now?"

Colin shrugged and took her hand in his, gently

massaging the back of it with his thumb. "I'm here for two weeks. We could … spend some time together and get to know one another." His dark brown eyes peered into hers pleadingly. "Please?"

"Alright," Lizzie whispered. "I … I'm not very good at this …"

"At what?"

She closed her eyes for a second, opening them to meet his. He was only touching her hand, but her heart was pounding, her pulse racing. She stroked the back of his hand with her fingers. "This."

"Ah. Me either."

"I'm not sure I believe you. I mean, look at you."

"You're a little bit mad, you know."

"Having second thoughts?" she challenged.

"Not a one. So … my lovely, mad, American … will you take pity on a weary traveler and show him some of your sights."

"See, now, when you put it like that, if I refuse I sound … inhospitable."

"And that would be bad?"

"Tragic. And … wrong … so, so wrong. Un-American, even. I guess … I guess I'll just have to agree to be … stuck with you."

"Careful what you say, Anna. I rather like the way that sounds."

Lizzie sighed and smiled softly. "Yeah," she breathed. "Me, too."

"Where the bloody hell have you been?" Colin's oldest friend, Court, growled into the phone.

Colin tossed the keys to his rental car on the nightstand and chuckled softly. "Cinema."

"Jesus, mate. Alone at the cinema on a Friday evening? When the hell are you going to learn to live a little?"

"Who says I was alone?"

"Humph. Let me think on that … your last date … and I use the term rather loosely since you barely made it through dinner … was more than three months ago. Lord knows how long it's been since you shagged someone."

"About a year," Colin admitted.

"Ah, yes. Sheila from Sheffield … and only because you were completely pissed. You lead a sad, sad life, my friend."

"Yes, well, not all of us are interested in the flavor of the week."

"It's a grand life," Court laughed. "Wouldn't kill you to make a bit more effort, you know."

"Perhaps I am."

"Right. You went to the cinema … on a Friday night. Alone."

"I wasn't alone." Colin tugged at his tie, pulling it loose and tossing it on the dresser. "I was with …" he paused, "a friend … or maybe more than a friend."

"How the … you've been there a day, mate …"

Colin sighed heavily and flopped down onto the bed. "Her name is Anna. She's been helping with my ever-changing travel plans for the last month. We … clicked."

Court snorted into the phone, and Colin knew he was probably rolling his eyes in frustration. "Define clicked."

"I reckon I drove her a bit … more than a bit … mad at first. I was … rude … I suppose."

"Ah, your usual charming self, then."

"Until she called me on it, yes. I like her. Quite a lot, in fact."

"Does she know how much you're worth?"

Colin frowned into the phone. Court was suspicious and slow to trust by nature, so the question wasn't a surprise, but he didn't have to like it. "She … she has an idea that I have money and, honestly, I think she's rather put off by it."

"Or so she claims. Listen, Col … you're only there for two weeks. Shag her if you must but don't make it into more than it is."

"Sometimes you're a complete arse," Colin mumbled. "I'm not interested in one of your patented limited-time-only relationships. I like her."

"You barely know her."

"We've chatted every day for a month. She makes me laugh, and she always says exactly what's on her mind, even if it means telling me I've been a pain in the arse. I want to know more about her. I want to know *everything* about her."

"Jesus. You need to get the woman in bed and get her out of your system."

"I don't want to."

"You don't want to get her into bed?"

"Well, no, *that* I do want," Colin admitted. "But I don't want to get her out of my system. I want … more."

"What the bloody hell does that mean?" Court muttered.

"I'm not sure. But I intend to figure it out."

"Don't do anything … stupid," Court said, his tone so carefully controlled that Colin knew he was biting his tongue.

"Define stupid."

"Don't …"

"Don't what, mate?" Colin prompted. Court didn't believe in love and romance, and Colin couldn't resist making him say the words.

"Don't … fall …" he gulped into the phone. "Don't fall in love."

"Ah, that. Concerned it will end up in heartbreak and misery? Or worse?"

"Jesus, Col, what could be worse than heartbreak and misery?"

"To you?" Colin chuckled, a smile spreading slowly

across his face. "An honest, real relationship that leads to … hmm … marriage, babies … the lot."

"A life sentence."

"Exactly," Colin said, smiling as he thought of Anna Kincaid's big brown eyes and shy smile, and imagined a lifetime of them. "A life sentence."

Lizzie rolled over and pounded on the pillow. Though she'd spent two hours cleaning until every surface in her apartment gleamed, and another hour putting away three weeks worth of clean laundry, after her unexpected evening with Colin D. Blake, sleep was impossible. She rolled from the bed, disturbing the two cats nestled against her, and switched on the light. Hugs gave her an icy stare and moved to the foot of the bed to curl up in a tight ball. Kisses butted his head against her hand, apparently hoping that a sleepless night might lead to some tasty treats.

"Sorry, boys," she yawned. "I know how you hate it when you don't get the full twenty-three hours of sleep you need in a day." She shoved her feet into her favorite zebra-striped slippers and padded to the kitchen.

She pulled open the refrigerator door to find the usual: one container of leftovers from her Mom, day-old Chinese take-out, a questionable-looking slice of pizza from God-knows-when, a carton of milk and, thanks be to God, a half-full bottle of chardonnay. "Hello, my lovely," she said as she cradled the bottle between her hands. "Perfect." She closed the fridge and set the chilled bottle on the chipped Formica countertop.

Balancing on her toes, she grabbed a wine glass from the cabinet and, frowning at the dusty surface, rinsed it quickly before filling it three-quarters full. She took a sip, savoring the tangy sweetness on her tongue, and lifted her glass. "To the craziest, most amazing day ever!" She took another long, satisfying sip and headed into the living room.

She set her wine glass on a corner of her computer desk and drummed her fingers on the faux-wood surface while she waited for the ancient computer to boot. It emitted a long, low whirring sound before the light began to flicker. "I'll bet Colin has a top-of-the-line laptop that jumps at his command," she mumbled. "Probably even does tricks."

She glanced around the living room. Her sofa, bought at a going-out-of-business sale, was a cheerful blue chintz, but there were claw marks from her naughty cats on the corners. The marble-topped end table was a yard sale find, and the three tall, heavily laden bookshelves were of the build-it-yourself, not-quite-wood variety. Still, the room was cozy and comfortable. She just couldn't quite picture Colin D. Blake, in his crisply tailored suit and Rolex watch there. It made her more than a little depressed.

A few more sips of wine and the antique cuckoo clock, a gift from an old neighbor, chirped two a.m. The computer whirred a little more, finally blinking to life with a ding. She quickly typed in her password and opened up her email, drumming her fingers on the desk again while two days worth of emails filtered into her inbox.

She managed a smile when she saw the name she wanted at the top of her list with the subject: *RE: Holy crap!* Sighing with relief, she double-clicked the email to open it.

Darl!

So the famous Colin Blake has finally arrived? Hot damn! Why the hell did Jess and I get dragged to this conference when our girl needs us? Oh, right, Jess has pointed out that we didn't get a choice.

So let's see ... not only does he have a voice that

makes you melt, but he's also a bona fide hunk who just happens to be a dead ringer for your favorite movie star. And you're COMPLAINING about this? WTF? If I were you, I'd drag him into the nearest empty office for a good long snog next time instead of pouring hot coffee all over the poor lad. I suspect you might BOTH enjoy it!

What have you decided? Are you going to be a coward and give him the brush off? Word to the wise, if you do, I will feed you to the sharks. (Jess says to tell you I'm not kidding as I'm wearing my patented evil empress of the universe grin. She's not wrong.) What's the worst that could happen?

Keep us posted. We'll be on booth duty most days and doing the forced socializing in the evenings (insert annoyed eye roll and fake smile here), but you know we're here for you, right?

Deep breath, girleen. You can do this, whatever it is that this might be.

Cuddles

Meg and Jess

Lizzie was grinning by the time she was done reading, grateful to have such good friends on her side. She clicked reply and began typing.

God, I love you girls! I'm still annoyed as hell that you're not around in my hour of need but, yeah, I know, it wasn't your choice. Besides, who knew that, for the first time ever, the guy with the sexy voice would turn out to be better than I could've imagined. (Big sigh, girls, big sigh.)

After the fiasco with the coffee, my day just got stranger and stranger. First he turns up in my office and forces me to 'fess up that the chick that spilled coffee all over him and his 'friend' Anna Kincaid are one and the same. I think he was a little hurt that I didn't say something right away, but I was freaking out at the time! (And injured, don't forget injured.)

Anyway, he wanted to take me to lunch, but I blew him off. Then he asked me to play tour guide and I offered to hire him a car and driver. And my pièce de résistance? He asked what a lonely traveler could do on a Friday night, and I suggested A. the hotel bar and B. a movie. He took it well, though, taking my hint to leave me alone.

Or so I thought.

I was too keyed up to go home. I mean, I love my boys but sitting home alone with two cats when I could've been hanging out with a guy who knocks my socks off was a less-than-appealing option. I decided on a movie. I wasn't the only one. (Yeah, I know, I did suggest it but, c'mon, I never thought a guy like that would go to the movies, alone!) It was ... dare I say it? the most magical evening I've had in ... yeah, ever.

He's lovely. Sweet, funny, a little shy beneath the surface. He makes me nervous, and he scares me to death, mostly because he's from such a different world, you know? He's the kind of man who thinks nothing of ordering a bottle of Dom, and I'm lucky if I can scrape together enough ones for a brew down at Flannigan's.

So when he said he wanted to spend the two weeks he's in town with me, I was going to say no. I mean, what else could I say? It's got disaster and heartbreak written all over it and ...

God help me, girls, I said yes! We're heading into the city tomorrow for the standard sightseeing and then ... who knows? I know, I know, I don't like open-ended questions. But here I go.

Wish me luck? I have no clue what I'm getting myself into. I'm terrified. But I'm also really excited. I like him, girls. Probably more than I should at this point, but I'm not sure I have a choice.

So have wine at the ready when you get home, just in case. I'll keep you posted.

CHAPTER 3

Colin pressed the buzzer by the door of the converted brick row house and took a step back, rocking on the heels of his tasseled loafers. He'd dressed casually in jeans and a golf shirt, but he suspected Anna would still consider him overdressed.

He heard a door slam, followed by the jingle of keys and the pounding of feet on the stairs. The heavy oak door swung open.

She'd paired a loose Phillies T-shirt with a pair of denim Capri pants and well-worn sneakers. In her hands, she held a canvas backpack with a baseball cap dangling from one of the straps. Her hair was pulled up into a high ponytail, swinging enticingly against her neck as she smiled at him. "You're shockingly prompt."

"Is that a bad thing?" He grinned at her, tempted to haul her into his arms and kiss her. Instead, he shoved his hands deep into his pockets. "Good morning."

"Morning." She raked her eyes up and down his body.

"Do I pass inspection?" he asked with a dimpled grin.

"Not too bad ... but ..." She glanced down at his

shoes and frowned. "Those won't work at all. Your feet will be aching in no time, and we've got a lot of city to cover. No sneakers?"

"Er … I left my trainers in … honestly, I don't quite recall where I left them. Tokyo? Bangkok?"

"It was the trip from hell," she laughed.

"Perhaps," he said. "Or not. The trip was arduous at best but … I rather like where I am right now. If the traveling was hell, what I've found at the end is …"

"Are you about to compare me to the pot of gold at the end of the rainbow?" she quipped.

Colin ignored her joke and searched her eyes. "What I've found at the end is pure heaven."

"Damn, you're good," she sighed. "What were we talking about again?"

"Trainers. Left God knows where and still missing." He wiggled a foot. "These are the most casual shoes I have at present."

"Then there's only one solution."

He gazed down at her expectantly. "And what's that, Ms. Kincaid."

"Wal-Mart. Before I show off the Cradle of Liberty, I think we need to visit America's Mecca for cost-conscious consumers. It can be … well, let's just call it educational … you never know what you might see."

"Sounds intriguing."

"Huh. So the oh-so-urbane Colin D. Blake is going to willingly follow me around while I show him the wonder-of-wonders that is Wal-Mart. You're a brave man."

"Perhaps. But there's something you should know, my lovely Ms. Kincaid."

"Yeah? And what might that be?"

"I'm quite certain … almost positive, in fact … that I'd follow you anywhere."

She shot him a quizzical look as she brushed past

him, only to pause on the second porch step, her ponytail tickling her neck as she whirled to face him. "Why?"

Colin peered down at her, smiling broadly. It was an impossible question to answer, but he knew she was waiting for some sort of response. "Because I want to."

"Ah. And you're *quite* used to getting what you want, aren't you."

"It's true; I nearly always get what I want. And I want to spend time with you whether we're wandering the aisles of Wal-Mart or exploring the wonders of Philadelphia. I like you, Anna Kincaid. I find you completely and utterly adorable and …" he felt his face color.

"And?" she prompted, looking him squarely in the eyes. "You like me. I'm adorable. And … what?"

"And you have the most luscious bum …"

It was her turn to blush, a rather fetching shade of rosy pink. "I … you … I don't …"

"Do so."

"Don't. It's, you know, too much junk in the trunk."

Colin's eyes dropped lazily to her curvy bottom. He moved down the steps to stand on the pavement in front of her and shook his head slowly. "Listen carefully, my dear *friend*, because this is an argument that you won't win." He leaned in closely, his lips brushing her ear. "You are lovely and you have the most enticing curves … *especially* your perfect derriere. So stop arguing and let me just … appreciate the view."

"I … well … if that's how you feel," she breathed. "Follow at will."

They spent the day exploring Philadelphia. Lizzie proudly showed off all the places where her Yanks stood up to his oppressive Brits. He laughed at her idea of history, informing her that his family home was at least two hundred years older than anything she could show him.

"Not much I can say to that. But older doesn't necessarily mean better, you know. And we did win the war," she said, grinning up at him as they stood in front of the Liberty Bell.

"We let you win," he teased. "It was all part of our master plan, you know."

"Ah. See, somehow I never pegged you as delusional. An annoying pain in the ass, yes. But I was still under the assumption that you hadn't completely lost your marbles."

"Humph. I can't possibly be crazy, you know." He took her hand and tugged her out of the Liberty Bell Pavilion onto the grassy mall in front of Independence Hall. "I can prove it."

"Can you?" Lizzie laughed softly, liking the feel of his large, warm hand covering hers. "What's your proof?"

"You." He tucked a strand of hair that had escaped from her ponytail behind her ear. "You're much too intelligent to waste your time on a raving lunatic. Since you clearly adore me, I can't possibly be mad."

"I ... you ..." Lizzie blushed hotly and punched him in the arm. "You may be sane ... the jury's still out ... but you're *still* a pain in the ass."

"And you still say exactly what you're thinking," he chuckled. "It's ..."

"Annoying?"

"Charming," he corrected. "Completely and utterly charming."

Lizzie blushed again, fighting the urge to throw herself into his arms and kiss him senseless. "So, are you ready to try Philly's finest gourmet treat?"

Colin grinned at her, his dimples dancing in his cheeks. "Changing the subject?"

"Avoiding the subject," she confessed.

"For now," he amended. "You can't avoid the subject forever. Now, I do believe you mentioned food ... so lead on, my lovely Yank."

Still holding hands, they walked through the city to Pat's Steaks in South Philly, where they gorged themselves on delicious, high-fat cheese steaks. "I'll bet you don't get these back home."

"Not a chance. English food in general leaves a lot to be desired." He took another bite and, after a moan of pure pleasure, wiped a dribble of cheese from his chin. "I may have to import these."

"Or maybe spend a little more time in the City of Brotherly Love?" she asked hopefully.

"Only a little?"

"I don't want to be pushy. A *lot* more time?"

"Perhaps ... Anna, I ..."

"What?"

"Nothing. I ... today was wonderful. It's been a very long time since I played tourist anywhere and ..." he stopped when she squealed and bolted from the table to launch herself at a tall, blond man in a police uniform. "Bloody hell."

A moment later she was tugging the officer to their table by his wrist. Though she certainly seemed fond of the man, he didn't sense anything romantic between the pair. "Found a friend?"

"Better! Colin Blake, meet my favorite cousin, Darius Kincaid."

"She says that about all of her cousins," he said, reaching out to shake Colin's hand. "Dare."

"He's a cop," Lizzie said. "Sorry, I guess that was pretty obvious from the uniform and the gun, huh?"

"So what brings you to the city? It's not really your thing."

"Dare's trying his best not to call me a country bumpkin," she laughed. "But I don't find that offensive at all. I like being near the big city for culture …"

"Meaning baseball," Dare told Colin in an aside.

"Hey! You love the Phils too, so shut your pie hole, officer. Colin here is … well … a client but …"

"We've become great friends over the last several weeks. Your cousin has been kind enough to show me around."

"Friends?" Dare said. His eyebrows shot up in disbelief. "That your story, too, Cuz?"

"Yep. Just showing a friend the sights."

"Just … be careful."

"I'm always careful. Besides, I had a great self-defense teacher."

Dare smiled proudly at his cousin. "And you were an excellent student. This one," he jabbed his finger at her, "can even flip me."

"I'm impressed," Colin said. Dare Kincaid was tall and muscular and had more than a foot on Lizzie. "Though I'm not surprised. I've already learnt that your cousin is … extraordinary."

"Mind that you don't forget it," he said gruffly while the radio on his belt squawked. "That'll be my partner." He kissed Lizzie on the cheek and shook Colin's hand once again. "Be good, kids."

When he was gone, Lizzie gathered up the remains of their lunch and tossed it in the can. "I know he's six-four, but I worry about him. Being a cop down here … it's not the same as out in the 'burbs. The criminals are better armed than the cops."

"He's a grown man and a trained police officer."

"I know, but he's still my baby cousin inside that overgrown physique."

"It's natural to want to protect the ones we love, even when they're old enough to take care of themselves. I think … it shows that you have strength and courage and …"

"You really do see all of that in me," she sighed. "Honestly, I wasn't sure I believed what you were saying before. Not to flatter myself, but I guess I thought you were saying some of those things to ... get me into bed."

"You give me far too much credit. To be perfectly honest, I'm rather hopeless at all of this. My friend, Court, he's the smooth talker. He'd have had you in his bed three minutes after the film ended last night, if not sooner. I've never been the sort of man who jumps from bed to bed without a care, and I don't intend on leaping into bed with you."

"You don't? But ..." She bit her lip, thoroughly confused. "You said you were attracted to me."

"I am. But I get the feeling that you're not exactly the sort of woman to have mind-blowing sex with a man she only just met."

"Well no, but ... mind-blowing?" She blinked up at him.

"Of *that*, I have no doubt. But ..."

"But you don't want to have mind-blowing sex with me?"

He laid one hand on her shoulder and tipped up her chin with his other. "Oh, I do. Very much so, but ... knowing who you are and being who I am, I ... I won't rush you into bed. Not until ..."

"Until what?" she whispered. "Help me out here."

"Until we figure out just what we're doing and where we're going. Or am I wrong? Should we head back to my hotel and see what happens?"

"Honestly? There's a part of me ... the part that can't quite breathe when you look at me ... who wants to do exactly that. But that would only complicate things, wouldn't it? I mean, it's already complicated, considering that you live in England and, I live here and ... " She smiled up at him. "You're a remarkable man,

Colin Blake. And you already understand me so well. I
… yes, you're right. A quick roll in the hay would
probably be spectacular but, it's not really who we are."

"So we're agreed? Until we sort things out, no sex."

"Not even kissing?"

Colin let out a heavy sigh and pressed a kiss to her
forehead. "I think … we'll have to take that as it comes
but … Anna?"

"Yes, Colin?"

"I'm almost positive that once I start kissing you I
won't be able to stop."

"Me too," she breathed. "So probably no kissing
either. At least we have this." She linked her fingers
through his and gave his hand a firm but gentle squeeze.
"We can hold each other's hand."

Colin squeezed back, the pad of his thumb brushing
softly across the back of her hand. "Your hands are small
and soft and yet … it's a perfect fit.

So they held hands as they wandered through the city,
a simple, gentle touch that, though it wasn't quite what
either one desired, seemed to be exactly what both
needed.

At least for now.

Colin gazed at her profile as she drove home,
memorizing the straight little nose and prettily bowed
lips. Not that there was a chance he would forget a single
detail of her face. After just over twenty-four hours, he
already knew that, for him, Anna Kincaid was
unforgettable. "Have dinner with me tonight?"

She gave him a sideways glance, careful to keep her
eyes on the busy Schuylkill Expressway. "I assumed that
was a given. We could grab something on the way or
…"

He shook his head. "A proper date."

"You're going to make me get dressed up, aren't

you?"

"You spent the entire day playing tour guide. Let me spoil you."

"I'm not used to being spoiled."

"I realize that. Which means it's long past time for someone ... me, that is ... to treat you like a princess."

"I gave up on expecting the princess treatment years ago," she sighed.

"Please?" he asked sweetly. "A proper date to the best restaurant in town ... wherever you'd go for a big celebration."

"That'd be the Sixpence Inn though I've only eaten there a handful of times. They have a Crème Brule that's divine. It's probably booked, though ..."

Colin whipped out his smartphone and searched for the restaurant and, after using every bit of his charm and business savvy, secured a table for two at eight o'clock. "They had a last minute cancellation."

"Liar. You must be some kind of shark in the business world if you can get people to do your bidding so easily."

"It's a useful enough talent," he smirked. "Pick you up at seven-thirty?"

"Make it seven. They have a great bar." She glanced over and grinned at him. "Or are you one of those guys who takes forever to get ready?"

"Definitely not me, love. I'll be there at seven ... if not before."

"Careful, Colin. Talk like that could turn a girl's head."

"Excellent," he nodded. "All part of my master plan."

Unfortunately, Lizzie had forgotten that she already *had* plans. Her three nieces arrived just minutes before Colin was due to pick her up. She'd promised to baby-sit while her brother and sister-in-law reconnected with an old college friend, but it had completely slipped her mind.

"Aren't you a little overdressed for babysitting?" her sister-in-law, Lisa, asked, eyeing her silky peach-colored dress and strappy gold sandals.

"Crap," Lizzie muttered. "I completely forgot. I ... well ... I have a date ..."

Lisa's eyebrows shot up in surprise. "You? Wow. How'd that happen?"

Lizzie narrowed her eyes at her sister-in-law, who loved to needle her about being single. "Let's see. I met a guy. He asked me out. It's not that complicated, really." She turned to her brother. "I'll figure something out. I know you haven't seen Ben in over a year and ..." The doorbell buzzed. "That'll be him."

She pulled open the door and offered Colin an apologetic smile. "I seem to be suffering from some short-term memory loss. Colin Blake, meet by brother, Pete, his wife, Lisa, and my gorgeous nieces, Dani, Rachel, and Sabrina."

"Pleasure." Colin shook Pete's hand, gave Lisa one of his dimpled grins and, to their delight, kissed each girl's hand in turn. Dani giggled loudly. Rachel offered him a shy smile. And nine-month-old Sabrina gurgled and clapped her chubby hands. "So ..."

"Awkward family moment?" Lizzie said, smiling hopefully. "I'm sorry. I guess dinner's out."

Colin grinned and surprised her yet again. "Let's see. My choices are as follows: go back to my lonely hotel room and order room service or have dinner with *four* lovely ladies. I'd be a fool if I didn't opt for the latter." He grinned down at the two older girls. "Pizza or Chinese?"

Lizzie looked down at nine-year-old Danielle and five-year-old Rachel. "Would you girls mind if my friend Colin joins us?"

"Sure," Dani shrugged.

Rachel regarded Colin for a moment, her head cocked to one side. She was the shyer of the pair. "Okay," she agreed.

Colin smiled at the girls as Lizzie took baby Sabrina from her brother, Pete. "Is that okay with you guys," asked Lizzie.

"I don't see why not." With that, they left, and Lizzie, Colin, and the girls climbed the stairs to her second-floor apartment.

She was grateful that, thanks to her nervous excitement and insomnia the night before, her apartment was spotlessly clean. She pushed open the door and caught a quick glimpse of her cats before they bolted to hide under the bed for the evening. She glanced over her shoulder at Colin. "Not sure if you saw my two blurry balls of fur before they took off. They're a little shy."

"I think I may have caught their clouds of dust," he joked, glancing around the room. "Cozy."

"Thanks. It's a great old building though it could use a little TLC."

"Wow, Aunt Lizzie, it's so clean!" Rachel exclaimed.

"I'm sure it won't be for long. It never is when you girls are here." Lizzie was about to hand Sabrina to Dani so that she could set up the portable playpen that Colin had lugged up the stairs, only to find that he had already done it.

"I'm impressed!" she said as she set the baby in the playpen. Sabrina promptly fell back onto her diapered bottom and gurgled happily up at them.

"I'm not exactly a novice."

"I keep forgetting that you have a daughter. Do you have a picture? Of course you do, she's your daughter, after all, and … I'm babbling."

Colin chuckled as he pulled out his wallet and retrieved a dog-eared photo of a pretty young teenager with his dark hair and dimples. "She's thirteen going on twenty-one."

"She looks just like you. It must be tough being away so much."

"It is. But she's away at school most of the time. I wish things were different. It's not how I planned to raise my child." He suddenly seemed somber and a little lost.

Impulsively Lizzie gave him a quick hug. "I'm sure she knows you love her."

"That she does," he said with a smile. "She's quite a young lady. Now, may I ask you a question?"

"Of course," said Lizzie.

"I know you as Anna, but this lot keeps calling you Lizzie."

"Oh, that. I've always been Lizzie to family and the people I grew up with, but when I started my job, there was already an Elizabeth and a Liz. To avoid confusion, they asked me to go by Anna."

"Which do you prefer?"

"Either works for me," Lizzie shrugged. "I answer to both."

"I suppose I'll have to work out which one feels right for me, then," he said. "Either way, Anna Elizabeth, I'm not going anywhere."

"He talks funny," Rachel said matter-of-factly, "but I like him anyways."

"Glad you approve, missy," Lizzie teased. "I'm afraid you'll be subjected to any number of Disney movies tonight," she told Colin apologetically.

"It's really quite alright, I don't mind at all. I'm happy to spend time with you, no matter what we do. But make no mistake, we will have a real date." With that, he took off his jacket, laid it across a chair, and loosened his tie. "You look lovely."

Lizzie glanced down at her dress, bought for a

wedding the month before, and gave a little twirl. "It was nice to get dressed up, even if it was only for a few minutes. Colin, I really am sorry for the mix-up …"

"It's perfectly fine and, somehow, exactly as it should be."

"Alrighty then." Reassured, she took everyone's order for Chinese food and phoned it in. "They'll be here in twenty minutes, so I'll just go and change."

Later, when the girls were engrossed in their movie and Sabrina napped in her playpen, Lizzie turned to Colin and grinned. "I'll never live this down you know. By tomorrow, my entire family will know all about you. They'll tease me about it for years to come."

"I think perhaps they'd best get used to the idea," he murmured. Somehow his hand had found its way to the nape of her neck and tangled in her hair. His eyes settled on her lips almost hungrily, then flickered back up to meet hers. "Anna Elizabeth," he whispered as his lips moved toward hers.

"Waaaaa."

"Damn," he swore softly. "I'll go." He crossed the room and plucked the crying baby from the playpen. "There now, love, you're alright. Uncle Colin's got you," he crooned as he carried her back to the sofa. "I think she's a bit wet."

"I'll take her."

"No, let me. It's been a while, but I think I can still remember how to change a nappy." Lizzie smiled and grabbed the changing pad and a diaper from the diaper bag and laid them on the sofa.

"All yours," she said, leaning back to watch. Somehow during the evening, Colin had morphed from formal and sophisticated to casual and very rumpled. His jacket and tie were gone, his shirt unbuttoned at the throat, the sleeves rolled up. He looked adorable and incredibly sexy.

He caught her watching him and smiled a dimpled grin that made her heart race. "All done," he said. He cuddled the baby to his chest and she nuzzled her face into his neck.

Lizzie sighed, longing to do the same. Instead she curled her body against his and laid her head on his shoulder.

Colin shifted his weight, his free arm curling around her shoulders, his hand on her hip. "Alright, then?"

Lizzie pulled her head back and smiled up at him, nodding. "Perfect. You?"

His arm tightened around her body, nestling her even more closely against him. He found her hand, linking their fingers, and rested his cheek against the crown of her head. "Perfect."

CHAPTER 4

Lizzie woke to the blare of trumpets somewhere near her right ear. Groaning, she rolled over to find the screen of her cell phone flashing as *Rule Britannia* continued to ring out. "What the …" She grabbed the phone and pressed answer. "I never pegged you for a sneak."

"Good morning to you, too, Anna Elizabeth," Colin chuckled. "Nothing like a patriotic anthem to start off the day."

"Trumpets, Colin?"

"Invigorating, aren't they?"

"And loud. Oh-so-very loud. So let me get this straight, you downloaded a ringtone and set it as yours, *and* you turned the volume all the way up?"

"Rachel made me do it."

"Humph. Well she is the sneaky one of the bunch, I'll give you that, but somehow I think this was all your idea."

"Guilty as charged," he laughed. "She was playing with your phone and told me that they like to change your settings to surprise you … it seemed like a good idea at the time."

"It's ..." Lizzie bit back a smile. True the trumpets were loud and ... trumpet-y, but there was something endearing about the playful prank. "I'm going to regret admitting this but ... it's charming and very sweet and ... you're a little bit crazy which I find very appealing. So ..." she squinted at the screen. "Why are you calling at the crack of dawn on a Sunday morning?"

"We have plans."

"At ten. It's barely seven-thirty."

"I ... but ten seems a dreadfully long way off."

"Right. You are *not* a patient man. That much I haven't forgotten."

"So ... name your poison?"

"Huh?"

"Coffee. I do recall that you drink it when you're not pouring it all over unsuspecting men."

"Humph. That was an accident, and you know it."

"Best coffee I've had in years. I believe that particular cup was pure, unadulterated black coffee. Is that your usual?"

"Most days, though I'll add some cream when I'm feeling a little naughty. And when I want the good stuff it has to be a skim milk latte with just a dash of vanilla, one packet of sugar-in-the-raw and two shakes of nutmeg on top. Bonus points if it's from my favorite coffee house downtown."

Colin laughed softly. "It wouldn't be called 'The Daily Jolt' would it?"

"Um ... yeah, but ... oh, man. You're there, aren't you? Right this second?"

"I needed coffee."

"Your hotel has a complimentary breakfast buffet, even on the weekends."

"They make a lousy cup of coffee."

"Right. Which meant you had to drive fifteen minutes to my sleepy little town, instead of hitting the convenience store just down the street from you, which *happens* to have fabulous coffee."

"I didn't want to wait until ten."

"Yeah, I figured that out already. So, you're about three blocks from my apartment, which means you'll be here in what? Fifteen minutes, after you wait for the coffee?"

"Er …"

"Damn it, Colin! I was still sleeping, and I haven't showered and … God … the idea that you simply can't wait a couple more hours is just … too damned sweet."

"So I can come over now?"

"Fifteen minutes. No less, buddy, or you are in *big* trouble."

Thirteen minutes and thirty seconds later, Colin leaned against the wrought iron railing to wait out the remaining ninety seconds until he could ring the buzzer.

She'd sounded so adorably sleepy when she answered the phone, her voice still low and raspy. He could picture her, her hair tangled about her face and her eyes only half-opened. He couldn't help hoping that the day would come, soon, when he'd wake up to her face beside his on the pillows.

But she wasn't ready for that. Neither was he. He glanced at his Rolex, watching the seconds tick by, determined to ring the buzzer at the promised fifteen minutes and not even a nanosecond earlier.

Finally, at fifteen minutes and one second, he retrieved the paper cup carrier and a bag of pastries from the small bench by the door and rang the buzzer. He heard the upstairs door open and shut almost immediately, followed by the pad of her feet on the wooden stairs.

"Seven-forty-five on a Sunday morning? Really?"

"Sorry?" he offered though he wasn't sorry in the

least. Her damp hair was loose about her shoulders, the ends just beginning to curl towards her face. She was adorable, from the chipped nail polish on her naked toes to the soft pink sweater that hugged her body, to her bright smile and rosy cheeks. "Good morning, beautiful," he said, unable to resist the urge to brush a soft kiss against her cheek. "You look lovely."

"You keep talking like that, and I may start believing you!" She stood on tiptoe to kiss the corner of his mouth. "Trumpets aside, I'm glad you're here." She turned and headed back up the stairs with Colin close at her heels.

But once inside she frowned at him, ignoring the latte that he held out. "On second thought, maybe we should get some fresh air."

"It's starting to rain," he informed her.

"I like the rain and ... well ..."

"What?"

"I don't have three cute little distractions here this morning and ..." she pointed at the open door to her bedroom. "I'm barely awake, and my bed's not made and since you woke me from a rather steamy dream ... *here* may not be the safest place at the moment."

"Meaning?" He understood what she meant, of course; he just wanted to hear her say it.

"Meaning, I'd like nothing more than to leave the coffee and pastries for later while I drag you to my bed and have my way with you. You are ..." she smiled up at him, blushing a fetching shade of pink. "You're dangerous at the moment. We could walk to the park and sit in the gazebo ..."

Colin tilted her chin up and smiled down into her chocolate brown eyes. He cocked his head towards the unmade bed. "Or perhaps *I'm* the one in danger," he teased, brushing a fluttery kiss against her mouth. "Let's have that walk in the rain."

Lizzie didn't hesitate. She thrust her feet into a pair of worn flip-flops beside the front door and grabbed an umbrella from its perch on the coat rack. "Just in case."

Colin eyed the oversized, rainbow-striped golf umbrella with a dubious grin. "In case of what? We come across a large family in need of shelter from a hurricane?"

"Scoff if you must," she huffed, "but this baby works!"

"I don't doubt it, as it's large enough for its own postal code. And such an understated design."

"You can be such a brat!" she laughed as she tugged him out the door and locked it behind them. "Make fun all you like, but if the skies open up, I have no doubt you'll be cozying up underneath it."

"Lizzie, love, I reckon I'll be cozying up whether the skies open up or not." He shot her a playful, dimpled smile and darted down the stairs to open the front door with a flourish. "Shall we?"

His hand captured hers, clasping it tightly as they walked.

"So ... you're going with Lizzie?"

"It suits you since you quite remind me of another Lizzie, one that I'm quite fond of."

"It had better not be an old girlfriend."

"A *very* old girlfriend," he chuckled. "Judging from your overstuffed bookcases, you're fond of reading."

"Have been since the moment I first opened a book," she sighed. "The whole world seems closer when you can dive inside the pages of a book, you know?"

"That I do."

"Hmm. Let me guess ... moldy old economics tomes?" she asked with a saucy grin.

"Perish the thought! When I need a bit of escape, I usually go for mysteries or thrillers."

"Ah ... you like the idea of inhabiting a world that's a

little less ... neat and tidy than the corporate world? Something that's kind of gritty and seedy. Interesting."

"Something like that. Now you ... I picture you as a pure romantic."

"Hey, I like a little blood and guts from time to time," she protested. But when he eyed her skeptically she admitted, "Were you perusing my bookshelves when you weren't downloading obnoxious ringtones? Fine, yes, when I need to escape, I read romance novels."

"She said apologetically," Colin frowned. "Many people do, you know. It's not exactly a crime."

"I guess ... it's just ... they're formulaic and predictable and yet ... they still have this magic. I may not have one of my own, but I like the idea of a happily-ever-after." She shrugged. "But what's my choice of reading material got to do with you calling me Lizzie?"

"You remind me a bit of Elizabeth Bennet from *Pride and Prejudice*."

"Really? But she's ... well, I love Jane Austen, but Lizzie is my favorite of all her characters. She's witty and smart, and she always says what she's thinking, even when she knows it will get her into trouble. And she's able to own up to her mistakes."

"Rather like you," he said, stopping in the middle of the sidewalk to smile down at her. "Anna was a friendly voice at the other end of the telephone. Lizzie feels more like a real woman and a beloved friend."

"I ..." Lizzie blinked back tears and smiled back. "That's the nicest compliment I've ever received."

"Good," he said, nodding as they resumed their walk. "But you did get one thing wrong."

"I did? What's that?"

"You forgot the *yet*. You may not have a happily-ever-after of your own ... yet."

"But you think I will?" she breathed.

His fingers tightened around hers. "Yes," he breathed.

"I think, perhaps, we both will."

The drizzle turned into a steady rain just as they neared the park, but Lizzie's rainbow umbrella kept them dry until they reached the shelter of the old gazebo. The white paint was peeling in places, and the benches were well worn, but neither of them cared. Colin curled his arm around her shoulders, and she snuggled into the warmth of his body.

"This is nice," she said, peering at him over the rim of her cup as she tore off a piece of flaky, chocolate-filled croissant. "It may be strange, but I've always liked the rain."

"That's me as well," he said, wiping a smear of melted chocolate from the corner of her mouth. "Which is just as well since business keeps me in London most of the time." He popped his finger into his mouth and sucked off the chocolate. "It's nice here."

"It's just a tiny local park," she laughed. "One in need of some serious upkeep."

"I dunno … it feels … like an all-American town park. Band shell for concerts on warm summer evenings … playground for the kiddos … dog run for the pups … quaint old gazebo for …"

"Good friends?" Lizzie whispered.

"Good friends for now," he replied.

"Only for now? What about later?"

"I …" he peered down at her, but she couldn't quite read the emotions she saw. "Later? I can't answer that yet, Lizzie, except to say, we shall see."

"I can live with that," she nodded. "So, what do you want to do today? I thought about Valley Forge or maybe Lancaster County, but since it's raining that's probably out. I guess we could head back to the city and check out the art museum or something … or … God … I'm a lousy tour guide!"

"Just because I happen to spend most of my time in

London doesn't mean I need city life to be happy, Lizzie. To be perfectly honest, I'm happiest when I'm at my family home in the country, especially when Tori is there. I don't need you to show me the sights, Lizzie. I need you to show me your world."

"My world is ... it's a simple place, Colin. It's a quiet town that's become a bedroom community since the steel mill closed when I was tiny. It's an even quieter village where the old timers like my parents sometimes grumble about the McMansions that are being built up the road. It's not that exciting."

Colin drained the last dregs of his coffee and crumpled up the empty pastry bag before getting to his feet and reaching out a hand to pull her up beside him. "It's your world, Lizzie. I don't care if it's simple or quiet or unexciting ... I care that it had a role in making you who you are." He placed his forefinger beneath her chin and tilted it up, his eyes smiling into hers. "Show me your world, Lizzie. Please?"

They walked the four blocks to the downtown area beneath her enormous umbrella. Lizzie giggled when Colin nestled his body much closer to hers than necessary, claiming he'd felt a drop of water on his hand, and he didn't want to catch cold. She showed him the abandoned steel mill buildings along the river, many of them dating back to the original mid-nineteenth century iron forge for which the town was named, and the crumbling, once-glorious hotel across the street. "I wish someone would fix this part of town up," she sighed, pointing down the street. "Another block that way, and you'll hit the roughest part of town. At least they've started attracting some new businesses to the next block up. We've got some decent restaurants and a few antique shops for the rich folks and ... um ... oops?" she said when Colin laughed softly in her ear.

"I didn't ask to be wealthy, Lizzie. I'm well aware

that I am much more fortunate than most and I won't apologize for it, even if it makes you uncomfortable."

"I don't need you to," she assured him. "I'm the one that has the issue, not you. I'll adjust. Just give me some time, okay?" She tugged on his hand, pulling him further down the block. "So ... do you like my little town?"

"Iron Forge is charming," he said, his dimpled smile proving to her that he meant it. "It's rather timeless, yet I can see that it's gaining new life." He tilted his head toward the old mill at the other end of the street. "That will as well. The right investor will appreciate the uniqueness of those old buildings and find a way to bring them back to life."

"Know anyone like that?"

"Possibly."

"Probably, more like," she sighed. "But don't worry, my friend, I won't pry into your secrets just yet."

Colin's eyes widened for a second before he eyed her quizzically. "Why do you say that?"

Lizzie just shrugged. "You're some sort of advisor for Consolidated, but I get the feeling you could buy and sell every single one of the bigwigs upstairs about ten times before breakfast. And no one that I've talked to seems to know exactly *what* you're here to do. But, honestly? I don't care. I'm just ..." she stopped walking and turned to beam up at him. "I'm happy. Happy that you're here with me. Happy that I get to spend some time with you. Hell, I'm even happy that you were a giant pain-in-the-ass at first. So keep your secret, whatever it is, if you must. It's only about Colin Blake the business tycoon anyway."

"Oh, that bloke? Forget about him. Boring as sin."

"As I suspected. And what about you? Are you boring and forgettable, too?"

He shook his head slowly, his eyes boring into hers. If he dipped his head, just an inch or two, their lips would meet. Lizzie held her breath, unconsciously licking her lips as she held his gaze. "Am I?" he challenged.

"I asked first."

"No, not boring and, I hope, not forgettable. I'm not a complicated man, Lizzie, though my life may seem that way at times. I will admit to a fondness for Cuban cigars and fine Scotch, and I won't pretend that I don't enjoy the luxuries that having a bit of money allow me. But the things that I value most are the people that I care about. That includes you, Lizzie. If that's boring and forgettable then so be it."

"I ... no ... it's neither. It's ... unexpected and ... honestly, I don't quite understand it yet, but it's completely wonderful." She glanced down at the hand she'd been holding almost nonstop since their walk to the park. "Whatever this becomes, I will always be your friend."

He nodded and kissed her on the forehead. "Yes. Whatever this becomes, I will always be your friend, too."

"So, basically, this is it!" Lizzie laughed as they drove down the main drag of Crossroads, where she'd grown up. She pulled into the parking lot and coasted into a parking space. "We can cover the rest of it on foot." She moved to open her car door, but Colin laid a hand on her arm. "What?"

"My mother would never speak to me again if I neglected to open the car door for a lady." He pushed his own open and darted around the hood to open Lizzie's and offer her his hand. "Like so."

"Ah, proper manners, huh? Don't get a lot of that around here, but it's a nice change. And ... bonus ... it's stopped raining." She let him help her from the car, savoring the little tingles that even the smallest touch sent coursing through her body. She swept her hand toward the three-story, gray stone building beside them. "This is the old Grange building, though the Grange disbanded about twenty years ago. Now it's home to Madame Tatyana's School of Dance – a fascinating woman who found her way here by way of the Bolshoi Ballet and a Cold War defection." She tugged at his hand pulling him out toward the street. "The grungy-looking building next door used to sell farm equipment, but it closed down when I was a kid." Next she pointed at the tiny brick train depot across the street. "My Dad and his brothers used to jump on the train and ride for hours when they were kids, all for free, because my Granddad knew the conductor."

They crossed the street and headed down a steep hill while Lizzie pointed out the old barbershop. "Mike's been cutting hair for about sixty years, I think. You should stop in ... but only if you have an afternoon to spare since he'll talk your ear off!"

"Hmm ... or if I have desire for a hairstyle reminiscent of the post-World War II Era?" Colin laughed.

"Chicken!" Lizzie giggled, taking off down the hill with Colin in hot pursuit. With his long legs, he caught her easily, wrapping his arms around her waist and lifting her off her feet. When he set her down, she twirled in his arms, her hands clasped behind his back, and peered up at him. "Hi there."

"Caught you."

"So you did. The question is, what do you plan on doing with me?"

His arms tightened around her waist, pulling her body firmly against his. Lizzie's heart began to pound as she tried to read the emotions in his dark eyes. Desire, for sure. Caring, yes, but she couldn't quite tell if it was friendship or something deeper. But there was a hint of uncertainty, too, and, just a touch of fear in the eyes that gazed so intensely into hers.

Lizzie took a deep breath and reached up to stroke his cheek. "Colin?"

He blinked at the sound of her voice, and the look in his eyes grew more heated. "Hold on," he breathed. "At the moment, I'm planning to hold on to you."

She stroked his cheek again before her fingers moved to tangle in his soft, dark curls. "Yes. Holding on is good." She let one of his curls wrap itself around her finger and grinned playfully. "I think I'll be keeping you and your gorgeous curls far away from good, ole Mike … cutting these would be a crime against nature." She took a step back, needing an inch or two of space between her overheated body and his.

"I cut them all off once when I was a lad," he admitted. "One of the older boys at school told me I looked like a girl, so I came home, grabbed Mum's scissors from her sewing basket and … snip, snip, snip."

"Your poor mother probably wept for days!"

"That she did though she allowed me to keep it a bit shorter after that."

"You obviously don't mind them now," she said as they began walking again.

"I reckon I grew into them a bit. Or perhaps I simply stopped caring once I was a bit surer of myself."

"What about the boy who teased you?"

"Ah, well, Mum saw him a few months ago, and it seems he's had a bit of payback. Poor bloke is completely bald now."

"Karma's a bitch," Lizzie laughed. "This is the Sixpence," she told him, pointing at a large white Colonial inn with glossy black shutters at its many windows. "It somehow manages to be elegant and homey all at once."

"It reminds me a bit of home," Colin said. "There's

an old coaching inn near my family home that was likely built around the same time. If you close your eyes, you can almost hear the sound of the horses' hooves and the rattle of the carriage wheels."

"Rumor has it the place is haunted."

"Many old buildings are. Nothing wrong with having a ghost or two to liven a place up."

"Ha ha, very funny."

"I'm not joking. I've had an … encounter or two."

"With a ghost?"

"Yes, Lizzie. With a ghost."

"Just when I think I have you all figured out, you go and surprise me yet again!"

"What's life without a few surprises?" he asked as they began walking back up the hill to her car.

"You think?"

"I know," he said firmly. "I like your world, Lizzie Kincaid."

"Not too simple and boring?"

"Are you always going to question every single nice thing I say to you?" he sighed.

"Probably," she laughed. "Sorry, sweetie, but you kind of throw me off-kilter."

"Good," he said with a nod. "Where to next?"

She turned and grinned up at him, wiggling her eyebrows playfully. "It's a surprise."

CHAPTER 5

"Lovely neighborhood," Colin said as Lizzie turned her car onto a quiet side street. It was an older community and, unlike the many developments they'd passed throughout the day, every house was unique – a cozy Cape Cod beside a quaint gingerbread cottage and, just down the street, a brick Colonial beside a low-slung rancher. The trees were mature, the lots large and, at times, uniquely shaped. There was no careful planning here, no rigid guidelines on door color or gardens; instead, the neighborhood gave the impression that it had simply happened that way, one house at a time. "Yours?" he asked, though he was sure he knew the answer.

"Mine. This neighborhood was all farmland until forty or fifty years ago, but the owner sold it off in bits and pieces, and this is how it turned out. My parents were some of the first to build here." She pointed at a gray stone rancher with a crooked pine tree in the front yard. "I ... we could go say hi, if you want."

"Why do I get the feeling you don't often bring friends by to meet your parents?"

"Because I don't. And I definitely don't bring a lot of men here. But they'll already know about you from Lisa since I have no doubt she was on the phone with Mom first thing this morning. Mom's already left a message on my cell, which I haven't bothered to return."

"Then let's get to it." Colin got out of the car and, just as he'd done earlier, darted around the hood to open Lizzie's door.

"You know, I could get used to this."

"I did say I planned to spoil you, did I not?"

"You did and … uh oh …" Lizzie's grip on Colin's hand tightened for a second before she dropped it as quickly as if it had just burned her. "Hi, Mom!" she said brightly.

Lizzie's mother, who shared her dark brown eyes and shy smile, glanced quickly from her daughter to Colin. "Lisa called me this morning."

"Yeah, somehow I thought she would," Lizzie mumbled. "Mom … this is my friend, Colin Blake."

"Pleasure, Mrs. Kincaid," he said, giving her hand a gentle squeeze before lifting it to his lips to press a kiss to her knuckles.

She giggled like a teenager. "Bev. Oh my! Lizzie, your sister-in-law left out quite a few details!"

"It's the dimples, isn't it Mom?" Lizzie laughed, smiling up at Colin. "They are adorable, aren't they?"

"Oh my goodness, yes! Now, where is your Dad? Jim … Jim Kincaid! Get your behind out front. Now!"

An hour later, Lizzie found herself in the kitchen with her Mom, slicing strawberries while Bev scooped vanilla ice cream.

Beverly glanced out the kitchen window at the two men, deep in conversation on the patio. "That Colin seems nice."

"He is nice, Mom."

"And you met at work?"

"I've been helping him with his travel for a month. We ... hit it off."

"Yes," Bev said as she let a scoop of ice cream drop into one of the bowls. "I think that much is obvious."

"But?" Lizzie prompted. "C'mon, Mom, I can tell there's a but in there somewhere."

"He lives all the way in England, sweetie."

"Oddly enough, I did realize that, Mom. But it's England, not Pluto. It might be a little complicated but ... I don't think it's impossible."

"Complicated can be painful, Lizzie. I can see that you like him and he obviously likes you but long-distance relationships are challenging at best."

"And you don't think I can handle the challenge? Honestly, Mom, we haven't even figured out if a relationship is where this is going?"

"Haven't you?" Bev asked. "When did you meet him?"

"Friday morning."

"And, let's see, you were together Friday night, all day Saturday, and again today? And he helped you babysit last night?"

"He likes kids. He has a daughter."

"And you're okay with that, right? Because if you're not ..."

"Honestly, Mom, I like the way he talks about her. Tori. He adores her. How could I not like a guy who treats his daughter like my Daddy treated me?"

"Just checking," Bev said as she dropped another scoop of ice cream into a different bowl. "So, just to make sure I have my facts straight ... you like this Colin, a lot. You're willing to accept a teenage daughter and a long-distance relationship."

"If that's what we both want, yes. I know it's complicated, Mom. I can deal with complicated."

"England's still a long way away."

"It's only a five-hour flight. And he does work for Consolidated, so he'll be back and forth a lot."

"For now, at least. What about when that changes?"

"Then we'll deal with it. Answer me this, Mom. Do you like him?"

"Of course I like him. He's got those dimples!"

"I like him, too, Mom. Because he's funny and charming and, okay, occasionally, a huge pain-in-the-ass and ... he makes me feel ..."

"Special?"

"Well, yes, he does make me feel special and beautiful and even a little sexy. But mostly he just makes me *feel*!" She touched her hand to her heart. "He makes me feel *so much*!"

"Then there's only one more piece of advice I can give you," Bev said as she put the lid on the ice cream and returned it to the freezer.

"What's that, Mom?" Lizzie asked as she divided the sliced strawberries between the four bowls. "Keep my feet on the ground? Be realistic?"

"No, my Lizzie-girl. I think maybe your Dad and I gave you that advice one time too often over the years. No, when the time is right, tell him how you feel. Tell him what you want."

"How do I know when the time is right?"

"Well for me it was after your Dad kept me out until three in the morning and landed me in a heap of trouble with your Gramps."

"Yeah, Mom, why's that?"

Beverly grabbed two of the bowls and motioned for Lizzie to get the others. "Because no matter how much trouble I was in, I knew that I would do it all over again. He was worth it. Still is. If you can say the same for Dimples out there ... that's all I need to know."

Colin leaned back against the bench and idly stroked the head of the small white poodle that had climbed up beside him and laid her head on his knee. He glanced toward the door to the house, where Lizzie and her mother had disappeared minutes earlier. "So, Mr. Kincaid ..."

"Just Jim, young man. I appreciate that you have good manners, but ... we're casual people."

"Jim, then ... I ..."

"You seem like a nice enough young man," Jim interrupted. "Hardworking, even if you *do* sit behind a desk ..."

"Thank you, I ..."

"My Lizzie ... she's one of a kind."

"I can't argue with you there, sir, er ... Jim. I happen to think she's rather wonderful."

"Good. Good. Here's the thing, kid. Though I've never understood it, she's never had much luck with men. Dated a bunch of idiots who treated her like dirt and then, well, I guess she just gave up. And then she shows up with you. Now, I know, you've been talking and emailing and texting and whatever else it is people do these days, but you only really met her two days ago. And yet ..." Jim took a long, slow sip of his iced tea. "She brought you here ..."

"We were walking around the village."

"So she said. But, see, Lizzie doesn't like to bring her friends around. I think she's a little embarrassed, you know? Bev and I, we both have our hobbies, and I guess we do get a little carried away. Lizzie calls us pack-rats. Too much clutter, she says."

"I suspect she may be testing me," Colin admitted. "Lizzie ... she worries that we're from different backgrounds."

"But you don't?"

"Not really, no. I think you've probably realized that

I'm not … a poor man."

"Yeah," Jim laughed. "I'm guessing that's not a fake Rolex on your wrist, eh? So you have a bit of money. I don't think you'd find a father in the world that would object to that. Now, if you were an unemployed ass who intended to mooch off of my girl … that'd be a different story."

"What I have and what I value are not the same. The most important things in my life are the people I love. I was raised to work hard in the hopes of making the world a better place because I should, and I was taught the importance of giving back. From what Lizzie's told me about her family, she learned the same lessons, or did you not spend most of your life serving your community as a volunteer firefighter?"

"I did. And Bev's always doing for others, baking and sewing and babysitting," Jim said proudly. "Lizzie, too, though she doesn't like to draw attention to it."

"That doesn't surprise me at all," Colin sighed. "If I ever meet the man or men who did such a number on her self-confidence I will happily beat them to a pulp."

"You and me both, kid. So, you like my girl?"

"Rather a lot," Colin admitted.

"What's that mean, exactly?"

Colin winced. It was an honest question from a loving father, but at the moment, he didn't have the answer, at least not all of it. "I reckon that's the bit we're trying to get sorted."

"Fair enough." Jim glanced through the window at his wife. "I had this feeling when I met Bevvy, but it took a while for my heart and my head to get on the same page. And we lived just across town from each other."

"Are you warning me off because of the distance?"

"Would it matter if I was? Because if you say yes, there's no way in hell, I'd let you date my little princess.

She deserves a man who will fight to be with her."

"Yes, she does."

"You planning to be that guy?"

"I ... it seems to be where we're heading." Colin frowned, wishing he knew all the answers that Jim needed to hear.

"Look, Lizzie's a grown woman who's more than capable of figuring out if you're the guy for her without her Mom and me interfering. We did a little too much of that when she was younger and ... it did more damage than good. Now, you work for Consolidated, right?"

"Yes."

"And you'll be coming back to Pennsylvania?"

"Quite often."

"And you're aware that Lizzie has three uncles and a cousin who are all police officers?"

"Lizzie's quite proud of them. And we ran into Darius yesterday in the city. Should I be concerned?"

"Not if you treat her well."

Colin took a deep breath and looked Jim Kincaid straight in the eyes. "I have a thirteen-year-old daughter who is, thankfully, not old enough to date. I can promise you that I will always treat Lizzie with the respect that I will demand for my daughter."

"Ah, that would change your perspective on things," Jim said with an approving nod. "They have a way of wrapping their daddy around their pretty little fingers."

"That they do. Not that I mind."

"Yeah, me either," Jim agreed. "I used to worry that there wasn't a man good enough for my girl."

"As a father, I can understand that. As the man who's more than a little interested in dating your daughter, it's not exactly good news, Jim."

"Relax, Colin. I said used to. I want my girl to be happy. The man for her doesn't have to be perfect; he just needs to want that, too."

"Happy," he nodded, remembering their earlier conversation. "Happy I can do."

"Did I pass your little test?" Colin asked as they drove back to her apartment.

"Test? I wasn't … "

"You're not a good liar, Lizzie Kincaid. Your Dad said you never drop by with people because you're embarrassed by their clutter."

"It's not exactly pretty," Lizzie mumbled.

"Perhaps not, but it's not a crime either. So they have a tendency to hold onto things a bit longer than they should. They're too busy doing what they love and living life to worry about being neat and tidy all the time. That's not a bad thing, is it? They're having fun."

"Well, yes, I guess." She stopped for a red light and turned to look at him. "You honestly don't care, do you?"

"I care that they are a lovely, down-to-earth couple who are still mad about each other and who obviously want the best for their daughter. They're good people, Lizzie."

"Well, I know that! It's just … I had this boyfriend my senior year in college, and he stopped by over spring break without calling first, and … he was appalled. Of course, he claimed he still loved me, but he broke up with me two weeks after graduation and took a job in Seattle."

"I was once foolish enough to be so taken in by what I saw on the outside that I completely missed that there was nothing real on the inside. I've been quite careful not to make that mistake again."

"Ah, inner beauty. The kiss of death." Her voice was cool, her eyes staring intently at the red light, but her lips quivered just the tiniest bit, and Colin knew at once that he'd said something to upset her.

"Christ, Lizzie, now what?"

The light changed, and she pressed her foot to the gas pedal without answering his question.

"Damn it, Lizzie. Will you talk to me?"

She shook her head, and he could tell that she was holding her breath to keep from crying.

"Please pull over and talk to me."

She clutched the wheel tightly, unwilling to look at him, but she pulled off into the parking lot of a fast food joint. When she still refused to speak, or even to look at him, Colin quietly turned off the car, removed the key from the ignition and opened his door. Once again, he walked around the hood to open her door and, when she ignored his proffered hand, he gently tugged her from behind the wheel. He steered her by the shoulders to a curb, pressed her down and sat beside her.

"Why is inner beauty the kiss of death?"

"H-had that sp-speech once," she croaked between sobs. "Y-you're a g-good p-person but … y-you …"

"Bloody hell." Colin wrapped his arms around her and held her while she sobbed against his chest. "So some stupid arse convinced you that you weren't worthy of his love because he didn't think you pretty enough?"

She nodded against his chest.

"We've agreed that we're friends, have we not?"

She nodded again and though she was still crying, her body felt a little calmer in his arms. "Good. Then you know that you can trust me to tell you the truth, so listen up, my girl. Firstly, just because you didn't live up to one bloody idiot's expectations does not mean that you are not attractive, pretty, or beautiful. I happen to find you all of the above and, since I suspect you think I'm merely trying to comfort you, you're going to listen while I tell you each and *every* physical trait that I find so completely and utterly irresistible. I'll start with your big brown eyes because they were the first thing I noticed the other morning. They're the color of dark chocolate with little flecks of gold around the iris, but what I like most about them is that I can always tell exactly what you're feeling. Shall I move on to your perfect little nose, or perhaps the exotic high cheekbones, or the gold-tipped eyelashes? Or the mouth? Such a lovely, kissable mouth."

"But you won't," she croaked. "You won't kiss me."

"Lizzie, I have every intention of kissing you."

"When?"

"When we know what this is between us. Or am I supposed to have that all neatly sorted out already? Do you?"

"No ... I ..."

"Whatever *this* is, it's special, and I don't mean to lose it by rushing into something that we're not quite ready for. That doesn't mean that sitting here, with you in my arms, isn't making my pulse race."

She lifted her tear-stained face, and he brushed the remaining tears from her cheeks. "Go on."

He kissed her forehead and cuddled her closer though he resisted the temptation to pull her onto his lap. "Where was I? Ah ..." He traced her lips with one finger and smiled softly. "These. So perfect. And all that in the loveliest, heart-shaped face." His hands moved down her body, skimming over her lush curves. "I seem to recall telling you how fond I am of your lovely, womanly body. Or do you need me to tell you again? I will, you know. Over and over until you believe what I say."

"I want to. Believe you, I mean. It's just hard ..."

"Yes, love, that it is, all for you," he joked with a throaty laugh that earned him a half-hearted punch in the arm. "Ah, your fighting spirit is returning. Hallelujah!"

"Brat."

"You like that about me," he laughed. "I hate that a few thoughtless, self-important morons managed to convince you that you needed to be someone else to be worthy of them. The thing is my lovely Lizzie, the fact that I find the outer package attractive is something of a bonus since I was already wildly attracted to you *before* I had a clue what you looked like. It was the girl who told me I was being a bit of an arse, the one who made me laugh, the one who apologized for flirting with me and then kept right on doing it, that I developed a crush on."

"You did?"

"Do you still doubt me, Lizzie?" he said, laughing softly. "I like you. I find you lovely and funny and bright and … I have a wild crush on you. Now, since you're looking a bit … fragile around the edges, I think it's time I take you home."

"Oh." She frowned, fresh tears glistening in her eyes.

"I'm not planning on leaving you there all alone," he soothed. "I'm going to make us some dinner."

"You cook?"

"I live alone in London much of the time, and as I travel so much, I try not to eat out when I'm home. I'm no gourmet, but I manage."

"I … there's nothing in the fridge."

"Righto. So a quick stop at the supermarket across the street and …" he frowned down at her puffy eyes and red nose. "You're a bit of a mess at the moment."

"I'm an ugly crier," she said with a laugh. "It's just the supermarket."

"Just … sit tight for a moment, alright?" He pushed himself up and darted inside the restaurant, heading into the men's room for a cool, damp paper towel and a wad of toilet paper.

"Customer's only," the teen behind the counter said as he walked past.

"Right. Fair enough." He handed the boy a fifty. "I'm not hungry, so your next few guests are on me."

"Dude, that's nuts!"

"Do you think? Tell me that after you've told a family or two that their meal has been paid for."

"Duuuude! You. Are. My. Hero."

Colin shook his head and pointed out the window to where Lizzie still sat on the curb. "I'm aiming to be *her* hero, mate, but thanks all the same." With that, he headed for the door, holding it open for a young mother with three whiny children under five. "Have fun," he mouthed at the cashier.

When he reached Lizzie's side, he held out his hands and pulled her to her feet. He offered her the toilet paper and, once she'd blown her nose, he gently wiped her face with the cool, damp paper towel. "Better?"

"Uh huh. You know, you were in there for quite a while."

"The lad behind the counter said I had to buy something."

"Um, Colin, I hate to tell you, but you got nothin'."

"Oh, but you're wrong." He turned her by the shoulders, indicating the now-grinning cashier and the open-mouthed young mother with a tray of free kids' meals. "I got to make my best friend feel better. My young friend in there got to experience the feeling of making someone's life just a little bit easier. And that young Mum and her little ones can stretch this week's paycheck a little farther. Everyone wins."

"You're a good man, Colin Blake."

"Even when I'm a pain in the arse?"

"Even then. So, you're making me dinner?"

"I am. And then we're going to get cozy on your sofa and watch mindless television until it's time for you to go to bed."

"Alone?"

"For now."

"But eventually?

"What do you think?" he said with a chuckle. "I'm a patient man, Lizzie, but I'm still a man."

"Eventually," she said with a smile. "Definitely, eventually."

"Hungry?" Lizzie asked as Colin loaded the shopping cart with produce. "Potatoes, asparagus, broccoli, spinach, tomatoes ... you're either really hungry or really indecisive."

"I'm planning ahead." He steered the cart toward the meat counter. "Two of the filets and ... hmm ... two of the New York Strips."

"Planning ahead for what?" Lizzie asked with a frown. "Ah ... you think I'll take pity on the weary traveler and cook for you every night if you fill up my fridge."

Colin took the two packages of meat from the butcher and let out an exasperated sigh. "You know, at times I wouldn't mind if you were a bit less like Lizzie Bennet, you know. You seem determined to woefully misunderstand me." He laid a hand on her shoulder. It was wonderfully warm and heavy as he stroked her jaw with the pad of his thumb. "I think I mentioned that I'm not overly fond of eating out all the time. I was wondering ... hoping ... planning ..."

"What?" she breathed.

"I like being with you, Lizzie, no matter what we're doing. I thought we could share our evenings and simply ... be. Cook *together*, do the dishes, watch some television. Get to know each other without having to make a show of it, though I will hold you to our date at the Sixpence. Or am I, once again, charging through your life like a crazed bull? If I am ..."

"You're not," she said, smiling softly. "I don't cook much when I'm alone."

"Hence the empty refrigerator?"

"I'm worse than your average single man," she laughed. "I do like to cook, and I'm actually pretty good, I just don't make the effort on a regular basis. But I like the idea of just hanging out with nothing particular in mind. I'm not ... I guess I've always been a homebody, which isn't always a good thing when you're single."

"I don't expect you to cook my meals for me."

"Yeah, I get that now. So, you've got beef covered? What else?"

He added Alaskan salmon, Chilean sea bass, and lobster tail at the seafood counter though Lizzie was careful to offset his pricey choices with some simpler fare. She tossed in a packet of ground beef and some chicken breasts, along with three kinds of pasta. "I'm letting you spoil me with all of the expensive stuff, so you're going to have to suck it up and eat some normal all-American meals."

"Steak isn't normal?"

"Not when it's filet mignon," she laughed. "Spaghetti and meatballs is normal. Chicken is normal. Filet is reserved for very special occasions."

"Then consider tonight a very special occasion."

"And what would that be?"

"Your birthday?"

"Nope. September. Yours?"

"October. Do we really need a reason, Lizzie? Can't the reason simply be because it's Sunday and you've had an awful day?"

"It wasn't an awful day, Colin. It was actually pretty damned amazing until I had a *minor* mental breakdown, which I am, thankfully, completely over. And ... I owe you an apology."

"What? Why? For having a ... moment?"

"For letting the past get in the way of the present. I do realize you're not all of the lousy men I've dated rolled into one, you know. And I can promise you that I'll do my best to leave the past where it belongs from now on."

"You don't have to, Lizzie. Everyone has some sort of residual damage that they cling to."

"I don't want it anymore," she said firmly. "I told you this morning that I'm happy when I'm with you. I want to hold on to that, Colin. I want to live in the present with you."

"Then we'll celebrate the present. Now, as we're having our very own special occasion, I think perhaps we need some wine."

"Then we'll need to hurry."

"Why's that?"

"Pennsylvania's antiquated Blue Laws," she laughed. "I blame the Quakers. The liquor store is only open 'til five, and it's already after four." She scanned the contents of the cart. "Honestly, though, I think we have enough food in here to survive for a couple of months."

"And your liquor store?"

"About five minutes back the way we came. Seems you live a charmed life, Mr. Blake."

"Me? Honestly, my life was dreadfully dull, apart from Tori, until you entered it. If it's charmed now, Lizzie, I'm afraid it's all your doing."

"Just to be clear, that's a good thing, right?"

"That, my Lizzie, is the most amazing thing of all."

CHAPTER 6

After that, they settled into a comfortable routine. There were the playful, flirtatious emails throughout the day that made both of them laugh out loud, and the chance meetings in the corridors that usually left one, or both, breathless and blushing.

And there were the long, cozy evenings at Lizzie's apartment, cooking side by side in her tiny kitchen, their bodies colliding so often that the food on the stove wasn't the only thing that sizzled. After dinner, Lizzie would wash the dishes while Colin dried them and put them away. Then they'd cuddle up on the sofa, Colin's long legs propped up on the coffee table while Lizzie's body curled into his.

Some nights they talked for hours, about books and travels and their childhoods. Others they barely spoke while they watched a movie, or Colin pored through stacks of work papers while Lizzie read her latest romance novel, sharing soft smiles and companionable silence.

They were playful and relaxed. Colin flirted. Lizzie teased.

Somewhere along the line, Lizzie forgot that they came from different worlds. It simply ceased to matter.

Somehow, they fit.

Both knew it, but neither one would broach the subject of what it meant and where it might take them. And the more carefully they avoided the issue, the more taboo it became.

Their second weekend together, they drove to Delaware to visit with her childhood friends, David and Kim Jameson. Kim had lived next door to Lizzie with her divorced mother and older brother Simon; their mothers were cousins and best friends. David had lived in the next house down with his little sister, Tessa. Dave and Kim had been childhood sweethearts, and now had three adorable daughters and an infant son.

While Colin and David bonded over Cuban cigars on the porch, Kim and Lizzie sipped wine in the living room.

"I'm so happy for you," Kim gushed. "You're happier than I've ever seen you."

"I am happy. But, I'm sad too. What happens next week? We haven't discussed it, and I don't have a clue how to bring it up."

Kim smiled gently and squeezed Lizzie's hand. "These things have a way of working themselves out. Whatever this is between the two of you, it's powerful. That's obvious."

Lizzie nodded mutely in agreement. "We haven't even kissed. We almost have a couple of times, but one of us always pulls back."

"Maybe it's because you both know it won't be any old kiss. Promise me you will not let him get on that airplane home without …"

"I don't know, Kimmy. I'm not sure I can, not if I don't know what happens next."

Colin watched as the smoke rings wafted slowly upward, widening before disappearing into the warm, evening air. He was happier than he'd been in years, thanks to Lizzie, but he wasn't quite sure what to do about it. "So ... you've known Lizzie for a long time."

"Since we were kids," David said. "The whole neighborhood gang. Kimmy and me. Kim's brother Simon. My baby sister, Tess. Lizzie's cousin Dare. The Brody's. We were always together."

"Getting into mischief?"

"Some of us," David laughed. "Mostly me, Matt Brody and Dare. Sometimes we dragged Matt's cousin, Sin along on our misdeeds."

"And Lizzie?"

"She was one of the older ones, her and Simon. They tried to keep us in line, but I'm not sure they were ever very successful. Still, Lizzie's always been something of a mother hen to the rest of us."

"I can see that," Colin said, glancing through the window at the two women on the sofa. "She's something special."

"She is," David agreed. "And she's family."

"Is that a warning?"

"It's just a fact. Lizzie, she's never had great luck when it comes to the guys she's dated. Just ... don't mess with her head."

"That's the last thing I intend to do," Colin said firmly. "But ..."

"Want some advice from someone who's known her forever?"

"Something tells me I'm going to get it whether I want it or not," Colin said with a laugh. "But honestly? Yes, I would welcome some advice."

"Look, you seem like a good guy, and I can tell you've got it bad for our Lizzie. I also know that you live in England. Just don't let it get too convoluted."

"What do you mean?"

"Don't leave without letting her know what you want. I know Lizzie. She'll second guess everything the minute you leave if you don't, and she'll probably end up convincing herself that it wasn't real." David took a long, thoughtful puff on his cigar. "I'm not wrong, am I? You do like her, right?"

"Mate, I more than like her, but it's complicated."

"Is it?" David asked with a snort. "Then I suggest you find a way to un-complicate it."

Lizzie reached for the remote and flicked off the television, blinking as the room grew darker. "Listen," she whispered. "It's thundering."

"The Weather Channel did say we might get some storms."

Lizzie laughed softly. "It still amuses me that you're a weather junkie."

"Laugh if you must, but when you travel as much as I, you learn to gather as much information in advance as possible. That includes the weather forecast."

"It's cute," Lizzie giggled. "Makes you fit in perfectly with my Dad and my brother." She held her breath for a second, hoping that she hadn't misspoken, but Colin either hadn't noticed that she'd included him as part of her family, or he didn't care.

God, she was hoping he didn't care. Or that he did care and that he liked that she'd included him. With a sigh, she nestled closer, and, when his shirt collar impeded her ability to nuzzle his neck, she pushed one button, then a second from its buttonhole. Her nose found the pulse at his collarbone. It quickened at her touch, "Mmm," she purred, inhaling his clean, masculine scent.

Colin laughed softly, his fingers skittering up and down her backbone. "You sound like a contented kitten."

"Almost," she murmured as she moved her lips over his smooth skin. "You taste as good as you smell."

"Lizzie, I … we …"

"Relax, Colin. I think maybe we can handle a little fondling without ending up tangled in the sheets." Her lips resumed their journey, traveling over his collarbone and up the strong column of his throat.

"Crazy girl," he laughed, shifting her body, so she was on his lap. "I reckon we can at that." His fingers slipped beneath her blouse, his fingers warm against the skin of her back. "Or maybe not," he croaked.

Lizzie tilted her head back and smiled up at him. "Maybe not," she began,

"Shush," he whispered. He dipped his head, and his teeth grazed the soft, sensitive skin of her earlobe. "Been wanting to do that for ages," he murmured against her ear before doing it again. "Ages and ages and ages and …"

Lightning flashed, followed quickly by a cannon boom of thunder and the clatter of a torrential downpour. "Mmm … now that's electric."

"Was that the storm, do you think?" he teased. "Or was it us?" His lips were hot as they trailed kisses down her neck.

"Us. All us," Lizzie murmured as lightning flashed again, brighter and hotter. This time, the thunder was almost instantaneous and, when the third bolt of lightning cracked only seconds later, the lights went out with a soft pop. "Wow."

Without thinking she began patting his body, shifting in his lap as she tried to figure out where she ended, and he began. One shift too far and she knew for sure where at least one part of him began.

"Unh! Lizzie, love, that's my …"

"You know, I actually had that figured out, but thanks

for the four-one-one," she laughed, moving as gingerly as possible, though her progress was somewhat hampered by the fact that his hand was stuck beneath her shirt and was, at present, all but cupping her breast. "Hand check?"

"Just … a … second … your bloody blouse is all twisted. Ah, success!" he shouted as he managed to free his hand. "So … what now?"

"Hmm. We could get all tangled up again."

"You did seem to enjoy it," he teased.

She slid her hand up his thigh, dangerously close to his still-erect penis. "I'm one hundred percent sure I'm not the only one. So, the question is do we get tangled?"

"We are both consenting adults."

"True enough. But …"

"But tangled would inevitably lead to more tangled and … "

"And it's Tuesday, and you're leaving on Friday," she whispered. "And as much as I want you, I don't know what that means for … for us. Do you?"

"I wish I did."

"So now what?"

"Now … we wait for the lights to come back on."

"And if they don't? If the power stays out?"

"Then maybe that's a sign."

"So … if the power stays off, it's a sign that we should sleep together?"

"And if it comes on, it's a sign that we need to wait."

"How long?"

He glanced at the illuminated face of his watch. "Two minutes?"

"Seems fair enough."

So they watched the seconds tick by.

Lizzie wanted the lights to stay out. It would mean at least one night in Colin's arms, one night of pure bliss.

Lizzie wanted the lights to come on. It might mean

delaying their pleasure for a few days, or even a few weeks, but somehow she knew that it would mean so much more.

At one minute, the lights were still out, and Lizzie was still vacillating between her two options.

At one minute, twenty seconds, the room was still dark. She could feel Colin's heart pounding beneath her hand, could feel her own thumping wildly.

And at one minute, fifty-five seconds, the lights flashed back on. "So," she said on a sigh.

"So, we wait."

"I think … honestly, I think it's better for us. I know some people can hop in and out of bed like it's nothing but it's not who I am. It never has been."

"Yes," he said, "I know. The funny thing is, as much as I didn't want the lights to come on, I think I *wanted* them to, even more. Does that make any sense at all?"

Lizzie kissed his cheek. "Yes. For you. For me. It makes perfect sense."

"And for us?" He rested his forehead against hers. "What about for us?"

"For us. For us. I think … I think if there's to be an *us* after … after you leave … it was the only real choice at all."

Their last night together, Colin and Lizzie snuggled on the sofa in Lizzie's apartment and watched *Pride and Prejudice.* "You know, you bear a striking resemblance to this particular Mr. Darcy, but I'm sure you hear that all the time," she teased, nodding at the actor on the screen.

He rolled his eyes. "It's been mentioned once or twice, I suppose."

"You're full of shit, you know. The pair of you could be twins, so my guess is it's mentioned all the time. Can I ask you a question?"

"Of course. You may ask me anything."

"What does the 'd' stand for? In your travel profile, you're Colin D. Blake, but your middle name isn't listed."

"By design," he chuckled. "I may have greased a palm or two for the privilege. Promise you won't laugh?"

"Why? Is it hideous?"

"Not hideous really … more … unusual and a bit embarrassing."

"Dilbert, Dexter, Duke?" she guessed.

"You'll never guess."

"Then you'd better just tell me, or I'll have to tickle it out of you," Lizzie laughed wiggling her fingers threateningly.

He grinned, his dimples dancing. "Darcy."

"No way!"

"I swear. Mum's an enormous Jane Austen fan, like you."

Lizzie started to laugh, unable to contain herself.

"You promised you wouldn't laugh!"

"Actually, I *didn't* promise, but I'm not laughing at *that*."

"What then?"

"Don't you get it? Anna *Elizabeth* and Colin *Darcy*?"

Colin was now laughing along with her, a loud bark of a laugh. "Good God, are we truly Darcy and Lizzie? Unbelievable."

"What a strange coincidence."

"Synchronicity," Colin corrected. "Some things are simply meant to be."

"Are we one of them, Darcy?"

"I'm coming back, Lizzie, a week from Sunday."

"Nicely deflected," she said with a frown. "I'm not trying to trick you into saying something you don't mean."

"I never believed that for a moment." He cupped her chin between his fingers and searched her eyes. "I'll be back before you miss me."

"I already miss you," she murmured. "And you haven't even left."

"Do you trust me, Lizzie?"

"You know that I do."

"I promise you I will answer your question the moment I set foot back in Pennsylvania, if not before."

"I'm going to hold you to that."

He smiled at her and kissed the tip of her nose. "I know. I'm counting on it."

He brought her flowers the next day, another Friday. Two dozen perfect red roses. The card read: *For my dearest, loveliest Elizabeth, your Darcy.*

Lizzie's friends at work were stunned. She'd kept their blossoming relationship a secret. Now that it was out, her friends wanted details, but she was too emotional to provide them.

She took a late lunch and walked Colin to his rental car. They clung to each other in the parking lot. She didn't know how to say goodbye or even if she *should* say goodbye. They hadn't talked about anything beyond their two magical weeks, and now it seemed too late. "Please don't let this be goodbye."

"Not a chance. A week from Sunday, remember?" He kissed her lightly on the top of her head and softly on her damp cheek. "My Lizzie," he whispered. "I've left a gift for you with your boss. What you do with it is completely up to you. I shall miss you dreadfully, but I *will* be back." With that, he was gone.

She watched his car until it disappeared, tears streaming down her face. "Goodbye, Darcy."

She stumbled back inside and flopped down in her chair so hard that it flew across the floor. Her boss,

Carolyn, stopped by her desk and handed her an envelope. "I'm supposed to give this to you. Anything you want to tell me?"

Lizzie shook her head and slipped her finger beneath the flap. Inside the envelope was a round-trip ticket to London and a note: *Lizzie, Please let this be only farewell, as we've just got started. Meet me in London next weekend. Yours, Darcy.*

It gave her hope.

"Thank you," Colin said, accepting a glass of scotch from the attendant at the British Airways Club at the Philadelphia International Airport. He set the glass on the table beside him without taking a sip.

His two weeks with Lizzie had been the best of his life. So why was he flying home with only a vague promise of a weekend? Why was he afraid to take her in his arms and kiss her?

He sighed heavily, raking a hand through his hair when his cell phone vibrated against his side. He smiled when he saw the number. "Hello, love," he said.

"You sound tired, Daddy," said his thirteen-year-old daughter, Victoria. "It's good you're on your way home, even if I'm not there to greet you."

"I … I'm not so sure about that," Colin said sadly. "I think, perhaps, I'm being a bit of a coward."

"Does this have something to do with your friend, Lizzie?"

Colin shook his head slowly, unsurprised by her perceptiveness. "It has everything to do with her," he admitted. "I …"

"She's more than just a friend, isn't she?"

"God, I hope so!" Colin groaned. "I …"

"You love her?" Tori suggested. "Had to happen sooner or later. So why are you at the airport when it's so obvious where you truly want to be?"

"And where is that?"

"With your Lizzie. Go, Dad. Tell her how you feel."

"Even if that means a lot of changes for all of us?"

"I'm not a *child*, Daddy. You've been alone for far too long. If she makes you happy ... and from everything that you've told me, I believe that she does ... go for it ..."

Hours after saying goodbye, Lizzie lay on her sofa listening to the pouring rain and watching *Pride and Prejudice* again. She poured a glass of Scotch, Colin's favorite, and took a tentative sip, coughing as it burned her throat, one more painful reminder that she was alone on the sofa tonight. With a dejected sigh, she turned her attention back to the screen.

She couldn't help the tiny smile that lifted her lips as on-screen Darcy and Lizzie purposefully lagged behind the others. And, just as Darcy confessed that his feelings and wishes had not changed, her doorbell buzzed. She glanced at the digital clock on the DVD player. It was nearly midnight, and she didn't know anyone who would stop by at that hour.

Anyone except ... Colin Darcy Blake.

She didn't bother pulling on a robe; she just flew down the stairs in her pink satin nightshirt and bare feet. She peeked through the peephole and suddenly couldn't breathe.

Lizzie yanked the door open. There, standing on her front step, drenched to the skin stood Colin!

"What ..." she swallowed her question as Colin pulled her into his arms and gave her the most soul-stirring, heart-pounding, earth-shattering kiss of her life. They stood there for a long time, oblivious to the cold, soaking rain, conscious only of each other. "You're on a plane!"

"Obviously not," he teased.

She swatted him playfully on the arm. "You're supposed to be."

"I couldn't. I couldn't leave without a proper kiss goodbye."

"And was that proper enough?" She ran her hands up the sodden fabric of his dress shirt, needing to feel his solid body beneath her fingers.

"Oh, no, very improper, I think. I believe we should try another one momentarily."

"Why did you really come back, Colin?" She had to know, had to hear the words, had to see the look in his eyes as he said them.

"Because my dearest, loveliest Anna Elizabeth, I'm completely in love with you. I couldn't leave with everything unsaid between us."

Tears stung her eyes. "You love me?"

He nodded, cupping her chin between his fingers and tilting it up. "I love you."

"I love you, too."

They kissed again. This one was infinitely sweeter and tenderer than the first, yet it burned just as hotly.

"Perhaps we should move this inside, my love," Colin suggested with a smile.

"Perhaps, we should," Lizzie agreed as she tugged him in from the rain. "Perhaps, we should."

CHAPTER 7

An awkward, if happy, silence filled Lizzie's tiny kitchen. She had just experienced what was undoubtedly the most romantic moment of her life. How often does one receive a midnight declaration of love in the pouring rain, after all? But now, in the glaring light of her apartment, she didn't know what to do next.

Colin didn't seem to know either.

She stared down at her bare, wet feet, suddenly wishing she hadn't allowed Rachel to paint her toenails in alternating colors of hot pink and turquoise blue. She peeked up at Colin. He was watching the ceiling fan spin and creating a large puddle on her chipped linoleum floor.

"So ..." Lizzie ventured, feeling the color creep into her cheeks.

"So," he repeated quietly. "I ..." He stopped then and opened up his arms. She stepped into them and he wrapped them around her waist.

The warmth of his embrace calmed her and gave her courage. She smiled up at him. "You're dripping," she teased.

"So are you," he reminded her.

She blushed again as she realized that her satin nightshirt clung to her body like a second skin. "I … we … maybe we should dry off? I'll get you a towel," she offered.

"I'll just go and get my suitcase from the boot of the car and be back directly." He squeezed her hand and kissed her on the forehead. "Back in a flash."

"Promise? I'm still not sure you aren't a mirage."

"I'm not a mirage, Lizzie," he chuckled. "I'll be right back. I promise you."

After the door shut behind him Lizzie grabbed a towel from the bathroom and headed to her bedroom. She stripped off her wet nightshirt and threw on a Phillies T-shirt and a pair of sweat pants. Part of her wanted to put on some make-up and a nice outfit, but given the time, she opted for comfort. Besides, she didn't want to pretend to be other than who she really was. She towel-dried her hair and slipped her feet into her fuzzy zebra-striped slippers, then walked back into the living room just as she heard Colin's footsteps pounding up the stairs.

"Crikey … it's blustery out there for the beginning of June. I'm chilled through," he said, shivering.

"I'll make us some tea while you change." Lizzie grinned at him, still not quite believing he was standing in front of her. Without thinking, she reached out a hand and touched it to his chest. He chuckled softly. "Just checking."

Five minutes later he joined her in the living room. They settled themselves on the floor in front of the sofa, his arm around her shoulders and her head on his chest. She took a deep breath and plunged in.

"What made you come back?" she asked.

"These last two weeks have meant everything to me. We connected in so many ways. I couldn't leave with everything so ambiguous between us. There I was, in the British Airways Club, and all I could think of was how much I'd been afraid to tell you. And I knew then that I had to tell you everything, straight away."

"I'm still stunned that you're here. I was wondering if I would be able to make that trip next weekend, not knowing where things stood. So … I guess you'll have to fly back tomorrow night, right?" She hated to think about it, but at least she knew she'd see him on the weekend.

"Actually, no."

"But what about your job? Don't you have to be at work on Monday?"

"Ah … there's something I should tell you about that actually. The … uh … purpose of this whole month-long trip has been to acquaint myself with all the particulars of Consolidated. I … uh …" he stammered, blushing hotly. "I bought it."

"Huh?"

"I bought the company."

"You … bought … it? But I thought … Aren't you just some kind of advisor?"

"I wanted things kept very quiet. I didn't wish to cause an uproar. People get upset when they learn that things are changing, especially when it concerns their livelihood. I'm not an advisor to the CEO or the Board of Directors or … anything, actually. I'm the CEO of Blake Enterprises. I … we … buy foundering companies and attempt to revitalize them and make them viable again."

"So … I guess since you're the boss you can work from wherever you please."

"Exactly. So, I'll stay in Pennsylvania and fly home next weekend. With you, if that's agreeable …" He glanced down at his hands and twisted the gold signet ring he always wore on his pinky.

The hint of nervousness only endeared him to Lizzie. "Of course it's agreeable!" She leaned in to kiss him softly, stroking his whiskered cheek with the pad her thumb. "So what took you so long?" she teased.

"What do you mean?"

"I booked your flight, remember? It was supposed to leave at eight-thirty, and it's only about forty-five minutes from the airport to here at that time on a Friday night."

"I had a bloody awful time getting another rental car for one thing. There's a big convention in town this weekend and every agency was booked, so it took me the better part of an hour to ... er ... charm my way into a rental. And if you hadn't noticed it's raining ... quite hard."

"Okay ... so that accounts for two hours. And the third?"

Colin grinned and rolled his eyes. "I had one other errand I needed to do which proved a bit tricky, given the hour."

Lizzie arched her eyebrows at him. "And that would be?"

"I suppose there's no time like the present." His dimpled smile was filled with mischief and mystery as he pushed himself up off the floor and crossed the room to rummage through his soft-sided leather briefcase. Lizzie couldn't tell what he retrieved, and he hid both hands behind his back as he knelt beside her.

"What are you up to Darcy?" she laughed.

He cleared his throat and swallowed nervously. "Funny you should call me that at this moment, my Lizzie."

Her heart started to pound.

"I only hope you are kinder to me than Elizabeth Bennet was to Fitzwilliam Darcy."

Lizzie's mouth went dry.

"I love you Anna Elizabeth. I need you. I …" Tears filled his warm brown eyes. "I can't live another day without you." He pulled his right hand from behind his back and held it out to her. On his palm sat a small black velvet box.

Tears streamed down Lizzie's face as Colin maneuvered onto one knee.

"Will you … would you marry me?" he asked softly. "Please?"

Lizzie couldn't speak, but she threw her arms around him and hugged him.

"Was that a yes?" he asked hoarsely.

She could only nod and hug him even more tightly. He removed the ring from the box and slipped it onto her finger. She glanced down at it and smiled. It was a simple round-cut diamond in an exquisite antique setting; two small sapphires, her birthstone, flanked the diamond.

"It's beautiful," she finally said when her ability to speak returned. "I love you, Colin Blake! Wow! I think we may surprise a lot of people."

"Undoubtedly."

"Since I doubt you had an engagement ring in your briefcase the whole time, how'd you manage to pull this off at midnight on a Friday?" She held up her left hand, beaming as the diamond glittered in the lamplight.

"Ah." He pulled a slightly crumpled business card from his pocket for 'Diamond Life Jewelers'. "I pocketed this the morning we wandered around town, so I rang up the old gent while waiting for my rental. Lovely man, your Mr. Visser. He was just closing up shop, but when I explained my situation, he was happy to wait for me."

"Charlie's the best," Lizzie sighed. "And something tells me you made it worth his while."

Colin shrugged. "He's a romantic at heart. So, Lizzie,

my love …"

"Umm, Colin? What about your family? What will they think of all this? Do they even know about me … us?" Though Colin had met most of her family, they'd barely even talked about his, aside from his daughter, Tori.

"Tori does. She's quite delighted and eager to meet you. She's been trying to marry me off for years. Her mother doesn't have any contact with her at all. Hasn't since she left when Tori was eight months old."

"You've barely mentioned her at all. Your ex, I mean. I don't even know her name."

Colin exhaled sharply and closed his eyes. "Her name is Lara, and I've known her most of my life. Our families moved in the same circles, so we saw quite a lot of each other as children, but then we were both off at school, and I didn't see her again until I was in my twenties. We ended up at the same party somehow or other and … one thing led to another, I suppose. She was beautiful, and we seemed to have a lot in common, so we drifted into a relationship."

Lizzie winced, knowing that meant that Lara would be her polar opposite. "I'll bet she's tall, blond, and skinny."

"She's beautiful enough, to be sure, but only on the surface. I expected her to be the same sweet child I remembered, so that's what I chose to see. I … ignored a lot."

"So you're trying to tell me that she's a bitch? But you're reluctant to completely trash her."

"Whatever else she is, she's the reason I have Tori. I can't hate her no matter how many awful things she's done." He shrugged before continuing. "After we'd been dating for a while she changed. Or more accurately, her real personality emerged. All the things I'd found so refined suddenly proved utterly artificial. I … I hesitate to speak poorly of the mother of my child, but she's a cold-hearted snob and … when I finally realized all of this and was about to break things off … she frostily informed me that she was pregnant. She knew me well, and she played me perfectly. We got married, of course, out of my somewhat misguided sense of duty and honor. I never really loved her, though I honestly did try. The marriage lasted … barely … until shortly after Victoria was born, then she was gone with a hefty divorce settlement and not a backward glance."

"I'm sorry. It must have been awful."

He nodded. "But I have Tori, and I wouldn't trade being her father for anything in the world. I think that's why I can't quite hate Lara."

"You haven't told me much about your family. I'm guessing they're very different from mine."

"In some ways, perhaps. But I think you'll find more similarities than differences. Just because we have money doesn't mean we aren't every bit as delightfully eccentric as the Kincaids." He glanced over at Lizzie's bookshelves, smiling at her collection of Jane Austen books. "You're quite a Jane Austen fan. Not only do you have her complete works, but you have the definitive biography of her."

"I majored in English. My favorite lit class was an in-depth study of Jane Austen and how she helped to shape the modern romance novel. That biography was one of the texts, but it's become one of my favorite books."

Colin walked across the room and pulled the book off the shelf. "I think I mentioned my Mum has a fondness for Jane Austen."

She laughed. "Yes, *Darcy*, you did."

He opened the book to the back and handed it to her. "You might want to read about the author."

"Helen Leigh is a renowned expert on Jane Austen," she read aloud. "I know all this, Colin, but what's it have to do with you?"

"Helen Leigh *Blake* is my Mum."

"Oh. Yikes. So she's more than just an Austen fan, she's the most knowledgeable expert on Austen's work and life there is. Wow. No wonder your middle name is Darcy. I guess you're lucky she didn't call you Fitzwilliam, huh?"

"Not for want of trying, I assure you. But Dad insisted on a 'normal' name for his son."

"Colin's a good, strong name," she said. "And Darcy makes it distinctive."

"Not a lot of people know about that," he laughed. "Would you like to know about my sisters?"

"You have sisters? How could you have never mentioned them?"

He grinned at her and kissed her softly. "I suppose I was a bit pre-occupied."

"Oh. Go on. How many sisters? Two, three?"

"Umm … it's good you're sitting down. Six."

"Excuse me?"

"I have six sisters."

"Six! Good God, I thought the filthy rich had one or two kids at the most!"

"That sounds like reverse snobbery to me," he protested.

"I'm joking! You kind of took me by surprise there. I'd been picturing you as an only child, or maybe having one or two brothers or sisters, like me. So where do you fall among these sisters?"

He rolled his eyes. "I'm the youngest."

"I'll bet you really got spoiled, then."

"Hardly. They tortured me every chance they got and always managed to get me blamed for everything."

She couldn't help but laugh. "Poor little Colin Darcy! So, what are their names?"

He grinned and glanced at her bookshelves again. "I

imagine you can probably guess."

"No! Really?"

"Yes. Elizabeth, Elinor, Catherine, Emma, Fanny, and Anne. You'll meet at least half of them next weekend, if not all."

"Now I'm *really* nervous."

"Don't fret, please. They all turned out well enough. And I daresay Mum will adore you! Anyone that can carry on a conversation about Jane Austen is quite something in her book." He smiled at her and then frowned and looked away.

"What aren't you telling me? Will your father hate me or something?"

"My father died three years ago."

"Oh, God, I'm so sorry. But someone's not going to be happy about us, I can tell."

"Nothing anyone can say will change how I feel about you, Lizzie."

"But someone will try to change your mind."

"I'm afraid my grandmother will feel she has to try. She's ... okay ... there's no way to sugarcoat this. She's an insufferable snob who believes that because her lineage is ancient that she's better than everyone. She'll likely accuse you of being a gold-digger or a trollop or both."

His admission made her laugh. "Great ... thanks for the warning. Now I'll have to reread *Pride and Prejudice* to memorize Elizabeth's responses to Lady Catherine de Burgh."

"Good idea, love. There's ... uh ... one other *little* thing about Grandmamma."

Lizzie rolled her eyes. "More? Good lord, what?"

"Her father was an Earl."

Lizzie had read enough historical romances to understand how the titles of the British aristocracy worked. "So that would make her Lady."

"Lady Frances. Although titles don't mean much anymore, they mean *everything* to her. She will insist on your using it."

"Jeez. Do I have to curtsy?"

"I think you can safely leave that out."

"Phew, cause my curtsy is pretty rusty, although Dani and Rachel make me do it sometimes when we play princesses ..." Lizzie stopped speaking when she realized that there was a new 'princess' in her life. She was about to acquire a stepdaughter. "Will I meet Tori next weekend as well?" she asked.

Colin nodded and squeezed her hand reassuringly. "I'm certain you two will like each other."

"But she's had you all to herself for so long. Are you sure she'll share you with me?"

"I told her all about you a few days ago. She seemed genuinely happy that I found someone. I rather think she worries that I'm alone too much. She's quite wise for thirteen."

"I hope you're right."

"I am, you'll see. She rang me whilst I was at the airport, and she helped me sort out exactly where I needed to be. She said 'go for it, Daddy.'"

"I would think she'd be anxious for you to get home."

"If she were home or at school she might be. But she's in France on a school trip. She's been far too busy to miss me at all."

"I missed you before your car even left the parking lot this afternoon. I'm so grateful you came back, Colin. It's been an intense couple of weeks." She glanced at the clock. It was now past one in the morning. Unable to help herself, Lizzie yawned. "'Scuse me."

"Am I keeping you up or something?" he teased.

"It's way past my bedtime."

Another awkward silence. She felt her skin color again. "I ... er ..."

"It's okay, my love. We're both emotionally drained. I think, maybe, we should save making love for another time." He pressed a light kiss to her forehead. "What I mean is … as much as a want to drag you into your bedroom and make wild, crazy love to you … and I really, truly want to … I think we're both …"

"It's okay. I understand and … I agree. My head is still spinning from your showing up and … Good God … proposing! I doubt I could handle anything more intense at the moment. But … I … will you stay? Here? With me?"

"There's nowhere else I'd rather be than cradling you in my arms."

Lizzie sighed and stood up, holding out her hand.

Colin took it and let her pull him to his feet. He tugged her into his arms and kissed her lingeringly. "Thank you," he murmured. "I should say more, but …"

She understood exactly what he meant. There were no words to describe all that had just happened. "You're welcome," was her simple reply. "You're very welcome."

CHAPTER 8

Lizzie woke up grinning like a fool. Colin was spooned against her from behind, one arm looped loosely around her waist. She rolled over carefully, not wanting to wake him, and studied him as he slept.

He looked young and surprisingly vulnerable. His dark curls were a tousled mess on her pale green pillowcase and his lips curled in the hint of a smile. Unable to restrain herself, she traced his mouth with her thumb and followed with a feathery-soft kiss.

His eyes popped open, and he grinned at her, his dimples dancing in his cheeks. "Good morning, love," he whispered, his voice still gravelly from sleep.

"Good morning, Darcy," she giggled. "I think from now on you'll always be my Darcy."

"I can live with that so long as you are always my Lizzie." His hand strayed from her waist and was now tickling its way up her bare thigh.

"Uh, Darcy?"

"Yes, Lizzie?"

"Whatcha doin'?" She could barely get the words out as his hand continued its tantalizing journey.

"I was thinking how utterly relaxing a good night's sleep can be." He grinned cheekily at her as his fingertips brushed her inner thigh. "I feel as if I could handle anything this morning."

"Is that so? And what, pray tell, did you have in mind?"

"A bit of this," he teased as he leaned in for a playful kiss.

"Oh, I like that. You may continue."

He grinned and rolled her onto her back, kissing her until she was breathless as his fingers found the hem of her t-shirt and slipped beneath it.

Lizzie's hands seemed to have developed a mind of their own as they learned the contours of his body, finally tangling in his soft curls. "Oh, Darcy," she murmured as she rained kisses on his eyelids, his cheeks, his nose ...

BUZZ

"What the ... oh, crap!" she muttered. "Just when things were getting interesting."

"What is it, love?"

"More like who. Today's Saturday and I completely forgot that I'm supposed to go shopping with Mom."

"I imagine she'll be a bit surprised to find me here?"

"That's the understatement of the century. I ... this would be a first for me. Getting caught with a man in my bed, I mean. Mom's a bit old-fashioned, so I've kept my love life pretty much under wraps. As far as she's concerned I'm a thirty-four-year-old virgin."

Colin chuckled. "This should be interesting then. Should we tell her, do you think?"

"I'd kind of like to tell them all at once. I thought maybe at dinner tomorrow ..." She wriggled into a pair of blue jeans and grinned as Colin did the same. "Ready to face the firing squad?"

Colin wiggled his eyebrows playfully, shot her an

adorable, dimpled smile, and followed her down the stairs to the front door.

Beverly Kincaid's shock was palpable as she stammered hello. To her credit, she managed a smile and a warm greeting to Colin.

"Hi, Mom. I ... uh ... forgot." Lizzie glanced up at Colin and grinned. "I ... um ... got a little sidetracked actually."

"So I see. Guess I'm on my own today?"

Lizzie nodded mutely. "Will you and Daddy be home later?"

"Yes." Lizzie rolled her eyes. Her family was not known for being great conversationalists, but something other than a monosyllabic response would soothe her jangled nerves. She looked up at Colin pleadingly.

"Maybe we should tell her," he whispered in her ear.

"I ... uh ... yeah. Um ... Mommy ... Darcy ... Colin, I mean ..." She couldn't seem to get the words out. "Shoot. Let me try this again. Colin asked me to marry him last night, Mom. And I said yes."

Bev's eyes widened, and her silent mouth fell open.

Colin slipped his arm around Lizzie's waist and kissed her softly on the cheek. "I love Lizzie very much, Beverly. I hope we have your blessing?"

Bev looked from Lizzie to Colin and back again. "Are you sure Lizzie? You haven't known each other very long."

"I'm sure Mom. I know everything I need to know about him, and I love him so much."

"Sweetie, I'm happy for you." She surprised Lizzie by hugging them both tightly, and Bev was not a hugger by nature. "I guess you'll want to tell your Dad yourself."

"Can you keep our secret for a while? We'll stop by this afternoon ... and I was hoping that we could get everyone together for dinner tomorrow. Would that be okay?"

Bev's method of agreeing was to quickly plan the menu. "I can do some steaks on the grill …"

"G'day, mate," Lizzie said when her friend Meg picked up the phone on the first ring. "How's Nebraska?"

"Flat," Meg said with a throaty laugh. "With cows."

"Hey!" Jess yelped. "Not nice!"

"Er, right. Nebraska is lovely," Meg amended. "Are you alright? Your email last night had us a bit worried."

"Oh, sorry about that." Lizzie had dashed off a long, self-pitying email after she'd gotten home the night before. "I was distraught."

"And yet you sound positively chipper this morning," Meg noted. "Did you decide Mr. Wonderful wasn't quite so wonderful after all?"

"Nope," Lizzie said, shaking her head and suppressing a laugh as Colin's fingers played in her hair. "He's amazing."

"Crikey. He's there, isn't he?" Meg gasped.

"He is. God, I've missed you two! You're *never* allowed to tag vacation onto a conference again. I needed you!"

"Aw, we're sorry," Jess said. "But the conference was in Chicago, and it's so close to home and I wanted to see how Gramps was after his fall."

"I know. I'm just teasing," Lizzie said. "How's Gramps?"

"Perking up," Jess said. "I think maybe it's because Meg's been … well … Meg, if you know what I mean."

"Let's see … sassy, funny and just a little flirtatious?"

"That about covers it."

"Humph," Meg blustered. "I can't help being me. And we weren't talking about me anyway. We were discussing how you went from being sad and depressed to downright bubbly. And why, exactly is Colin Blake, who my sources tell me is, in fact, our new boss, with you when he's *supposed* to be in London."

"Let's see. In reverse order, he changed his mind about flying home, he is your new boss, but that's not public knowledge until it's announced on Monday and he's here because, well, he can't resist my charms. I ... he showed up late last night, kissed me senseless, and proposed."

"Proposed?" Meg and Jess whispered together.

"I said yes," Lizzie added though it probably wasn't necessary.

"Not messing around, eh?" Meg asked. "Good for you."

"I do have one question, though," Jess said. "Any chance he's got a brother or two?"

"Sorry, ladies, no brothers," Lizzie laughed. "Now, when are the two of you going to get your butts back to Pennsylvania? No more side trips."

"Flying home tomorrow, back in the office first thing Monday," Jess assured her.

"Three girls and a bottle of wine next week?" Meg suggested. "Got a case of wine from my mates in Margaret River just before Jess and I left town."

"I ..." Lizzie hesitated and glanced at Colin.

"It's fine," he whispered. "I've had you all to myself for two weeks, and I've no doubt that I'll have mountains of work to keep me occupied."

"But ... well, okay, I do need some girl time, but would you two mind if Colin joined us later?"

"You're kidding, right?" Jess said with a laugh. "Meg's been salivating at the idea."

"That true, Meg?"

"Abso-bloody-lutely! It's my job to make sure this lad's worthy of you. If he can make it past my bullshit detector then you know he's a keeper."

"You know, Meg, as much as I appreciate your bullshit detector, this time, I don't need it. He's the best man I've ever known and I plan on keeping him … forever."

When she ended the call, Colin was smiling softly at her. "Good answer, love. And in case you've any doubts, I plan on keeping you forever, too." He whipped out his phone and touched the screen. "Shall I have a go? Seems you're having all the fun." He quickly tapped on the number labeled 'Mum'.

Lizzie clutched his hand tightly as she listened to his half of the conversation.

"Hallo, Mum … Yes … change of plans. I have some wonderful news … are you sitting down? Good … good … Mum … do you recall me mentioning my travel agent Anna … yes … the one that loves Jane … yes … well … we've been seeing quite a lot of each other while I've been here … She's wonderful, Mum … You'll love her … yes … she's flying home with me Thursday night … great … a dinner party sounds lovely … slow down, Mum … there's something I need to tell you … are you sitting down? All right then … I've … um … I've asked her to marry me … and … well, she said yes …"

Lizzie giggled as she heard Helen's cry of excitement.

"Yes … Mum, quite … I … do you think you could break the news to Lady Frances for me? I know … it'll be bloody awful … yes … I've warned her … glad to know I can count on your support … think you can rally the rest of the troops? Right-o … excellent … what's that? Let me ask her …" He put his hand over the mouthpiece and informed Lizzie that his mother wanted to say hello. Lizzie nodded yes. "Here she is Mum …" he said as he handed her the phone.

"H-hello Mrs. Blake," Lizzie stammered.

"You must call me Helen, my dear." Her voice was warm and inviting, and Lizzie liked her at once. "Do you prefer Anna or Lizzie?"

"Either is fine, although Colin calls me Lizzie. I'm sorry, I'm a bit nervous at the moment," she admitted as she chewed on her lower lip. "Kind of a weird thing to announce by phone, but we couldn't wait."

"That's the best kind of love, dear, the kind that makes you rush right in. I trust my son was suitably romantic when he popped the question."

Lizzie rolled her eyes and grinned at Colin. "She's asking if you were romantic," she mouthed. To Helen, she said, "very romantic. He told me just how ardently he admired and loved me … though I think he used slightly different words."

"Good for him. And about time, if I might say so. He's warned you about my mother-in-law, Lady Frances, I hear. Don't worry, the girls and I will back you one hundred percent. Tori too, I dare say. I'm so looking forward to meeting you in person, Lizzie."

"Me too."

"I've told Colin to bring you straight away to the country house. See you Friday morning, my dear. And welcome to the family."

"Thank you, Helen. See you Friday," Lizzie said as she handed the phone back to Colin.

"Right, Mum. Cheers." He ended the call and flashed her a dimpled grin.

"Stop it!"

"What?" he asked feigning innocence.

"Those damned dimples of yours make you irresistible and you know it!"

"Good to know, Lizzie, good to know."

"So … what does one wear to a simple dinner party in your neck of the woods?" she asked with trepidation.

"Suit and tie for me, probably some sort of nice frock

for you."

"I can see I'm going to have to go shopping. I'm sure I don't have anything that would be even remotely appropriate."

"I think you look lovely as you are," he said, eying her baggy t-shirt and blue jeans.

"That's sweet, but somehow I doubt this will cut it, even at your country house. I'm afraid to even ask about that! Suddenly I'm picturing Pemberley or at the very least Netherfield."

Colin chuckled, and a slight blush tinged his cheeks.

"I'm right, aren't I?"

He nodded slowly. "It is more than just a house in the country. But I'll let it speak for itself."

"Should I assume that if it speaks it also has a name?"

He flashed her a smile. "Yes. It's called Snowhill. It's just a house, Lizzie, with a few gardens."

"I'll take that under advisement, Darcy. I suspect our ideas of *just a house* are a little different," she added wryly. "Mid-century American rancher versus ancient English country estate?"

"We may differ in background and circumstance, but in the things that matter most, we're much the same. Lizzie, please don't let my wealth affect how you feel about me. What makes me a rich man ... and a lucky one ... is my family ... my daughter ... and now you."

"How did I get so lucky?"

"I keep asking myself the same question. I suppose we'll spend a lifetime trying to determine the answer."

"I love you, Darcy," Lizzie said as she kissed him. "Um ... don't you have another call to make?"

"I do, indeed. Brace yourself for this one, though. She's a bit of a whirlwind, my Tori." He dialed quickly and paused as the phone was answered on the other end. "Victoria Blake, please. Yes ... her father," he said into the phone. "They've just gone to fetch her."

Once again Lizzie found herself listening to half a conversation.

"Hallo, sweetheart. Having fun? Oh … on your way out are you … I'll be quick then … wouldn't want your old Dad to get in the way of all that fun … you will be home next weekend won't you? Good … there's someone I want you to meet … yes … that's right, Lizzie … the one I told you about … yes …well, I took your advice and went for it … .she said yes … yes … I'm sure! Of course you may … " This time, he didn't ask, but just handed her the phone.

"Hi, Tori," Lizzie murmured, her heart pounding. "I've heard a lot about you."

Lizzie was quickly brought up to speed on Victoria Blake's life and recent travels. She certainly had no reason for nervousness, since she couldn't get in a word if she'd tried. The two pieces of information that she remembered from the conversation were that Tori and her friends met Leonardo DiCaprio in Cannes and that she was elated for her Dad because "he spends far too much time all alone, so now I won't worry so much."

She let out her breath as she hung up the phone. "That went much better than I hoped. She certainly can string a lot of words together without taking a breath!"

"That's my girl. She's more reserved and quiet in person. I think there's just something about adolescent girls and telephones … brings out some sort of mutant chatty gene, I suspect."

"I remember what it was like. Actually, I understand that concept pretty well. I'm much more outgoing on the phone than I am in person. Much easier to talk to someone when you don't have to look them in the eye. God … that day I ran into you … I was so nervous. Our conversations and emails meant so much to me … I was so afraid you'd be disappointed."

"Do you know you became my best friend over those

few weeks? I found myself looking forward to talking to you … and making up the lamest excuses to call. You know … I think I started to fall in love the moment you told me off."

"You apologized so sweetly. I guess that's when it started for me too."

Lizzie's father, Jim, took the news well, but she'd expected him to. He respected Colin because he worked hard even though he didn't have to. For Jim Kincaid, that was the truest measure of a man's worth.

"So what do you want to do tonight," Colin asked as they drove back to Lizzie's apartment.

"Well, I had plans to go out with my work friends. But we can do something else if you'd rather. They were only trying to cheer me up when they saw how bummed I was after you left yesterday. And they don't even have a clue how we really feel about each other. To them it's a harmless flirtation, maybe a mutual crush … nothing serious at all."

"I imagine they'd be surprised if I arrived with you?"

"You imagine right. So, are you game? I should warn you in advance … it's just Flannigan's, the local watering hole, very down-to-earth … *and* it's karaoke night too … you might be called on to perform."

"Oh, I intend to perform my love, but that will be later, when we are quite alone."

"That had better be a promise, Darcy."

"You can bank on it, Lizzie."

Hours later, Lizzie walked into the smoky, dimly lit bar alone and joined her friends at the table they'd claimed. "I hope you don't mind, but I brought … a friend." She was careful to keep her left hand jammed deeply into her pocket for the moment.

"Do you have an imaginary friend now, Lizzie?" her friend Karen asked, peering over Lizzie's shoulder and seeing no one.

"My friend is parking the car." Lizzie maneuvered her way around the table and grabbed a stool where she could keep her eye on the door. She was excited to see her friends' faces when Colin arrived and they shared their news. She was also curious to see Colin's reaction to her idea of a good time. In a way, she was testing him again, giving him one last chance to see who she really was. She only hoped that a smoky bar, cheap beer, and amateur entertainment wouldn't scare him off completely.

He grinned as he walked through the door, and Lizzie fell in love all over again. He was twisting his ring nervously as he neared them and she sighed, adoring the innate shyness that lurked beneath his confident exterior.

Her friends were deep in conversation and didn't see him approach. When he wrapped his arms around her possessively from behind and kissed the nape of her neck, they stared wide-eyed and open-mouthed.

Carolyn, Lizzie's boss, was the first to recover. "Mr. Blake ... I ... uh ... thought you flew home last night."

Colin grinned at Lizzie's friends then turned his eyes to her. The warmth of his gaze made her heart pound. "I forgot something."

She arched her eyebrows at him. "Some*thing*, Darcy?"

"You know what I forgot, Lizzie."

"Anyone gonna tell us?" Joanie pouted.

"Shall I tell them Lizzie or do you want to?"

"You tell them, Darcy. They'll never believe it, coming from me."

"Believe what? Jeez, you're driving us nuts, Anna," Karen moaned. "And why do you keep calling Mr. Blake Darcy anyway."

Colin grinned at Lizzie and rubbed her neck gently. "Here goes. First of all, please call me Colin. Second,

Darcy is my middle name and since Lizzie and I are both great Jane Austen fans we found it an amusing coincidence …"

"Jane who?" interrupted Joanie.

Lizzie rolled her eyes at Colin. "Jane Austen! Come on Joanie … I talk about her books all the time."

"Oh, yeah, the old ones with no sex. Go on, Colin."

"Thank you, Joanie." Colin took a deep breath. "The … er … thing I forgot was … *is* … extremely, *vitally* important to me."

"So are you gonna tell us sometime this century?" Karen asked. She looked from Colin to Lizzie and her eyes widened. "No way!"

Lizzie nodded. "Way."

"I couldn't fly back to Britain because I hadn't told Lizzie how I feel about her." He smiled and glanced around the table at her friends. "I'm in love with Lizzie." He leaned forward and kissed her softly.

Lizzie's friends stared at the pair in stunned silence.

"There's more," Lizzie sighed. "I love him too."

"I think we already knew that Anna," Joanie informed her with an approving nod.

"I guess I wear my heart on my sleeve, huh?"

"I'll say," Carolyn agreed. "You were moping around all afternoon after Mr. Blake, I mean, Colin, left."

"Sorry about that. I know I was pretty useless. So … um … do you guys want to hear the rest of the news?" Lizzie asked, a broad grin plastered on her face.

"Well, we already know about the trip next weekend. It makes a lot more sense now. Don't tell me … you're quitting?" Carolyn asked with a frown.

"Nope." Lizzie pulled her left hand from her pocket and laid it casually on the table.

Joanie noticed the ring first. "Jesus Christopher! You're engaged?"

"That we are," Colin said grinning proudly.

They chatted happily over pitchers of beer for a while. Colin was perfectly at ease, unperturbed by her friends less than perfect manners, Joanie's chain smoking, or even the occasional belch.

Lizzie beamed at him. He leaned back in his chair, a grin spreading slowly across his face. "Did I pass your latest test?" he asked so that only Lizzie could hear.

Lizzie groaned. Damned perceptive man! Defeated, she simply nodded her head. "Sorry," she muttered.

"No apologies necessary. Just know that nothing you throw at me will change how I feel about you."

When it was time for karaoke, Lizzie fought through the crowd to Seamus Flannigan, the young bartender, and gave him her name and her selection. "Thanks, Seamus." She was up third - not too early and not too late. She wove her way back to the table and happily held Colin's hand as they listened to the first performers – a pot-bellied man who offered up a mediocre rendition of *Friends in Low Places* and a superb folk singer whose whiskeyed voice evoked Janis Joplin. As she sang her last note, Lizzie kissed Colin on the cheek. "My turn," she said, escaping before he could remark.

Lizzie loved music and singing, something she hadn't mentioned to Colin. Never completely comfortable onstage, she felt vulnerable and exposed and yet, once she began singing, once the adrenalin started to pump, she felt a high like no other. Tonight was no exception.

She closed her eyes and took a deep breath, listening for the slow, bluesy chords of Etta James classic, *At Last*. It was one of Lizzie's favorites, but she'd never sung it knowing it was true before. Her eyes searched the smoky bar and found Colin's. "For you," she mouthed.

The heartfelt words of the song washed over her as she sang, feeling every word, knowing that she had, at last, found her soul mate. The loneliness and disappointment of the past faded with each syllable, allowing Lizzie to finally embrace all the possibilities of her future with Colin.

He smiled at her, his dimples carved deeply in his cheeks as he listened and watched, both surprised and deeply touched.

Tears stung her eyes as she lingered on the final note, tears she found reflected in Colin's eyes.

The normally noisy bar was silent when Lizzie finished. Her eyes remained locked with Colin's as he wound his way through the crowd and joined her on the small stage. "Thank you," he said simply. "I had no idea you sang so beautifully. You touch my soul in so many ways, Lizzie. Thank you for sharing this with me."

"Oh, Darcy," she whispered as he swept her into his arms. She lost herself in his kiss. It was only when she heard the whistles and catcalls of the crowd that she realized where they were. "Good lord, Darcy, we're onstage," she whispered against his lips.

"So we are my love." He kept his arm firmly around her waist and stepped up to the microphone. "I won't offend your ears by attempting to sing, especially not following my beautiful Lizzie. I will, however claim a kiss, and tell her once again, how much I adore her."

"What a night," Lizzie laughed as they left the stage.

Darcy grinned, his dimples dancing devilishly. He leaned in, close to her ear and whispered, "the night is still very young, my love."

She couldn't stop herself from blushing again. "So it is," she whispered back. "So it is."

CHAPTER 9

Lizzie was silent for most of the drive home. Pensive. Anxious. She loved Colin more than she'd dreamed possible and knowing that they were about to make love for the first time had her feeling as if a million butterflies had been released into her belly. She closed her eyes and took a deep breath.

"... do you think?" Colin said as they waited at a red light.

"Huh?" He'd obviously asked her a question, but she'd been so lost in thought she hadn't heard. "Sorry."

"I asked what you thought about getting married at the end of the summer."

"I ... honestly, Darcy, I haven't thought about it at all."

"What's the matter, love?" Colin asked uneasily. "You're not ... please tell me you aren't having second thoughts ..." Even in the darkened interior of the car, Lizzie could see the worry lines furrowing his forehead.

She ran her hand reassuringly down his arm and squeezed his hand. "Nothing like that. Pretty much the opposite, in fact. I ... I'm feeling a little ... actually, a lot … nervous … about us making love. You have to admit, this is all incredibly intense. I'm not used to intense."

"Would it help if I confessed I'm a bit edgy myself, Lizzie?" He smiled gently, and she felt her anxiety ease.

"It does help. This is miles out of my league. I'm not exactly a woman of vast experience. I mean … I've had a couple of serious boyfriends … I am over thirty after all … but … it's … um … been a while … a long while."

"I haven't exactly been setting the sheets afire myself, Lizzie."

"That's reassuring and … surprising. I mean … look at you … you're one sexy man, you know," she teased. She was feeling better now, knowing that Colin shared her nervousness. "Are all the women in England blind and stupid?"

Colin chuckled and quirked an eyebrow. "Hardly. Truthfully? After Lara, I was so busy building my business and raising my daughter I scarcely had the time, let alone the inclination. And, at the time, I was less than willing to gamble on love. I stayed far away from anything that could be deemed a serious relationship."

"So why now? Why … me?" she asked, needing to hear the answer.

"It's quite extraordinary really. I felt the connection between us from the start. I *wanted* to trust you, to love you, to need you. Once you were in my life, I suddenly couldn't picture it without you. When I tried, it looked bleak and empty. I knew without you I'd be … incomplete."

"I felt it too. Needed you. Wanted you." She felt the car slow, as Colin parallel parked in front of her building. "We're here," Lizzie gulped.

"We are," Colin replied. He pushed open his door and got out, sprinting around the hood of the car to open

Lizzie's door and help her out. He tugged her gently into his arms and lowered his lips to hers. "I need you so much, Lizzie." His voice caressed her ear like fine silk, making her shiver.

Lizzie gave herself up to the heady pleasure of his kiss, losing herself as sparks flew between them and ignited. Flames of passion licked her body, and as their hearts pounded in synchronicity, her apprehensions waned. This was the man she loved, her one true love, her soul mate. In a heartbeat, she knew that with Colin she was safe, happy, cherished. Whatever miracle had brought them together, she knew with certainty that they were meant to be.

"Um, Darcy? I think maybe we should take this indoors before we get ourselves arrested or something," Lizzie said giggling as she grabbed his hand and pulled him inside.

They laughed and kissed their way up the stairs, barely shutting the door before they began fumbling with each other's clothes, struggling to find buttons and zippers, desperate to shed the barriers between them. They stumbled into the bedroom and tumbled onto the bed, a happy tangle of arms and legs.

Making love with Darcy was so much more than Lizzie had ever experienced or even dreamed possible. More intense. More playful. Hotter. Sweeter. Pure bliss. She felt as if a corner of Heaven had touched her soul as she learned the contours of his body. Sinewy muscles, taut abdomen, strong arms to hold her for a lifetime. "I'm a lucky woman," she whispered against his cheek. "Who knew you were hiding all of this beneath those expensive suits of yours?" She skimmed her hands over his powerful shoulders and skittered them down his backbone to the firm muscles of his butt.

"For your eyes only," he chuckled as he trailed hot kisses down her neck and across her collarbone. His tongue swirled slowly around her nipple, making her gasp loudly. "Mine. Every luscious inch of you is all mine."

"It's a lot of inches," she said apologetically.

"Don't you dare," he growled. "You're perfect." He kissed her, his mouth moving over hers fiercely, scorching her lips. "Perfect," he whispered as he thrust inside her.

Lizzie sighed, reaching up to cup his cheek. "Perfect," she murmured, rocking her hips against his.

He laughed softly, his dimples deeply etched in his cheeks as they rocked together, each movement bringing them closer, binding them. Gentle touches. Soft sighs. A vortex of pure pleasure.

Heat coiled in Lizzie's belly, whirling, splintering, shattering as wave after wave of bliss left her teetering on the edge.

They toppled together, their bodies shuddering to climax. They were connected, mind, body and soul. They were one.

In the afterglow, Colin rolled onto his back and held her tightly in his arms, lovingly caressing her skin. "You're dazzling," he whispered as he kissed the tip of her nose. "My Lizzie."

"I'm just an ordinary woman, but you make me feel spectacular."

"You *are* spectacular, my love."

She giggled and kissed him softly as they lay nose to nose on the pillow. "I'm short and chubby and always a mess, that hardly qualifies me for spectacular, though I do think you're the sweetest man I've ever known for saying so."

"I believe you're the first person besides my mother to ever call me sweet."

"You are sweet, no matter what you, or the rest of the world thinks. The sweetest man I've ever known."

"And you are my beautiful Lizzie, no matter how often you try to tell me otherwise."

"I'm a realist, Darcy. I don't pretend to be other than who I am."

"I wish you could see yourself as I see you."

"What do you see?" she asked.

"I see a lovely woman, all generous, intoxicating, enticing, irresistible curves. A woman who values substance over superficiality, who loves with intensity and generosity. I see … someone who's unafraid to tell it like it is and who's willing to put up with me for the next fifty-odd years, knowing full well that I can be a right pain in the arse."

"God, I love you!" Lizzie said as she rained soft kisses on his face. "I love you, I love you, I love you!"

Colin woke to a soft scratching on the bedroom door. He angled up onto one elbow, smiling down at Lizzie's sleeping form.

She was curled onto her side, her hands beneath her cheek. The sheet had slipped down to her waist, exposing her soft, generous curves to his hungry eyes. She was beautiful, with lush, full breasts and sweetly rounded hips. "One day you'll believe that not all men want a skeletal model, my Lizzie." He kissed the curve of her shoulder and brushed her hair back from her face.

Lizzie's eyes fluttered open, and she smiled dreamily up at him. "Hey." She reached up to sift her fingers through his hair. "Now this is what a woman should wake up to," she said as she tugged his head down.

He chuckled softly as his kissed her. His tongue tangled with hers, silky and demanding, and his clever fingers swirled over her taut nipples. His lips left hers, burning their way down her throat to replace his fingers. His tongue swirled around her nipple, his teeth grazing the sensitive skin.

Lizzie moaned softly. Colin laughed. His lips moved to her other breast and his fingers slid beneath the sheet and skimmed over the soft skin of her belly to dip into her slick, wet folds. Her eyelids fluttered as he swirled the pad of his thumb over her throbbing nub. "God, how I love you …" he murmured, trying to ignore the persistent scratching at the door. "Bollocks."

"Cats," Lizzie giggled. "They're curious."

"They've hidden every time I've been here," he grumbled against her breast. Ignoring the noise, he returned to the task at hand. Lizzie wriggled against his hand, arching her back and purring with pleasure. He swirled his thumb over her mound in slow, sensuous circles, watching her face as passion and joy and bliss flickered across her features.

She shivered and moaned as his mouth and his fingers continued their tantalizing play. "More," she murmured. "More."

Without a word, he slithered up her body, settling his hips between her thighs and balancing above her on his forearms. He entered her slowly, one scintillating millimeter at a time.

"More," she repeated.

"Patience, love," he murmured. "We have a lifetime together. I mean to savor this moment."

Lizzie let out a long impatient sigh and tilted her hips ever-so-slightly, pulling him deeper. "Savoring is good but let's not get crazy." She wrapped her legs around his waist, urging him deeper still.

Colin groaned and gave in to her demands, thrusting deeply. "Happy now?"

"Ecstatic," she said on a sigh. "You?"

He laughed softly, his dark eyes bright and his dimples dancing, and withdrew slowly to thrust again. "Perfect." He thrust again and again, loving the way her body enveloped his, warm and slick and throbbing, loving the way her short fingernails scratched and clawed at his shoulders, loving how she trembled and gasped and cried his name.

Colin plunged forward once more, his body shuddering as he exploded within her. With a grunt, he collapsed on top of her. He nuzzled her neck with his nose before rolling onto his back and gathering her into his arms. "I've waited a lifetime for one morning like this."

"Get used to it, my adorable Brit, because I'm planning to fill the *rest* of your lifetime with mornings just like this."

"It seems we're of one mind, then," he said softly. "Promise me something?"

"Anything. Whatcha need?"

"A very short engagement," he laughed.

"I'm already yours, you know."

"I know but I want it official, legal, blessed by God and man and ..." he stopped speaking as the scratching at the door resumed with increased fervor. "Bloody hell, do they do that every morning?"

"Well, no," Lizzie said, coloring slightly. "They're not used to the door being shut, so they usually come in for a snuggle."

Colin laughed softly. "I reckon I'll adjust, but for the record, I prefer to snuggle with you and you alone."

"They'll adjust, too," Lizzie said with a smile. "We all will."

There was another round of persistent scratching before the door burst open. Colin had just enough time to pull the sheets over their naked bodies before Lizzie's two cats jumped lightly on the bed. He quirked an eyebrow at them. "Morning, lads."

Kisses, a silky black longhair, trotted up the bed and rubbed his chin against Colin's shoulder. Seemingly satisfied with his presence, he curled up on the pillow and began purring loudly in his ear.

"Aw, my baby likes you!" Lizzie gushed. She snapped her fingers and Hugs, her Siamese-tabby mix padded up the bed. He sniffed the air tentatively, taking slow, measured steps before lowering his head and rubbing his ears against Colin's hand. "Even my shy boy is smitten. Boys," Lizzie said, addressing the cats, "I know you've been avoiding my Darcy, but it's time you get used to him." She smiled up at Colin, reaching over to stroke Kisses's soft head, then scratching behind Hugs's ears. "He's part of the family now."

"So what's your big news?" Lizzie's cousin Dare asked as he kissed her on the cheek.

"Soon," Lizzie said, grinning up at her brawny blond cousin. "Dare often forgets that it's not polite to interrogate family. Still enjoying the quiet life in the city?"

"Eh, you've seen one dirtbag drug dealer, you've seen them all."

"He also likes to pretend that his job is just a few boring dirtbags, and wants us to forget that it's actually incredibly dangerous."

"Lizzie's a worrier," Dare said. "She forgets it's my job."

"A dangerous job," Colin said with a nod. "You're a brave man."

"Something tells me you're no coward." Dare eyed Colin shrewdly, his gray eyes narrowed. "Or you wouldn't be facing off with a family of cops."

"It's not so different from convincing someone to see my side of a deal," Colin said evenly. "Protective lot," he whispered against Lizzie's ear.

"Overprotective," Lizzie said, rolling her eyes at her cousin. "He means well. They all do. They just …"

"Want the best for you? Trust me, love, I understand.

Perhaps we should just jump in feet first?"

"Go for it," Lizzie breathed, clutching his hand nervously.

Colin took a spoon and tapped it on the neck of his beer bottle. When he had their attention, he smiled and wrapped his arm tightly around Lizzie's waist. "I reckon you're all curious about this impromptu gathering ..."

"I'm never curious about a free meal," Lizzie's Uncle Neil yelled.

"Sad, but true," added his younger brother, Phil.

"But I'm more curious about the strange man who's got his arm around my favorite niece," shouted her Uncle Ed, who just happened to be the local Chief of Police. "Your intentions had better be honorable, young man."

"Sorry about them," Lizzie mumbled. "They're *mostly* lovable."

"Shush," Colin said with a finger to her lips. "I can handle the lot of them." He surveyed the crowd with the confident eye of a man who knew exactly what to say to charm his opponents into seeing his point of view. "Gentlemen," he said nodding to Lizzie's trio of uncles and her overgrown cousin. "I can fully appreciate your desire to protect the ones you love. I have six sisters and a teenage daughter, after all, so I'm well acquainted with the need to fully vet the men in their lives. It's caused me more than a bit of trouble over the years, to be perfectly honest and ..."

"You're losing them," Lizzie hissed in his ear. "Honorable intentions, remember?"

"Right. Sorry, got a bit off track for a moment. To answer your question, Chief Kincaid ... yes." He held Lizzie's left hand up high enough for everyone to see. "I reckon that's as honorable as it gets."

"You *are* a brave man," Dare said later as he clapped him on the shoulder. "Not for marrying my cousin ...

Lizzie's the best … but, well, we Kincaids can be a handful and …"

"And?" Lizzie asked with a grin.

"Welcome to the family, cuz."

It was the first time that Lizzie had ever truly surprised her family. Reserved, play-it-safe, predictable Anna Elizabeth Kincaid was taking a chance on love - and on life - for the first time. The overprotective uncles and cousin gave Colin their unanimous approval and support.

It didn't take long for the conversation to turn to the prospect of more grandchildren. Lizzie could tell that her parents were a little concerned at her becoming an instant stepmother, but their concern was tempered with joy over having another grandchild to spoil. This naturally led to a discussion of *her* having a baby, which made both Colin and Lizzie blush uncomfortably. It was one of many vital subjects they had yet to discuss.

"So when's the wedding?" Lisa asked.

Lizzie glanced at Colin and shrugged. "We haven't decided. Maybe the end of the summer."

"Are you nuts? That's only two months away! You'll never plan a decent wedding in two months," she replied authoritatively.

Lizzie rolled her eyes and grinned at Colin. "I've learned that with Darcy anything is possible." She hadn't told her family the details of Colin's life, especially not the extent of his wealth. It would make them uneasy and possibly affect how they treated him. She wanted them to get to know him better first.

"Okay, whatever. Where?" she asked, continuing her interrogation.

"Not sure. Possibly here. Maybe over there. We'll figure it out." Yet another subject they hadn't touched on. Lizzie smiled uncertainly at Colin. He shrugged his shoulders and gave her hand a reassuring squeeze.

"Well, here's an easy one for you. Where are you going to live?" she questioned.

"Jeez, Lis, you should've been a cop like the rest of the family! We've only been engaged for two days!" Lizzie said, sighing with exasperation. She looked pleadingly at Colin, hoping for a rescue.

Her hero didn't disappoint. "You promised to show me more of the neighborhood, love."

"You're right, I forgot." She stood up and held out her hand to him. "Come on, then." To her family, from whom she desperately needed a breather, she said, "we'll be back in a while."

"I guess we have a lot of decisions to make, huh, Darcy?" Lizzie mused as they walked hand-in-hand down the winding, tree-lined road.

"We'll sort things out. So, where are you taking me?" he asked with a dimpled grin. "You've already shown me most of the neighborhood."

"It's a secret. Now this," Lizzie said indicating the tree-lined street, "this was the site of my first great enterprise."

"Care to enlighten me?" he asked.

"My paper route. I was … twelve, maybe thirteen. Used to ride my bike and toss the papers in the driveways."

"Did you make your fortune as a newsgirl?" he teased.

"Hardly," she snorted, "but it gave me some spending money. Money was always kind of tight when I was a kid."

"You haven't told them, have you?"

"That you're rich? Nope, not a chance. I …" She hung her head shamefully.

"My money embarrasses you?"

"It makes me a little uncomfortable," she answered

truthfully. "I suppose I'll get used to it in time," she laughed. "I want them to know you a little better is all. They're already shocked enough at what I've done. Any more truth might kill them!"

Colin laughed heartily. "Wouldn't want to be the cause of that, my Lizzie." He caught her hand and lifted it to his lips, tenderly kissing the tip of each finger. She shuddered with pleasure. "Tell them whenever you think they can handle it."

They continued walking slowly, still holding hands, past her old stone elementary school and down a winding hill toward the creek. A weathered, red covered bridge spanned the gently flowing water. Lizzie tugged Colin down a narrower lane, walking until they reached the restful spot that she wanted to show him.

They made their way carefully down a steep hill toward the broad, flat, gray rocks where she'd spent many dreamy afternoons growing up. A smaller stream joined the creek there, its water tripping merrily over the rocky streambed to merge with the more sedate rhythm of the creek.

Lizzie plopped down on the sun-warmed stone and grinned up at the man she loved. "Welcome to my secret place."

"It's a warm, soothing spot. It suits you, Lizzie." He settled beside her, his arm looped loosely at her waist.

"I did all my best thinking here when I was a kid."

Colin nodded in understanding. "I have quite a similar haven at Snowhill. It inspired most of my great dreams ... and one or two truly stupid ones."

"I know what you mean. I'd disappear from home for hours on end and wander back just before dark. This place got me into more trouble ... but I've always made my best decisions here."

"Then perhaps we might try to make one or two?" Colin suggested.

"Good idea, Darcy. So, end of the summer? August?"

"Is it too soon?" he asked impatiently. "Do you need more time to plan?"

"I don't think so. I want a simple wedding. I always have. As long as you and I are there, I'll be happy." She traced a finger down his cheek and outlined his lips, then angled up and kissed him softly.

"Simple sounds lovely to me," he sighed.

"I take it your first wedding wasn't simple?" she asked as curiosity got the better of her.

"Quite the opposite," he said, his voice tinged with sadness. "Lara and her father demanded the wedding of the year."

"I'm sorry, Darcy."

"Sorry? For what?"

"That she treated you so badly. Look, sweetie, I'm realistic enough to know that life won't be perfect. We'll both have some adjusting to do. I'm sure we'll have our share of arguments, but I promise you'll always be able to trust me and to talk to me about anything. I see marriage as a partnership. And I don't take those vows we'll make lightly. You and I, this is a forever thing."

"You never cease to amaze me, Lizzie. Now, tell me what sort of wedding you have in mind," he said deftly changing the subject.

"I know most women have lifelong dreams about their wedding, but I'd pretty much convinced myself I'd never have one. It's been a long time since I let myself dream about it."

"Then tell me what you dreamed on your sunny afternoons, lying here on these rocks."

"How can you know me so well?" she sighed. She took a long, deep breath and closed her eyes, allowing the long-banished dreams to flood her mind. "For a long time I pictured my wedding in the little church on the hill. Small, just family and close friends. Now I think I'd rather have a garden wedding ..."

"Where would you like to be married, Lizzie? If you wish for a garden, I can recommend Snowhill. It's particularly lovely in August."

"I don't know, Darcy, it's so far away. Most of my friends and family couldn't afford ..." She glanced up at Colin and blushed. He could easily afford to transport whomever she cared to invite. "I know you'd fly over anyone I want there. My mother won't fly, though. She flatly refuses."

"We'll book her on a transatlantic cruise, then. Please say you'll consider us getting married at Snowhill."

"I'll consider it. Of course, I'll consider it if it's important to you."

"Okay ... so we've got the when - late August - and possibly the where. What's left?"

"The biggest decision of all."

"Where to live?"

Lizzie nodded. She was a small-town girl at heart and the thought of living as far away as England scared her. "Here?" she asked hopefully. "But I guess you need to be there for your business."

Colin grinned and squeezed her hand reassuringly. "It's my business. I can manage it from wherever I choose. There's this rather amazing contraption nowadays, you know. It's called an airplane ..." he teased.

"Don't be a pain in the ass," she said swatting him playfully on the arm. "This is serious!"

"I know it is, Lizzie," he said with a contrite smile. "We're deciding where to call home. It's not a decision to take lightly."

Lizzie's eyes locked with Colin's and she realized that as long as she was in his arms, anywhere she was would be home. "Where do you want to live?"

"Anywhere that you are, my love."

"Funny, I was just thinking the same thing. Home is wherever you are."

"What if we look for someplace here? I'll have to spend the majority of my time here to get Consolidated back on its feet. It's in a bad way."

"I'd like that, Darcy. I'd like that a lot."

"I do hope you'll come to think of Snowhill as your home, too."

"I'm sure I will once I've seen it and I can picture little Colin Darcy Blake sliding down the banister or tracking mud all over the parquet floors," she said, grinning. "What about Tori? This affects her too."

"How would you feel about her living here, with us?" he asked quietly. "I miss her dreadfully when she's away at school."

"Would she be okay with moving here? God ... that makes it sound like I don't want her and that's not true at all. I hope she can consider me a friend or ... something."

"I'll let the two of you work that bit out on your own, but I've no doubt you'll be good friends. Despite her mother's absence, she's never lacked a female influence in her life thanks to my mum and sisters, but she has always wanted a *real* family. As for moving to America ... she's a teenager. America is her idea of heaven on earth."

Lizzie laughed softly. "I can't wait to meet her. Now ... about that real family idea ... how do you feel about that ... a baby I mean? My pesky biological clock is ticking after all, as my sister-in-law delights in reminding me *every* time I see her."

"I've always loved being from a large family," he said. "And I've always regretted that Tori is an only child though she's always had plenty of cousins to run about with. I'd like to give her a brother or sister or two ... and just think of the fun we'd have making them," he said seductively as his lips found hers. "Such fun," he whispered softly.

"Yes," she whispered as his lips covered hers. "So much fun …"

CHAPTER 10

The weekend was over far too soon. Monday morning arrived with depressing regularity and Lizzie found herself wide-awake at five am dreading the day. She knew that her relationship with the new boss would be fodder for office gossip by mid-morning. The thought of it made her stomach lurch, but the warmth of Colin's body nestled tightly against hers calmed her. She snuggled into his embrace, loving the way he held her as if he would never let her go, loving his musky, slightly spicy scent, loving the soft tickle of his breath on the nape of her neck, and his soft snore in her ear.

Careful not to wake him, Lizzie slipped out of bed and put on a pot of coffee. As the rich, heady aroma filled her kitchen, she padded back to bed.

Colin was smiling in his sleep. She sat down cross-legged beside him, content to watch him as he slumbered. She reached down to brush a stray curl from his forehead, allowing her fingers to tangle in the tousled mess. He sighed deeply and began to stir. Lizzie leaned forward and brushed a soft kiss on his temple. "Soon time to face the firing squad," she whispered in his ear.

Ever so slowly, he opened his eyes, regarding her with amusement. "I reckon so."

"You reckon?" she chuckled. "I'm a little worried about going to work today," she murmured. "People will talk."

"People always do."

"Not about me, they don't. The idea of being water cooler gossip ..."

"I can't imagine it will be as bad as all that."

"No, not for you, it won't be. You'll be the sexy stud who seduced the lowly corporate travel agent. But me? I'm the slut that's sleeping with the new boss."

"No, you're the sweet, lovely woman who's *marrying* the new boss. Anyone I hear suggesting otherwise will be looking for a new employer."

"You'd fire someone for me?"

He shrugged. "If it came to that. Do you really think it will be so bad?"

She nodded slowly. "I'm afraid so."

A slow smile spread across his face. "I didn't seduce you. You seduced me."

Lizzie laughed and rolled her eyes. "Oh get real! I wouldn't have a clue where to start."

He gave her hand a gentle tug and pulled her down beside his warm, firm body. "Then you've not earned the office slut title, have you?"

"Hmmm ... I guess I'll have to try a bit harder," she teased as she raked her fingers through the crisp, springy hairs on his thigh. "Wouldn't want to disappoint the office stud, would I?"

"No, you wouldn't," he said against her mouth. Their lips met in a fiery kiss. Lizzie moaned as his tongue slid against hers.

They made love slowly, delighting in each tender caress, relishing each delectable kiss, treasuring their unique rhythm, until they spiraled to an earth-shattering climax.

If Lizzie had her way, they would have taken separate cars, and she would have slunk in the back door and avoided everyone for as long as possible.

Unfortunately, Lizzie didn't get her way. Colin insisted that they drive in together and he held her hand tightly as they walked through the lobby, past the gaping receptionist, to the travel office. "I'll pop in 'round one for lunch, if that suits you?"

"Ah … one is fine. I … I'll see you then," she stammered.

Colin just grinned and leaned in for a sweet, lingering kiss. "G'bye."

It was past ten before Lizzie felt brave enough for a trip to the kitchen for a much-needed boost of caffeine. She took the back way, wanting to meet as few people as possible, and slipped into the kitchen, looking this way and that, giggling at her silliness.

She poured herself a cup of the steaming coffee and cradled the chipped ceramic mug in her hands. Leaning back against the hard edge of the counter, she closed her eyes as she remembered their first meeting.

"Careful you don't burn yourself again."

Lizzie opened her eyes to find Colin grinning wryly at her. "Hey you."

"Fancy meeting you here," he teased.

"Hey, well I do work here after all. I … I missed you," she admitted sheepishly. "I can't seem to focus today for some strange reason."

"Nor can I," he said as he drew her into his arms for a kiss.

"What if someone walks in?" she asked nervously.

"They can bloody well find someone of their own to kiss," he growled.

Lizzie gave in and wound her arms around his neck, tangling her fingers in his dark curls.

"A-hem!" came a loud voice from the doorway.

Reluctantly, they pulled apart and looked up to find two people gaping at them, Lizzie's beaming friend, Meg, and Meg's smarmy, obnoxious boss, Dan Highland.

Dan raked his eyes over Colin and Lizzie and sneered. "Glad to see *someone's* benefiting from this buy-out," he said snidely.

"I'd be cautious if I were you, Dan," Colin warned. "There's still *much* to be decided."

Dan paled beneath his spray tan and stalked from the room. Once he was gone, Meg threw her arms around Lizzie and hugged her tightly. "Darl! I'm so thrilled for you," she said with her charming Aussie twang. "The pair of you look like you're in the midst of a happy attack."

"Definitely a happy attack, Meg. It's been such a whirlwind."

"So it would seem," she said drolly, grinning at the pair. "Word has it you're some sort of brazen hussy, Lizzie."

Lizzie laughed and thumped Colin playfully on the arm. "Told ya so."

"So what's his highness got stuck up his ass today?" she asked Meg.

Meg rolled her eyes. "Who knows with him?" She glanced up at Colin. "I will tell you he's none too happy about the changes here."

"Yeah, probably because he might have to do some *actual* work for once. God, Meg, I don't know how you put up with him."

"Mostly I just ignore him and do my job."

"I suspect you do your work and most of his, Meg."

She just rolled her eyes and tucked her strawberry

blond hair behind her ear. "Seems that way sometimes, darl."

"I'm finding this all quite fascinating," Colin murmured. "Obviously, I've been talking with the wrong people around here."

"*Always* start at the bottom," Meg said sagely. "We minions always know what really goes on, you know."

"Yup. We know who works, who coasts, and who's stealing you blind," Lizzie added.

Colin regarded them thoughtfully. Despite their playful banter, there was a lot of truth in what Meg and Lizzie were saying. "I'm grateful to have you two ladies in my corner."

"As you should be. Well kiddos, duty calls. Mr. Blake ..."

"Colin, please, Meg."

"Colin, you've got yourself one hell of a lady here. Treat her right or I'll have you thrown to the sharks."

Colin snorted. "Protective lot, you Aussies."

"Don't you forget it."

"Um, Meg, maybe you shouldn't threaten your new boss on his very first *day* as your new boss," Lizzie teased.

Meg grinned and shrugged her shoulders. "Eh, easy come, easy go. I'm kidding by the way," she assured Colin.

"I'm relieved to hear you say it." He glanced at his watch. "Bloody hell, I'm late to my own meeting." He kissed Lizzie quickly on the cheek. "See you at lunch, love. Bye, Meg."

"Damn, woman, you are one lucky chick!" Meg sighed when he'd gone.

"Don't I know it. Now, keep your mitts off him!" Lizzie threatened. "He's all mine."

Colin pinched the bridge of his nose as the numbers

on his screen blurred. His head was pounding, and his eyes were bleary from staring at the screen for three hours straight. He blinked and stretched and rolled his chair away from the desk then strode from the office in search of a couple of aspirin.

He poked his head into the office next-door, pleased to see a friendly face at the desk. Meg held up one finger while she finished up a phone call. "Bloody moron," she muttered as she ended the call.

"I hope that wasn't meant for me," Colin said with a pained smile.

Meg rolled her eyes dramatically. "One of Dan's partners in crime," she muttered. "That man! Good thing he's at one of his three-martini lunches."

"Three martini lunches?" Colin asked with a frown. "We'll come back 'round to that, Meg. I was hoping you could point me in the direction of some aspirin."

"You are a bit green around the edges," Meg said peering at him closely. She pulled open her top drawer and tossed him a bottle of Tylenol then wheeled across the room to grab a bottle of water from the mini-fridge. "Dan's private stash. But as he orders them on the company dime, I reckon that means they're technically yours." She wheeled back to her desk and offered him the plastic bottle. "Not eco-friendly, mind, but that's Dan, though he can talk a good game about how environmentally-conscious Consolidated is. In case you haven't figured it out, this company is no friend to dear old Mother Earth."

"It will be. It will also be profitable and a decent place to work."

"I believe you," Meg said with a grin. "I Googled you after I spoke to Lizzie the other day. Your career is … impressive to say the least. Have you made your first billion yet?"

"Not quite," Colin laughed. He poured a pair of

tablets onto his palm and tossed them in his mouth, following with a gulp of the icy water. "Is that important?"

"To me? No. To Lizzie? Definitely not. In fact, my guess is that our girl would be much more comfortable if you weren't an almost-billionaire. No, Colin, what impressed me most is the focus you place on giving back. The Blake Foundation is quite the philanthropic endeavor."

"Thank you. Apart from my daughter, it's what I'm most proud of. Will I see you at lunch?"

"Not a chance," Meg sighed. "A weeklong conference followed by a week's holiday equals an inbox filled to bursting. I'll be eating at my desk this arvo."

"I'll allow it this once, but don't make a habit of it. Everyone needs a mental break from time to time … except perhaps the ones who do little else. When Highland gets back from his lunch, send him to my office."

"Will do, boss," Meg said with a mock salute. "Let me know if you need anything else."

He returned an hour after his lunch with Lizzie. "I'm sorry, Meg. I know you're buried but …"

"What's up?"

"I need a favor. I … I'm supposed to take Lizzie shopping tonight for our trip this weekend, but I've hours more work to do …"

Meg held up a hand. "Say no more. I've got this."

"You're a lifesaver."

"Nah. I'm not sweet and fruity with a hole in the middle. I've always thought of myself as more of a Sweet Tart, you know … much more interesting and …"

"Meg?" Colin murmured.

"Yes, boss?"

"I owe you one." He tilted his head toward the door to Dan Highland's office. "Still at lunch?"

Meg nodded. "Likely on his third martini about now, and trying to sweet talk the nearest female with his unique charms," she shuddered.

"While you do the bulk of his work and he takes all of the credit?" Colin muttered. "I guarantee that won't continue and nor will the long, alcohol-fueled lunches. I'm not overly fond of the part of my job that requires me to, shall we say, prune away the dead wood, but in this case I've a feeling I'm going to enjoy it immensely."

It was well past five-thirty when Lizzie finally shutdown her computer for the night. It had been an emotionally draining day. She had never discussed her personal life - her love life - so often or with so many people.

Wearily she gathered her things, murmured a soft goodbye and slipped out the door to the elevator. Once the doors slid open, she leaned against the back wall, savoring the peace and solitude as she coasted to the fourth floor where Colin had claimed an office.

As Lizzie stepped from the elevator, her friend Jess grinned at her and held up a finger as she put her caller on hold. "Damn it! It's almost quitting time, and there are six calls on hold. I'll be here late for sure. Ugh!" she moaned as she adjusted her headset and crossed her legs to reveal a tattoo of a musical note on one ankle. She raked a hand through her brown hair and rolled her eyes.

"I feel your pain, Jess!" Lizzie said, smiling her understanding.

Jess shrugged her shoulders and pasted a smile on her face. "That's life, I guess."

"Um, Jess? You may want to unclench your teeth." Lizzie chuckled.

"Good point, Lizzie. Hey, don't go anywhere! I need

the scoop!"

Lizzie nodded as Jess turned back to her computer and pressed the hold button to finish her call. "I'll be right back," she mouthed as she wandered down the corridor toward Colin's makeshift office.

She didn't get far before smarmy Dan, carrying a box of his belongings, accosted her. "Well, well, if it isn't Blake's little tramp," he sneered.

Lizzie smiled angelically at him. "Why Dan Highland I do believe that's the nicest thing you've ever said to me!" she gushed, her voice sugary sweet. "Going somewhere?" she asked archly.

"That bastard fired me because of you, you little bitch!"

"Oh, Dan! I'm sure Colin fired you because you're a lazy son-of-a-bitch who puts his work off on his assistant and pads his expense reports," she said reassuringly. "I'm sure I had nothing to do with it!"

Meg emerged from Colin's office, grinning broadly as she watched Dan Highland step into the elevator. "Strewth, what a kerfuffle!" she laughed. "He was mad as a cut snake when old Colin gave him the sack."

"English please, Meg?" Lizzie pleaded.

"Sorry, love!" she laughed, "thought your command of 'strine was improving. Shall I translate?"

"Hmm, no … I think I've got it. Let's see … Gosh, what a commotion. He was furious when Colin fired him?"

"Perfect! You know, Jess is dying for all the gory details."

"Humph, as if you haven't already told her. So, where's Colin?"

"In his office. I think he's a bit done in, really, the poor lad."

"Ugh. And I'm dragging him shopping tonight."

"I wish," Colin said dejectedly from the doorway.

"I'm sorry love, but this place is more of a disaster than I realized."

Lizzie wrapped her arms around his waist and hugged him close. "It can wait."

He grinned down at her. "Actually. I have a small surprise for you."

"Another surprise," she squeaked. "I'm not sure I can take that, Darcy."

"You'll have to learn to adjust. I plan to surprise you quite frequently."

"Oh, you do, do you?"

"Yes, I do."

"So ... what's the surprise?"

"If I tell you that will spoil all the fun. But your friends Meg and Jess will be going along."

"Oooh! I love a good mystery. Okay ... I'll accept your surprise on one condition."

He arched one eyebrow. "And that is?"

"Wherever you're sending us, promise to meet us later for a drink or two?"

"Already arranged, love. Now go, have fun."

"All right." She stood on tiptoe to kiss him soundly. "Try not to work too hard, okay?"

"I won't."

"Liar," she called over her shoulder as she flounced back down the corridor to where Meg stood. Halfway there, she turned and smiled at him. "I love you, you crazy, workaholic millionaire stud!"

CHAPTER 11

Jess finished up her last phone call, pulled off her headset, and tossed it on the desk. "Okay, ladies, are we ready?" she said.

"I'd be more ready if I had a clue where we're going, but hey ... after the weekend I just had I'm game for almost anything!"

"No worries, mate!" Meg assured her. "You're in excellent hands. Muah ha ha ha ha."

"I'd feel better without the evil laugh, sunshine," Lizzie said as she followed her friends to the elevator. "Can't I even get a tiny clue?"

A black stretch limo was waiting for them in front of the building. "He didn't!"

The chauffeur stepped out and opened the door with a flourish. The trio climbed in.

"Hey girls, look what I found!" Jess said pulling a bottle of champagne from the mini-fridge. "Shall we?"

"Why not? We're not driving."

Jess grinned and popped the cork, chuckling as the champagne bubbled over her hand. "Did you know he even gave us tomorrow morning off?"

Lizzie rolled her eyes. "That man!"

"You're a lucky woman," Jess sighed.

By the time they arrived at their destination, they were all giggling and more than a little tipsy. The chauffeur opened the door and helped them from the limo.

They'd arrived at ... the mall. But not the mall Lizzie frequented, the one with K-Mart and Target. No. This one had Bloomingdale's, Macy's, Neiman Marcus and Nordstrom's, luxury stores that Lizzie had never even browsed.

"He sent us shopping? Well, I can't say I blame him for finding a way out of it."

"Come on, Lizzie, it'll be fun," Jess encouraged as she and Meg tugged Lizzie ever so gently through the doors of the most daunting store of all, Neiman Marcus.

"I can't go in there," she said as the color drained from her face.

"What'd you do, shoplift or something?" Jess teased.

"I just ..."

"C'mon, Lizzie. She'll be apples." Meg said.

"Fine. But this has disaster written all over it," Lizzie grumbled.

They walked briskly through the store, not even glancing at the expensive, high-end designer displays, and carefully ducking from the overzealous perfume testers. "Where are you taking me?" Lizzie moaned as they took the escalator to the top floor.

She groaned when they reached their destination. Personal Shopping.

"Oh, Christ! Doesn't he think I can pick out clothes on my own?" Lizzie whined. She glanced around and took a step toward the down escalator.

"Lizzie! That's not it at all!" Meg said, grabbing her by the arm before she could make her escape. "Colin mentioned to me that you wanted to find some things for your trip, but he couldn't break away from the disaster that is Consolidated. The personal shopper was our idea, since we know how much you detest shopping. Did you *not* say that you wished someone would dress you up and tell you what looks good when you had to buy a dress for that wedding last month?"

Jess nodded her agreement. "What she said. C'mon, Lizzie … it'll be just like *Pretty Woman!*"

Lizzie groaned. She was beaten and she knew it. "Hey with all the chatter around the office I *feel* like Vivian Ward today! Okay, fine, I *may* have mentioned how fabulous it would be to get a makeover."

Meg and Jess exchanged identical, slightly evil grins. Lizzie's forehead crinkled as she eyed her friends nervously. "I'm not a Barbie doll you know."

"You are now," Meg said with a devilish laugh. "Ooh! This will be fun!"

"Miss Kincaid?" asked a cool, professional voice.

"That would be me."

"Good evening. I'm Kaitlin. Welcome to Personal Shopping. If you and your friends would follow me …" She ushered them into a posh, but comfortably decorated room with a large dressing room in one corner.

"Mrs. Blair will be right with you," she said with a smile.

Madeline Blair was an attractive woman in her late forties; she was dressed to impress in a belted silk blouse and pencil skirt paired with five-inch stilettos.

"I'm not wearing those," Lizzie mumbled, motioning at the shoes. "I'm all about comfort."

"They're not as scary as they look," Madeline laughed. "But we can work up to these. We'll get you some training heels. Just relax, honey," she said, her charming Southern drawl as soothing as warm honey. "I'm here to build you up, not tear you down. I don't want to change you. But I will help you appreciate what you've got and learn to love it."

Lizzie smiled nervously. Madeline wasn't what she'd expected at all. She was down-to-earth and funny and the four women were quickly laughing like old friends. "I'm afraid you've got your work cut out for you," She plucked at her baggy tunic and one-size-too big trousers. "I'm fashion-challenged."

"Only because, like most women, you've bought into the idea that you have to look like you haven't eaten in years to be considered sexy." Madeline smoothed a hand over her perfectly fitted skirt. "I'm not exactly a size two, you know. I've got hips and a booty under this."

Lizzie eyed the fitted skirt skeptically. It enhanced Madeline's natural curves without making her look lumpy and dumpy. "I'm at least two sizes bigger."

"Size doesn't matter," she said with a wave of her hand. Meg and Jess exploded into a fit of the giggles. "Okay, maybe it does in *certain* situations, but not when it comes to clothes. You two, giggle twins, front and center."

Meg and Jess snapped to attention, still laughing. "See, both of your friends have classic hourglass figures that men just pant over. Dress them in baggy, shapeless clothes and they look … forgive me, ladies … chubby." She grabbed a handful of loose fabric on Meg's shirt and twisted, making it mold to her full breasts. "But put them in clothes that fit and … *voila* … grown men will weep with joy."

"Va-va-voom!" Meg said, nodding at her reflection appreciatively. "Reckon I'll be doing a cull this weekend. Time to let my girls shine!"

"That's the attitude!" Madeline grabbed Lizzie's wrist and pulled her up to the mirror. "Too much material," she said, pulling on her shirt. "God gave you boobs for a reason."

"Breastfeeding?" Lizzie said drily. "I'm not that well-endowed. I'm more of a pear."

"Honey, look in the mirror!"

Lizzie did as she was told. With the shirt hugging her body, her breasts looked rounder and fuller. "Hmm. That's not bad."

"When we get you in the right bra, it'll be even better," Madeline promised. "Now can you tell me why in the *hell* you're wearing trousers that are at least three sizes too big? And pleats? What were you thinking?"

"That I desperately need to do laundry but ... well ... I've been busy. I gained a few pounds after a bad break-up and ... these were on the clearance rack and ... well ..."

"Never again," Madeline said with a grimace. "Pleats don't work on anyone with hips, thighs or a belly. You think they're camouflage, but they're actually making you look bigger. Now ... as far as size, don't worry about the number on the tag. It's meaningless since every brand has its own chart. And accept that practically nothing off the rack will ever fit perfectly unless you're a fashion model with zero body fat. A good tailor is worth their weight in gold."

"Yes, ma'am," Lizzie said with a salute. "Help me?"

"My pleasure!" Madeline disappeared for a few minutes, returning with a rack of pre-selected clothes. "Do you remember how much fun it was to change Barbie's clothes a hundred times an hour?"

Lizzie swallowed hard. "Maybe."

"Liar," Meg teased. "You still play Barbies with your nieces, and you love every second of it."

"Fine," Lizzie grumbled. "Have your fun. I'll be your very own, living Barbie."

She spent the next two-and-a-half hours trying on outfit after outfit, amazed to find that the right style and cut really *could* take off ten pounds. True, there was a large pile of rejects, but there was an even larger one of yeses and, as Madeline pointed out, it was as important to learn what didn't work as it was to learn what did.

Lizzie twirled in front of the mirror, pleased, for once, with her reflection. "Still no price tag?" she laughed. It had upset her at first, but now she found it amusing that Colin had asked that everything be brought in with the price removed.

"He thought that the price tags might distress you," Madeline confided with a sigh. "He seems like a very nice man!"

Lizzie nodded quickly in agreement. "He is."

"He's a bit of alright as well," Meg chimed in.

"That means he's a real hottie," Jess translated.

"I may be married," Madeline sighed, "but there's no harm in appreciating the rest of the male species, right?"

"No harm at all," Meg assured her with a nod. "So, Lizzie, how are you feeling about all of this now?"

"Honestly? I'm stunned at how many amazing outfits we found …"

"Outfits that you look stunning in," Jess added. "Admit it."

"For once, I can. And I've never had so much fun shopping. I may," Lizzie gulped. "I *may* have enjoyed it."

"Well ladies," Madeline said, clapping her hands with satisfaction. "It looks like our work here is done. Kaitlin's kept track of everything you've selected, so we'll just send the bill to Mr. Blake."

"Any chance you'd tell me just how much I've spent here?" Lizzie asked though she was sure she knew the answer.

"Sorry, honey. Your man wants to give you the world," Madeline said. "I say let him."

"He made them take an oath over the phone," Meg informed her. "I was his witness."

Lizzie giggled. It would take her a lifetime to get

used to Colin's overwhelming generosity, but she was ready to give it a try."

The following evening, they went house-hunting. Lizzie was nervous and excited at the thought of owning her first real home.

"I understand you two are recently engaged," Gia, the real estate agent said with a smile. "Congratulations! Buying a house together will make it feel even more real."

"I'm counting on it," Lizzie sighed. "I'm still feeling swept off my feet."

"Get used to it," Colin murmured. "I plan to sweep you off your feet as often as possible."

Lizzie let out a dreamy sigh. So did Gia. "Wow. You two are … wow!"

"We get that a lot," Lizzie giggled. "Okay. We're looking for someplace that feels warm and homey."

"Comfortable and cozy, with a bit of property," Colin added. "And perhaps some historical significance."

"Mm-hmm," Gia said. "You've got a lot of things on your wish list. Modern kitchen, at least five bedrooms …"

"He has a huge family," Lizzie explained. "Including a boatload of nieces and nephews that will all want to visit."

"Uh huh. Swimming pool …"

"That's not a must," Lizzie said quickly. "But it would be nice."

"Okay. And budget?" she asked peering at them over the rim of her glasses.

"Not an issue," Colin said with a shrug. "We're more concerned with finding the right house for us."

Gia's eyes widened, and Lizzie suspected that she was mentally calculating the commission on a sale with no set budget. "Hmm. Alright, then. Location?"

"I grew up in Crossroads, so something in the general area would be great. But we'd go a little farther out if it felt right."

Gia nodded, making notes as she paged through the listings that she'd pre-selected. "I have a few ideas where we can start."

Unfortunately, the realtor focused more on the size of Colin's bank account than their specifications of comfort and coziness; her choices were definitely not what Colin and Lizzie were looking for.

The first was an enormous mausoleum of a house on the Main Line. Though it was over a hundred years old, it felt as if no one had ever lived in it. It gave Lizzie a cold, lonely feeling that matched the austere marble of the foyer. "It's a little ..." Lizzie began.

"Frosty?" Colin supplied. She grinned at him, grateful to find that they were on the same wavelength. "My family home in England is older and grander, but it still feels like a home."

"This doesn't, at least not for us," Lizzie said. "Although it's a beautiful property."

"Hmm. Okay, well I'm sure you'll love the next one. It's new construction ..." she said confidently.

It was, indeed, a beautiful home, designed to be a showplace and located in an exclusive, gated community. "It's nice," she reassured the frustrated realtor, "just not what we're looking for."

"We want something more ... homey," Colin explained. "A place where we can raise a bunch of loud, messy, rambunctious children."

"Oh. I ... I see. Could I show you one more property? It's *just* come on the market."

"That's fine," Lizzie agreed, "but then we'll have to call it a night."

She was thrilled when they ended up not far from her parents' neighborhood. They pulled up in front of an old stone farmhouse. Built in the eighteenth-century, it had been restored and remodeled just a few years before. Among other things it had served as a schoolhouse and a stop on the Underground Railroad. Lizzie grinned at Colin. "I've always loved this place," she whispered.

They wandered around the house, appreciating the cozy, high-ceilinged rooms, stone fireplaces, and the gleaming hardwood floors.

The property was ten acres, a rare find in the increasingly sub-divided neighborhood and had an old stone barn, a small pond, a modern stable, and a charming carriage house with a loft apartment. It was everything Lizzie had ever dreamed of and never expected to have.

"Um … could you give us a few moments to discuss things?" Colin asked.

The realtor smirked, dollar signs flashing in her eyes. "Sure. Take all the time you need. I'll just … go out to my minivan and make a few phone calls."

"So?" Lizzie asked hopefully. "Please say you love it!"

"It's a stunning home! I could use that addition off the back as a home office."

"And Tori could have a horse. So, do you think this is a place we could raise those rambunctious kids?" Lizzie asked, biting her lip as she looked up at Colin.

"Yes," he answered softly. "Welcome home, Lizzie."

With their future falling neatly into place, Lizzie was happier than she'd ever believed possible. Even the daunting task of meeting Colin's large, extended family and his dragon of a grandmother couldn't dampen her spirits.

Work, however, was not going so smoothly.

Colin was working long hours trying to find ways to revitalize Consolidated. He formed an advisory council with members from all areas and levels of the company; Lizzie was pleased when she learned that he'd included Meg and Jess among the group.

Lizzie's clients treated her differently. Gone was the friendly banter and the occasional complaining about their job; she was, after all, marrying the boss. Her work friends felt the effects in an increased workload and they were getting understandably grouchy; it didn't help that her boss, Carolyn, kept having hushed conversations with *her* boss, bandying about the phrase 'conflict of interest'. Lizzie hated that her happiness was causing extra work and stress to her friends.

Thursday morning she gave her notice. Though Carolyn seemed genuinely sad to lose Lizzie, she also seemed relieved. Lizzie would spend the summer planning the wedding, setting up the house, and getting to know her new stepdaughter. For the first time in her life she had the luxury of not having to work and she planned to enjoy it.

Lizzie laid her head on Colin's shoulder and gripped his hand as the British Airways jet sped down the runway and took to the sky. He squeezed her hand reassuringly. "I forgot you told me you're afraid to fly," he murmured.

"Not so much afraid as I just don't care for it. But I hate taking off," she admitted. "Now flying like *this* I could get used to!" she joked, indicating the spacious business class cabin.

"We could go back to coach if you prefer," he offered.

"Not a chance, buddy." Lizzie scrunched around in the roomy, comfortable leather seat. "As if I could sit back there, packed in like sardines, after experiencing the wonders of Business Class! Now I understand why my clients were so rabidly insistent on their upgrades."

Colin chuckled, then became more serious. "Are you sure you want to give up your job?"

Lizzie rolled her eyes and giggled. "Are you kidding? Aside from meeting you, I haven't enjoyed that job in a long time. You know ... if you'd told me last Thursday that a week later I'd be flying off to England to meet my future in-laws, I'd have had you hauled off to the State Mental Hospital."

"It has been a bit of a whirlwind I suppose."

"A bit? Darcy in one week you declared your love, asked me to marry you, bought me a house, and whisked me off to Merry Olde England to meet the family. And on top that, I quit my job! Not that I'm complaining mind you ..." She gazed tenderly into his deep brown eyes and sighed softly. "I've never been happier."

"Nor I. I'm crazy in love with you, Lizzie."

"I'm crazy for you, too, Darcy."

"You going to break into your Madonna act now, Lizzie?" he teased.

"Humph. Hardly," she said swatting him on the arm. "Whatever happened to the oh-so-serious Colin Blake I first talked to on the phone a few weeks ago? All quiet reserve and careful control."

He smiled charmingly at her and brushed a stray lock of hair behind her ear. "He met this extraordinary woman who taught him how to laugh again," he said sweetly. "You truly make me a better person."

"Oh, I don't know about that, Darcy. I think he was lurking there beneath the surface, longing to come out and play. I suspect I'll find out you were quite a naughty little boy when I get your Mum and your sisters alone."

Darcy groaned and rolled his eyes. "I swear I was a perfect angel."

"I'm not buying it. Besides my family's already filled you in on all of my less than glorious moments. Turnabout's fair play."

"I suppose if you must," he conceded. "I hope you like them, Lizzie."

"I'm sure I'll love them. If they're anything like you, I know I will. I'll even find a way to love crusty old Lady Frances," Lizzie vowed.

"Jesus, Lizzie, if you can do that you'll qualify for sainthood. She may be my grandmother, but she's not an easy woman to love."

"Your grandfather did, though, right? Or was it one of those neat and tidy, upper-crusty arranged marriages?"

"You know, family legend says that it was true love," Colin said with a chuckle. "Though it's difficult to envision the old girl as a dewy-eyed romantic."

"See. The old girl does have it in her. I just need to find a way to make her adore me."

"You know, my love, if anyone can do it, it's you."

"You think?" Lizzie asked with a grin. "Why's that?"

"Because you made me adore you."

"Only after I told you off," she laughed. "Should I tell old Lady Frances off?"

"Probably not. But Lizzie?"

"Yes, Darcy?"

"If you do, promise me I get to watch!"

Five hours later, they touched down at Heathrow, made their way through Customs, and headed to the terminal. They were greeted by a loud, high-pitched, enthusiastic shriek as Victoria Blake launched herself into her father's arms. "Daddy you've been gone far too long," she scolded.

He kissed the top of her head and turned her to face Lizzie. "Yes, love, but look who I've brought with me. Tori, this is Lizzie."

Tori Blake bore a striking resemblance to her father. At thirteen, she was as tall as Lizzie and had a coltish figure that suggested she would soon tower over her. Her hair was the same wildly curly brown as Colin's and flowed halfway down her back. She shared his intense, deep brown eyes and charmingly dimpled grin. Lizzie's future stepdaughter was a lovely young lady. She was also, apparently, a very nervous young lady, dancing from foot to foot at her father's side.

She bit her lip and smiled shyly. Lizzie smiled back and extended her hand in greeting. "It's nice to meet you, Tori," she said. "I've heard so much about you!"

Tori took her hand, tentatively at first, but when Lizzie gently squeezed it, she squeezed back. "I've heard a lot about you too," she murmured, glancing at her father with a dimpled smile. "I hope we'll be friends," she said shyly.

"I hope so, too." Lizzie glanced up at Colin and smiled softly. "We've already got someone we love in common, right?"

"Righty-o," she chirped. "Um ... Auntie Nora was right behind me with Sam," she explained. "Where can they have gone?"

"Just here," huffed an attractive blond in her late forties or early fifties. "I wish you wouldn't dash off like that, Victoria," she chided.

"My sister Elinor," Colin supplied, "also known as Nora. And her eldest son, Samuel Mason. Sam works for me. Nora, Sam, meet my fiancée, Anna Elizabeth Kincaid."

"It's lovely to meet you, Anna," Nora gushed. "High time my baby brother settles down!"

Lizzie couldn't help but laugh. It was difficult to think of a man as self-assured as Colin as someone's baby brother. "It's lovely to finally meet some of Darcy's family!"

"Darcy? You call him Darcy?"

"It's a long story ..." Lizzie laughed.

"It's a *long* ride to Snowhill."

Lizzie giggled and rolled her eyes. "Then I guess we'll have to tell you, huh?" She turned to the handsome young blond man at Nora's side. "Nice to meet you, Sam. You know, I have this friend back home ..."

"Crikey, Lizzie, you playing matchmaker already?" Darcy sputtered.

"Can't help myself. I want everyone to be as happy as us. And you have to admit, he'd be perfect for Jess."

"I don't mind, Colin," Sam said pleasantly, his green

eyes twinkling. "Reckon I wouldn't mind an introduction once I'm stateside."

"Why'd you call her Lizzie, Colin," Nora interjected.

Tori, who'd followed the conversation to this point and had already heard the story, quickly filled them in, her eyes sparkling merrily. "I think it's romantic," she sighed dreamily.

"Very romantic," Nora agreed.

"So … Aunt Lizzie are you ready to head to Snowhill?" Sam grinned. "Are you sure you're up for meeting our eccentric clan?"

Lizzie glanced up at Darcy for reassurance, and he smiled warmly. "As ready as I'll ever be. Oh and Sam?"

"Yes, Aunt Lizzie?"

"If you ever call me *Aunt* Lizzie again you'll be sorry. I'm *way* too young to have a nephew your age."

"That's not an idle threat," Colin warned. "Be frightened. Be very, very frightened."

She swatted him playfully on the arm causing him to yelp, feigning much more pain than she'd inflicted. "See what I mean?" he moaned.

"Point taken. Lizzie it is," Sam said emphatically. "Now … off to Snowhill."

Colin couldn't stop grinning. Lizzie, who was not always at ease around strangers, was chatting with his sister and nephew as if she'd known them her entire life. She filled them in on her small-town childhood and her family of police officers. If she was still concerned about her middle-class background, she was hiding it well.

But the best moment of the day was her reaction to his daughter, and Tori's to her. They were currently head-to-head, sharing a whispered conversation and, at some point, they'd held hands.

"What?" Lizzie said as she caught him staring.

Colin just shook his head and kept smiling.

"Darn it, Darcy, You're smiling at me again."

"And smiling is bad?" he asked, his dimples deepening. "I'm happy, Lizzie. Can't a man be happy?"

"He can," she said, grinning back. "But you know those dimples of yours make me swoon and ... well ..." She laid the back of her hand on her forehead and threw her head back dramatically. "Swoon."

"Wow." Nora glanced from Colin to Lizzie and nodded her approval. "If I had any misgivings about your whirlwind romance, you've both calmed them."

"You had misgivings?" Colin frowned. "Why?"

"Hmm. Let's see. When you left on your most recent trip, you were a confirmed bachelor and showed little interest in changing that fact. Oh, you've dated off and on over the years, but we all knew your heart wasn't in it. And then ..."

"Me?" Lizzie laughed. "Honestly, Nora, I'm still in shock myself." She glanced over at Colin and smiled softly. "The best kind of shock, but still ..."

"Good to know I can still surprise you, Nora," Colin laughed. "And you're right. I didn't set out to fall in love. It just ... suddenly, there it was. The best surprise of my life."

Nora shook her head slowly. "You do know he's not always this nice?" she told Lizzie.

Colin chuckled softly. "Trust me, Nora. My Lizzie did not fall in love with me the moment she heard my voice."

"Let's see ... thoughtless, demanding, and impatient come to mind," Lizzie laughed.

"Until you called me on it."

"And you apologized and ... honestly? I think at that point I knew I was in trouble."

"Me too, Lizzie."

Sam made an exaggerated retching sound, earning him a hard whack on the shoulder from Tori.

"It's romantic," she protested.

"Maybe," Sam groaned. "But that kind of behavior makes us other poor blokes look bad in comparison."

"No worries," Colin reassured his nephew. "When you meet the right woman, the rest will follow on its own."

Lizzie had never related so completely to Elizabeth Bennet as when she caught her first glimpse of Snowhill, Colin's 'country house'. She could well imagine her heroine's surprise and delight on her first visit to Mr. Darcy's home, and her excitement and trepidation on her subsequent return as Pemberley's mistress. Lizzie felt all of them.

They rounded a bend, and the limousine slowed as the house came into view. Her mouth fell open, and she sat mutely for a long moment, taking in the beautiful scene before her.

Snowhill perched atop a verdant hill, glistening as the sunlight touched her weathered golden stonework. It had three stories, with massive windows stretching from floor to ceiling, making it appear to be constructed of glass. Four towers soared skyward, lending the building an unparalleled grace and beauty. A small lake sparkled invitingly at the foot of the hillside. Despite its grandeur, Snowhill looked warm and friendly, as if she had always been waiting to welcome her home.

Too awed to speak, Lizzie could only sigh.

Colin lifted her hand to his lips and kissed it. "How do you like the house, Lizzie?" he asked, his eyes twinkling mischievously.

"It's magnificent!" she murmured, smiling. "It's stunning, Darcy. Like every stately home in every cheesy romance novel, I ever read, only better because it's real."

Colin's mother, Helen, greeted them warmly in the main entranceway. She was a tiny, birdlike woman in her mid-seventies with silver gray hair, vivid blue eyes and a warm, engaging smile. She giggled like a schoolgirl when Colin lifted her off the floor in a huge bear hug.

"Hallo, Mum," he said with a cheeky grin. "I've brought you my Lizzie."

"Hi," Lizzie said nibbling nervously on her lower lip. "It's lovely to meet you."

"It's lovely to meet you as well, my dear girl!" She turned to Colin, nodding her approval. "I'm happy to see you've finally found your Lizzie, Son."

"No happier than I," he said smiling adoringly. "I'm just praying she doesn't run off after she meets the lot of you!" he teased.

"Being naughty as usual, little brother?" said the attractive, if slightly mussed, blond beside Helen. "Hi. I'm Anne, youngest of the sisters, but most everyone calls me Nan."

"Hi, Nan," Lizzie said, searching her brain for what she knew about Nan. "Hmmm. You have three boys?"

"Impressive," she said with a broad grin. "If you can keep track of this clan you'll fit in just perfectly." She laughed softly and looked around the hall. "Two of my little monsters just ran off toward the courtyard ..."

"Jordy and Benjy?" Tori interrupted.

"Victoria," Colin said sternly. "You've better manners than that."

"Sorry Daddy. Sorry Aunt Nan. So ... may I go and find them, please?"

Colin smiled indulgently and ruffled her dark curls affectionately. "Go on then. But Tor ... I'd love it if you'd help me show Lizzie around Snowhill later, so mind you don't get too lost."

"Sure Daddy, but only if I get to tell her about Ruby."

"Ruby?" Lizzie asked.

"Our ghost," Tori giggled as she ran off.

"Your ghost?"

"What sort of grand old house would this be without the requisite ghost. But I've promised to let Tori tell you the story ... so I mustn't," Colin teased.

"Please?"

"Sorry. Besides, Tori tells it much better than I. Now ... I thought perhaps you might like to freshen up before the rest of the clan descend on us."

"I'd kill for a hot shower," she admitted.

"Hmm. I quite like the sound of that," he whispered wickedly.

"Ahem?" Nan said clearing her throat loudly. "Did you honestly imagine you'd get off so easily? Grandmamma expects to see the pair of you in her sitting room this morning."

Lizzie clutched Colin's hand as he ushered her into Lady Frances's formal sitting room. The old woman's cold gray eyes dismissed Lizzie as inconsequential as Colin bent to kiss her wrinkled cheek. "Good morning, Grandmamma," he said as pleasantly as he could muster.

"Perhaps for you. I suppose this is your *American*?" she asked frostily. "Tell me, young woman, what makes you think you're good enough to marry my grandson?"

Lizzie beamed up at Colin and shrugged her shoulders as her eyes locked with those of Colin's fearsome grandmother. "Oh, I'm not. But by some miracle, he loves me as much as I love him."

"Pah. You love his money," she accused.

"Am I that unlovable then, Grandmamma?" Colin countered. "Lizzie would be much happier if I were poor rather than rich."

"Believe what you will, but you'll never have my blessing," she vowed.

"I hardly need your approval, Grandmamma. With or without it, Anna Elizabeth Kincaid is going to be my wife."

"Humph," she snorted. "What sort of name is Kincaid?"

"Scots-Irish but I'm basically a mutt. I think I might even have a little Gypsy blood in there somewhere ..." She smiled cheekily at the imperious old lady. "You remind me a lot of my grandmother," Lizzie informed her. "She was a Slovak peasant, as tough as nails!"

"Well!" Lady Frances sputtered. "Such impudence!"

A slow dimpled grin warmed Colin's handsome face. "Yes, quite," he agreed, still smiling at Lizzie. "My Lizzie is refreshingly honest about everything. It's one of the things I love most about her." He kissed Lizzie lightly on the cheek and smiled at Lady Frances. "I hope you'll come to the party tonight. I don't expect that you will, but I do hope it."

"This is unreal!" Lizzie breathed as she glanced around the elegantly furnished suite. "What did you say it was called?"

"It's the Queen's Room."

"And who slept here?"

"Queen Elizabeth."

"The First?"

"Yes, Lizzie, the First."

"Still love me for my impudence?" she teased.

Colin just flashed her a sexy grin as he leaned against the open door connecting her room with his. She started giggling uncontrollably.

"What's so bloody funny, Lizzie?"

Still giggling, she climbed into the huge four-poster canopy bed and pulled the covers up to her chin. "Her magnificent bosom heaved as she kept her eyes glued to the door, which connected her room to Lord Colin's. She gasped as the door creaked open … God! It's a bodice-ripper come to life."

Colin laughed softly, strode across the room, and dove onto the bed. "If that's the case … I believe Lord Colin is supposed to make mad, passionate love to her … er … you?"

"Well now, if you insist on being accurate …" she teased as his mouth found hers. "My, my Lord Colin! You naughty, naughty man!"

CHAPTER 13

She twirled in front of the mirror, pleased with her reflection. She had tamed her unruly hair into an elegant French twist, with soft tendrils framing her face. Her leaf green silk dress hugged her curves in all the right places and fluttered softly to just above the knee. "Thank you, Madeline," she whispered as she smoothed a hand over the flared skirt.

"Ready, love?" Colin asked from the doorway.

She took a deep breath and turned to face him. "Ready. Do I look okay?"

"You're beautiful, Lizzie. Truly beautiful."

"Thank you, Darcy. For once, I *feel* pretty."

"I have something for you," he said handing her a long black velvet box.

She flipped it open to find an exquisite pear-shaped emerald pendant. "You told me you were wearing green," he explained as he fastened the chain around her neck.

"Thank you, Darcy," she sighed. "It's stunning. So is it … you know … one of the family jewels?"

Colin blushed and nodded sheepishly. "I hope you

don't mind that it's slightly used?"

Lizzie grinned up at him. "Nah. You know me, I'm used to hand-me-downs and second-hand stuff."

They were halfway down the grand staircase when Lizzie realized she'd forgotten her lucky bracelets. "I'll be back in a sec," she said over her shoulder as she darted back up the stairs.

"I'll wait here."

"No, it's okay, really. Go. Mingle. I'll be down in five minutes tops."

True to her word, she entered the party in less than the promised five minutes and quickly spotted Colin, in his charcoal suit, talking to Helen. Feeling playful, she slipped an arm around his waist and sneakily pinched his behind.

"Goosing other men's bums now, Lizzie?" asked an eerily familiar voice at her back. She turned slowly to meet the very amused eyes of her fiancé.

"Shit," she muttered as the man she'd publicly fondled turned to face her. It was her Hollywood crush, Griffin Brookes.

"Hello, Colin," he said over her head.

"Evening, Griffin," her future husband replied. "I see you've met Lizzie?" he asked unnecessarily. "Lizzie, I don't believe you've *officially* met Griffin Brookes."

"Bloody Hell!" Lizzie muttered as the color drained from her face. "I ... uh ... ummm ... crap!"

"Uncanny resemblance?" Griffin supplied helpfully.

Lizzie nodded mutely. The actor's hair was a slightly lighter brown, his face a little broader, and he currently sported a rakish goatee, but otherwise they could be twins. "Sorry?" she murmured.

"No apologies necessary. I ... er ... *quite* enjoyed it," he chuckled.

"Oh, well good," she said without thinking. "Damn it,

Darcy why didn't you warn me?"

"Lizzie, I swear I had no idea. Mum met Griff on the set of *Pride and Prejudice*; she was a technical consultant. They've been friends ever since."

"Oh, well ... ah ... nice to meet you, Mr. Brookes," she chirped as she regained her composure.

The actor shot her a cheeky grin. "Since we're *intimately* acquainted perhaps you might call me Griffin?"

Lizzie chortled. "Griffin it is. Any more surprises, Helen? Is the actress who played Lizzie lurking behind the draperies?"

"I believe you're quite safe for the moment," Helen assured her.

"Good," Lizzie said sighing heavily as Colin embraced her from behind.

"You might be safe for the moment," he murmured wickedly in her ear, "but later I do believe *Lord* Colin may have to ravish you again ..."

Despite her initial concerns about fitting in, Lizzie had a wonderful time at the party. After her accidental goosing of Hollywood heartthrob Griffin Brookes, he entertained them with tales from his movie shoots and proudly showed off pictures of his family. She was surprised to learn that he and Darcy were quite good friends. "So why didn't you mention it?" she asked later as they danced.

"I dunno really. I suppose because the difference in our backgrounds troubles you so. I was concerned that adding a famous friend on top of everything else might scare you off."

"You might have been right, at least before."

"Before what, love?"

"Before coming here. See, I finally get it. Yes, we grew up in completely different worlds, but the things that matter to me - family, friends, home, love - they're the same things that are important to you. I mean … I knew that before, I just didn't understand it. And I was afraid to trust in it completely."

"And now?"

Lizzie shrugged and let out a heavy sigh. "Snowhill, for all of its splendor, is very much a home. Despite the antiques, the great masterpieces, and the formal gardens it's comfortable and inviting. I assumed I'd feel very uneasy and out of place here, but I don't, not a bit."

"Thank God!" he said, relief evident in his voice.

"You were worried?" she asked with surprise.

He nodded. "A little."

"I'm sorry, sweetie. I should have trusted my feelings more and my insecurities less."

"And I shouldn't have made so light of them. I tend to take all of this for granted," he said glancing around the room.

"You know I never did get that tour you promised me." she pouted.

"We … er … got a bit sidetracked," he said with a sheepish grin.

"Delightfully sidetracked," she giggled. "Then by the time we resurfaced the rest of your family had arrived."

Colin's remaining sisters and their families had turned up throughout the afternoon. They were a laid-back group who loved to laugh and took great pleasure in teasing each other. Nora, who she'd met at the airport, administered the Blake Foundation; her husband Jack and his brother Lance were Colin's business partners. Elizabeth, whom everyone called Bets, and her husband Thomas were both doctors and had recently returned from a two-year stint in Africa. Fanny was a human rights attorney, her husband, James, a member of the House of Commons. Emma, much to Lady Frances's chagrin, wrote a very popular advice column for a

London newspaper. Catherine, known as Cate, lived in Scotland with her husband, Daniel, and helped oversee his family's centuries-old distillery. Nan was busy with her young family, but in her spare time, she helped manage Snowhill. Before meeting them, Lizzie had almost let their list of achievements overwhelm her. But, like Snowhill, they were warm, friendly and eager to welcome her to the clan.

"My family adores you, you know," he grinned.

"Everyone but Lady Frances that is," she sighed.

"Yes, but she dislikes everyone that doesn't fit into her tidy little world."

"That's a relief! You know, she does remind me of my Grandmom. I suspect beneath that cold, haughtiness she's not so bad."

"Ever the optimist, Lizzie? I suppose she cares for us all in her unique way, but if I were you, I wouldn't get my hopes up. She still barely speaks to Nan's husband, Matt, though they've been married ten years."

"Just watch me, Darcy. I'll have her eating out of my hand in no time. She'll be apples, as Meg would say. Don't worry, I won't let one crotchety old woman run me off."

"Glad to hear it, Lizzie."

"Your family's lovely, Darcy, though I don't think I'll ever get down all of your nieces' and nephews' names. How many of them are there again?"

Colin paused for a moment, squinting his eyes as he mentally ran through the list. "Twenty-one."

Lizzie groaned and laid her head on his chest. "God, I'll never keep them straight."

"Don't worry. They're used to that. I've no doubt you'll get to know them all very well in time since I overheard them planning lengthy visits to America."

"Actually, that sounds like fun! Although, no visitors for at least a month after the wedding. I want us to have some time to get used to being a family."

"Tori seems quite fond of you already."

"She's a great kid, Darcy. You've done an amazing job raising her all alone. Are you sure she'll want to move three thousand miles away? I mean ... I really want us to be a family, but if she doesn't want to move ... I ... I'd move here ..."

Colin hugged Lizzie tightly and kissed her softly on the forehead. "You would do that for me?"

"Sure. I think you once reminded me of this wonderful invention, the jet airplane? And I do know a thing or two about how to book a flight."

Colin lowered his mouth to hers and kissed her until she was dizzy with desire. "Wow."

"I love you, Lizzie."

"Wow."

He chuckled softly. "For the foreseeable future, I need to be based in Pennsylvania; Consolidated's in quite a bit more trouble than I expected. Jack will oversee things here. Lance and Sam will join me in the States, at least temporarily, and Court will likely end up commuting."

"Just promise me you won't become that grouchy, rude, workaholic again because I really didn't like him very much."

"I promise."

Colin pushed the door shut and turned the lock. "Lord Colin pulled Lady Anna into his arms and plundered her soft mouth with hot, seductive kisses ..."

Lizzie giggled as his lips trailed fire along her jaw. "Lady Anna pressed her body tightly against his, gasping as she felt his powerful manhood stirring beneath his close-fitting breeches ..."

"Powerful manhood? I do like the sound of that, love," he said as he nibbled her ear. "You've a way with words. Go on …"

"Boldly, her trembling fingers moved to the waistband and carefully unbuttoned the straining fabric …"

"Good Lord, Lizzie!" Colin groaned as she slid down his zipper. "Er … Lord Colin stilled her hands and kissed her tenderly as he scooped her into his strong arms and carried her to the bed …"

"Anna sighed as Lord Colin slowly eased her silken dress from her body, tossing it carelessly to the floor … 'I need you,' she whispered frantically as she pushed his shirt from his broad shoulders …"

"I need you too," Colin breathed as they collapsed together onto the bed. "I love you."

Lord Colin and Lady Anna's story was abandoned as their alter egos made love slowly, savoring each silken caress. Languid kisses shivered against heated skin and fiery lips. Fingers teased and tickled as they rocked together until, sated, they collapsed in a tangle of limbs.

"I love you," she whispered as they held each other close. "We're so incredibly lucky to have found each other."

"I know, love. I never expected this. I wasn't looking for it."

"I gave up on love a long time ago. Too much heartache. Funny how things happen when you least expect them. If I hadn't taken that phone call …"

He laughed softly. "Somehow, my Lizzie, I think *you* had to take that phone call. Call it Fate or Destiny or whatever you like, but you're my true love."

"Soul mates?"

Colin nodded.

"I love you, Colin Darcy Blake."

"Are you sure you wouldn't prefer Griffin Brookes?" he teased. "He's just down the hall …"

"Hilarious, Darcy. Besides, he's a married man. Now

that Lord Colin … I'm growing pretty fond of him …"

"Are you?" he said as his lips blazed a path to her breasts.

"Uh-huh," she moaned as his mouth continued its tantalizing caress. "Again, Darcy?"

"And again and again …"

CHAPTER 14

Colin smiled down at Lizzie as she slept, curled tightly on her side with her hands folded together against her chest. Tempted as he was to slide back between the cool sheets and wake her with soft kisses, he had work to do. He laid his handwritten note on his pillow and topped it with a single red rose plucked from one of last night's floral arrangements and, with one more lingering, needful glance at his sleeping bride-to-be, he headed out the door.

He entered the library a few minutes later, balancing a plate of pastries atop his coffee cup. "Morning, lads."

"Bit early for a Saturday," his oldest friend and corporate attorney, Willoughby 'Court' Courtois said lazily. "Shouldn't you be cuddled up with your future wife?"

Colin narrowed his eyes at his friend. Court's early life had been difficult and painful, and he was slow to trust or to let people get too close. Though he'd been his usual charming self to Lizzie's face, Colin suspected that he hadn't quite given their whirlwind romance his approval. And Lizzie had seemed less than impressed with Court's wandering eye and open flirtatiousness. He only hoped that, in time, the two of them would see each other as he saw them. "Mate, it was a wrench pulling myself away," he said. "But there's quite a lot to sort through with our newest acquisition. Lance, you've seen the reports on the Turkish copper mines?"

"Production is down, injuries are up, and rumors are flying that the workers want to strike. Jesus, Colin, it's a miracle Consolidated is still afloat ..."

"Barely," Sam added. "Mismanagement at its worst."

"With a touch of embezzlement," Court said as he read through the financial statements. "We should sue for breach of contract. None of this was disclosed."

"We could," Colin frowned. "But the company was turning a profit as few as five years ago. I'd much rather focus on repairing the damage than waste resources on a costly legal battle. I've already eliminated most of the worst offenders and a fair few others have been put on notice."

"You're being far too nice," Court complained. "Don't tell me all this romantic nonsense has made you soft."

"You think I've lost my edge?" he asked with a wry grin. "I can assure you I haven't. However, I no longer intend to spend every waking hour strategizing and plotting my next move. Is Jack weak because he loves my sister?"

"Well, no but ..." Court admitted.

"Since I met Lizzie I've realized that I haven't truly been living all these years. Oh, there's the thrill of the next big deal and Tori, of course, but I reckon I forgot how to have fun. She gave me that back."

"It's about time," Jack said with an approving nod. "A bit of balance is a good thing."

"Humph," Court snorted.

"I dunno," Sam said with a grin. "Sounds tempting to

me."

"Wouldn't mind a bit of domestic bliss myself," Lance said with a sigh.

"Hopeless," Court muttered.

"No. Hopeful," Colin corrected. "You might give a real relationship a try one day, mate."

"When pigs fly."

"You know, my friend, never say never. If you're too busy saying no, you might just miss the love of a lifetime."

"It's not for me," Court vowed. "Now can we get back on topic? I must be back in London by six."

"Hot date?" Sam asked with a grin. "You might leave a few women for the rest of us."

"Turkey," Court said firmly, ignoring Sam's remarks. "I suggest we send someone over to have a look …"

Lizzie was alone when she woke up. She stretched and sighed dreamily as she recalled their sweet, playful lovemaking. She rolled over to find a single red rose and a note on Colin's pillow.

Morning, love
  Wish I was there to kiss you awake, but duty calls. I'll explain later.
  Meet me in the breakfast room? (See attached map!)

I miss you already.

Love, Darcy

P.S. Crikey - I sound like a lovesick schoolboy.
P.P.S. Oh - I am lovesick?
P.P.P.S. Griffin Brookes will be at breakfast so keep your hands to yourself!

Lizzie giggled as she turned the note over to find a carefully drawn map and directions to the breakfast room. She slipped from the bed, showered and dressed, and, note in hand, headed out the door.

Colin never made it to breakfast. According to Nora, he was holed up in the library with Jack, Lance, Court, and Sam discussing a labor dispute at the Turkish mine. "Sounds serious," Lizzie said.

Nora shrugged. "Perhaps. It seems probable that one of them will have to go over, most likely Lance and possibly Sam."

"As long as it's not Colin," she said with relief. "We've got too much planning to do."

"Just remember you've got heaps of enthusiastic volunteers," said Nan. "We'd love to help."

"We'd about given up hope on him," said Cate.

"I've never seen him so happy and relaxed," added Bets.

Lizzie grinned at them. "Thanks, chickies. I knew there was a reason I always wished for a sister!"

"Now you've got them in spades," teased Emma.

"Hey, one of you is missing," Lizzie said, counting only five sisters in the room. "Where's ... shoot ... who's missing? Fanny?"

"Fanny had to get back to London. She has a major case going to court next week," said Helen. "She left early this morning."

"But I'm still here," Griffin Brookes said, grinning as he entered the room. "Mind you, I've quite a bruise on my arse this morning!"

"Hey! It was an accident, remember? A case of mistaken bums," Lizzie reminded him with a huff.

"Is that the story you're telling Colin?" he asked with a cheeky grin. "Right, right. Accidental fondling. I'll back you completely," he assured her with an audacious wink.

"Naughty boy!" said Helen. "Behave yourself, Griffin, or I'll put you over my knee."

"You would, wouldn't you? And you'd quite enjoy it! Fine, I know when I'm licked," he said.

"So, Lizzie, have you given any thought to your dress?" Nan asked.

"Truthfully? Not a bit. I guess that will be top of the list when I get home."

"If you're interested there's a collection of antique gowns here, all of which I've had reproduced for display. We could take a look after breakfast. Perhaps you could find something there to inspire you."

"Take a look at what?" Tori asked as she dashed into the room with several of her cousins. She paused to kiss Lizzie on the cheek, a sweet gesture that touched her deeply. "Good morning Lizzie!"

"Morning, Tori."

"So what are we looking at?"

"Gowns," said Nan.

"Ooooh," Tori squealed. "May I come?"

"As long as Lizzie doesn't mind."

"Of course not!"

The gowns were stored in one of Snowhill's four tower rooms. The view from the window was spectacular and somewhat dizzying. "Long way down," Lizzie said, breathing heavily. As she gazed down at the flagstone driveway, she heard what sounded like faint sobs and felt an overwhelming sense of sadness.

"Yes. Especially for poor Ruby," said Tori.

"This is Ruby's Tower," Nan explained.

"You hear her, don't you?" Tori asked. "Crying?"

Lizzie nodded her head as the skin on her arms prickled. "Yes. What happened to her?"

"Ruby was the daughter of the first owner of Snowhill, our ancestor John Blake. By all accounts, she was lovely and kind and desperately in love with William Travers." Tori pointed out the window, to a manor house atop a hill on the other side of the valley. "Their fathers were bitter enemies, and they were forbidden any contact with each other."

"They found ways, though," Nan added. "As young lovers often do."

"Yes," Tori murmured. "William sent Ruby a letter telling her he would meet her at midnight, and they would run off together. She was to wait in the tower and watch for him."

"But he never came?" Lizzie asked.

"He tried. He was coming around that bend," she said pointing again, "when Ruby's father met him. They fought, and William was killed. Poor Ruby watched it all from this window, and as her father pulled his bloodied sword from William's chest, she screamed and threw herself to the ground."

Tears streamed down Lizzie's face. She could feel Ruby's despair as if it were her own. "Poor Ruby."

"She'll likely visit you tonight. She recognizes true love and guards it," said Bets.

"Legend has it that a marriage blessed at Snowhill will *always* be a happy one," Emma sighed. "It's certainly been true for all of us."

"Even Grandmamma had a happy marriage," said Nora.

"But what about ..." Lizzie nodded in Tori's direction.

"They weren't married here," said Cate. "And Colin's more than a bit superstitious about that fact."

"I had no idea. I guess that settles that - the wedding will be at Snowhill."

Lizzie felt like a princess as she tried on the exquisite gowns. Dress-up had always been a favorite game of hers and, truth-be-told, she still enjoyed playing it with her nieces.

Each dress was a forgotten treasure. An elegant Edwardian ivory lace. A heavy, high-necked Victorian silk. An opulent Georgian satin. An ornate Elizabethan brocade. Each was unique and beautiful, but none felt quite right.

Not until Nan pulled out a soft, golden ivory silk gown in the Regency style, that is.

The simple, elegant gown suited Lizzie perfectly and the dress fit as if it had been made for her. "It's lovely," she sighed.

"You should wear it, Lizzie," Tori declared.

"I believe I shall," she said in her best imitation of Elizabeth Bennet. "Are you sure it's okay to wear?"

"It's a reproduction, used for some of our public events," Nan assured her. "And it looks as if it already belongs to you."

"You're the expert, so I'll bow to your judgment. Now, I'm going to see if I can track down my errant husband-to-be."

Lizzie found him in the library talking to Lady Frances. She was about to enter when the old woman's request caught her attention.

"I insist you have her sign a prenuptial agreement, Colin. If you intend to go through with this marriage, the least you can do is protect yourself and your family from a fortune hunter."

Lizzie gasped and hid behind the door, not wanting to miss a syllable of the conversation.

"Your fears are unjustified, Grandmamma."

"Humph ... then it would be a mere formality."

"I'm only going to say this once," he said tightly, "so I suggest you listen. I love Lizzie, and I trust her with *everything* that's precious to me. I will not begin our marriage with a plan for it to end. Ours will be a 'til-death-do-us-part' marriage … for both of us. If you used half the energy to get to know her that you've used to condemn her, you would know that she's sweet, gentle, loving, shy, funny, irreverent, impudent and, to me, quite perfect."

"Bravo!" Lizzie said clapping her hands as she walked through the door. "Thanks for sticking up for me, sweetheart. Lady Frances, FYI, I would sign a prenup if Darcy would agree to it. Not because I think we'll ever need it, but just to let him know for sure that I love him for him."

"I never doubted it for a moment, Lizzie."

She grinned at him. "There you go being all sweet again. Better not let it get around the business world that Colin D. Blake is a big, romantic softy."

"Nope. Not."

"Foolish boy!" said Lady Frances.

"If you say 'you'll rue the day' I'll laugh my arse off, Grandmamma."

"Humph," she snorted as she shuffled from the room.

"She means well," Lizzie offered weakly.

Colin rolled his eyes. "She means to try to run my life, as usual."

"She's just an old lady who's trying to look out for her family, no matter how misguided her attempts."

"I know," he sighed. "I just wish she'd give you a chance and maybe show a little faith in my judgment for once."

"Grandmamma will come around eventually."

"I hope you're right."

"Of course, I am, I'm always right!" she teased. "Isn't that the first lesson in the husband handbook?"

Colin laughed and snaked an arm around her waist. "I believe you're right. Now, what say we find that daughter of mine and talk to her about moving?"

"Daughter of *ours*," she corrected.

He smiled down at her and kissed her softly on the forehead. "Ours. I do like the sound of that, Lizzie."

Though Lizzie had seen quite a bit of Snowhill, she was still astounded by her grand tour. She'd been an avid reader of romance novels since her teenage years, but she especially loved historical romances. And every romance reader knows that in all of the best historical romances the stately ancestral home of the hero is as much a character as the innocent, beautiful young woman and the handsome-if-devilish lord of the manor.

For Lizzie, Snowhill was very much like stepping into her fantasy world. She found it difficult to conceive that it was now her home, at least part-time. It was decidedly elegant but retained a lived-in warmth throughout. Colin was quick to point out the scratches on the ballroom floor, from the time he and his sisters had turned it into an indoor roller-skating rink, and the chipped mantelpiece in the music room, result of an ill-advised indoor soccer game gone awry. He grinned cheekily as he showed her the small dent in the wall at the foot of the grand staircase's polished banister.

"That must've hurt," she said sympathetically.

"I had a knot on my head for about a week," he admitted. "It was jolly good fun, though."

"Still is, Daddy," Tori said as she ran to the middle landing. "Look out, Lizzie!" She flew quickly down the polished banister and landed gracefully on her feet.

"The things I missed growing up in a rancher," Lizzie laughed, shaking her head. "I might have to give that a whirl."

In the Long Gallery, she gazed in wonder at the portraits of Colin's ancestors. She paused in front of a young man dressed in Regency style to whom Colin bore a strong resemblance. "Who's this?" she asked.

He shrugged absently. "I'm not certain," he said

peering at the brass plate on the frame. "Charles Blake. I think he's my great-great-great-great grandfather."

"You've missed a great, Daddy," Tori supplied.

"Have I, Poppet? You're much better at keeping all this sorted out than I."

"I know, Dad." To Lizzie, she said, "would you like to see a portrait of Ruby, Lizzie?"

Lizzie nodded and followed Tori to the far end of the gallery. The young woman in the painting was lovely, with elaborately styled dark hair and a mischievous gleam in her dark eyes. She was dressed at the height of Elizabethan fashion, in an elaborate red brocade dress, but her only jewelry was a simple ruby cross. "You look like her, Tori," she said.

"A little I suppose. I wish she'd appear to me!" she said.

"You *want* to see a ghost?" Lizzie asked. "I think I'd be a little freaked out."

"No, you mustn't be frightened of Ruby, Lizzie. She would never hurt you."

"Still, a ghost? I'm not sure I even believe in ghosts."

"You heard her crying in the tower," she reminded her.

"She's quite real, Lizzie," Colin stated. "I've seen her."

"You have?"

"Yes," he said nodding. "When I came back here with Tori after everything fell apart I was ... a bit of a mess."

"More than a bit according to Gramma, Dad," Tori corrected.

"Right. I was a complete wreck," he admitted. "Anyhow, one night after a dreadful bout with colic, I'd finally managed to get Tori to sleep, and I was completely knackered. I fell asleep in the rocking chair and woke up around three to the faint sound of sobbing.

My sisters had told me of their encounters with Ruby, but she'd not ever visited a man that I was aware. If you haven't noticed, our suite of rooms is just below Ruby's tower. I checked on Tor, who was finally sleeping peacefully and made my way up into the tower room."

"She was sitting on the chaise, gazing out the window. She turned and smiled at me, and told me not to worry, that everything would work out in the end. She assured me that Tori and I would be fine and that I would find happiness someday." He smiled at his daughter, then at Lizzie. "Seems our ghost was right."

After her tour of the house, the three of them walked through the gardens and Colin and Lizzie shared their plans with Tori. As Colin had predicted, she was thrilled with the idea of moving to America and begged for details on the house.

"So I can have a horse?" she asked. "Yay! Will you ride with me sometime, Lizzie?"

Lizzie bit her lip and sucked on it for a moment. "I don't know how."

"We'll teach you then, won't we, Daddy?"

"What do you think, Lizzie?" Colin asked.

"Well, I'm game for just about anything, so why not?"

"Yippee!" Tori exclaimed.

"Are you sure you want to move to America," Lizzie asked. She needed to know that Tori was okay with such a major upheaval in her life. "You'll have to change schools."

"I know," she grinned. "It'll be brilliant!"

Colin beamed at Lizzie over Tori's head, his deep dimples dancing in his cheeks. "I'd take that as an enthusiastic yes, love."

"Seems that way," she agreed. "I do have one favor to ask you, Tori."

"Sure … Li … um … what *should* I call you?" she asked, her brow furrowed.

"Lizzie's fine. I wouldn't expect you to call me Mom or anything like that. I mean, you do still *have* a mother …"

"I've *never* had a mother, not really," she said matter-of-factly. "I … I was hoping … wondering rather … I …" she blinked and looked away, then shyly looked back at Lizzie. "May I call you Mum?"

"Oh, Tori!" Lizzie's voice broke as tears streamed down her cheeks. "I'd be honored. I hoped that maybe someday … but I didn't want to push you." She pulled her future stepdaughter into her arms, hugged her tightly and kissed the top of her head. Her eyes met Colin's, and she was surprised to find tears glistening there. "How'd I get so lucky?"

CHAPTER 15

Much later that night, Lizzie lay on her side, watching Colin sleep. She loved the soft sound of his breathing, his gentle rhythmic snore, the way his long, dark lashes lay against his cheeks. Unable to resist, she reached out a hand and gently cupped his face. "I love you so much," she whispered.

"He loves you too," said a soft, gentle voice.

It startled her. She glanced around the darkened room and saw a figure outlined by the moonlight streaming through the window. She was darkly pretty and wore a red gown. "Ruby."

"'Tis I. I've been waiting for you."

Lizzie sucked her bottom lip into her mouth and nibbled softly, not sure how to address a ghost. "I'm honored to meet you," she said as she slipped from the bed and moved toward the pretty spirit.

"And I you, Miss Lizzie. True love is a rare gift, would you not agree?"

"Yes."

"You and your Colin are meant to be. You shall be happy together, but you will face a difficult trial before you are wed."

"What?" A difficult trial was *not* what Lizzie wanted to hear.

"You are strong. Your love for each other is stronger. All will be well."

Why, Lizzie wondered, did ghosts have to be so annoyingly non-specific? "What's going to happen?"

"I do not know. Your strength and your love will see you through."

Lizzie felt tears burning her eyes. "Please?" she begged, her voice quivering.

"I am most remorseful, but I do not know," she said sadly. "Do not be afraid, all will be well."

"I can't lose him."

"You shall not." She reached up and unclasped the plain ruby cross around her neck. "Hold out your hand."

Lizzie did as the ghost asked, gasping as she felt the cold, solid gems of the necklace in the palm of her hand. "How …?" Had a ghost just given her a gift?

"Wear it and I shall be with you. Do not make yourself uneasy, Miss Lizzie. You and your Colin belong to each other. You shall be together."

"Thank you," Lizzie whispered. She closed her eyes and brushed the tears from her cheeks. When she opened them, she was alone. "Ruby?"

Ruby was gone. Lizzie opened up her hand and stared down at the ruby cross. Instinctively, she fastened it around her neck. It felt cool against her skin. She fingered it gently, wondering at the feeling of protection it gave her despite Ruby's warning. "Thank you, Ruby," she whispered.

"What's that, love," Colin mumbled sleepily from the bed. "Lizzie?"

"I'm here. I've had a visitor."

"Ruby."

"Yes. The ghost of Snowhill."

"What did she tell you?" he asked as Lizzie snuggled back under the covers, cuddling against his warm, solid body.

"That we'd be happy, but we have to face some sort of trial before we can be."

"Trial? Did she elaborate?"

"No. Are ghosts always so vague?"

Colin laughed softly. "I suppose it's in the spectral code. Are you all right?"

"Yeah, I'm fine. I think she likes me," she murmured as she drifted back to sleep. "I love you, Darcy."

Lizzie woke up wrapped tightly in Colin's strong arms. She rolled over onto her side, facing him and kissed him awake. "Good morning, Darcy," she trilled.

"Good morning, Lizzie," he said as he nibbled his way down her throat. "What's this?" he asked, gently fingering the ruby cross. He looked puzzled at first, then stared at her as realization dawned. "Crikey. It's Ruby's cross, the one from her portrait."

She nodded. "She gave it to me last night."

"Jesus, Lizzie, this is impossible!"

"What? Why impossible?"

"Because … to the best of my knowledge, Ruby's cross was buried with her."

"Oh. My. God. Then … how the hell …"

"I've no idea, Lizzie. Ruby's never done anything like it before."

"I think she's trying to protect us, Darcy. I just wish I knew from what."

Before leaving Snowhill, she made one last attempt to change Lady Frances's mind about Colin and her. Lizzie knew it was probably futile, but her refusal to accept their relationship hurt like hell. Right or wrong, she wanted her approval.

She rapped softly and smiled nervously as Lady Frances's maid opened up the door. "I would like to see Lady Frances, please," she said as politely as she could.

The maid stepped aside, unsmiling, and ushered Lizzie into the sitting room. "Miss Kincaid to see you, Ma'am."

Lady Frances eyed her coldly. "Say your piece, then, if you feel you must."

"Thank you," She said, hoping she appeared more confident and calm than she felt inside. She took a deep breath and fingered the ruby cross for comfort. "I know you don't trust me. That you believe I'm after his money."

"I believe what I see."

"Excuse me? How can you make a judgment like that without even *trying* to get to know me? Do you base it on the fact that my family's hopelessly middle class? What is it that you object to? I think I'm a good person. I'm not afraid to work for what I want. I'm kind to children and animals and try not to knowingly hurt others. Why do you see me as some sort of horrible, money-hungry monster?" She was fighting an internal battle to maintain her sense of calm. So far she was winning.

"My grandson is not prone to such impulsive behavior. He would never behave as he has with you."

"I'm not exactly a living-on-the-edge kind of woman either, Lady Frances. Love can make even the most rational heart indulge flights of fancy. Haven't you ever been in love? I thought Nora told me that you had. Do you remember how it feels? The fluttering in your heart when you think about him? The way your pulse races when you catch his gaze? That need to know every little thing about him? I love Colin because he's Colin. All I want is to spend my life with him."

Lady Frances said nothing and there was no hint of a

thaw in her frosty gray eyes.

"Okay, then. I've said what I wanted to say. I knew my chances of changing your mind were slim to none anyway. For what it's worth, Lady Frances, beneath that tough as nails, snooty exterior of yours I suspect that deep down you love the whole noisy bunch of them. Maybe you'd be a little less grouchy if you'd show them from time to time." She rose from her seat and gave the old lady a quick peck on the cheek. "Bye."

"I hope you don't mind the princess decor," Lizzie said as she ushered Tori into her guestroom.

"It's sweet," Tori said as she flopped onto the bed. "Lord, I'm knackered," she sighed.

"Why don't you take a nap?" Lizzie suggested. "I'm ordering us a pizza for dinner."

"Pizza sounds perfect," she yawned as she stretched out. Hugs and Kisses jumped up onto the bed and, after a few sniffs, curled up contentedly beside her.

"You've found a couple of new friends."

"They're lovely boys," she said as she scratched Kisses's chin. "I've always wanted a cat."

"Well, now you have two, since they've adopted you." She smiled as a thought crossed her mind. "Funny how things can feel right so quickly, isn't it?"

"Umm hmm," Tori yawned, her eyelids fluttering shut.

Lizzie leaned down to brush her hair back from her face and kissed her lightly on the cheek. "I'll holler when the pizza's here." She pulled the door shut behind her and joined Colin in the kitchen, leaning into him as he wrapped his arms around her waist.

"I'm a little worried about us living together, Darcy. I'm old-fashioned, and it's something I never thought I'd do, especially not with an impressionable teenager in the house."

"It's the only practical solution. It wouldn't make sense to set up two households for such a short time. Besides," he said with a sexy, dimpled smile, "I'm not willing to spend my nights without you."

"That's not what I want either. I just … I want to be sure this is right for all of us, but especially for Tori."

"Lizzie, love, Tori's bright enough to know the difference between shacking up and a genuine commitment. She understands that we're a family now, except for a few legalities."

"Speaking of legalities …" she began.

"Please tell me you're not bringing up a prenup again."

"Nope. Furthest thing from my mind. Besides, I know when to give up. I'm afraid you're stuck with me for life, sweetie."

"God, that sounds wonderful. So what did you want to discuss, then?"

"Tori. She's a wonderful young lady, Darcy."

"Thank you. I think so, but I'm a bit biased. What about her?"

"I want to be a real mother to her."

"She seems to want that too, *Mum*," he teased gently.

"I want to make it legal. Darcy, I'd like to start proceedings to adopt her."

"You want to adopt my baby? Oh, love," he murmured as tears shimmered in his eyes. "I'd hoped that maybe in time you'd want to … I never dreamed … are you certain, Lizzie?"

She hugged him tightly and reached up to brush the tears from his cheeks. "I think I love her almost as much as I do you. What do you think?"

"I think I'll call Court in the morning. He'll know how to begin the process.

CHAPTER 16

Lizzie's last two weeks at work were blessedly uneventful.

Colin was busy re-organizing Consolidated, but he made a conscious effort to keep regular hours. Sam and Lance arrived after a week in Turkey, relieving some of his burden and catching the eyes of her friends, Jess and Meg.

Life was good. The wedding plans were falling into place, and they were able to make settlement quickly on the farmhouse. Court had begun a search for Lara, who would need to consent and sign some papers. That made Lizzie nervous, but Colin assured her that his ex-wife didn't have a motherly bone in her body; he couldn't imagine her raising any objections.

"Why do I suspect that a proper send-off means getting me totally plastered?" Lizzie moaned as they entered Flannigan's hand-in-hand."

She was, of course, right. Meg and Jess had a round of drinks waiting at their table. "But what if I don't *want* to get drunk?" she complained to them as she nursed her cocktail.

"Too bad, darl. Besides, Jess and I want to get Sam and Lance pissed and take advantage of them," she said, gazing longingly at Colin's business partner. He caught her staring at him and winked, causing Meg to turn six shades of pink. "Cheeky man!"

"That'd be just your type, Meg. Now Sam there, he's a bit quieter, but I think our Jess can liven him up."

"I'd sure as hell like to try," she sighed.

"Go for it. Though it would be a little weird because theoretically, Meg and I would be your aunts."

"I can live with that," Jess shrugged. "I'm gonna say hi." She grabbed Meg by the arm and tugged her along.

Lizzie grinned as her friends sidled up to the handsome new imports at the bar. "Funny how when you're happy and in love you want everyone else to be, too."

"I've been telling you that for years," Joanie laughed, tossing her bleached blond curls and downing a shot. "You should get married in Vegas."

"Nope. Traditional all the way for me. I want the fairytale."

"And you shall have it," Colin promised. He nodded toward the bar. "How about that then?"

"They have great taste?" Lizzie laughed.

"And love is in the air," sighed single mom, Karen. "I wouldn't mind a little romance."

"I know, sweetie." Lizzie squeezed Karen's hand. "Just have a little faith."

"I'm trying," Karen sighed.

"Uh oh, looks like I'm in trouble now," Lizzie moaned. The waitress, a pretty blond named Mollie, stopped by the table with a tray of tequila shooters.

"We'll miss you," said Carolyn.

"I'm gonna call you every time I have to change a ticket, you know," said Joanie.

Lizzie laughed. "You'll have to find me first. Tori plans to keep me very busy during the day."

"And I intend to keep her very busy at night," Colin quipped.

"Promises, promises," she giggled.

"Who do I bitch to now?" moaned Jess as she returned to the table with Sam in tow.

"You still have Meg. And I'll be around. My husband-to-be owns the joint, in case you've forgotten."

"And we're eternally grateful to him for importing Lance and Sam," Meg said, wiggling her eyebrows playfully.

Lance grinned at Meg and quirked an eyebrow. He lifted his glass in a silent toast.

Sam smiled down at Jess, who'd wriggled into a seat beside him. He blushed slightly but winked at her and it was Jess's turn to blush.

Self-conscious, she raised her glass. "To Lizzie and Darcy."

Everyone clinked glasses and downed their shots in one swallow. "Speech, speech, speech," they chanted.

"Er … okay, I hate public speaking, but here goes nothing. I wish I could say I'm sorry to be leaving, but I've never been less sorry about anything in my life." She smiled up at Colin and he bent his head to kiss her softly. "I'll take the summer to get to know my new daughter, plan the wedding, get our house together, try to keep this insatiable hunk satisfied. And maybe write a hot and steamy romance novel."

"Will this novel require research?" Meg asked with a playful grin.

"Oh, God yes!" Lizzie laughed. "Lots of research!"

"Does this research involve Lord Colin?" Colin whispered hopefully in her ear.

"Oh, definitely, my Lord. Definitely!"

"What are you two whispering about?" Lance asked.

"Research," Colin said with a sly grin. "Lots and lots of research!"

They moved into the farmhouse the first weekend of July, but it was a different kind of move for Lizzie. Gone was the backbreaking labor and exhaustion; this time, aside from packing, she barely had to lift a finger. Brand new furniture, her first ever, was delivered and set up wherever she told the deliverymen to put it. Lizzie, Colin, and Tori spent an entire Saturday at the furniture store choosing what they wanted, along with hours at Home Depot selecting paint colors.

"I'm glad this place has a pool," Lizzie sighed as she mopped the sweat from her forehead; July had arrived with high humidity and hundred degree temperatures. "I can't believe we're home, Darcy," she said as she hugged him.

"Seems to me this place needs a name."

"You Brits and your need to name your houses," she teased. "Okay, what'll it be? Snowhill West?"

"Make fun all you like, Yank, but a house is like a part of the family. It deserves a name."

"Sorry! Jeez, touchy, touchy. You've never *really* forgiven us for winning the war, have you?"

"Humph."

"Ahem?" Tori interrupted. "The pair of you sound like a proper married couple already. I have the *perfect* name," she announced with a dramatic flourish.

Colin and Lizzie looked at her expectantly. "Well?" Lizzie asked.

"Okay. Now I've got your attention. Since you're Darcy and Lizzie there's only *one* possible name for your home. It has to be Pemberley."

"Pemberley Farm," Colin amended.

"Perfect," Lizzie agreed. "Now, what do you say we try out that swimming pool?"

181

Colin loved being a part of Lizzie's world. Her family was as open and loving as his, and their constant teasing made him feel at home. He learned that he wasn't the only one with a famous friend or two. Lizzie had grown up with acclaimed portrait artist Tessa Jameson and was the second cousin of crime novelist Simon Prince. "And here I thought you'd be intimidated because I'm friends with Griffin Brookes," he laughed as they walked down the road toward the picturesque white church on the hill.

"My fantasy man," Lizzie sighed, but when she caught his frown, she reached up to stroke his cheek. "As much as I love his interpretation of Mr. Darcy, you have to know that it's only a pale imitation of my very own Darcy."

"Good answer, Lizzie." He gave her hand a squeeze. "So … church?"

"I know it's corny and old-fashioned these days, but I've always gone and I've been missing it since we met. You've kind of kept me a little busy."

"Sorry?" he offered.

"It's not me you have to apologize to, it's the minister."

"Reckon I can handle the old guy."

But the old guy turned out to be young, good-looking and a little too friendly with Lizzie. Colin eyed the young pastor warily as he pulled Lizzie into a long, tight hug after the service.

"Calm down, Daddy." Tori took his hand and tugged him over to where Lizzie and the pastor stood.

"There you are!" Lizzie beamed, reaching for his hand and pulling him to her side. "This is Matt the Brat Brody," she said grinning at the pastor. "I used to babysit him when he was a little hellion."

"I was a pastor's kid," Matt said with a crooked grin.

"I had to be a brat, or I'd have been labeled a goody-goody."

"Which would be the kiss of death," Lizzie laughed. "Thankfully, Matt outgrew his brattiness and is now a fine, upstanding citizen. Matt, this is Colin Blake, the love of my life, along with my new daughter, Tori."

"Good to meet you," Matt said, shaking both of their hands in turn. "You're a lucky man, you know. Our Lizzie is one special girl."

"Don't I know it," Colin said as he snaked his arm around Lizzie's waist. "I can't wait to make it official."

"Wise as well as lucky," Matt said with a nod. "If a little … impatient."

"When it's right, you just know," Lizzie assured him. "One of these days you'll find out for yourself that you don't need to spend years with someone to know their heart. I know Colin's heart."

Colin drew her into his arms and kissed her softly on the cheek. "That's because it belongs to you, love. Always."

"See?" Lizzie said, grinning triumphantly at Matt. "He's all mine!"

CHAPTER 17

Getting to know Victoria Blake was a unique pleasure. Lizzie's new daughter was bright and articulate and shared Colin's combination of shyness and confidence. She was a fearsome soccer player, a bold horseback rider, and an exceptionally graceful ballerina. Lizzie spent a great deal of time chauffeuring her from one lesson to another, but she didn't mind. Tori's enthusiasm for all of her interests was inspiring.

The more she knew her, the more she loved her. She was a patient horseback riding teacher and she loved playing dress-up with her new cousins as much as she loved keeping up with the current Hollywood heartthrobs. Without missing a beat, she skipped from daydreaming about her favorite movie star to discussing Jane Austen.

Tori was a charming young woman, and Lizzie felt privileged to be called her Mum.

One late July afternoon, they decided to paint the room beside Tori's as a guest room for her nieces. The vibrant pink, chosen by Dani and Rachel, made them feel as if they'd been trapped in the Barbie aisle at Toys

'R Us.

They spent the morning painting and by noon they were exhausted and overheated. Colin had taken the train to New York for a meeting, but Meg and Jess were both in his home office, working on a special project. "Want to call it a day?" Lizzie asked Tori.

"Mm hmm! I'm dreadfully hot and tired."

"I'm an evil step-mother, working you to the bone," she teased. "What do you say we talk Meg and Jess into joining us for a swim?"

"Brilliant idea, Mum!" she squealed. "I'll run and ask them now."

"I'll just clean things up a little and be right down." Lizzie closed the paint can and carried the brushes into the bathroom to rinse them out. She glanced at her reflection in the mirror and giggled. She had a streak of pink paint on one cheek and a splotch in her pony-tailed hair. Her pink tie-dyed t-shirt had a rainbow of paint stains on it, and her shorts were a pair of cut-off black sweatpants with one leg ever so slightly shorter than the other. "Eh, it's only Meg and Jess. They don't care if I'm a hot mess."

She bounded down the stairs just as the doorbell rang. 'Probably just Jeff again,' she thought to herself. Jeff was the Express deliveryman. They'd become good friends since he stopped by daily with another housewarming or wedding gift. She grabbed a few dollar bills from the hallstand as she hurried down the hall.

"Whatcha got for me today, babe? Toaster oven? Blender?" She was grinning as she pulled open the door.

Where she'd expected to find redheaded Jeff in his brown shorts uniform, stood a tall, model-thin, very elegantly dressed woman. Her blond hair was pulled tightly back into a chic chignon, her make-up flawless. Her cold blue eyes looked Lizzie up and down and quickly decided that she was of no consequence.

"May I help you?" Lizzie asked.

"I'm here to see Colin Blake. He *does* live here, doesn't he?" she said, wrinkling her nose.

"He lives here, but he's not home at the moment." Something about the woman put her on her guard. She wasn't about to give up more information than she had to. "Can I help you with something?"

"Hardly. Perhaps if the *lady* of the house is home?"

"I *am* the lady of the house," she offered reluctantly.

"Well, well. Seems Colin's gone slumming," the blond sneered.

"Just who the *hell* are you?" Lizzie asked, already suspecting that she knew the answer.

"Darling, I'm Lara," she said with more artificial sweetness than saccharin. "Colin's wife."

"Don't you mean *ex*-wife?"

"Fine, ex-wife then. Why is Colin trying to find me?" she asked coolly.

"*We* have something to discuss with you." Lizzie said as politely as she could muster. She couldn't afford to be rude to the woman, and she was, after all, Tori's birth mother.

Footsteps echoed on the hardwood floors, making Lizzie jump. She swallowed hard as Tori called out to her.

"Meg and Jess are just finishing up. Who was that at the door? Was it Jeff with another toaster ov- ..." her voice trailed off as she recognized their unexpected visitor. "What are *you* doing here?" she asked, her voice trembling. "Mummy?"

"Yes, Victoria, it's your Mummy ..."

"I wasn't talking to you, *Lara*. I was talking to my Mum." She threw herself into Lizzie's arms, suddenly very much an abandoned little girl. "Make her go away."

"But darling ..." Lara began.

"I'm *not* your darling," she shouted, wrenching

herself from Lizzie's arms and stepping forward to stand toe-to-toe with Lara.

"Tori ..." Lizzie cautioned. She didn't approve of children shouting at adults, but she sensed that Tori had some things she needed to say. "Never mind. Go on."

"I don't want you," she spat out. "I don't need you. I have my daddy, and now I have a *real* mum, one that bakes cookies with me, and takes me to ballet class and likes to play Marco Polo in the swimming pool. You left me. I don't want you."

"I will not be spoken to like this," Lara shrieked. "You little witch!" she raised her hand as if to strike her. Lizzie quickly stepped in between them.

"I think you should leave now." She was so angry that she was shaking.

"Very well. But I'll be back."

"Colin will be home at seven. Victoria won't be here, so we'll be able to have a nice, long chat."

"Fine," Lara shouted as she slammed the door behind her.

Tori crumpled to the floor, bawling. Lizzie knelt beside her and gathered her in her arms, the two of them rocking slowly as they wept.

Meg and Jess found them huddled in a heap on the floor, sobbing uncontrollably.

"Who the fu-udge was that?" Jess asked as they hunkered down beside them.

Meg grabbed a box of tissues from the hallstand and waved it in Lizzie's face. Grateful, Lizzie pulled out a few tissues, wiped her eyes and blew her nose. "That was Lara," she mumbled.

"Oh shi-sugar," Meg said. "You all right, darl?"

"I'll survive. I'm furious, and when I'm furious, I cry."

"Me too," Tori sniffled. "I hate that. Mummy, what

are we going to do about ... *her*?"

"I'm not sure, sweetie. But I'll do everything in my power, so she never hurts you again. I love you, Tori."

"I love you, too, Mum."

"C'mon, mates, what say we see about some tucker? I think your Mum here needs to make a few phone calls," said Meg. "We'll meet you by the pool, okay?"

"That's perfect. I need to call Darcy. And ... I don't want Tori here when she comes back ... unless she wants to be, that is ..."

Tori shook her head vehemently.

"How about the three of us take in a movie?" Jess suggested.

"That would be lovely," Tori said, sighing tiredly. "Is that all right, Mum?"

"It sounds like a brilliant plan to me," Lizzie said gratefully. "You guys are the best!"

The trio headed off to the kitchen, allowing Lizzie to make three phone calls in rapid succession.

The first, of course, was to Colin. He picked up his cell phone on the first ring. "Hello?" he answered briskly.

"Darcy, we've got a problem."

"What's wrong, love?" he said, his voice tight. In the background, Lizzie heard him explaining a family emergency to his business associates.

She took a deep breath, closed her eyes and slowly let the breath out. "Lara."

"Bloody hell! She was there?"

"Uh huh. Tori and I are okay, just a little shaken. She's ... she's coming back at seven tonight ..."

"Christ. Okay, call Court and have him meet us at six. And try to get Tori out of the house. I don't want her to deal with ... that woman ... until we've settled things."

"Court's my next call. And Meg and Jess have already offered to take Tori to a movie."

"Remind me to give them both hefty raises," he sighed. "Gentlemen, ladies, I have an urgent family matter that requires my immediate attention. I'm dreadfully sorry to cut this short ..." Lizzie could hear the murmurs of his business associates in the background as they rescheduled the meeting for the following week. "Lizzie, love, I've wrapped things up here. If I can hail a cab, I'll make the one o'clock Acela."

"That will put you home by three, three-thirty at the latest," she said with relief.

"Will you be all right until then?"

"Well, she is pretty frightening, but I think we'll survive."

When she hung up from Colin, she immediately called Court. He did his best to calm her fears and assure her that her adoption of Tori would go through as planned. "Trust me, Lizzie, I've dealt with the bitch before. I know her weaknesses, and so does Colin."

Her final phone call was to Madeline for a true fashion emergency. She seemed shocked as Lizzie described what had happened. "It doesn't help that I was covered in paint at the time," Lizzie moaned. "So do you sell armor?"

"What I sell is better that armor, Lizzie. Sugah," Madeline said in an exaggerated southern accent, "I've got Armani!"

Colin leaned back against the seat, staring out the window as the high-speed train left the Manhattan skyline behind. He hadn't seen his ex-wife since their last, acrimonious meeting to sign their final divorce agreement, but he'd heard plenty of stories. He'd seen her photographed on red carpets from Cannes to London to Hollywood. He knew about the glittering parties, the celebrity friends, and the endless days of shopping for expensive designer clothes. To the best of his knowledge, Lara Winthrop had never done a single day's work nor made any effort to make the world a better place. She was spoiled, cold, and selfish.

He suspected she was also bitterly unhappy beneath the icy façade though he knew she would never admit it.

As a little girl, she had followed him around like an over-eager puppy, a small girl with a big crush. She'd been sweet then, open and friendly, even if she was a bit over-indulged. As a young woman, she'd proven to be utterly fake and completely heartless. She'd turned his life upside-down in a whirlwind of deception and lies and, when she'd run off with another man, she'd left him shattered.

Yet amongst the painful shards of refuse, she'd somehow managed to give him Tori. Because of Tori, he had no regrets. Because of Tori, he couldn't hate Lara. He pitied her.

But pity didn't mean he would allow her to threaten his family. He knew her far too well to believe that she had developed a sudden interest in motherhood. Lara was reacting to Court's attempts to find her. At best, she was intent on causing mischief simply because she could. At worst, well, Colin didn't even want to think about that.

His cell phone buzzed in his pocket. He whipped it out and answered brusquely. "Blake."

"So the bitch is back."

"Please tell me you have everything in hand," Colin asked Court. "I can't believe she's just … shown up."

"Can't you? When has Lara Winthrop ever been able to resist the chance to cause a bit of mayhem?"

"She's managed to stay well out of my way for thirteen years."

"Because she had millions of reasons to," Court reminded him.

"You've never forgiven me for giving her a settlement."

"It's not as if she needed it. She does have her dear old daddy's millions. Perhaps she's hoping for another installment?"

"I reckon we'll know soon enough," Colin said tiredly. "I don't like the way Lizzie sounded when we spoke."

"Can you blame her, mate? We both know that Lara's capable of bringing grown men to their knees. From the sound of it, your Lizzie is preparing for war."

"You're beginning to like her, aren't you?"

"She's … something."

"She's many things," Colin said with a smile. "All of them quite wonderful."

"She's … fierce."

"She's protecting her family. Our family. You have the papers?"

"Ginny's faxed everything – divorce decree, custody papers – everything's in order, just as it's always been. Lara can stir up as much as she cares to, but she won't take Tori away."

"She could refuse to sign the papers to allow the adoption."

"I've no doubt she'll threaten exactly that," Court said.

"I'll appeal to her better nature."

"She doesn't have one."

"Perhaps not now …"

"Crikey, Col, are you still convinced there's a decent person buried beneath all of that ice?"

"She's a part of Victoria, Court. I *need* to believe that there is something good inside of her."

"If there is, it's *deep* inside," Court said with a laugh. "So I take it you plan to play nice?"

"Don't sound so disappointed. I've no doubt that if

the situation requires it, you'll be more than happy to play the bad cop. You do enjoy a good adversary, after all, and Lara has always been that."

"True enough, but something tells me your protective mama bear of a fiancée may just prove the fiercest opponent my old adversary Lara has ever faced. It should be an interesting evening."

"It had better end with her signature on those papers."

Lizzie tried her best to relax and not dwell on what had happened earlier. Tori, at least, seemed content to play in the pool, and Lizzie was unbelievably grateful to have such supportive friends with her.

"How do I deal with this woman?" she asked them.

"Pretend she's just a nasty client that you have to be nice to," Jess suggested.

"I hate kissing ass, especially when it's someone like her," she muttered. "Ugh."

"Just keep in mind that once she's signed the papers you can tell her to piss off," Meg said.

"You discussing the dragon lady?" Tori asked as she climbed out of the pool.

"Dragon lady?" Meg asked, one eyebrow raised questioningly.

"Yes. That's what the Aunts call her," she said. "I even heard great-grandmamma call her that once."

"Tori, I don't think you should talk about Lara like that. She did give birth to you, remember," Lizzie chided gently.

Tori shrugged her shoulders and began towel-drying her hair. "Seems it's about all she's ever done for me. She didn't stick around long enough to change even one nappy," she said, her voice flat and devoid of emotion.

"I'm sorry, sweetie," Lizzie said, feeling helpless to ease her pain.

"Don't be, please. I've not been deprived at all. My

Dad's wonderful and I've had Gramma, the aunts and my cousins. I did wish for a real Mum, and now I've got that." Tori plopped into her lap and kissed her on the cheek. "I don't even hate her. I feel sorry for her."

"You're pretty wise for a thirteen-year-old, you know that?"

Madeline arrived barely an hour after Lizzie called her with five incredible outfits for her to choose from.

"Hey, honey!" she called in greeting. "Why's there a frigid looking blond sitting in a car down the road?"

"Shit. Oops, sorry Tori."

"Like I've never heard that before," she said, rolling her eyes. "No worries, Mum. I can't believe she's not gone!"

"The frigid blond would be Lara," Lizzie explained.

"Oooooh ... lemme at her!" said Madeline.

"Down girl!" said Jess.

"I'm very protective of my friends."

"I've noticed that. And I'm extremely grateful," Lizzie said with a sigh. "God, what a day."

"So are you just gonna let her sit there?" Madeline asked insistently.

"Hmm. I have an idea." She grabbed her cell phone from the table and punched in a number.

"Crossroads Police, how may I help you."

"Officer Kincaid please."

"Officer Neil Kincaid, Officer Phil Kincaid, or Chief Ed Kincaid?"

"Who's on duty at the moment?" she asked with a laugh. "Aunt Margaret, it's Lizzie."

"Hey you! Congrats, by the way."

"Thanks. So are any of my uncles working today?"

"Uh huh. Neil is. I'll patch you through."

Once her uncle was on the line, she quickly outlined the situation for him. "Anything you can do to make her leave?"

"Sounds like good old-fashioned loitering to me. I'll take care of it."

"Cool. When you're through, stop up for a glass of iced tea."

She ended the call and leaned back against the chaise. "Ah, it's good to have friends in high places. *This* should be an interesting show."

They turned their lounge chairs to face the road where Lara's rented silver Mercedes was parked. Within five minutes, Neil's police cruiser sped up the hill, lights flashing and sirens blaring. The car screeched to a stop behind Lara's. They watched, amused as she stepped out of the car and gestured wildly at Lizzie's uncle. Lizzie giggled as he scribbled out a ticket and thrust it into her hand. She slunk back to the car and tore off down the road.

Three minutes later, Uncle Neil climbed the stairs to the deck. She poured him a glass of iced tea and handed it to him. He took several long, satisfying gulps and leaned back against the railing. "Trouble in paradise, kiddo?"

"Hardly. More of a glitch."

"Rhymes with glitch anyhow," Meg said glibly.

"Yeah, but starts with 'b'", Jess added.

"Did you Mirandize her?" Meg asked hopefully.

"Nah. Just gave her a ticket. But she wasn't too happy about it."

"I imagine not," Tori said. "But then from what I've heard, she's rarely happy about anything."

CHAPTER 18

Colin arrived home at three-fifteen, Sam and Lance in tow. He glanced at Meg, Jess, Tori, and Lizzie lounging by the pool, smiled and shook his head. "And I thought I was coming home to mass pandemonium."

"Nope, boss man, we're just chillin' by the pool," joked Jess.

Sam raised one eyebrow and flashed Jess a playful grin. "And looking quite fetching if I might say so."

"Oh, you might," she said sassily.

"Humph. Seems *I'm* not fetching in my togs," Meg pouted.

Lance smiled crookedly at her. "On the contrary, love, you're so fetching I was momentarily at a loss for words."

"Good answer," she said, blushing deeply.

"Darcy, we need to talk strategy. Court will be here at five, so I'm ordering out for dinner. Meg and Jess will get Tori out of here by six for the movie ..."

"Movie?" Sam asked. "I'd love a movie."

"Me too," said Lance.

"Okay, but it's a chick flick," Meg warned.

"Ahem!" Lizzie cleared her throat in an attempt to get them back on topic.

"Sorry, Lizzie," Sam said ruefully.

"Okay, Madeline has provided me with an amazing suit of Armani armor … so I feel like I can face Lara on her turf."

"You're so far beyond her reach. She could never compare to you, Lizzie," Colin said sweetly.

"God. How is it that you always manage to say exactly the right thing?" Lizzie sighed. "Marry me?"

At six-forty-five, Lizzie checked her reflection in the mirror. The black Armani suit fit like a glove and made her feel classy and confident. Her only jewelry was her engagement ring and Ruby's cross. She fingered the cross, feeling once again the sense of calm it always gave her.

She took a deep breath, squared her shoulders and stepped into the hallway.

"Let's go," she breathed as Colin took her hand in his.

Her heart pounded in her chest as, promptly at seven, Lara rang the doorbell. "At least she's on time," Lizzie murmured.

She greeted Colin and Court coolly and eyed Lizzie in surprise. "Well, well, don't *you* clean up nicely," she said snidely. "Armani?"

She fought the urge to retort and merely smiled pleasantly. "Won't you come in?" she said motioning toward the living room.

"Let's keep to the subject, shall we, Lara?" Colin said coldly.

"And the subject would be?" she asked.

"You know bloody well why you're here. We need to talk about Victoria," he said.

"Ah, yes. *Our* daughter. What about her? You know,

she's *quite* an impertinent child."

"*My* daughter is a lovely young woman. If I ever hear that you've raised a hand to her again ..."

"What, darling? You'll have me arrested? Throttle me?" she laughed. "What is it you want? I'm feeling quite bored by all of this, you know, and some rustic police officer related to *her* had the balls to give *me* a ticket."

"Perhaps you shouldn't be where you don't belong," Lizzie said, her voice tight.

"Ah, but if I recall the details, *you* were looking for me. I did get a rather official-looking letter from him." She shot Court an icy glare. "Surely you're not shocked to see me?"

"I'll get straight to the point. Lizzie and I are getting married next month. She would like to adopt Tori."

"We want to be a real family, in every way possible."

"How quaint. What if I say no?" she threatened.

"Why the bloody hell would you say no? You haven't seen her since she was an infant," Colin growled.

Lizzie put her hand on his arm, hoping to calm his anger.

"Perhaps I'm feeling motherly all of a sudden," she said.

"Stop, Lara. Please. For once in your life do the right thing. Look, if Tori wants to see you at some point, we won't raise any objections," Colin said.

"But it would have to be her choice," Lizzie said firmly. "We won't force her, not if she doesn't want to see you."

"She hates me," Lara said. "She'll never want to see me."

"She doesn't hate you. But she doesn't know you either," Lizzie said calmly. "Please, we, all three of us, we want to be a real family."

"I never understood all of that silly family nonsense,

but then I'm an only child. Colin's family certainly never welcomed me."

"Because you never gave them a chance."

"Humph," she snorted. "Very well. Have your cozy little family. Give me the bloody papers."

Court presented the papers to her with a flourish and handed her a pen before she had the opportunity to ask for one. She scrawled her name quickly where he indicated and when she was through, she rose to leave.

"Thank you," Lizzie said gratefully.

"Yes, thank you," Colin echoed as he curled his arm around her waist. "It's the right thing to do."

"Well, then," Lara said as she moved towards the door. "I suppose I should offer my congratulations to you both." With that, she was gone.

"Phew," Lizzie said, mopping her brow.

"Congratulations, it's a girl," Court grinned. He shook Colin's hand and kissed Lizzie on the cheek. "You know … I believe it's traditional to smoke a fine cigar …"

"Outside," she reminded Colin as he pulled two Cuban cigars from his humidor.

Colin flashed her a dimpled grin. "As if I could forget that? Care to join us, love?"

"Hmmm, no on the cigar, but I could do with a nice glass of wine. I'll be out in a few minutes. I have *got* to get out of this get-up!"

"See you outside then," he said as he bent to kiss her softly. "Mum."

"Thanks, mate," Colin told Court as he offered him a cigar. He snipped the end off of his own and handed Court the cutter. "I never expected Lara just to turn up."

"Nothing that woman does would surprise me. It's not as if she had a sudden urge to spend time with Tori. I noticed that her left ring finger was bare, so perhaps her latest conquest has moved on." He twirled the cigar in his fingers and tucked it into his shirt pocket. "I'll enjoy this later."

"Let me guess," Colin said, eying his friend as he warmed the tip of his cigar. "With a leggy blond and a glass of Talisker?"

"Redhead. You don't mind if I take off?"

Colin shook his head. "Of course not. Hell, Lizzie and I will have the house to ourselves so ... why are you still here?"

"Point taken," Court laughed. "Er ... I realize I gave you a rough time about all of this ... romantic nonsense, but mate?"

Colin clamped his cigar between his lips and watched the conflicting emotions on his best friend's face. Court didn't want to admit that there might be something to this romantic nonsense, but Colin could see that his viewpoint was softening. He lifted the lighter to the tip of the cigar and quietly waited.

"Not making this easy, eh?" Court grinned wryly. "I don't know that I've seen you like this since we were lads. Lizzie, she makes you happy."

"She makes me happy," Colin echoed. "She makes me laugh and not take life so seriously. That's not a bad thing, you know."

"For you, at least," Court admitted. "Your Lizzie, she's quite something."

"Are you giving us your blessing?" Colin smirked as he puffed on his cigar. "I reckon Lizzie will appreciate that!"

"You think?" Court chuckled. "I realize that you don't *need* my approval, but you have it all the same. Now, I should be off. I've a stunning redhead waiting on me in the city and you've got your adorable Lizzie and an empty house ..."

"That I do," Colin said as a grin spread slowly across

his face. "See yourself out?"

Court shook his head. "Humph."

Colin just kept grinning as he extinguished his cigar and rested it on the ashtray to finish later. "I'm not sorry to be rude, mate. Enjoy your evening."

Once upstairs, Lizzie stripped off the black suit and slipped into a pair of cotton shorts, an oversize tee shirt and her favorite Birkenstocks. "Much better."

"I quite agree," Colin said, dimples dancing in his cheeks as he leaned in the doorway.

"I thought you were smoking a cigar with Court."

"Seems we were keeping him from a hot date with a sexy redhead," he laughed. "He took his cigar to go."

"Hmm. So ... we're all alone then," Lizzie said with a sly smile. She tilted her head, raking her eyes over him. "You're overdressed," she said as she unknotted his tie, slid it off and tossed it on the floor.

"Am I?" he said with a lazy smile.

"Oh, definitely." Her fingers moved to the buttons of his dress shirt, and she pressed her lips to the warm skin at the base of his throat.

Colin groaned softly. "How long did you say this picture was?"

"Probably not long enough," she sighed. "Of course, they might go out for ice cream after ..." She quickly found herself scooped up and deposited unceremoniously on the bed.

"I believe we'll have to make the most of our time then." His impatient hands skimmed over her bare legs and tickled teasingly at the hem of her shirt.

Ring.

"Damn," she breathed as Colin nibbled seductively on her earlobe. She felt blindly for the cell phone on the nightstand. "H-hello?" she answered breathlessly.

"Darl? You alright?" Meg asked.

"Oh ... er ... yeah ... everything's wonderful," Lizzie gasped, struggling for words as Colin's mouth continued its assault. "Um ... oh my ... um ... aren't you supposed to be watching the movie?"

"Sam and Lance made us a bit late, so we've had to wait for the next show. Not that Jess and I mind, of course. So ... what happened? Did she give in, in the end?"

Perfect, Lizzie thought, Meg wants to have a chat *now.* "Yes. Everything's perfect but ... um, Meg?"

"Yeah?"

"Can I fill you in on the details later?" she murmured as Colin trailed hot kisses along her jaw. "Oh, my!" she gasped as his gently seeking mouth found the sensitive hollow of her throat.

"Hullo? Darl, if it's okay, we'll stop for an ice cream cone on the way home."

Lizzie giggled as Colin's fingers tickled the skin of her waist, teasing the fabric higher and higher over her stomach. "Take all the time you need."

"You sure? You sound a little ... odd ..."

"I ... uh ... sure I'm sure? I mean ... yeah ... it's fine ... bye, Meg." Somehow, Lizzie managed to end the call as Colin kissed his way up her bare belly, his silky hair tickling her hypersensitive skin.

He tugged at the hem of her shirt. She wiggled on the bed, trying to help as he pulled the shirt over her head. Cool air caressed her skin, quickly followed once again by the sensual heat of Colin's mouth. She gasped, her fingers tangled in his hair as his tongue licked playfully at one taut nipple. A soft moan escaped her mouth as they quickly shed their clothing.

They lay quietly for a moment, hip to hip, heart to heart, bared body and soul. Lizzie traced Colin's mouth with a finger, rewarded with a kiss that began with infinite gentleness but quickly intensified to mind-blowing heat.

He lifted his lips from hers for a moment. She opened her eyes slowly, bereft by the sudden loss. He kissed her eyelids, the tip of her nose and smiled the sweet, dimpled smile that she loved so much. "I love you, Lizzie," he said.

"I love you, too, Darcy. So much …" Her body burned as they moved together, passion tempered by a deepening love, hearts thundering as they rocked and kissed, thrust and nibbled, each bringing the other to heart-stopping, blissful climax.

Colin collapsed on top of her. She laughed softly, loving the feeling of his solid weight atop her, their bodies slick with sweat.

"You know, we're pretty good at that," she teased as Colin rolled onto his back, pulling her with him, and cuddled her close.

"Only pretty good?" he said, trying to sound hurt. "I tend to think we're rather *amazing* at this."

She laughed and kissed the hollow of his throat. "Amazing, huh? We're amazing at … what is it you call it again?"

"Shagging," he answered with an adorable blush. "Care to give it another go?"

"Well … we've got the place to ourselves for a few more hours. Kind of seems like it'd be a crime to waste it."

"Wouldn't want to commit a crime now, would we, love?" Colin teased. "Although there might be one or two illicit things I'd consider …"

And consider them they did.

CHAPTER 19

Knowing that the obstacles to becoming a family had been resolved, Colin, Tori, and Lizzie began to feel like one.

Their little family grew quickly. They adopted a chocolate Labrador puppy named Hershey and a black and white lop-eared bunny called Muffin from a nearby shelter and a weekend excursion to Amish country to meet with a young Amish farmer named Jake, yielded three horses and a pony. Lizzie loved her little menagerie and joked to Colin and Tori that next she would buy a cow named Bessie, a couple of chickens, and a sweet little lamb to make Meg feel at home.

Life was good. They were happy. But Ruby's warning remained in the back of Lizzie's mind.

As the wedding date neared, she began to have a recurring dream.

She was alone. Tired. Hungry. Lost. Searching. Trying desperately to find Colin. She would wake up in a cold sweat and Colin would gently rock her back to sleep. She tried to focus on how truly happy she was, but the warning and the dream left her feeling vaguely unsettled.

It was three weeks until the wedding. Tori was camping with a friend from ballet class and Colin and Lizzie were anticipating a quiet evening alone.

But they'd no sooner settled cozily onto the sofa with a movie and a couple of bottles of beer when the doorbell rang. It was Meg and Jess who, as usual, were followed closely by Lance and Sam.

Lizzie shot Colin an exasperated, longing look. He rolled his eyes and shrugged. Though they treasured their time alone, they loved that their friends felt at home with them. "Come on in," she said with a wave.

"Hey guys!" Jess said cheerfully.

"It's surface-of-the-sun hot!" Meg said, mopping her brow dramatically. "Feels like home."

"We were hoping for a swim, mate," said Lance.

"Sounds good to me. We're a bit low on beer though," Lizzie said holding up the bottle in her hand.

"We've got you covered, Lizzie," said Jess.

Sam grinned. "Ice cold beer!" He held up a large box.

Lizzie burst out laughing and shook her head slowly. "Sam, sweetie, that's a beer ball. Do you have any idea how much beer's in one of those things?"

"Not a clue," he said.

"A lot. Jeez ... there's only six of us!"

"Make that eight. You may as well call it a party," said Abby Brody, entering with her brother, Matt.

"I'm so glad to see you!" Lizzie said hugging her hello. "I'll need your help tapping this thing. It's been a long time since college, and I'm pretty sure none of *these* guys has ever tapped a keg."

To Colin's amazement, Abby and Lizzie installed the tap and had cold, frothy beer flowing quickly. "I'm impressed, ladies," he said. "Where'd you learn how to do that, love?"

"Did you think I spent all my time in college reading Jane Austen?"

"Rumor has it, she had a wild side," teased Matt.

"Shut up, Mattie," Lizzie warned. "Darcy doesn't need to know the sordid details of my misspent youth."

"On the contrary, love, I need *all* the details I can get. Cigar, Matt?" Colin offered.

"Resorting to bribery, honey? That is so not nice!" she complained. "Humph."

"Not to worry, Lizzie. It's just ... I have this insatiable need to know everything there is to know about you."

"But ... I have to have one or two secrets. I have to maintain that air of mystery after all."

"Mystery? You?" Jess said incredulously.

"Darl, you're an open book," Meg agreed.

"Yeah, Lizzie, you wear your heart on your sleeve," said Abby.

"But ... you mean I'm not mysterious?" Lizzie sighed.

"Not a bit," said Jess.

"Oh." She frowned dejectedly. "Darn."

"I think you're very mysterious and fascinating," Colin whispered in her ear. "Not to mention incredibly sexy."

"Good answer, Darcy. Very, very good answer," she said as she stood on tiptoe to kiss him on the mouth. "We're so lucky," she said. "Even with an otherworldly warning of doom ... I still feel so blessed."

"Look, love. We've made it this far without any catastrophes. Maybe Ruby's wrong this time.

"She's never been wrong before, has she?"

"Not that I'm aware of."

Lizzie reached up to finger the ruby cross, as she so often did when she was nervous. "Then I'm sure she's not wrong about this. The nightmares ... they scare me.

Darcy … whatever it is … we'll make it, won't we?"

"We will, love. I'm certain of it. I love you too much to doubt that."

"Thanks. I needed to hear that. I love you too."

"Aw … look at the lovebirds," cooed Meg.

"Jealous, Meg?" Lizzie teased.

"Hardly, darl. I've got Lance here just where I want him."

"That true, Lance?" Colin asked.

Lance grinned crookedly at Meg and kissed her on the cheek. "Fair dinkum, mate. But I'm not the only one." He nodded in the direction of the hot tub, where Jess and Sam looked more than a little cozy.

"Love is in the air," Abby sighed. "I think that calls for a toast," said Abby. "To love."

"Cheers," Colin said as they clinked glasses.

"Are we done with the mushy stuff now?" Matt whined. "I'm hungry. Can we order some pizzas?"

"Sounds like a plan, Matt," Lizzie laughed as she tossed him her cell phone. "Romano's?"

"Best in town," Matt nodded. "And fast."

"Imperative when you have unexpected visitors popping in without warning," Colin quipped, adding quickly, "not that we mind."

Forty-five minutes later, Lizzie was in the kitchen with Jess and Meg, standing on a step stool searching for paper plates when the doorbell rang. "Can you girls get that? It's just the pizza, I'm sure. The money's on the hall table, in the basket."

"No worries, mate," Meg called as they headed toward the front door. Lizzie grinned at her and went back to her search.

"Hey there pizza …" began Jess. "Oh …"

"My …" continued Meg.

"God!" Jess finished. "You're … you're …"

"Jesus!" Meg exclaimed. "What kind of pizza

delivery service did you call, Lizzie?"

"Not Jesus or the pizza man," came a familiar, very amused voice, "I'm a friend of Colin's."

Laughing, Lizzie climbed from step stool and joined her friends in the front hall. They stood, open-mouthed, staring at a befuddled Griffin Brookes, who held four pizza boxes. "Griffin!"

"Hello, Lizzie," he said as he kissed her on the cheek. "Er … your friends seem a bit confused."

"Well, this is a bit of a shock. What the hell are you doing here?"

"I was in New York taping The Late Show. Since my flight home isn't until tomorrow evening, I thought I'd pop round for a visit."

"Ah," Lizzie said, trying to sound as if that was the most normal thing in the world. "Well, hi! Um … these are my friends, Jess and Meg. I think you guys recognize Griffin Brookes."

"Uh huh," they murmured in unison.

"Ladies," he said with a charming smile. "Lovely to meet you both." He glanced at the three women in wet swimsuits with towels wrapped sarong-style around their hips. "I seem to be a bit overdressed," he said indicating his open-necked white dress shirt and blue jeans.

"We've been swimming, obviously. Would you care to join us in the pool? I can get you one of Darcy's suits,"

"A swim sounds perfect, then I'll drive back to my hotel in New York."

"Not a chance, buster. You're staying here."

"Lizzie? What's taking so long with the pizza?" Colin called as the door slammed shut behind him.

"We've got another visitor, Darcy." By this time, he had joined them in the hall.

"Hullo, Griff," he said. "I heard you were in New York this week. Good of you to stop 'round."

"So, swim?" Lizzie asked.

"Why not?"

"Good. Follow me. I'll show you where you can change."

"Crikey! Is Griffin Brookes really here?" Meg whispered, her voice tinged with awe.

"I thought you were shitting us when you told us about the party," Jess said.

"I would *never* lie about Griffin Brookes," Lizzie breathed.

"She wouldn't," Colin sighed. "If he wasn't happily married I'd be jealous."

"Ha. You're just upset because I goosed his butt."

"I can't believe you did that," laughed Jess.

"Neither can I," Lizzie smirked. "I swear I thought it was Darcy."

"Still sticking to that mistaken identity story, Lizzie?" teased Griffin as he joined them.

"Absolutely," she chuckled.

"Not to worry, Lizzie, your secret's safe with me," he teased again.

"Phew. At least I'll be able to sleep at night. So … you going in?"

"I dunno. Is it safe do you think?" He glanced nervously at her salivating friends.

"I think you'll be alright. No sharks here." She glanced over at Meg. "Well, maybe one, but she's pretty well spoken for these days."

"That is a relief." He dropped his towel on one of the lounge chairs and, moving to the deep end of the pool, dove in gracefully. All of the women let out a deep, collective sigh.

"You lot are too much," Lance moaned, shaking his head.

"We know," Meg admitted. "But we've all been

carrying a torch for Griffin for a very long time now."

"He's a hottie," Jess agreed. "Sorry Sam."

Sam shrugged his shoulders and grinned at her. "I just find it hard to believe you've a crush on old Griff."

"Well, we're not exactly used to hanging out with the rich and famous," said Jess. "You've known him for years, so it's different for you."

Sam glanced at Griffin, eyes narrowed jealously. "As long as it's just an innocent crush, Jess."

"Of course it is, silly!" She thumped him playfully on the arm. "You know very well who I have the hots for."

Lizzie glanced from Meg and Lance to Jess and Sam and beamed at Colin. "Looks like everyone's exactly where they belong."

The dust choked her throat and burned her eyes as she stumbled blindly through the rough terrain. "Darcy," she called hoarsely. "Darcy. Where are you?" she stumbled again as the earth rocked beneath her feet and knocked her off her feet. Crouched on the ground, she pummeled the arid soil with clenched fists. "I have to find him," she muttered. "I have to."

"Lizzie," called a soft voice. "Follow me."

She forced her eyes open. In front of her, resplendent in her scarlet gown, stood Ruby. Her ruby cross was missing, fastened around Lizzie's own neck. "Ruby. Help me, please! I have to get to Darcy!"

"Shhh ... there now. Did I not promise all would be well? Come with me and you shall find your love ..." She held out her hand

"Thank you," Lizzie murmured over and over again. "Thank you." She took her proffered hand and stumbled to her feet ..."

"Lizzie! Lizzie! Love, wake up," Colin whispered as he gently nudged her awake.

"Wha ... huh?" she mumbled groggily. "What's

wrong?"

"You were calling for me. Did you have the nightmare again?" His voice was soft, gentle, and full of concern.

"Yes. Ruby was there, leading me …"

"Leading you? To where?"

"Not to where, to whom. She was helping me find you. Darcy, something's going to separate us."

"Wrong, love. Something's going to *try* to separate us. There's a difference. Whatever it is, together we're stronger than it is. Do you believe that?"

"I believe it," she said with conviction.

Colin reached up a hand to trace the cross where it hung between her breasts. "Besides, you have a protector."

"*We* have a protector, Darcy. Ruby's promise is for both of us."

Colin gathered her tightly in his arms and kissed her tenderly. "You're right. I … I need to tell you something …"

Lizzie sat up in the bed and switched on the lamp, turning to stare at him expectantly. Colin dragged a hand through his dark curls and let out a weary sigh. "I'm not sure where to begin." He took one of her hands and gave it a gentle, reassuring squeeze.

"The beginning's usually a safe bet."

"Right. Have I ever mentioned that Snowhill has another ghost?"

"Nope. I think I'd remember that. Who is it?"

"It's William. Ruby's love. He haunts the grove by the lake. I suppose he's still trying to make it to Ruby after all this time."

"How come no one ever mentioned it?"

"Because, to the best of my knowledge, I'm the only one who's ever seen him."

"Tell me what happened, Darcy."

"When I was, I dunno ... ten or eleven ... I was out riding. I was a bit of a daredevil in those days, reckless and convinced of my own immortality. I sailed my horse easily over the hedgerow but something spooked him. He stopped short and threw me arse over head. I'd got quite a nasty concussion and passed out. When I regained consciousness, a young man was holding the reins of my horse, stroking his nose to calm him. He never said a word, just handed me the reins and walked away. I didn't realize at the time who it was."

"But you saw him again?"

Colin nodded. "More than once. Always in the same spot."

"And he never spoke to you?"

"No. That is to say ... not until recently."

"What? How? When?"

"About the same time that you started having your nightmares, I've been having some as well. I'm trying desperately to get back to you but something's immobilizing me." His head dropped as he idly twisted his signet ring.

"Why didn't you tell me?" Lizzie asked, unable to keep the hurt out of her voice. She stroked his cheek softly with her thumb and forefinger. "You should have told me."

"I didn't want to frighten you any more than you already were. You've been sleeping poorly from your nightmares. I didn't want to add to your burden."

"Isn't that the point of all this? To share the burdens as well as the joys?" Tears slipped down her cheeks to splash on their joined hands.

"You're right, of course. I ... I'm sorry, love."

"It's okay. Just ... remember in the future that we're in this together? For better or worse, okay? No more secrets."

"I promise," Colin said, his voice husky with emotion.

"How do we get past this, Darcy? I don't want to be constantly waiting for some sort of catastrophe. I want us to enjoy these last few weeks."

"Then that's what we'll do," Colin vowed. "I love you, my Lizzie."

CHAPTER 20

"It's not like we have a vast number of choices, I'm afraid," Lizzie said when Griffin offered to take them to breakfast. "But if you're up for some local color, there's the Iron Forge Diner. I can guarantee that no one there will have a clue who Griffin is."

"That's not exactly reassuring, Lizzie," Griffin said dryly.

"Don't worry, Griffin. Most of the regulars are eighty if they're a day. They probably haven't actually been to a movie since the seventies."

The diner was exactly as she remembered it, the quintessential greasy spoon, complete with paper placemats bearing a map of Greece, and a raspy-voiced waitress named Flossie. To her surprise, along with the geriatric set, was a couple that she recognized from high school.

"Crap," she muttered.

"What's wrong, Lizzie?" Colin asked.

"See that couple sitting two booths up on the left? The dark-haired woman with the clean-cut guy?"

The two men nodded. "Friends of yours?" Griffin

213

asked.

"Not exactly. Laurel Ford and Kevin Gragson. They were in my graduating class, but Laurel and I ... I've told you, Darcy, I wasn't exactly popular in high school."

"Their loss, love," Colin assured her. "Was she dreadful?"

"Yup. Your basic mean girl," Lizzie sighed.

"Perhaps you might have the last laugh?" Colin suggested with a devious grin.

"I love it when your shark side comes out, Darcy. Very sexy. What do you have in mind?"

"See if you can catch her eye, but pretend that you don't recognize her," Colin said.

Lizzie glanced casually around the restaurant as if she was trying to locate their waitress among the noisy throng of patrons. She caught Laurel's eye and it was instantly apparent that her old nemesis remembered her. "Phase one complete," she said with a mock salute. "What now?"

The two men exchanged nearly identical, grins. "Wait for her to come to you," Griffin suggested.

It didn't take long. In less than two minutes, Laurel and Kevin approached their table, their eyes widening as they recognized Griffin Brookes and Lizzie's look-alike fiancé.

"Lizzie?" Laurel said hesitantly.

Lizzie looked at her without blinking, playing it very cool. "Have we met? I'm sorry, I'm terrible with faces."

"Sorry," Kevin said. "We thought we went to high school together. Class of ninety-two?"

"Choir? English lit class? Ringing any bells?" Laurel asked tapping her foot.

"Sorry," Lizzie said frowning and shaking her head. She tilted her head and regarded the pair of them intently. "Wait a minute! Laurel and Skippy?"

"Skippy?" Colin mouthed with a smirk.

"Yes, it's us. We're married now, you know. Kevin and I have been *so* busy with our law practice and our family."

"How nice for you."

"So what have you been doing with yourself, Lizzie?" Kevin asked. He was the kinder of the pair.

"Well, I've had an incredibly busy summer," she grinned. "I'm getting married in three weeks."

"Well, congrats," said Laurel coolly. "Who's the lucky guy?"

"Sorry, I guess I should introduce you. Laurel Ford, Kevin Gragson meet Colin Blake."

"That name sounds familiar," Kevin said.

"Colin is CEO of a multinational corporation," she informed them. "Oh! I should introduce our very good friend, Griffin Brookes. He's an Oscar-winning actor."

"Er ... uh ... I ... I ... yeah," Laurel muttered. "Holy crap!"

"I know!" Lizzie grinned. "If anyone had told me six months ago he'd not only be a dear friend but a houseguest, I'd have sworn they were nuts."

"How special for you," Laurel muttered.

"You look great," Kevin said in an attempt to smooth things over and change the subject.

Lizzie smiled at him, proud that over the course of the summer she'd learned how to dress her curves to look her best. "Thanks, Kevin."

"Well, we'd better get moving," Kevin said. "Good to see you, Lizzie. Congratulations."

"Kevin," Laurel barked. "Let's go!" She was already halfway out the door.

"Er ... you better go, Kevin. Looks like Laurel's not too happy."

"Yeah," he sighed. "She never is."

"We're so lucky," Lizzie told the two men after

they'd gone. "I'm so glad I held out for the real thing. How sad that some people settle for a second-rate imitation."

The following Monday, Colin, Sam, and Lance met in his home office. Though Consolidated was now on its way to recovery, the problems with the Turkish mines had escalated again. The three of them were on a lengthy conference call with the local management when Lizzie wandered in.

"Not a good time, darl," Meg warned.

"Turkey again?"

"Uh huh. I expect one of them will have to fly over to sort things out," she said.

"Damn," Lizzie mumbled. "I don't even want to think about that." Though both Lance and Sam had visited the site and a new contract had been signed, the workers were still far from happy.

"You're worried about Ruby, aren't you?" Meg asked.

"Yeah, I am. If someone has to go …" Lizzie's voice trailed off as tears sprang to her eyes. "Damn."

The three men concluded their call and joined them in Meg's office. "Hey, Darcy," Lizzie said, hugging him tightly. "Rough day?" Fighting to keep her uneasiness from showing, she forced a smile and tilted her head back to get a better look at him. There were deep creases etched into his forehead. "Darcy?"

He pulled her close and kissed the top of her head. Wearily, he leaned against the edge of Meg's desk, holding tightly to both her hands. He glanced up, his intense brown eyes searching hers. "Lizzie," he said softly. "I'm going to Turkey …"

"Does it have to be you?" Lizzie asked. She didn't mean to be selfish, but Ruby's warning weighed heavily on her mind. "Sorry. You wouldn't be going if it didn't."

"Look, Lizzie. The last thing on earth I want to do right now is travel to a remote village in the mountains of Turkey. But ..." He squeezed his eyes shut and pinched the bridge of his nose.

"But you have to?"

"Yes. Cengiz ... he's the foreman who speaks for the workers ... he's insinuated that the local manager isn't adhering to the contract they signed when Lance and Sam were there last month."

"One of the miners was badly injured last week because of some faulty equipment," said Sam.

"Equipment that should have been replaced according to the terms of the new contract," Lance added angrily. "That bloody bastard Adil!"

"I've got to go, Lizzie. I have to make this right. Those men deserve a safe place to work."

"Of course they do," she agreed readily. "Just, be careful, Darcy. I'm scared."

"I will, love. I should be home by Saturday at the latest."

Lizzie spent the next hour on the phone with Carolyn, working out a flight itinerary and car rental. Colin was leaving that night for Frankfurt, where he would catch a connection to Istanbul, then on to Trabzon on the Black Sea coast. From there they'd dug up an SUV for the two-hour drive into the Caucasus Mountains to the copper mine. Once it was settled, Jess offered to drive over and help Meg prepare the documents Colin needed to take with him.

Though she put on a brave face, especially when they told Tori about the trip, Lizzie's heart felt as if it had been ripped in two.

She trudged up the stairs to help Colin pack, needing something mundane to keep her mind occupied and sniffed back tears as she handed Colin a stack of clean socks and underwear.

He chuckled softly at the size of the pile she'd given him. "Good God, Lizzie, I'm only going for a few days."

"S-sorry ..." She sputtered as tears splashed down her face. "Are you sure you have to go?"

"Lizzie, you know that I do."

"That doesn't mean I have to like it."

"I'll be fine, love."

"Maybe I should come with you," she suggested.

"As much as I'd love that, it's not practical. It's a full day's travel getting there, and I'll be tied up every minute. I'd never see you."

"I ... I'd feel better if we were already married."

Without saying a word, Colin crossed the room and went into the bathroom. Lizzie heard him rummaging through the medicine cabinet. He returned quickly, hiding something in one hand.

With the other, he took her hand and led her over to sit on the bed. His deep brown eyes held hers in a caress as he lifted her left hand to his mouth, his lips lingering on her ring finger. He smiled and she saw the love they shared shining in his eyes. "Dearest, loveliest Lizzie," he said softly. "You own my heart."

A tear trickled down her cheek. Colin reached up to gently wipe it away with the pad of his thumb.

He gazed into her tear-filled eyes. "I, Darcy, take you, Lizzie, to be my wife. For richer, for poorer, in sickness and health, to love and to cherish as long as we both shall live."

"Oh, Darcy!" she said as a fountain of tears poured from her eyes.

He opened his clenched hand to reveal two Band-Aids. He slipped off Lizzie's engagement ring, removed the backing from one of the Band-Aids, and placed it on her ring finger. Then he slid the ring back on.

Lizzie's fingers trembled as she took the other Band-Aid from him. Her voice husky with emotion, she repeated the words back to him. "I, Lizzie, take you, Darcy, to be my husband. For richer, for poorer, in sickness and in health, to love and to cherish as long as we both shall live." She applied the Band-Aid to his finger and lifted his hand to her mouth. "I love you!"

Colin grinned cheekily and wiggled his eyebrows at her. "I may now kiss the bride," he announced.

Lizzie giggled as his lips found hers. She relished each moment of that kiss; the firm gentleness of his mouth, the silky seductiveness of his tongue, the prickle of his whiskers on the skin of her chin.

They fell back on the bed, lost in each other. She gasped as she felt the buttons on her blouse giving way. "Door?"

"Shut."

"Tori?"

"Out riding."

"Excellent," Lizzie whispered as she pulled his mouth back to hers. "Can't take wedding vows and not have a proper wedding night, now can we?"

"That would break all the rules," Colin laughed.

Buttons popped. Zippers slid open. Clothing was flung helter-skelter around the room until skin met skin.

Wildly, almost frantically, they made love, saying with their bodies all they were afraid to put into words. Love mingled with fear, passion with commitment, joy with heartache. Colin's sensual lips branded every inch of her skin as his own until she could feel the microscopic end of every nerve.

Her own lips were bold and brazen as they traveled over the firm muscles of Colin's body. The contrast between the taut muscles and his smooth, silky skin pushed her to the brink. She moaned softly as Colin rolled her onto her back and plunged inside her, his need as primal as her own. She wrapped her legs around his hips, moaning again as their bodies moved together until, trembling and slick with sweat, they shuddered together in an explosive climax.

"Wow," she said when she finally regained the ability to speak. "That was …"

"Beyond words?"

"Uh … yeah … I'll say," she sighed. "You know … I'm not sure I can make it until Saturday night." She licked her way down his chest and swirled her tongue around his nipple.

Colin groaned and sucked in his breath. "I … uh … don't I have a plane to catch?"

"Plane shmane," Lizzie teased as her lips moved to the other nipple.

"Lizzie, please!"

"Please? So polite, Darcy. I may have to punish you for that."

"Promises, promises," he teased seductively as he rolled her onto her back. He nipped at the tender skin of her breast.

"Er … plane?" she murmured.

Colin angled himself up to glance at the clock radio on the nightstand. "We've got at least an hour."

"An hour you say? Well, well, Darcy, whatever will I do with you for an entire hour?"

"I'm sure you'll think of something."

Lizzie thought of several.

At three o'clock that afternoon Colin lugged his suitcase down the stairs to the front porch. Lizzie couldn't handle the idea of a public goodbye, so she wasn't going to the airport. He kissed Tori tenderly on the cheek and told her to be good. He turned to Lizzie and pulled her into his arms for a fierce, fiery kiss. "Time to go," he whispered. "I love you, Lizzie."

"I love you too, Darcy." She kissed him again, tasting the salt of her tears. Colin brushed them away, squeezed her hand and walked slowly down the steps toward his car. He turned to smile and blow her a kiss as he got into the car and drove off.

As his car disappeared from view, Lizzie couldn't help but wonder just when she'd see him again.

Self-pity was not an option. She knew that if she stopped moving, even for a second, she would wallow. Lizzie grabbed Tori's hand and squeezed it. "What do you say we have a girls' night in? Junk food and chick flicks?"

"Just us, Mum?"

"Yeah. Just the two of us. What to do you think?"

"I think it sounds perfect."

They spent an hour deciding what movies to watch. Lizzie insisted on a classic Doris Day movie while Tori chose one starring the latest teen heartthrob. And they both agreed to end the evening with a musical.

"Er … perhaps we're being a bit overzealous," Tori laughed when she realized that they had a seven-hour marathon planned.

"If we fall asleep we can stay in our pajamas and finish them tomorrow night. Deal?"

"Deal!" Tori threw her arms around Lizzie and hugged her tightly. "I love you, Mum, just so you know."

"Yeah, kiddo, I love you, too."

Once they had their entertainment planned, they headed to the grocery store, where they filled the shopping cart with every junk food known to man. "Chips?" Lizzie asked.

"Barbecue," Tori said, tossing them into the cart. "Cookies?"

"Has to be chocolate chip," Lizzie said. Tori nodded and lobbed a bag into Lizzie's hands. "Now, ice cream?"

"Mint chocolate chip," they said in unison.

Tori giggled and raced the cart to the frozen foods aisle.

"I think we've got all of the food groups, you know, salt, sugar, and fat," Lizzie joked. "I know it looks bad but it's girls' night and … eh … a woman can only eat so much rabbit food. What do you think?" Lizzie asked, assessing the array of food in their cart. "I should probably feel guilty for feeding you this crap."

"It's fine, Mum," Tori assured her. "How much harm can one night's indulgence cause?"

"Hm." Lizzie suddenly remembered how the fat clung to her thighs and how the salt made her feel bloated. "Maybe we should rethink this idea."

"Mu-um! It was your idea in the first place!" Tori took control of the cart and steered it toward the checkout lines. "We'll eat real food the rest of the week, alright?"

"Fine," Lizzie sighed, jumping as her cell phone vibrated in her pocket. "Hello?" she whispered.

"I miss you already," Colin said sadly.

"Darcy! Where are you?"

"I'm at my gate. How're my girls doing?"

"We're okay. But we miss you, too, and you haven't even taken off. Darcy, how the hell am I supposed to make it through five days without you?"

"I dunno, love, I've been wondering the same. Listen … I forgot to tell you something."

"What?"

"Court's got some papers to drop off today. I completely forgot about them. He met me here so I could sign them."

"What sort of papers?" she asked nervously.

"Nothing to worry about, I assure you. It's all been in the works for weeks, really, just some legalities. Court will explain everything. Lizzie, love, I don't want you to get upset, but one of them is …" he paused, "my will."

"Oh. That's more than a little freaky, Darcy, considering."

"Please don't let it worry you. It's all routine."

"My head knows that, but thinking about it now … it gives me the creeps."

"Nothing's going to happen."

"Can you give me a guarantee on that?" There was silence on the other end, making Lizzie feel a twinge of guilt for her petulance. "Sorry, sweetie. That was bratty. What time should I expect Court?"

"Within the hour, I should imagine. Is Tori with you?"

"Yes." She handed the cell phone to Tori.

"Hey, Dad … Righto … Yes … the school tour's on Friday, I think …" she glanced at Lizzie for confirmation, who nodded. "Yes, Friday … What's that, Daddy? … uh huh … I reckon so … Love you too … Here's Mum back …" She handed the cell phone back to Lizzie.

"What are you two up to?" Lizzie asked.

Colin chuckled softly. "I asked Tori if she could keep you out of trouble for me."

"Oh." She smiled in spite of her tension. "I think maybe you've given her an impossible job. Darcy …"

"Damn. They're calling my flight, love."

"Darcy … I love you so much," she murmured. "Keep yourself safe for me, okay?"

"Your wish is my command."

"If only it were that simple. At least I know you've got a guardian angel looking out for you."

"I'll call you between flights in Frankfurt, alright? That's my final boarding call. I must go."

CHAPTER 21

True to his word, Colin called between flights in Frankfurt and again when he arrived in Istanbul. Once he reached the small mountain village where the mine was located, they were lucky to manage one short, fuzzy phone call a day.

During the days, she maintained her calm. But the nights were terribly lonely and sleep was impossible. She'd barely slept since Colin left, but she didn't realize that Tori wasn't sleeping well either.

In the early hours of Thursday morning, Lizzie lay in bed, reading the same paragraph of her romance novel over and over again. She jumped when she heard footsteps creeping past her bedroom door and down the stairs. Without a second thought, she rolled out of bed and threw on her robe.

Muted piano music drifted from the living room. Lizzie leaned in the doorway, listening as Tori played. "I love that song," Lizzie whispered, recognizing the piece. "It's like a goodnight prayer."

"I ... I couldn't sleep. I hope I didn't wake you."

"Nope. I'm not sleeping too well these days either,"

she admitted. "Will you sing it with me?"

Tori nodded and began playing the "Prayer" from Engelbert Humperdinck's *Haensel and Gretel* from the beginning. Her sweet contralto merged with Lizzie's lilting soprano as the song conjured a host of protective angels.

Lizzie pressed a kiss to the top of Tori's head as they sang. Tori smiled up at her and somehow she knew that they would both sleep a little easier.

She slid onto the bench beside Tori, who laid her cheek on Lizzie's shoulder as they finished the song.

"I love you, Tori," Lizzie said as she hugged her. "Shall we send those angels to watch over your Dad?"

"Yes, please," she said softly. "And Ruby and her William, too, Mum. I miss Dad. I know it's probably silly since we spent so much time apart, but after this summer, with the three of us together, I can't help it. I miss him."

Colin called just after midnight on Friday morning to tell them that the situation was finally resolved. "I'll not make the flight connections today, so I'll wait until tomorrow as planned."

"I'm so relieved you're coming home!" Lizzie said.

"Me too. So what have you got planned for the day?"

"Tori and I have the tour of the middle school at ten, then Tori's babysitting for Lisa, and I'm running some errands. What about you? Is there anything to do there?"

"Not much, really. Cengiz has offered to take me into the mine." His voice was filled with boyish enthusiasm.

Lizzie shook her head, not surprised that he was excited about exploring the open pit mine and playing with some really big toys. "You boys and your toys! If that's your idea of a good time ..."

"Hardly," Colin said, laughing huskily. "But I've dozens of ideas for when I get home."

After the middle school tour, Lizzie dropped Tori at her brother Pete's house and headed off on her errands. Each minute closer to Colin's return made her feel calmer and more at ease. He called her cell phone promptly at noon to inform her that he was packed and ready to fly home. "I land at three-thirty tomorrow afternoon."

"We'll be there."

Lizzie's first stop was the liquor store. Darcy's homecoming warranted champagne and, though the two-hundred-dollar price tag gave her pause, she took a deep breath and presented her credit card. Next she headed to the mall to pick up the gifts that she'd ordered for her bridesmaids. After a quick bite at the food court, Lizzie was ready to head home.

She sang along with the radio on the way, glancing at the clock on the dashboard. It was three-twenty-three pm. A poignant song tugged at her heart and, for some unfathomable reason, she burst into tears. "Good thing Darcy will be home tomorrow," she muttered to herself. "I am definitely losing it. And now I'm talking to myself." She laughed softly, brushed the tears away, and grinned as the next song came on.

It was a cheerful song, and she was singing at the top of her lungs as she pulled up to a traffic light. The young male driver beside her laughed and shook his head, but Lizzie merely shrugged and beamed at him as the light changed.

She was still smiling and singing when she pulled into the driveway and headed straight back to the office to say hello to Meg and Jess and attempt to drag them away for a swim. She pushed the door open, grinning like a fool and shaking her butt in her version of a happy dance. "Woohoo … Darcy's coming ho-ome …"

"Lizzie," Meg croaked.

Lizzie stopped dancing and stared at her friends. Their faces were pale and stained with tears. "What's happened," she breathed.

Neither of them could speak. They just stared at her, open-mouthed, as if willing the words to come out.

"Please, just tell me," she begged.

"Lizzie … it's Colin," Jess began.

Meg took a deep breath and wrapped her arm around Lizzie's waist. "Love, there's been an earthquake."

She felt the color drain from her face. "No," she whispered. "No."

Meg and Jess guided her to the sofa and sat down on either side of her, each of them holding tightly to one of her hands. "I'm so sorry, love," Meg soothed.

Lizzie began sobbing, her body heaving as the pain stabbed at her like a white-hot knife. "What happened?" she managed to croak between sobs.

"It happened just after three," Jess began.

"Three-twenty-three," Lizzie breathed, remembering the unexplainable sadness she'd felt in the car.

"There's no easy way to tell you this," said Jess, glancing over her head at Meg.

"The mine is right at the epicenter. They … they say it more or less swallowed up the entire village." Meg expelled a long, slow breath. "We've had no news at all."

"Just what we heard on CNN," said Jess. "Sam and Lance have gone to the office to try to get through to their contacts over there."

"What can we do, Lizzie?" Meg asked. "How can we help?"

"I … This isn't real. It *can't* be real. It's all another fucking nightmare," Lizzie shrieked. "Oh, God! Please tell me this isn't real." Her body heaved with deep, hiccupping sobs. "I have to find him. I … I'm going to find him."

"Lizzie, you can't go over there," said Jess.

"I'm going," she vowed.

"Then we're going with you," Meg promised as she got up and walked to the credenza.

"No," Lizzie said quietly. "No, you're not."

"You're in shock, Lizzie," said Jess.

"Of course I'm in shock!" Lizzie shouted. "The man I love is God knows where! How the hell would I not be in shock?"

"It's normal," Jess assured her, "all part of the …"

"What?" she shrieked. "Part of what? The grieving process? I'm *not* grieving. Grief implies that Darcy's gone. I won't believe that. I'll *never* believe that!"

Lizzie jumped as Meg pressed a glass into her hand. "Drink it," she ordered.

"What is it?"

"Whiskey."

Lizzie swallowed it in one gulp. It burned her throat, somehow cutting through the haze of pain and bringing her to her senses. "Get Lance and Sam on the phone. Please."

Meg dialed without question and, when Lance picked up, pressed the button for speakerphone. "Any news?" she asked.

"Not a bloody word. The phone lines in eastern Turkey are down," said Lance. His voice was tight with worry.

"Damn," Lizzie said softly. She took a deep, steadying breath. "Okay, here's what we're going to do. Guys, I think under the circumstances it's best if you stay here to keep things calm at Consolidated. Meg, Jess … as much as I love you both for wanting to come, I think Lance and Sam will need you more. I'm going to Turkey. Alone."

"What about Tori?" Sam asked. "Does she know?"

"I … I don't think so. She's babysitting, so there's

not much chance she's watching the news. I … I'd appreciate if you would pick her up and bring her home. This isn't news I want to give her over the phone." Lizzie took a deep breath, wondering where this unexpected reserve of calm had come from. "I think it would be easier for her if she could stay here." Lizzie turned to Meg and Jess. "Will you guys stay with her?"

"No worries, mate," Meg said.

"Of course we'll stay," said Jess.

"Thanks. Okay, I've got to figure out how to tell Tori and … break the news to Helen …" Fresh tears streamed down her face. "God this sucks."

"I'll call Mum," Sam offered. "I think Gram would take the news better in person."

The numbness Lizzie felt somehow kept her going. Her heart had been ripped in two, but she kept breathing, kept moving, kept, inexplicably, living.

In a daze, she made travel arrangements and packed some clothes and essentials in a backpack. The closest she could get by airplane was Istanbul, which left an almost nine hundred mile drive through rugged terrain still suffering strong aftershocks. Lizzie had no idea what she'd find when she arrived and she was terrified, but not going, not trying was simply not an option.

"Why Darcy?" Lizzie screamed, shaking her fist at God. "Why now?" she threw herself on the bed and gave in to the fear and despair that threatened to swallow her up. "Please, God … I need him," she prayed. "I can't lose him." She picked at the Band-Aid on her ring finger, and then reached up to touch the ruby cross at her throat.

"Okay, Ruby. It's you and me. Look, I know ghosts don't make command performances, but I *really* need to know that you're on my side. So if you feel like haunting someone, now would be a really good time."

Lizzie lay there for a long time, her head buried in the pillow, sniffling back tears. "Dearest Lizzie," said a soft voice, "have I not promised that I would help you? You shall not be alone."

"Please tell me he'll be okay."

"I know only that you will find him, and you will marry. He is a strong man, is he not?"

"I just hate to think of him alone … in pain …"

"I do not know where he is, my friend. I do not know if he is whole and well. It is not for me to know but …"

"But?"

"I do not believe he is alone, not really. Your Colin, he has met my William, has he not? William has kept a watchful eye on Colin since he was but a lad."

"You knew about that?"

"I am trapped within Snowhill. I know all that happens within and without. I have seen my William wandering in the grove of an evening."

"If you're trapped at Snowhill, how are you here, with me?" Lizzie sniffled loudly and blotted her eyes with a crumpled up tissue.

Ruby sighed softly. "I do not understand why, but I was allowed to attach myself to you, my friend. It is a rare gift for one such as I, but I am most grateful to be of use. I shall stay with you, Lizzie, as long as you wear my cross about your neck. Remember that even if you do not see or hear me, I am with you. I will help you."

"I'm scared, Ruby. I'm afraid I won't find him. Or that I will and …" She took in a long, slow breath. "I'm going to find him. I'm going to bring him home. And we will get our happily-ever-after."

"You have great courage, Lizzie. You are not afraid to fight to keep what is precious to you as I was. You will not suffer regret as I, my dear friend. I shall help you to find your love and your happy ending. That is my promise and my vow."

Telling Tori was the hardest thing Lizzie had ever done. Tori sobbed in Lizzie's arms as she wept fresh tears on her daughter's slender shoulders. "Please let me come with you!" she pleaded.

"Tori, it's not a good idea. Honestly, it's probably not even a good idea for me to go. I don't know what I'll find there. I won't take you into that kind of turmoil. But I promise you, I will do all I can to find him and bring him home."

"I don't want you to go all alone."

"I won't be alone." Lizzie's voice was soft as she held up the cross. It glowed fiery red as it glinted in the sun. "Ruby will help me."

Colin gasped for air, choking as he inhaled a thick cloud of dust. Coughs racked his body, each one adding another layer to the blinding pain in his leg. He closed his eyes, willing himself to slow his breathing until his lungs cleared.

He took a slow, careful breath and opened his eyes to … nothing but suffocating darkness. He could move his arms and upper body but his legs were pinned beneath something large and heavy. He held his breath and wiggled the toes on his right foot, relieved to find that, though the leg was pinned, it seemed to be in good working order. He let his breath out in a loud puff and took another cautious breath, holding it while he attempted the same exercise with his left foot. He managed to move his big toe but even the tiniest motion caused searing pain to shoot up the length of his leg.

"Right. That's shattered then." He said it aloud to no one but himself. "Bloody hell." With a grunt he pushed and clawed at the rubble that covered him, determined to find some connection to the world above.

His nails scraped the fractured wood above his head,

splinters piercing the flesh beneath his fingernails. The rough wood abraded his hands and he could feel a trickle of blood sliding across his knuckles, but he kept moving, ignoring the darkness, the dust, and the excruciating pain in his leg. "I will get out of here. I will."

A blast of icy air shivered across his skin. He squeezed his eyes shut, imagining Lizzie's warm smile and Tori's bright laughter. He could see the rolling hills of Pemberley Farm and feel the warmth of the late summer sun on his face as they relaxed by the pool; his world, his life, hidden from him by the mound of rubble that held him hostage.

He remembered how it had felt when the earth had rumbled and roared. He remembered the panic and the screams and then the silence and the darkness. He'd felt the aftershocks, each one burying him more deeply, taking him farther away from the ones he loved. "I will get out of here. I will."

Colin repeated the words over and over in his mind like a mantra. He was too stubborn to give up without one hell of a fight, and he had far too much to fight for. "Lizzie. I need Lizzie."

"Your Lizzie needs you, too, Master Colin." The voice was soft, barely above a whisper, and though he'd never heard it before, Colin knew at once to whom it belonged.

"William Travers."

"Aye. 'Tis I."

"How are you here? You belong at Snowhill."

"I do not understand it. I have not left the grove since old John Blake thrust his sword into my heart. I do not know this place."

"It's a long way from the wonders of Derbyshire, to be sure. Did Ruby send you?"

"I have not seen my dearest Ruby, but I know that she is tied to Snowhill as I am to its grove and, perhaps, its master. I know only that the earth beneath my feet shuddered, and I was at your side. Many souls are departing this place, and many more are entombed beneath the rubble."

"Would you mind not using the word entombed?" Colin mumbled. "I've no intention of dying in this bloody hole in the ground. I will get out."

"You will," William assured him. "It is not your time to leave this earth."

"I don't suppose you can help me get out."

"I am not of this world, Master Colin. I cannot move something as solid as that beam."

"I was afraid you'd say that. So ... what now? Am I just supposed to lie here and hope someone thinks to look in this pile of dirt and stone? Do I just ... wait in the dark and the dust with a roof beam pinning me to the floor?"

"Aye, Master Colin."

"That's not exactly reassuring, William. I'm not a patient man. I can't breathe properly for all the dust; I can't see my bloody hand in front of my bloody face, and my leg ... Jesus ... you can't imagine the pain."

"Is it worse than a sword through the heart? You are alive. You will survive. You will see your lovely daughter and your beautiful betrothed. This much I can promise you though I cannot say when. Will you trust me?"

"Do you swear it?"

"By all that I hold sacred. You will survive. And until you are found, you are not alone."

CHAPTER 22

Lizzie made the late flight from Philadelphia to London. She leaned back against the leather seat as the jet sped down the runway and lifted effortlessly into the air. It seemed strange that a hunk of metal could hurtle itself through the atmosphere, thousands of miles above the earth's surface, a simple feat of engineering, while at the same time the earth itself was shuddering and groaning, consuming mountains and villages.

She squeezed her eyes shut, willing away the images of dust and rubble, the cries of the injured, and the howls of pain for the lost. "Stay with me, Darcy," she murmured to herself. "Wherever you are, don't you dare give up!"

She stared out the tiny window at the endless black of the night sky. Somewhere down there was the man she loved, lost, alone, hurting. What they'd found together was beyond anything she'd ever allowed herself to dream of having; she wasn't about to give it up without one hell of a fight. "I will not go gentle into that good night," she vowed softly. "And I won't let Darcy go either." She brushed the fresh tears from her cheeks and sniffled softly.

"Hot towel, Ma'am?" the flight attendant asked.

"Thanks," Lizzie said gratefully. She buried her face in the warm, moist towel, breathing deeply as the heat rejuvenated her and eased the numbness, at least for a moment.

"You haven't touched your dinner," she reminded Lizzie gently. "It's not bad for airplane food."

"I'm not hungry."

"Are you quite all right?" Her voice was soft and kind. "You're a bit pale."

"I ... I've had better days," Lizzie mumbled.

"Well, love, a proper holiday will have you right as rain in no time."

Lizzie burst into tears. The flight attendant sat down in the empty seat beside her and laid a hand on her arm. "Sod it! I've upset you, now." She patted Lizzie's arm helplessly. "You're not on holiday, are you, love?"

She shook her head mutely, then blotted her eyes with a crumpled tissue and blew her nose. "There was an earthquake today."

"In Turkey," the flight attendant said. "I saw it on the news."

"My fiancé is there. I ... we haven't heard a thing so ..." The story tumbled out with all the force of an aftershock. "I have to find him," she said with renewed determination as she finished telling the story.

"They say love can move mountains," the flight attendant said.

"I just hope it can move a mountain that's crumbled."

Lizzie sat sleeplessly in the darkened cabin, listening to, but not hearing the Turkish language course that Lance had loaned her. Restless, she threw off the headset and pushed herself out of her seat. She wandered up the aisle to the galley where the flight attendants were enjoying a break while most of their passengers slept.

"Sorry to bug you," she said. "Any chance I could get a Coke?"

"Can't sleep?" asked Molly, the flight attendant she'd unloaded on earlier. She flicked open the can of soda and poured it over a cup of ice.

Lizzie shook her head mournfully. "I'm afraid to close my eyes."

"You should try, though. You've got a difficult trek ahead of you."

"I know," she said leaning against the wall. "I just ... can't. Not when I don't know ..."

At Heathrow, Lizzie was met at the gate by Helen, Nora, and, to her shock, Lady Frances. They walked through the concourse to a small cafe where they could discuss details. Nora ordered her a buttery croissant and coffee though Lizzie tried to protest.

Lizzie took Helen's hand and gave it a gentle squeeze. Her face was ashen, tear-stained and etched with fear; for the first time since Lizzie had met her, she looked like a woman in her seventies.

Nora, she learned, had been extraordinarily busy since Lizzie had boarded her flight. The Blake Foundation had arranged for a huge airlift of medical supplies and emergency personnel to the stricken country. Bets and her husband, Thomas, had already flown over to set up a field hospital in a neighboring province. They even had a specially equipped helicopter fueled and ready to transport the most critically injured patients to Istanbul or beyond.

"Bets has already started making inquiries, but they've not had any luck. The searchers haven't even been able to make it to the village," Nora said.

"Oh, God!"

"You'll find him, Lizzie. I know you will. Now, in

Istanbul, you'll meet up with a contingent of doctors, nurses, and rescue workers. Bets said for you to ask for Marida. She's American but married to an Italian. She's to help organize triage closer to the site, so you'll travel with her and some other rescue workers to a small town called Oltu. From there, they're planning a rescue mission into the most damaged areas. The mine's one of them."

Lizzie blinked back her tears and played with the flaky croissant in front of her. She'd managed to eat a few tiny bites and to take a few sips of her coffee. Now, as the reality of the situation struck her again, she felt the croissant rebelling in her belly. "I'm going to be sick." She clapped a hand over her mouth and bolted from the table to the ladies room.

Tears streamed down her face as she heaved the minimal contents of her stomach into the toilet. When she was done, she rinsed her mouth out and splashed her face with cold water. Sighing heavily, she glanced up at her reflection in the mirror. Her face was white as a sheet, she had dark circles under her eyes, and her hair resembled a rat's nest. She finger combed the tangled tresses back from her face, slipped a scrunchy from her wrist, and fashioned a messy-but-serviceable ponytail.

Wearily, she headed back to the table and laid her head on her arms.

"Poor Lizzie," said Nora. "You look done in."

"I ... I'm not sure I can do this ..." she said weakly.

"*You* are the only one who can do this," Lady Frances said. She placed a finger under Lizzie's chin and lifted it gently. The gray eyes that met hers were far from cold.

Lizzie's eyes widened with surprise. It was the first time that the old lady had addressed her since she'd arrived in the terminal. "Excuse me?"

"Miss Kincaid ... *Lizzie* ... you are the sort of woman who stands up for what she believes in, are you not? You did, after all, defend yourself to me. I may have …" she glanced at Nora and Helen, then back at Lizzie, "*did*, in fact, misjudge you. I understand that my grandson loves you. I've never seen him happier, nor Tori. You're good for him." Tears sparkled in the eyes that had so often seemed cold and disdainful.

"He's everything to me," Lizzie murmured.

"Then you must find him. Bring him back. Tell him his Grandmamma would like to dance with him at his wedding."

Lizzie managed a weak smile as the duo waltzed through her head. "I … I will. Th-thank you, Lady Frances."

"We're to be family, child. You must call me Grandmamma."

After tearful goodbyes, Lizzie boarded her second flight in twenty-four hours. She slept in short bursts throughout the flight. Fragments of dreams, visions of Darcy, haunted her, and no amount of hopefulness could latch on to the happy ending she yearned for. She played with Ruby's cross, drawing from it strength and resolve. With the cross between her fingers, she closed her eyes and visualized her ghostly protector. "It's you and me, Ruby," she whispered.

The plane touched down uneventfully in Istanbul. The sky was a cloudless, azure blue; it seemed wrong that in the face of tragedy there should be any beauty at all. Frowning, Lizzie trudged into the terminal, lugging her backpack and made her way through customs.

In the arrivals lounge, she glanced around nervously, breathing a sigh of relief when she saw a pretty Turkish woman holding a sign with her name on it. Lizzie approached her and tilted her head in greeting. "*Merhaba.*" She pointed to the sign. "I'm Miss Kincaid."

"*Merhaba*. I am Huri. Welcome, Miss Kincaid. I am sorry you must come to Turkey for such tragic reasons." She picked up Lizzie's backpack from the floor and hoisted it onto her shoulder. "You are tired, no?"

Lizzie nodded silently and followed Huri through the busy terminal to a roped off area. "Miss Marida?" she called.

An attractive brunette looked up from the medical supplies she was counting. "Yes, Huri?"

"Miss Kincaid has arrived."

Marida pushed herself up from her cross-legged position on the floor and walked over to Lizzie. "Hi. I'm Marida, but my friends call me Mari."

"Lizzie."

"I know. I've heard all about you. Bets and Thomas are good friends of mine. Come on, let's get you settled." She guided her through a maze of camping supplies and medical equipment and out the back door. "Huri, I'm going to take Lizzie to the hotel to get settled for the night. I'll be back in a couple of hours."

"No, Miss Marida. You have been here since the moment you arrived, and we have a long trip in the morning. You stay with Miss Lizzie and rest. All is in good order here, many thanks to you."

"Okay, then. I'll see you early tomorrow morning. Come on, Lizzie. Something tells me you need a decent meal, a hot bath, and a lot of sleep."

Lizzie pushed open the door of her hotel room and dropped her heavy backpack on the floor with a thud.

"Hey, *cara*, I'm right next door," said Mari. "Why don't you run a hot bath and I'll order up some dinner."

"I'm not really hungry."

"Look, hon, I know food is the last thing on your mind right now, but you have to keep your strength up. Tell me the truth, when was the last time you ate anything?"

"I had some coffee and a croissant at Heathrow this morning, but I threw it right back up. I just want to get moving, you know."

"I know you do, but we've got a long trip ahead of us tomorrow. You need a good meal and a decent night's sleep."

"I know. I just … can't. I haven't slept much since he left … and barely at all since …"

"Since the earthquake?"

Lizzie nodded miserably, fighting back tears. "He has to be all right."

"From what Bets has told me about her brother, he's not one to give up on anything easily. And with you to fight for? I have no doubt he'll do whatever it takes to make it back to you."

"He's an amazing man, Mari. I can't wait for you to meet him," she said wistfully.

"Now you're talking, *cara*! Okay, time for you to run a bath and have a nice long soak. Oooh … wait a sec …" She rushed through the connecting door and breezed back in carrying a small bottle of lavender scented bath oil. "I usually save this for the end of an assignment, but I think you need it more."

"Thanks," Lizzie said, sighing as she took the bottle. "I should call Tori first." Lizzie retrieved her cell from the front pocket of her backpack and touched the screen to make her call.

Meg answered the phone on the first ring. "How are you holding up, mate?"

"I'm still pretty numb. How's Tori?"

"She's worried about you both, but she's a strong kid."

"Would you put her on?" Lizzie heard the muffled sounds of the phone being handed over. "Tor?"

"Mum? Are you okay?"

"I'm exhausted from traveling, but I'll be alright. How are you doing?"

"I … I'm okay. Meg and Jess are being super nice. I … I just want you and Daddy home safe," she said with a sniffle.

"That's what I want too, sweetie."

"Have … have you had any word?"

"Nothing yet." Lizzie wanted to be as honest with Tori as she could without scaring her too much. "But, he's alive. I can feel it. Besides, didn't Ruby promise that everything would be all right in the end?"

Tori sniffled loudly. "I remember, Mum. And Ruby's never been wrong."

"She won't be this time either. I love you, Tori."

"I love you too." She hung up the phone and yawned, rubbing her stiff, aching neck.

"Go," Mari ordered, pointing at the bathroom door. "I understand that you don't want to feel good at the moment, that feeling tired and miserable is strangely comforting, but if you attempt this trip tomorrow in this condition, you won't be helping Colin, or yourself, at all.

Lizzie nodded her understanding, shuffling into the bathroom. She closed her eyes as the sound of the water filling the tub somehow soothed her frayed nerves. She poured a generous amount of the bath oil into the steaming water and inhaled the comforting aroma of lavender. Stripping quickly out of her clothes, she lowered herself into the scented bath. The hot water penetrated the numbness that had enveloped her for the last twenty-four hours and began to ease the tension from her weary muscles.

She washed the travel grime from her body and lathered her hair liberally with herbal-scented shampoo, sighing softly as the gentle pressure of her fingertips against her scalp massaged away the dull pounding in her head. Satisfied, she held her breath and ducked her head under the water to rinse out the shampoo.

Lizzie closed her eyes and leaned back against the tub, remembering the night she and Colin had made love in the swirling waters of their newly installed hot tub. The sweet, sexy memory made her smile.

A soft knock on the door lifted her from her reverie. "*Cara*? Dinner's here."

"I'll be right out." She stepped from the tub and pulled the plug, toweling herself dry as the water gurgled down the drain. She pulled on the soft terry robe that hung on the back of the door and knotted it around her waist.

Feeling human again, she went back into the bedroom and rummaged through her backpack for a comb, dragging it gently through her tangled hair. "So what's for dinner?" she asked, inhaling softly, surprised to find her stomach grumbling at the savory aromas.

"Pita with hummus, stuffed grape leaves, lamb kebabs, rice pilaf ... and for dessert, baklava."

"That's a lot of food," Lizzie said eyeing the heaping table.

"You'll find the Turks to be overwhelmingly generous, Lizzie," said Mari with a soft laugh.

"Like your friend, Huri? She seems like a real angel."

Mari laughed again. "Cute."

"What's that supposed to mean."

"Huri is Turkish for angel. It seems an appropriate name since she's studying to be a doctor."

They talked quietly over dinner. Lizzie told Mari about the first time she spoke to Colin and about the night he'd swept her off her feet. Mari told Lizzie about her life on Italy's Adriatic coast with her Italian husband and nine-year-old son. Lizzie was unbelievably grateful to have found a new friend amid such chaos in her life.

"Well, look at that! You belong to the clean plate club, young lady."

Lizzie glanced down at her plate, surprised to find it empty. "I must've been hungrier than I thought."

"Your body knew it needed food, *cara*. Are you feeling a little better?"

"Slightly less queasy and a bit more relaxed. If you can make me get a decent night's sleep, you're a miracle worker."

"Hmm … I'll be right back." She went back into her room through the connecting door, and Lizzie heard her digging through her bags. She walked back in carrying a small medicine bottle. "Take one and I'll have to call you in the morning."

"I've never taken sleeping pills."

"It's only a mild one. You need to get a decent night's sleep. Our trip tomorrow is at least eighteen hours of driving. They'll drive straight through with just a few stops for food and bathroom. It's not going to be an easy trip."

"Are you sure it's safe?"

"I promise."

Lizzie popped one of the pills into her mouth and swallowed it with a long gulp of cold water. "See you in the morning then."

A sharp knock on the connecting door woke Lizzie before dawn. "Wha?"

Mari pushed the door open, peeking her head in. "Sorry, but we're moving out in an hour. I'm going to turn the light on, okay."

"Uh huh." Lizzie squeezed her eyes shut to block out the bright light. Slowly, she eased them open, rubbing the sand from them as she yawned.

"How are you feeling?"

"Better. Almost normal."

"*Perfetto*! They've sent up some breakfast, so we can eat while we get ready."

Forty-five minutes later, fortified with a hearty breakfast and a flask of sweet, strong Turkish coffee, Mari and Lizzie made their way downstairs. A convoy of trucks and old U.S. Army Jeeps waited along the curb. On the sidewalk, a virtual United Nations of rescue workers milled about, yawning and sipping from steaming Styrofoam cups.

"We're in this one, Lizzie," Mari said, grabbing Lizzie by the sleeve. They climbed into the backseat of a rickety old Jeep. "Not exactly comfortable, but it'll get us there."

"I reckon," Lizzie said, smiling to herself as she realized she'd picked that up from Colin. "Let's go. I have a mountain to move."

CHAPTER 23

"Is it morning, do you think?" Colin asked his ghostly companion. He'd lost his watch in the aftermath of the quake and without even a sliver of light, he was losing track of time. His parched mouth and empty stomach suggested that a lot of time had passed, but he couldn't be sure.

"I do not know the hour."

"Yeah, I thought as much."

"Does your leg still pain you?"

"It's gone numb. Something tells me that's not a good sign. Damn it." At first, he'd welcomed the respite from the searing pain, but now he'd give anything to feel something. Frustrated, he pulled at his injured leg, twisting it back and forth. "Fuck!" he screamed as the change in position brought back white-hot waves of pain. "Right then, nerve endings still functional."

"You wish to be in pain?"

"Strange, eh? I reckon as long as it hurts the leg isn't beyond repair and, no offense, mate, I'm still amongst the living."

"I would not wish my existence on anyone, my

Lily Dobb

friend."

"May I ask you a question?"

"You may."

"I've seen you many times since that first time when I was a lad, but you've never spoken and yet now ..."

"I was not welcome on Blake land, yet I was cursed to remain there. I was not allowed to speak. This is not Blake land. Here, I may speak as I wish."

"You may always speak as you wish, William. I can't repair the damage done by my ancestor, but you are welcome at Snowhill. Perhaps you'll even find your way back to Ruby."

"I thank you kindly. I ... I do not know if it is possible, but it is a worthy dream."

"I know about those," Colin said. "Have I told you about my Lizzie? She's the most amazing woman ..."

It was still dark as the convoy of vehicles crossed the Bosporus Strait into Asia. Lizzie yawned tiredly and allowed her eyes drift shut. "Yow!" she yelled an hour later as the Jeep struck a pothole, making her head hit the roof. She winced and rubbed the small bump on her head. "That hurt."

"You okay?" Mari laughed.

"Yeah. I'll live."

"Good, because you wouldn't want to miss this." She pointed out the front window of the Jeep to where the sun was beginning to peak over the horizon. "Looks like the weather's going to cooperate."

Lizzie nodded and leaned back against the seat to watch the sunrise. It was a symphony of colors as the black night sky tinged with lavender, rosy pink and fiery orange. Witnessing the sun's emergence from the darkness brought her hope; it rose out of the depths of shadows and gloom to bathe her in warmth and light. It reminded her that life could and did go on. She wondered if Colin could see and feel the sunshine. "Even if you can't, my Darcy, you will. I promise you a lifetime of sunrises. Together."

With the sun up, Lizzie found herself watching with interest as they sped through the Turkish countryside. She was surprised to find that she could appreciate the rugged beauty of the landscape, even under the bleakest of circumstances.

Turkey was a study in contrasts. It had a rich history steeped in traditions, yet it embraced the modern. Ruins from the time of Alexander the Great sidled up to remnants of the Ottoman Empire and, just across the street, you could find a forty-story skyscraper. Flowers seemed to bloom everywhere, the cloudless sky laden with their intoxicating perfume. The highway on which they traveled was modern and well maintained, yet Lizzie could see a man driving a mule-drawn wagon down a dirt road.

"I had no idea it was so beautiful," she said to Mari.

"You should come back someday, under better circumstances," Mari said.

"I'd like that. I'd love to explore the bazaar in Istanbul with Darcy and Tori," she sighed, smiling wistfully.

"You will. You'll see. And when you do, you must stop and visit me in Italy. Deal?"

"That sounds like too good an offer to refuse."

They stopped for lunch in the city of Çorum around one in the afternoon. It had been nearly eight hours since breakfast, and it didn't take long for the aromas of roasted lamb and strong coffee to make Lizzie's mouth water.

It seemed as if the convoy was met by everyone in town, from the Mayor on down to the tiniest children. Since they'd known that a convoy of rescue workers would be passing through, they'd organized a hearty feast to keep them going as they traveled eastward.

Over the delicious meal, Lizzie got the chance to meet and talk with some of the rescue workers as well as with some of their Turkish hosts. The Turks were friendly and generous by nature. They went out of their way to make sure the group was as comfortable and well fed as possible before sending them back on their way.

The rescue workers, though, were a different breed. They minimized the sacrifices and the dangers of the job they'd come to do and only wished that they were already digging through the rubble or treating the wounded. They didn't consider themselves heroes at all though Lizzie knew that they were.

She had a special place in her heart for people like them. Her family had a strong history of service in the local fire and police departments and her Dad, Jim, had been the local volunteer fire chief for most of her childhood. She understood these angels. They, rolled out of their warm beds on freezing nights, risking their lives for someone else's.

And they did it for the simple reason that *someone* had to do it.

It was an unbelievable mix of people. They came from as far away as Australia and California, called from their comfortable lives because someone they'd never met needed their help. The Blake Foundation, working closely with the International Red Cross, oversaw the setup and day-to-day operations of the rescue mission.

The vastness of it amazed her. Surely, with so many people on his side, Colin would be all right!

After lunch they piled back into their vehicles and continued their trip east. Each hour, each mile brought her closer to finding Colin and bringing him home. Lizzie was grateful for Mari's company and friendship. She was realistic, but reassuring.

By the time they reached Erzincan, where they

stopped for dinner, they'd ascended into the mountains of eastern Anatolia. After sunset, the air became chilly, making her glad she'd thrown a lightweight fleece jacket into her backpack.

Dinner was somber and quiet. They were tired from the long hours on the road and beginning to focus on the difficult tasks at hand. They joined hands and prayed, asking for guidance, for patience, and for strength. They ate quickly, without the friendly banter of lunch, eager to get back on the road.

From Erzincan, they drove another three hours to Erzurum, where Colin's sister Elizabeth and her husband, Thomas, had established their field hospital. Lizzie was relieved to see some familiar faces.

Thomas helped her down from the Jeep and gave her a brief hug hello. Bets squeezed her tightly and held her for a long time. Finally, she stepped back, but kept a tight hold on Lizzie's hand.

"Any news?" Lizzie asked.

"The road to Oltu is clear now, so the rest of your trip should be smooth going. We've not heard if they've made it to the village."

"Are they setting up the camp at Oltu?" Marida asked.

"They've started, yes," Bets said.

Lizzie blinked as she suddenly saw two of Bets in front of her. She pressed her thumb and forefinger to the bridge of her nose as a sharp headache and a wave of nausea hit her.

"You alright, Lizzie?" Bets asked, wrapping her arm around Lizzie's waist. "You've gone a bit pale."

"I … headache," Lizzie breathed.

"Probably the altitude, love. It takes time to adjust," Bets said.

"Are you sure you want to go on?" Mari asked. "I'm sure you could get a ride up in the morning."

"No," Lizzie said firmly. "I need to go now."

"We've got a bit of time, Lizzie, while they unload some supplies. Why don't we go for a walk?" Mari suggested. "It might clear your head a little."

Lizzie nodded and they headed down the road toward town. As they walked, she focused on the motion, on putting one foot in front of the other. Gradually, her headache began to fade and her nausea subsided. "Whew."

"Feeling better?" Mari asked.

"Yeah. I guess we should get back before they leave without us."

Mari nodded and they turned back toward the makeshift hospital. Without warning, the earth shifted beneath their feet, tossing them both to the ground.

"You okay?" Mari asked. The rumbling ended as abruptly as it had begun.

"Yeah. You? Was that …?"

"Just an aftershock. We're close to the epicenter here. Thomas said they've had a few, but they're getting less severe and less frequent."

"That's a good thing, right?"

The remainder of the trip was two and a half hours of steep, curvy mountain roads littered with rocky debris. The air was cold now and Lizzie could see snow blanketing the highest peaks, glistening in the silver moonlight.

It was two in the morning when they reached the town of Oltu. A mobile medical unit had been set up by the Turkish Army on the outskirts of town, nothing more than a small cluster of olive drab tents.

With the arrival of the rescue workers, it bustled with activity. Medical personnel, led by Mari and Huri stocked the supply shelves with bandages and drugs. The search and rescue teams, forced to wait until morning to begin the trek to the village, found their tents and went immediately to sleep. Not knowing what else to do, Lizzie began making up the cots in the small ward tent until Mari ordered her to go to bed.

"But ..." Lizzie protested.

"*Cara*, you've got another long day ahead of you. The road to the village isn't passable by car, so you'll be traveling on foot. And it's seven miles, mind you."

Knowing she was beaten, Lizzie made her way into the tent she was sharing with Mari and Huri and collapsed on the cot. She fingered the ruby cross as she stared up at the olive drab roof of the tent. "Okay Ruby, we're here. Now what?"

"Now you rest, Lizzie. And tomorrow we shall find him."

Reassured, she allowed her eyes to close and, within minutes, she was sound asleep.

Lizzie was awakened at dawn by the buzz of activity in the camp. With a groan, she rubbed her eyes and rolled from the cot.

She grabbed a pitcher and stumbled outside, filled it with icy water from the pump and went back into the tent to pour it into a small basin. Bracing herself, she splashed her face with the frigid water, trying hard not to screech and wake up Mari and Huri. She dried her face with a small towel and dragged a comb through her hair before securing it in a high ponytail.

"You're up early," Mari mumbled sleepily.

"God, I'm sorry! I was trying not to wake you. I've got to get going."

"Take care, Lizzie. Go find your Darcy."

Generous as always, the townspeople had loaned the rescue workers every available horse, donkey, and mule to make the arduous trek up the mountain to the village. Lizzie was grateful to Tori for teaching her to ride over the summer, but the cantankerous mule she was currently riding was a far cry from her gentle mare.

As they made our way slowly up the steep mountain road, they began to meet the walking wounded threading their way slowly down. They were battered and dusty and clutched what meager belongings they'd been able to salvage. As they passed, Lizzie searched their faces, desperate to find the one she needed to see.

Sadly, Colin wasn't among them and, though she was truly happy to see so many people alive, her own pain intensified. She reached up to finger the ruby cross. "Please tell me he's alive, Ruby," she pleaded.

Ruby's soft voice echoed in her head, "he's alive, Lizzie. He's alive and he needs you."

"Lizzie," Colin mumbled as he woke from a fitful sleep.

"Dreaming again?" William asked.

"Yes. No. I … perhaps. I feel as if she's closer, somehow. Is that odd?" He shook his head slowly, chuckling at himself. "Right. It's all odd. Here I am, trapped in the remains of a house with a ghost for company and …" He let out a heavy sigh and let his head fall back against the pile of rubble that had become his pillow. "Blimey … have I gone mad?"

"No. You have a dream. You have hope. You have a reason to fight, to live. And your Lizzie …"

"She's a fighter and for some unfathomable reason, she loves me."

"Then you are a fortunate man. A love like that can move mountains."

He could see her face in his mind, could feel the softness of her touch and hear the sweetness of her voice. He remembered how she had stood up to his dragon of a grandmother and how fiercely she had fought for his … their … daughter. Anna Elizabeth Kincaid was strong and brave and she would not leave a single stone or piece of rubble unturned until she'd brought him home. "I'm counting on it," he said, as, once again, he began to claw at the debris above his head.

About a mile outside of the village, the convoy of rescue workers met a young family. Although he was covered with dirt, the man was handsome, with thick, black hair and piercing dark eyes. His right arm hung limply at his side and his left looped around the waist of his hugely pregnant wife. A tiny little girl clutched her mother's hand tightly with one hand and gripped a small, wriggly puppy with the other.

Lizzie's eyes met the young woman's and held. She could feel her fear and pain. Remembering how long the trail had been, how far they had to go until they reached Oltu, Lizzie slipped from the mule and handed the reins to the young man. "Take her."

"Many thanks," he murmured.

"You speak English," she gasped. "Tell me, please, do you know Mr. Blake?"

His eyes widened in shock. "I know Mr. Colin Blake, yes."

"Do you ... do you know if he's ..." Lizzie couldn't make herself finish the sentence. There were too many possibilities, each one worse than the last.

"I ... I have not seen him since it happened. He was at our home ... he helped me get my family out ... but the house ... it ... it fell before ..." He took in a deep gulp of air. "I could not reach him."

"Oh, God no! Please ... you have to tell me where ..."

"I will help you. I am Cengiz. My wife is Fatma and our daughter is Yasemin. Mr. Blake ... he is a good man. I will help you find him. I ... I meant only to take my family to safety and then return to help with the search."

"But … your arm …" She called to one of the EMT's from the trip from Istanbul. "Can you take a look at this man's arm?"

"It's dislocated," he said matter-of-factly after a quick exam. "You have to get to the triage center, sir."

"No, I must help this lady," he said indicating Lizzie.

His wife screamed in pain and clutched at her pregnant belly. "Cengiz!"

"Christ, she's in labor," the EMT said.

Cengiz paled noticeably. "Our Yasemin, she came very fast."

The EMT called to one of the passing wagons. "I'm going to need your help," he said to Lizzie as he helped Fatma to lie down in the wagon bed. She screamed again as another contraction hit.

It was a surreal experience as, on a dusty road amid chaos and tragedy, Fatma gave birth to a strong, healthy baby boy. His lusty cries reaffirmed to all who heard them the importance of what they were doing.

"You should get her down to the triage center," Lizzie urged Cengiz.

"No. I will help you. "

"You really should get your arm looked at," the EMT reminded him.

"You fix it now. I must help this lady find Mr. Blake. My brother-in-law, Mehmet, will help his sister." He called to a young man barely out of his teens and the pair had a quick, hushed conversation in Turkish.

"You want me to fix it here?" the EMT asked. "It's gonna hurt like hell."

Cengiz nodded. Lizzie looked away as the EMT yanked the injured arm until it popped loudly back into the socket. Cengiz kissed his wife, daughter, and newborn son goodbye as they headed down the mountain in the back of the horse-drawn wagon.

Sam and Lance had once shown Lizzie pictures of the mining village. It was a tidy, cozy place with small but comfortable houses clustered around a central square.

Now, there was nothing left but piles of rubble and a deep scar marring the earth.

With tears in his eyes, Cengiz led her, along with a canine rescue worker to the pile of wood and stone that was once his home.

"Darcy!" Lizzie called out. "Darcy!"

She jumped when she heard a faint, weak sound from inside the rubble. The search dog sniffed around and began pawing at the rocks. Cengiz, the rescue worker, and Lizzie worked gingerly in the ruins of the house, moving the stones one by one, calling out to Colin.

It was hours of slow, backbreaking work, but with each handful, Colin's voice sounded closer. It was raspy and weak, but it was unmistakably Colin.

The first thing Lizzie saw was his left hand, the Band-Aid still fastened around his ring finger. "Darcy, it's Lizzie!"

"Lizzie," he said hoarsely.

They continued to claw at the rubble until they could pull him free. His forehead was caked with dried blood, his face covered in filth.

Lizzie had never seen anything more beautiful in her life.

Cengiz and the rescue worker lifted him gingerly onto a litter and lowered him from the pile of rubble. The EMT that had delivered the baby came over to assess him.

The wound on his head was just a superficial cut. The real problem was his left leg. It had been pinned under a heavy beam and was badly broken. Colin moaned softly as his leg was splinted. Lizzie squeezed his hand, surprised when he pulled it back with a yelp of pain. "Oh, Darcy, your poor hands," she said, noticing that they were scratched and bloody. It took a minute for her to realize why. "Oh my God! You were trying to dig your way out." She held one of his hands gently between her own. It was cold and bloody and scarred. "You're alive, Darcy."

"Lizzie, what the bloody hell are you doing here?" he demanded weakly.

"Well, we did say for better or worse, didn't we?" She traced her finger carefully over the Band-Aid on his left hand.

"I reckon we did, my Lizzie."

She leaned forward to kiss him gently on the forehead. "You're mine," she breathed.

"How are you here? I seem to remember an earthquake?" He managed a smile.

Lizzie giggled happily when she saw the dimples she adored dancing in his cheeks once again. "Earthquake you say? Well, did you honestly think I'd let a measly little mountain of rock keep us apart?"

"Crazy!" he rasped, wincing as they moved the litter toward a horse-drawn cart.

"That's me," she said cheerfully. "Crazy for you. Now … what do you say we blow this Popsicle stand?"

CHAPTER 24

Lizzie felt like singing. Knowing that Colin was safe, that he'd be okay, made her want to burst into song. Instead, she grinned happily down at Colin as she sat beside him in the bed of the cart.

She reached out to gently trace the features of his handsome, dirt-stained face. "You're a sight for sore eyes, Colin Darcy Blake. You know that?"

He smiled weakly through his pain. "And you're the bravest, most amazing woman I've ever known," he murmured. "I can't believe you've come all this way."

She simply shrugged and leaned down to kiss him softly on the mouth. "I had to come. I love you, Darcy."

He reached up one wounded hand to cup her face. "And I love you, my Lizzie."

The trip back down the mountain was arduous and, for Colin, extremely painful. Each bump and pothole made him pale and wince with pain in spite of the generous dose of painkillers he'd been given. Lizzie sat cross-legged beside him, carefully holding one of his injured hands, soothing his forehead, whispering soft words of reassurance, and wishing desperately that she could take away his pain.

"I wish I could do something," she said sadly. "I hate seeing you hurting."

"I reckon I'll survive, love. Especially now you're here to hold my hand."

"I'll hold your hand forever, Darcy. But, are you sure there's nothing I can do to make you feel at least a little better?"

"You could sing to me."

"What, here? Maybe they're wrong about that cut on your head not being serious, Darcy."

"Please," he pleaded softly. The wagon hit another pothole, jolting his litter and making him yelp with pain.

Lizzie smoothed her hand across his forehead and started singing a Beatles song they'd once danced to. Colin's eyes held hers, and he seemed to breathe a little easier as she sang.

She was surprised to find him humming along softly. Somehow listening to her voice was helping him focus on something other than the pain. So she kept going, singing an eclectic variety of songs from her favorite old standards to country to Broadway show tunes and pretty much everything in between.

Finally, they reached the triage center. It was abuzz with activity. Medical personnel ran back and forth, assessing the wounded and treating them or sending them by helicopter for more acute care.

The wagon ground to a stop outside of the hospital tent. Lizzie was thrilled to see Mari running towards them. She stopped when she saw Lizzie, clutching Colin's hand and grinned.

Lizzie smiled back. "Ready for another patient, Mari?"

"So this is the legendary Colin Darcy Blake, huh?"

"Yup," she said happily. "And somewhere underneath all that dirt is the sexiest man you've ever seen."

"Let's have a look." She instructed two medics to move the litter into the hospital and set about examining Colin. "No signs of concussion, but we'll keep an eye on that gash on his forehead." She fastened a cuff around his upper arm and quickly measured his blood pressure, then looked at the cuts and bruises on his knuckles. "These don't appear to be too bad. Now ... are you ready for me to take a look at that leg?"

Colin nodded, biting down on his lip. His hand gripped Lizzie's tightly as Mari gingerly cut his jeans to check the condition of his leg. He moaned as she gently prodded the shattered bones. "Okay, kids, hang tight for a few minutes. I'm going to get Dr. Goddard ... he's an orthopedic surgeon from Johns Hopkins ... we'll shoot some x-rays and get that leg set." She started to move away, but Lizzie put a hand on her arm to stop her.

"How bad is it?"

She glanced from Lizzie to Colin. "It's a bad break, but it will heal."

Dr. Goddard confirmed what Mari had said. "Okay, I need to repair some of the damage. There's a spot here," he said pointing at the x-ray, "where the bones aren't where they should be. I need to go in and put them back where they belong and then I'll use some metal pins to keep them in place. It will take a while to heal, but you'll be fine in a few months."

"Can we have a few minutes? We need to call our daughter and tell her that her Dad's okay?"

"Of course ... but ... well there's still no phone service out here."

"Bugger that," Colin muttered.

"Can we get a message to Erzurum? Dr. Elizabeth Fauconbridge is Colin's sister. She's heading the hospital there."

"I know Bets. Wonderful doctor. Let me see what I

can arrange."

When he'd gone Lizzie pulled a folding camp chair up beside the cot. "Don't worry, sweetheart, we'll get word to everyone."

"It's not that … I … I've just realized we'll have to postpone the wedding," he said sadly. "I'm so sorry, Lizzie."

"I … it's alright, Darcy. We'll push it back until you're on your feet again. I'm not letting you get away, you know."

"I've no intention of going anywhere but straight into your arms, my beautiful Lizzie. But I am sorry about the wedding. I really don't want to postpone it."

"I don't see where we have much choice …" Lizzie paused, suddenly grinning broadly. "Unless …" she giggled and stood up, moving the chair out of the way. Still laughing, she knelt on one knee and took Colin's left hand in hers.

"Lizzie, what are you up to?" Colin asked with a raised eyebrow.

"Colin Darcy Blake," she said softly. "I love you. The past three days, not knowing where you were or if you were okay, they nearly killed me. I don't want to live another day without you. Will you marry me? Here? Now?"

"Are you certain, Lizzie? Don't you want the fairy tale wedding with all of our loved ones there?"

"I do want that. But there's no rule that says we can't have another wedding when you're better. So, what do you think?"

"Yes, Lizzie. Yes, I'll marry you."

"Phew!" she said wiping her brow. "I was worried there for a minute."

Dr. Goddard returned with the news that they'd be able to relay a call by radio on to the United States. "Thank God! I promised our daughter I'd let her know the moment you were safe. It's a promise I'm excited to keep."

It took a while for them to rig up the radio, but after half an hour Lizzie held the transmitter in her hand and pressed the button. "Bets?" she asked over the scratchy radio connection. "That you?"

"Yes, Lizzie, it's me. Any news?"

Without a word, she handed the transmitter to Colin with a grin. "Well, there's been a small earthquake," Colin deadpanned.

"Colin!" she shrieked. "You're alive!"

"You've always been such an astute observer, Bets. Yes, alive, if not quite kicking."

"It's wonderful to hear your voice, little brother. Have you talked to Tori yet?"

"No. We can't get a direct line through … still no phone service out here." He explained to Bets what they needed to do and within minutes Bets put the call through.

Meg answered the phone on the first ring. "Cheers!"

"Meg? It's Lizzie."

"Darl! It's wonderful to hear your voice. So … how are you?"

"I'm wonderful. Meg … Darcy's here … holding my hand!"

"Oh, Lizzie," she sniffled. "I'm so happy for you!"

"I'm in the middle of the biggest happy attack of my life, Meg. Is Tori there?"

"Of course. I'll give her a shout." Lizzie heard her cover the mouthpiece with her hand and call Tori's name. In a matter of seconds, she heard Tori's quick footsteps on the hardwood floors.

"Mum?" she said breathlessly.

"Hi, sweetie. There's someone here who'd like to say hello."

She handed the transmitter to Colin again, tears of

happiness trailing down her dusty cheeks as father and daughter shared a reunion. "Hallo, poppet," he said softly.

"Daddy! You're alright!"

"Yes, love, I'll be right as rain in no time at all. Nothing worse than a broken leg. I love you, Victoria," he said softly, "We'll be home as soon as can be."

While Colin was in surgery, Lizzie found herself at loose ends, wandering around the camp. She paused at the open flap of the morgue, her own happiness tempered by the knowledge that so many families weren't as lucky. She ignored the morbid curiosity that made her want to go inside and instead continued walking.

A few yards away, she came across a tent that had been designated as a chapel by the rescue workers. She pushed the flap aside, drawn inside by a need to thank God for giving Colin back to her. She took a seat in one of the rickety wooden chairs and bowed her head in thankful prayer.

She realized that there was someone else that she needed to thank. "Ruby," she said softly. "How can I ever thank you?"

"Be happy," the spirit said simply. "As my William and I could not. Do not take the love you've been given for granted as we did. Fight for it, guard it with everything inside you. You will be happy, Lizzie. I will, perhaps, share a little in your joy."

"I wish there was something I could do for you, though."

"There is not. I was not brave like you. I would not stand up to my father. And my William, he was too reckless. We let ourselves be torn apart, Lizzie. I've learned that from centuries of watching lovers fight to be together."

"Surely there's something?" Lizzie smiled softly as an idea came to mind. Perhaps they could have William moved to lie beside his Ruby. She stored the idea in the back of her mind to discuss later with Colin.

Ruby smiled back at her. "Perhaps there is," she said quietly. "You are fond of stories, are you not? Perhaps you might write us a happy ending."

It was an extraordinary idea. "I think I might just do that, Ruby."

She left the chapel and headed to the tents that had been set up for the displaced villagers, where she visited with Cengiz and his family. A sling immobilized his injured arm, but he proudly showed off his handsome new son with his good arm.

"He's beautiful," Lizzie said as her eyes grew misty. "And a miracle. Will you bring him with me to see Colin? He should be waking up soon."

Colin was awake and propped up in bed when they entered the ward. "He came through very nicely, Lizzie," Mari informed her. "And you're right, he does clean up quite handsomely."

Lizzie bent to kiss his clean, smoothly-shaven cheek. "I've brought you a little surprise. Cengiz and Fatma had a special delivery this morning." She took the baby from Fatma and placed him in Colin's arms. "Isn't he beautiful?"

Tears shimmered in Colin's eyes as the baby wrapped a finger around his pinky. "Gorgeous little lad."

"Your Lizzie, she helped my Fatma," Cengiz said gratefully.

"I didn't do anything, really," Lizzie protested.

"You did," Cengiz insisted. "Both of you have saved my family. I am forever indebted to you."

"And you helped me dig Colin out stone by stone. I'd say we're even, Cengiz."

"My son will always know that his namesake is a true hero to us."

"You've named the baby Colin?" Lizzie glanced at Colin. He was smiling softly, clearly as touched by the gesture as she was.

"My son is named for a strong, brave man," Fatma said softly.

Lizzie smiled at Colin over the baby's downy head. "He sure is."

News of their wedding spread quickly through the camp. In short order, the local magistrate provided them with a marriage license, and a Lutheran pastor, chaplain of one of the search and rescue teams, offered to perform the ceremony.

Fatma's sister, a vivacious twenty-year-old named Layla offered her a beautifully embroidered silk kaftan to wear, the only thing she'd managed to save. "It's lovely," Lizzie said gratefully, "I'll give it right back after the ceremony."

"No, no! You must keep it, please." Layla smiled brightly and fingered the soft silk. "To remind you that my country is a place of beauty."

"Okay then, name anything you'd like from America and it's yours."

"Levi's," she said with a grin. "I would like a pair of Levi's button fly jeans."

It was a strange preparation for a wedding. The day after finding Colin, Lizzie sat on a cot in her tent while Bets, who'd arrived by helicopter, braided her hair into a pretty French braid and slipped fragrant fresh flowers into it. She stepped into the silky kaftan, sighing as the fabric slithered over her body.

"You look stunning, Lizzie," Mari said.

"Have we got everything covered? Old, new,

borrowed and blue?" Bets asked.

"The cross is old, I have blue flowers in my hair and in the bouquet, the dress is new, at least to me ... I guess I just need something borrowed."

Bets reached up and removed the simple pearl earrings she always wore. "These should fit the bill."

"Perfect. Now I just wish we had some rings, but I suppose if that's all we're lacking, I can't complain."

"Knock, knock," Thomas said from outside. "Everyone decent in there?"

"Come on in," Lizzie called out. "I guess we're ready. They've got the radio rigged up, right?"

"Check," Thomas said.

"And that girl from Georgia ... what's her name ... Melinda ... she's going to play the guitar, right?"

"Check."

"You've helped Darcy get ready?"

"Check."

"Er, Thomas, darling?" Bets said.

"Che- ... Yes, my pet?"

"If you say check one more time I may just have to hurt you."

"Che ... Righto, love. Oh ... Lizzie, I think you might need this." He dropped a simple gold wedding band into her hand. "Compliments of Yusuf, the town mayor and a talented goldsmith to boot."

"I guess that's it then."

Lizzie took a deep breath as Melinda softly strummed her guitar in the flower-bedecked town square. Though she didn't know most of the guests at her own wedding, she knew that both her family and Colin's were huddled around hastily rigged up short-wave radios for their impromptu ceremony.

She took a step forward and smiled at Colin. Dr. Goddard and Cengiz helped him stand up. He was

265

leaning heavily on his crutches, but he'd insisted that he'd be married standing on his own two feet.

She ambled down the aisle, and when she reached his side, she laid her hand over his on the crutch. "I love you," she whispered.

He stroked the back of her hand softly with his thumb. "I love you too."

The minister began with a simple prayer, then smiled at them. "I have not had the privilege of knowing Colin and Lizzie for very long, but I have witnessed a profound love between them. They have already *lived* the vows they are about to speak." He turned to Colin, asking if he promised to love, honor, cherish, and protect her.

Colin smiled down at Lizzie, his deep dimples dancing in his cheeks. "I do," he said huskily.

He brushed a tear from her cheek as the minister turned to her. It was her turn to make her vows.

"I do," she murmured. "Absolutely."

The minister smiled and blessed the plain gold bands, and handed one to Colin.

His fingers trembled as he took the ring from the minister and slipped it onto her finger. "It's fitting that we will always wear a piece of this place."

Lizzie nodded and bit her lip to keep the tears at bay. "I, Lizzie, take you, Darcy …" Like Colin, her fingers trembled as she slipped the thick gold band onto his finger.

"Colin and Lizzie, I now declare you to be husband and wife. Colin, you may kiss your bride."

Lizzie wrapped her arms around Colin's waist to steady him as he bent to kiss her. It was a soft, gentle kiss, sealing the promises they'd just made to one another. Her head was spinning when Colin lifted his lips from hers.

Colin blinked and stumbled a little. Worried that he'd

overdone it, Lizzie helped him back into the wheelchair and perched carefully on his good leg. She brushed his dark curls back from his forehead. He grinned up at her. "That was some kiss, Mrs. Blake. Seems you've knocked me off my feet."

Two days later, Dr. Goddard agreed to let Colin go home. They flew by helicopter to Istanbul, then caught a nonstop flight to JFK. "It feels incredible to be going home."

"I know. I can only imagine the greeting committee that'll be on hand. They've all been very secretive and mysterious about what's gone on there while we've been gone. I'm sure they've planned some sort of surprise."

"I love surprises," Colin said with a grin.

"Do you?" Lizzie asked with a secretive smile. "Well, maybe I've got one more for you."

He shot her a questioning look. "Oh?"

She shifted in her seat and tucked her legs under her bottom. "I thought I'd lost you, you know."

"I know," he whispered. "You've been through quite an ordeal, my courageous Lizzie."

"Well, yes, I guess I have, but it's nothing compared to what you went through. Darcy, you haven't really talked about it much but ... I ... I want to know what you survived. I think ... I think I need to know."

Colin took a deep breath and reached up to tuck a loose strand of hair behind her ear. "I suppose I've been coming to terms with it. I'm not certain I know where to begin."

"I know that you were with Cengiz and his family," she said. "What was that like?"

"We'd had a productive week. I sent Adil packing and worked out a plan for the miners to purchase an interest in the mine ... to be paid in sweat equity. They're good people, Lizzie, simple, hard-working men trying to feed their families."

"I know, sweetheart. I think giving them some control over the operation is a wonderful plan."

"I'm glad you approve, love. Last Friday, after we spoke on the telephone, Cengiz and I went into the mines. We made a list of needed improvements and when we were done, he invited me home for dinner with his family. So I went. After dinner, we sat around chatting ... Fatma put Yasemin to bed with her little puppy round about ten o'clock. I started to say my goodbyes ... I had a long drive in the morning to catch my flight home. It was all so ... ordinary. And then it wasn't. There was ... I dunno ... this god-awful rumbling ... and the floor seemed to disappear from beneath our feet. Cengiz ran toward Fatma, but he was thrown to the ground, hard - I guess that's when his shoulder was hurt. Fatma screamed for Yasemin ... so I went to get her while Cengiz got Fatma out of the house. She was still in bed, wide-eyed and howling. I scooped her up and ran with her. When I handed her to her parents, she was crying for her little puppy. I ... I didn't think about it really. I just ran back inside to grab the little dog ... but the blasted thing had hidden beneath the bed. I finally managed to grab him, but he wriggled out of my arms ... and ran off ... I think he got out ..."

"He did."

"I was almost to the front door when an aftershock hit. It was almost as intense as the earthquake. One of the beams fell from the roof and pinned me to the floor ... then ... I guess the roof caved in on top of me. In a strange way that bloody beam saved my life because it kept the debris from killing me. I tried to claw my way out ..."

"I know," she whispered. "You're poor hands!" She lifted one of his bruised, scarred hands to her lips and tenderly kissed each wound before taking the other and doing the same. "How did you manage to survive?" She whispered the word, in awe of how close she'd come to losing him forever.

He caressed her cheek with the back of his hand. "I had a promise to keep."

"That's what kept me going too. I ... you know that feeling after we make love when it seems like our hearts beat as one?"

Colin smiled softly. "Uh huh."

"I could feel your heart beating, right along with mine. I guess I knew as long as I felt that, you were alive. What ... what was it like?"

"Dark, cold, suffocating. I ..." His eyes locked with hers. "I was frightened Lizzie. It was every terrifying childhood nightmare come to life. If not for William's company, I might've gone mad. But ... I knew you'd be searching for me. I suppose that's what kept me going. I could hear them above me you know, calling for me, but I'd screamed for so long when it first happened that I lost my voice. It wasn't until I heard your voice calling for me that I managed to find the strength to call out again."

"Hearing your voice was the most beautiful sound I've ever heard, Darcy. You know, the villagers, they tried to find you, but they had no equipment and half of them were pretty bad off."

"I don't think there's a family among them that hasn't lost someone."

"It's so sad, but they're determined to rebuild."

"I suppose that's a natural reaction to that sort of devastation. One wants to recreate a sense of normalcy as quickly as can be."

"We can help them can't we?" Lizzie asked.

"Of course we can, and we shall."

"You're a good man, Darcy. How did I ever get so lucky?"

"I keep asking myself the same question, my love."

"It amazes me that in the middle of all that suffering, life kept right on moving," she murmured.

"It was a beautiful wedding, even under less than ideal conditions."

"It was," she agreed. "Perfect. I can't believe we're actually married."

"'Fraid so, love. You're stuck with me now."

"Good. Because I have no plans to ever let you go."

Colin grinned happily and leaned forward to kiss her softly. "You're amazing, do you know that?"

"Who me? Nah. I'm just an ordinary chick with the incredible good sense to fall in love with you."

"Lizzie, my love, there's nothing ordinary about you at all. Do you realize you helped deliver a baby in a wagon on the side of a mountain road?"

She grinned and rolled her eyes. "I just did what had to be done. He's a miracle baby, though, isn't he?"

"He is. I can't believe they've called him after me," he said with a grin. "I guess that makes us honorary something-or-others to the little lad."

She chuckled softly. "You like that idea, don't you?"

He shrugged and smiled his dimpled smile. "You know I love children. And making them," he added wickedly.

"Yep. I do."

"If I wasn't laid up with this bloody cast, I'd prove it to you. As it is, we'll likely have to wait weeks." He let out an exasperated sigh.

Lizzie grinned broadly and let out an unrestrained giggle.

"What's got you grinning like the Cheshire cat?" he asked, eyeing her suspiciously. "Something to do with my surprise?"

"Maybe," she teased.

"C'mon, Lizzie, spill it."

She giggled again and tangled her fingers in Colin's dark curls. "After you left, I started feeling a little under the weather. I figured I was just feeling lonely for you. It got worse after I heard about the earthquake. I started throwing up, but I've always had kind of a nervous stomach. Now, I'm not so sure. You're safe, and we're on our way home, but I still feel a little queasy. This morning I realized something else." Colin frowned, and she leaned forward to give him a brief kiss. "I'm late, Darcy."

"Late? For wha ... oh!" his eyes grew wide. "Really?"

"Well, I'm not positive, but yes, I think we're having a baby."

Colin pulled her into his arms and kissed her thoroughly. When they parted, breathless, he linked his fingers through hers and twisted her wedding ring. "Good thing I made an honest woman of you then, don't you think?"

"A very good thing, Mr. Blake," she agreed. "So ... I take it you like your surprise?"

"Like?" he croaked. "My dearest, loveliest Elizabeth, I love my surprise."

CHAPTER 25

They landed just after four in the afternoon and made their way through customs. Colin's face was pale, and there were deep shadows beneath his eyes. Lizzie was anxious to get him home. She pushed the borrowed wheelchair into the main terminal, laughing when she heard Tori shriek happily and dash towards them.

She threw herself into her father's arms. Colin hugged her tightly, as if he never wanted to let go. "Dad! I can't breathe!"

"Sorry, poppet. I'm just so happy to see you."

"Me too, Daddy." She extricated herself from Colin's arms and gave Lizzie a long, tight hug. "Thank you. Mum."

"Tori, sweetheart, I had to bring him home. For all of us."

Lance, Meg, Sam, and Jess appeared just after Tori. There were long, heartfelt hugs all the way around and by the time they'd finished, they were all crying. It wasn't until they turned to make their way to the baggage carousel that Lizzie noticed the television cameras. "What the …?"

"Er … the press got word that Colin was in Turkey. They've been all over us!" Meg said.

"Yeah, but we've managed to use them to our advantage," said Jess.

Lizzie looked at Colin, not sure what to do or say.

"Mr. Blake," said a lacquered blond reporter as she shoved a microphone in Colin's face, "what was it like?"

Colin took a deep breath and squeezed Lizzie's hand tightly. She squeezed back, hoping to comfort him. "I'd be happy to make a statement at a later time, but at the moment I'm just delighted to be home. Now if you'll excuse us, I'd like to spend some private time with my family."

"Crikey," Colin muttered as they pushed their way through the crowd. "Has it been that way the whole time."

"More or less," said Lance.

"But as Jess said, we've used it to our advantage," said Sam.

"What have you lot been up to?" Colin asked, his eyes narrowed.

"I reckon you'll find out when you get home, Colin," Meg said, smiling mysteriously.

"Secrets, Meg?" Lizzie asked.

"Possibly."

"Hmmm." Lizzie leaned forward to press her lips to Colin's ear. "I'll bet their secret doesn't beat ours, though."

Colin chuckled softly and winked at her. "Not a chance."

"Hey! What's all the whispering?" Tori protested.

"Nothing, poppet," Colin said. "Let's go home."

Though the ride was just over two hours, to Lizzie it felt endless. All she wanted was to collapse on the sofa with one arm around her husband and the other around her daughter. If she had her way, she wouldn't move for at least a month. She laid her head on Colin's shoulder and tilted it back to smile up at him.

He was happy, laughing and chatting with everyone, but she could tell he was exhausted and uncomfortable. His broken leg was propped up on the facing seat in the stretch limo that Meg had hired for the trip, and he winced every time it got jostled.

"Sweetie, are you sure you don't want one of the pain pills Dr. Goddard sent with us?" Lizzie asked with a frown.

"No. I'll be fine. I don't want to depend on them," he said.

"How about some wine?" Meg suggested. "As long as you haven't taken anything that is."

"I haven't. Wine would be great. Thanks." Meg poured him a glass of Merlot and pressed it into his hand.

"You're welcome. How about you, Lizzie?"

"None for me, thanks. I'm so tired it would put me right to sleep." She winked at Colin who winked back at their shared our secret.

"What's all that about, then?" Sam asked. "The pair of you look mightily pleased with yourselves."

"We're just happy to be home," Colin said grinning at Lizzie.

It was dusk when the limo turned off the Pennsylvania turnpike and drove through the countryside to Pemberley Farm.

"Should we stop and pick up something to eat?" Lizzie asked.

"Nah," said Jess with a shake of her head. "We're all set."

"Still being mysterious, huh?" Lizzie laughed. "Fine!"

She squeezed Colin's hand when they turned down

their street. When he squeezed back, Lizzie realized that she'd hardly let go since he was pulled from the rubble. Funny how something so simple could bring her such immense joy. "It's so good to be home."

"It is," Colin agreed. "What's with all the cars? Someone having a party?"

"Er … that would be you, I'm afraid," Lance said.

"Well, not a party exactly," Meg amended.

"Welcome to command central," said Jess.

"Huh?" Colin and Lizzie asked in unison.

"What they're trying, badly, to say is that since you've been gone, we've been very busy," said Tori. "When people heard that Dad was missing and that you'd gone after him, they started stopping by with all sorts of things. Money, clothes, food … stuff like that … to send over to Turkey."

"It's unbelievable," said Jess.

"They've also been trying to feed us," said Meg. "We had so many casseroles and whatnot that we've been feeding a homeless shelter."

The limo pulled up to the front door. Lizzie was surprised to see that temporary ramps had already been installed on the steps, good news since Colin's use of crutches was to be extremely limited for the time being. "My Dad?" she asked.

"Uh huh," said Tori. "Grandpop and Uncle Neil did it. I … uh … may have helped," Tori admitted. "I was so relieved and happy when you found Dad that I was … a bit hard to contain."

Lizzie smiled softly and kissed Tori on the cheek. "Trust me, sweetie. I can relate."

"Me too," Colin said. "It's good to be home."

The house was filled with people sorting through the various donations. It seemed as if Lizzie's entire family was in on the activity, along with many familiar faces from Consolidated. "Wow!"

"It's unreal," Colin murmured as he surveyed the piles in the living room. "How did all this come about?"

"Once the local media learned that an area resident was involved and it hit the news, people started showing up," Meg shrugged.

"How about a tour?" Lizzie suggested to Colin.

"It's a bit tight in here for this thing," he said tapping the arm of his wheelchair in frustration.

"If you're very good and promise to take a pain pill before bed I'll let you use your crutches," she indulged.

"I promise," he said solemnly.

"Be back in a flash, then." She hurried off to retrieve his crutches.

On the way, she grabbed one of Meg's hands, and one of Jess's. "Thank you both. For everything. I need another favor …"

"Anything, darl. What's the favor?"

"Not here." She tugged them through the kitchen and onto the deck. "Sorry."

"What's with the spy routine?" Jess laughed.

"It's silly really. I just … I don't want everyone to know until I'm sure, and there's no way I'll get out of here tonight before the drugstore closes.

"What do you need us to do?" Jess asked.

"I need you to pick something up at the drugstore, but you can't tell anyone, not even Lance and Sam, okay?"

"We swear!" they said in unison.

"Hell, I'll pinky swear if you need me to," Meg laughed. "Now, what is it that you need?"

"I need … girls, I need a home pregnancy test." Lizzie whispered, grinning from ear to ear.

"Woohoo!" Meg screamed. "Oops. Sorry. Secret. Shhh. Okay … We'll just be off then … back in a flash." They hugged Lizzie tightly and disappeared back into the house.

Lizzie took a moment to breathe, leaning back against the railing. The air was moist and heavy, holding the promise a hot and humid day to come. It was scented with freshly mown grass and late summer roses, and a symphony of crickets and cicadas provided a merry welcome.

Colin was home. Her family was whole again. Lizzie let out a contented sigh and headed back into the house, retrieved Colin's crutches, and joined him in the hall. "I know it's a little insane, but it's good to be home."

Colin nodded, arranging the crutches beneath his armpits and leaning forward for a soft kiss. "I was home the second I heard your voice."

"Yeah, I know what you mean." She stood on tiptoe to kiss him again and they followed Lance into the organized chaos of their living room.

Meg and Jess returned a half-hour later with a brown paper bag that they handed to Lizzie covertly. "Here you go," Jess whispered.

"Smooth," Lizzie grinned. "I think you two missed your calling. I hear the CIA's recruiting …"

Their laughter echoed as Lizzie climbed the stairs to hide the bag in her closet. Before she tucked it behind a stack of undies, she snuck a peek inside to take a quick look at the instructions. She burst out in a fit of giggles and poured the contents of the bag on the closet floor. Overachievers that they were, her friends hadn't bought just one pregnancy test. They'd bought six!

Lizzie was giggling when she found them chatting with Colin in the living room. "Six?" she grinned.

Meg shrugged, her bright blue eyes twinkling mischievously. "We wanted you to be really sure."

Lizzie and Colin laughed. "I think we're good to go!"

By eleven, the crowd had dwindled to just Colin, Tori and Lizzie. They were reclining quietly on the living room sofa, watching television. "I love them all for what they're doing, but it's nice to have some peace and quiet," Lizzie sighed.

"I agree," Colin said tiredly. "I'm especially proud of you, Tor," he said as he ruffled her hair.

"Keeping busy helped, especially before Mum found you. It made me feel like I was helping too," Tori said.

"You are. I can't believe what people have donated. There are enough supplies here to completely rebuild the village and then some."

"Your Dad told me that the local building supply company is donating several truckloads of lumber."

"I know. And one of the construction companies wants to send over heavy equipment and manpower to help them rebuild. It's good to know Cengiz and his family will have a warm new home before winter."

"Are they the ones with the baby you delivered, Mum?"

"I didn't deliver him. I just helped. Would you like to see a picture?"

Tori nodded and Lizzie got up and rooted through her purse until she found her cell phone. She paged through photos until she found the snapshot she wanted. It was a picture of Colin and Lizzie cuddling with baby Colin. "He's lovely, isn't he? I think it's sweet they've named him after you, Daddy." She yawned. "Lord, I'm knackered." Tori tilted her head and scrutinized her parents. "I think it would be lovely if you two had a baby." With that, she kissed them both good night and dashed up the stairs to her room.

"Tori Blake, queen of the bombshells," Colin chuckled.

"Still, it's good to know we have her blessing."

"I'm a bit knackered myself, love," he yawned.

"Let's get you settled then." She wheeled him into the hall bathroom and handed him his crutches. "Sure you don't want that sponge bath I promised you?" she asked with a cheeky grin.

"Perhaps tomorrow?" he said with a sly smile. "Not exactly our dream honeymoon."

"As long as I get to wrap my arms around you, I'm happy."

"But it will likely be weeks before we can make love properly," he said. "I'm sorry, Lizzie."

She wrapped her arms tightly around his waist, disregarding the crutches and stood on tiptoe to kiss him soundly. "I love you, Darcy. I just need to be with you. I think I can handle a few weeks without sex, amazing as it is between us. Besides … we're creative people … I'm sure we'll think of something."

Colin laughed and kissed her hungrily. "All I could think of the whole time I was trapped was how much I longed to hold you in my arms."

"Then let's go to bed."

The den had been converted into a temporary bedroom for them until Colin was able to manage the stairs. He shuffled behind Lizzie on his crutches and plopped wearily onto the side of the sofa bed. She handed him the pain pill and a glass of water. He swallowed it in one gulp. She fussed around him, trying to help him get comfortable before sliding into bed and snuggling up to him. With a contented sigh, she curled an arm around his waist and laid her head on his shoulder.

"It feels wonderful to have you in my arms," he whispered quietly as his fingers traced circles on her back.

"It feels wonderful to be here." She pressed a soft kiss into his collarbone. "G'night, Darcy. I love you."

Lizzie woke at dawn and sprinted up the stairs to grab one of the pregnancy tests then ran back downstairs, slipping into the half bathroom in the hall.

She tore open the box and read the instructions. It sounded simple enough, just hold one end of the stick and pee on the other. "Mission accomplished," she said to herself as she laid the stick on the edge of the sink. "Now what can I do that takes two minutes?"

She shuffled quietly into the kitchen and put the coffee on to brew. By the time the coffee maker began to gurgle she was heading back to the bathroom to check the results. She grabbed the stick, careful not to peek, and headed back into the den.

She slipped carefully back onto the bed and sat cross-legged beside her gently snoring husband. "Darcy, wake up," she said quietly. He didn't stir. She nudged him gently on the shoulder. "Darcy!" she said a little more loudly. He merely grunted and swatted her hand away. "Hmmm, drastic times call for drastic measures," she mumbled. She leaned forward and kissed him. One eye popped open, then the other. "Good morning, Sleeping Beauty," she said with a cheeky grin.

"Now that's how a man should wake up in the morning," he said lazily. "Good morning, Mrs. Blake."

"Hi," she laughed.

"You look very happy this morning, love."

"Incredibly happy for a woman who just peed on a stick. So … don't you want to know?"

"Huh?"

"You're a little slow this morning, Darcy. But you're injured and on pain meds, so I won't be too tough on you. I thought maybe you'd want to know if you're going to be a Daddy."

"Crikey!" he blurted as he eased himself into a sitting position. "Well?"

"I don't know yet. I thought we should look together." Very slowly, she moved the hand that covered the results. There were two parallel lines. A slow smile spread across her face.

"We're having a baby," she whispered.

Colin hugged her and kissed her tenderly on the lips. "We're having a baby?"

"Uh huh," Lizzie nodded.

"Wow," he sighed before kissing her again.

"Yup," she said softly. "Wow."

They held each other contentedly for a long time, savoring the shared secret. "I can't believe I'm having a baby," Lizzie said as she burrowed her face into Colin's neck. "I never thought I'd have one child let alone two."

"Speaking of our other child, I hear Tori moving about upstairs. How do you feel about sharing our news?"

"Well, she seemed pretty interested in being a big sister last night."

"True enough. Just realize that once Tori knows, the entire universe will be privy to our secret within seconds."

"I can live with that, I think. It's not like I could keep that big of a secret for very long myself."

A few minutes later, they heard Tori running down the stairs, their puppy, Hershey, trotting close at her heels. They expected her to come bursting in with her usual cheerful good morning, but she crept quietly past the door to the den.

"What's up with that?" Lizzie asked Colin with a frown.

"Probably gone to let Hershey out."

"Maybe." She snuggled more deeply into Colin's arms and pressed a kiss to the throbbing pulse at the base of his neck. "God, I missed this," she sighed.

"Me too," he whispered as his lips found hers. "I never want to let go again."

"Me either, but I guess we'll have to eventually.

Otherwise people will start to think we're a little strange," she laughed.

"Fair enough. Just promise me you'll forgive me if I forget to let go?"

"I promise," she said solemnly. "And, Darcy?" Lizzie tilted her head back to stare into his eyes.

"Yes, love?"

"You may have to occasionally pry me out of your arms too."

"Not a chance, love," he grinned.

A half-hour later, there was a soft knock at the door. "Come in then," Colin said. "We were hoping you'd pop in."

"Good morning!" Tori sang as she pushed the door open and poked her head into the room.

"Morning, poppet," Colin smiled. "Why don't you come in? We have something to discuss with you."

"Alright, but first things first. I thought since this is technically your honeymoon you deserve ... drum roll please ..." Colin and Lizzie laughed and he playfully drummed on the end table. "Breakfast in bed."

With that, she pushed open the door the rest of the way and strode into the room carrying a heavy tray of food. She set it carefully on the bed between them. There were fresh strawberries with whipped cream, fluffy scrambled eggs, buttered toast cut carefully into triangles, freshly squeezed orange juice, and the steaming coffee Lizzie had started earlier. "Tori, this is so sweet!"

"My daughter the gourmet," Colin said proudly.

"It's just eggs, Daddy," Tori said, rolling her eyes. "So, what did you want to talk to me about?" She perched on the edge of the bed and plucked a strawberry from the bowl on the tray.

Colin and Lizzie grinned happily at each other, then burst out laughing.

"What's so funny? You're acting awfully odd this morning. Perhaps it's jet lag."

"Perhaps," Lizzie grinned.

"Then again, it might be something else," Colin teased.

"Argh! Out with it already!" Tori demanded.

"We're just happy to finally be a real family," Lizzie told her.

"Oh. Because you and Dad are married now?"

"That and me adopting you and … the fact that we're having a baby," Lizzie announced.

"Pardon? Did you say …?" Her eyes widened, and her mouth fell open. "Hurrah! A baby … that's … that's brilliant! Brilliant!" She hugged them both tightly. "A baby. Wow!"

"That's more or less what we said," Lizzie admitted with a laugh.

"Does anyone else know?"

"Nope, you're the first." Colin reached up to ruffle her curls. "Big sister."

"Is it a secret?" she asked.

Colin and Lizzie beamed at each other. "Not for long."

"You hate this, don't you?" Lizzie asked Colin as she helped him get dressed.

"I don't like feeling helpless, no."

"It's only temporary. You'll be back on your own two feet in no time. Then you can feel free to pamper me throughout this pregnancy." He leaned heavily on her as she helped him back into the wheelchair.

"Careful what you wish for, Lizzie," he said with a wry grin. "I'll apologize in advance for being a lousy patient. I'm afraid you might be in for a rough couple of weeks."

"Thanks for the warning," she laughed.

The telephone rang, but as Lizzie moved to answer it, she heard Tori pick it up. "Who is it, Tor?"

"Just Aunt Nan. She's ringing to say that Gramma and Great-Grandmamma are on their way here."

"Crikey," Colin swore softly. "When?"

"Er ... now," Tori laughed. "Nan said they took the morning flight out of Heathrow and that Sam's picking them up this afternoon."

"Talk about timing!" Lizzie chuckled. "I guess we can tell everyone at once."

By ten in the morning, the house was once again humming with activity. Friends, neighbors, co-workers, even strangers were pitching in to help. Everything was being coordinated through the Blake Foundation, and they expected to airlift the supplies by the following weekend.

"I still can't believe all of this," Lizzie said to Meg and Jess as they packed a box of soft, fleecy blankets.

"It just kind of happened," Jess said. "And once it started it just kept growing."

"Darl, we've gone global you know."

"What? How?"

"Let's see ... apart from what the Foundation has organized in the UK, your friend Matt's sister set up a drive at Princeton, which has spread to quite a few other large universities. And do you recall me mentioning my friends, Fiona and Andrew?"

"The dancers?"

"Righto. They arranged a benefit performance for last night. She rang me up just before I came over. They've raised a very tidy sum ... something in the neighborhood of $50,000."

"That's amazing."

"I know. And we've received donations from other countries as well," Meg said.

"And all over the US and Canada," added Jess.

"I'm so glad people want to help. I hear Sam and Lance are going over with the supplies. You two should consider going with them," Lizzie suggested.

"Maybe," Jess said cautiously. She glanced at Meg, and the pair of them began to blush.

"Okay, what's going on?"

"Oh nothing," Meg said.

"Humph. I don't believe you for a second. You two are up to something."

"Aren't we always?" Meg said with a cheeky grin.

Lizzie chuckled. "More or less. And thank God for that!"

Colin agreed to an interview with one of the local news teams that afternoon. Lizzie wasn't wild about the idea of appearing on camera, but he wanted her beside him, and that was all the encouragement she needed.

Sam arrived from the airport with Helen and Lady Frances while Lizzie was upstairs changing. When she finally came downstairs, casually but carefully dressed in trouser jeans and a soft, pale green sweater, she found them in the living room with her parents. Lady Frances seemed to have conveniently forgotten her earlier objections to Lizzie and her family as she sat beside Lizzie's mother folding used baby clothing. Lizzie caught Colin's eye and nodded in their direction with a wink. "Will wonders never cease?" she mouthed.

She hugged Helen hello, relieved to see that her vivacity had returned. "I'm glad you came, Helen."

"Thank you for giving me a reason to come," she said, her voice quivering.

"I told you that you could do it, girl," Lady Frances said gruffly.

"Yes, you did. Thanks for giving me the push I needed that day to keep going," she said as stooped to kiss the old woman's wrinkled cheek. "As you can see,

I've brought home one Colin Darcy Blake, only slightly damaged."

"So you have, my dear. And quite properly married, I understand."

"Yes, ma'am."

"I don't approve," she said. "I would have liked to dance with my handsome grandson."

"You'll get your chance, Lady Frances … I mean … Grandmamma. I promise. I just have to get Darcy back into top dancing form."

An hour later, a very nervous Lizzie perched beside Colin on the deck, clutching his hand tightly as she faced the television camera. "Are you sure we have to do this?" she whispered.

"Just this once, love," he murmured. "I promise."

"And you don't break your promises, do you?" She smiled softly. "Having you back in our home is worth facing my fear of cameras."

"Ready you two?" asked the producer.

"Ready," Colin and Lizzie said in unison.

"I'm here with British multimillionaire and local resident Colin Blake, who recently returned from Turkey. Blake, who is CEO of both Blake Enterprises and the locally based Consolidated Mining Corporation, was involved in labor negotiations with a mining operation in eastern Turkey when the earthquake struck late last Friday. He spent three days trapped in the rubble before being unearthed on Monday by rescue workers and his fiancée, Anna Elizabeth Kincaid," said local reporter Ashley Thomas.

Colin described his terrifying ordeal to the reporter, unabashedly admitting just how terrified he'd been. "But then I heard the most amazing sound … the woman I love calling my name."

"Miss Kincaid, how did you feel when you realized you'd found him?"

"At the time all I could think of was getting him out, but once I knew he was going to be okay, I was overjoyed, incredibly grateful and … completely overwhelmed."

"I understand you were married there?"

"We were faced with the reality of having to postpone our wedding," Lizzie began.

"Neither of us wanted that. We'd come so close to losing each other. So with the help of our new friends, we had a small, simple ceremony."

"It may have been simple," Lizzie said, smiling at the camera, "but it was beautiful and romantic."

Ashley sighed dreamily. "Er … sorry, I think I got a little caught up in your love story. So now that you're home safely, married, what does the future hold?"

"Aside from getting back on my feet, we've got this incredible relief effort to help with …"

"And we're still going to have the wedding we had planned, this time with all our family and friends there. We've just decided to postpone it until Christmas," Lizzie said. "Mostly, though, we just want to start our life together as a family." She glanced at their family and friends, most of whom were a little teary-eyed, then smiled brightly and winked at Colin.

He grinned back, clasping her hand tightly in his. "My family is the most important thing in the world to me. Especially my brilliant daughter Tori, my beautiful wife Lizzie and, of course, the new baby we're expecting sometime next spring." He leaned in to kiss her softly.

Lizzie lost herself in the gentleness of his kiss, unaware of the stunned silence surrounding them. Finally, he lifted his lips from hers. "Well, my Lizzie, seems we've surprised everyone," he said with a chuckle.

Lizzie's eyes skimmed over their audience. Their eyes were wide, their mouths agape, but nearly all of them were beaming at the news. "Looks like it," she laughed. "Um, guys?"

The reporter was the first to recover. "Now that's a happy ending!"

"No," Colin said, shaking his head. "It's a happy beginning."

CHAPTER 26

The newlyweds struggled to settle into a routine. Their quiet, comfortable home was currently a collection center for a major international relief effort. Though Lizzie loved and appreciated what was being done, she longed for peace and privacy; the constant stream of visitors, however well-intentioned, was hard to cope with.

Dealing with her recuperating husband was a challenge, too. Colin was frustrated by his immobility, yet he seemed incapable of obeying the doctor's orders. Aside from bedtime, he wouldn't take his pain medication and, although Lizzie knew he got a little freaked out in the dark, he wouldn't ask her to leave a light on for him. He stubbornly tried to do things for himself, instead of asking her, or anyone else, for help.

So she hovered, hoping to anticipate his every need. She was so elated to have him home safely, that she wanted to do everything for him. She forgot that the last thing he wanted from her was mothering.

"Bloody hell, Lizzie! I can bloody well pick up the

blasted book that I dropped myself," Colin yelled. "I'm not a damned invalid so you can bloody well stop coddling me."

"Fine," she screamed back. "Do it all yourself and don't let anybody help you. Make yourself worse instead of better. You really can be a pig-headed ass, you know that? I'd almost forgotten." Her eyes stung with tears as she turned and stomped up the stairs, well aware that he couldn't follow her.

She slammed the bedroom door behind her, thankful that they were alone. "Crap," she muttered as the tears began to fall in earnest. She threw herself onto the bed and buried her head in the pillow, intent on having a good, old-fashioned self-pitying cry.

As she lay there, sobbing into the pillow, she let go of all the fear and pain of the past week. Colin was the most important person in the world to her and she'd come within a hair's breadth of losing him forever. Instead, he was downstairs, probably pacing on his crutches even though he shouldn't be walking at all, her stubborn, sweet, sexy impatient patient.

She wiped her eyes and stroked a hand over her belly, where their baby nestled unaware of their current turmoil. She pushed herself off the bed, padded to the bathroom, and splashed her face with cold water.

She grimaced at her image in the mirror. Her face was splotchy, her eyes bloodshot, but she just shrugged and headed back downstairs to find her husband.

He was in the kitchen, sitting on the kitchen floor, leaning against the cabinets, his crutches a foot beyond his reach.

"Need some help?" she smirked.

"I … uh … tripped over the dog dish," he said sheepishly as he indicated the puddle from Hershey's overturned water bowl.

"So I see. Darcy … I'm … I'm sorry if I've been …

hovering. I did warn you I might get a little clingy."

"Yeah, you did. And I remember warning you I'd be a bit of a pain in the arse."

"A bit? Come on, sweetie, you've been more than a *bit* of a pain in the ass. Are you *supposed* to be wandering around on your crutches?" she chided.

"Er ... no. But damn it, Lizzie, I detest that miserable chair."

"I know, sweetie. Just remember that it's only temporary. We've got an appointment with that orthopedic surgeon Doctor Goddard referred us to on Tuesday. He said you'd probably get upgraded to a walking cast."

"I know. But you know patience isn't exactly my strong suit, love."

"Oh, I remember," she said with a grin. "I remember *exactly* how annoying you can be, sweetheart."

"Gee, thanks, Lizzie. Now ... uh ... do you think you might give me a hand up?" he asked with a sheepish grin.

"I thought you'd never ask." She held out a hand to pull him up, shocked to find herself tugged, very hard, to land on his lap.

"Um, Darcy?" She said as his hands moved lightly over the bare skin of her lower back. "Why'd you do that?"

"I missed you," he said quietly. "I hate when we fight, Lizzie."

"Me too," she said as she trailed hot kisses over his stubbled jaw line. "But making up's kind of fun."

"Uh huh," he murmured as their lips fused in a slow, passionate, intense kiss. "I reckon making up is worth a fight or two."

His lips teased hers in another searing kiss. She moaned softly as their tongues collided, savoring the prickly tickle of his whiskers on her chin. Colin groaned and deepened the kiss, one hand sliding beneath her t-shirt to cup her breast.

"What is it about the pair of you and kitchens?" Meg snorted. "Crikey."

"Yeah, get a room," teased Jess from behind her.

Lizzie glanced down at Colin, who hastily withdrew his hand, and blushed hotly. "Bloody hell," he muttered.

She burrowed her head into his shoulder then sneaked a peak at her friends. "Guys ... not that I'm unhappy to see you, but what's up?"

"Lance and Sam wanted to discuss some business with Colin," Meg said.

Colin rolled his eyes and grinned at Lizzie. "Tell them to handle it. In addition to recuperating from a broken leg, I happen to be on my honeymoon."

"Righto," Meg said. "Duly noted, boss. Er ... maybe we should reconsider some of the logistics of this operation?" she suggested.

"Isn't there an empty warehouse at Consolidated?" Jess pondered.

"I think you're right!" Meg agreed. "Guys, I believe that we can safely promise to be out of your hair in no time."

"Good," Lizzie said a little too quickly. "Sorry ... I didn't mean it like that."

"Yeah, right. Come on Meg, somehow, I sense they want us to leave," Jess said with a fake sniffle.

"Well, now you mention it," Colin said with a cheeky grin.

"Righto, getting lost," said Meg.

"By-ee," said Jess.

"I am truly sorry for being such a pain in the arse," Colin said as they sat on the floor, still holding each other. "I've never been much good at being sick."

"So I've noticed," she teased. "But I can live with that."

"I'm delighted to hear it. Er ... Lizzie?"

"Yes, Darcy?"

"I've a confession to make."

"What kind of confession?"

"Do you remember this morning when we got up, and you were wondering how the light got turned on?"

She nodded. "Uh huh. Care to shed some *light* on the subject?"

He groaned at her pun. "Very funny, Lizzie."

"Sorry. Go on. How'd the light get turned on?"

"I turned it on. After being trapped in the dark for so long, I ... I find I'm not so fond of the dark." He looked away, embarrassed to meet her eyes.

"Aw, honey, it's okay." She placed her fingers on his chin and turned his face back to hers.

"Are you certain you can respect a grown man who's afraid of the dark?" he muttered.

"Darcy, nothing could ever make me think less of you. You're the bravest man I know. Besides, you've gone and knocked me up, so you're kind of stuck with me."

The following week was a busy one. Colin's x-rays looked so good that his full leg cast was replaced with a walking cast, and he had his first session with the physical therapist. They also had their first appointment with the ob-gyn, Dr. Silver, who confirmed her pregnancy and assured them that everything appeared perfectly normal. Lizzie was six-weeks along, and the doctor estimated her due date as early May. Tori flew to England with Helen and Lady Frances for a short visit before school started and, with the relief effort moved to the warehouse, their friends respected their need for privacy.

"It's so quiet," Lizzie whispered reverently.

"If I could, I'd sweep you into my arms and carry you

upstairs to our bedroom," he said with a wicked grin. "I'd toss you on the freshly laundered sheets and kiss every inch of your delectable body ... then make sweet, wild love with you."

"Hmm ... well, the carrying and the tossing may have to wait a while, but I think we could probably manage the rest." She laced her fingers through his and walked slowly up the stairs as he limped behind her.

Once they reached their bedroom, Lizzie pushed the door shut with her foot as Colin hauled her into his arms, bodies colliding, lips fusing amidst a symphony of sighs and soft whimpers. Seeking hands tickled their way beneath clothing, teasing and caressing until the unwelcome barriers whispered to the hardwood floor.

"I've missed you, Lizzie," Colin murmured as he sat on the edge of the bed. "I've missed us." He tugged her forward, so she was standing between his thighs. She bent forward to kiss him, moaning as he took control, his tongue boldly thrusting against hers.

Lizzie shivered, smoothing her hands over his firmly sculpted shoulders and arms. "Me too," she said peering into his deep brown eyes. "Are you sure you're up for this?"

He laughed, a sexy throaty laugh that made his dimples dance and left her breathless with longing. "I should think that's quite obvious, love," he teased as he tugged her into his lap.

She blushed and laughingly punched him in the arm. "Well ... er ... yes ... I guess it is. But, well, your doctor didn't say we could ..."

"He didn't say we couldn't, either," he reminded her.

"True enough." She slipped off his lap and slithered into the center of the bed to recline on a pile of pillows.

Colin scooted up beside her and laughingly tugged her back into his arms. "So what would you like to do about it, my Lizzie?"

"There's always this." She straddled his thighs and leaned forward to graze his chest with her breasts. "Or this," she whispered as she angled her body up to take him deep inside. "Or possibly, this," she said as she began to move ever so slowly.

"Oh, definitely that," he whispered as they rocked together in the rhythm that was uniquely theirs. Hands, lips, bodies remembered the secrets their minds had forgotten in almost three weeks of separation.

She laughed huskily, her fingers laced through his dark hair, pulling his lips to hers for a searing kiss. Colin's hands trailed down her back, traced the curve of her waist, the swell of her breasts as they spiraled wildly out of control, finally collapsing in a tangled, satiated heap against the mound of pillows.

"I believe that was *just* what the doctor ordered," Colin said as he gently cupped a breast. "Hmmm … are these new?" he asked, laughing down at her.

"Um … sort of," she giggled. "One of the benefits of pregnancy."

His hand trailed down her abdomen to rest on her belly. "I can't believe our baby's in here," he murmured. "What does it feel like?"

"It's pretty surreal, knowing that our baby is growing inside me."

"Can you feel him moving around?"

"Him?"

"Or her. Can you?"

"Not yet. I think that's a few weeks away. Mostly I feel queasy, and I have to pee about every five minutes. Haven't you been through this once before?"

"Not really. Lara wouldn't let me near her for most of the pregnancy. I never even felt Tori kick."

"Well, this time around you'll be in on everything. I swear. Just promise me you'll still love you when I'm as big as a house."

Colin dipped his head and reverently kissed her belly, just below her belly button. "I'll always love you, Lizzie. Every delightful inch."

"Every inch, huh? Didn't you say something about kissing every inch of me earlier? I think I'll hold you to that little promise …"

"That will be my distinct pleasure," he said as he rolled her onto her back, his lips branding hot kisses on her already overheated skin.

CHAPTER 27

"Feeling a little frisky this morning, Darcy?" Lizzie giggled as he blindfolded her with a silk scarf.

"I'm simply prolonging the mystery. Shall we?" He placed her hand in the crook of his elbow and guided her carefully out the back door, carrying his crutches in his free hand.

Once they were on the deck, he removed the scarf and whirled her around. "No way!" she gasped.

"Way," he laughed. "Happy birthday, love."

A rainbow-striped hot air balloon was tethered in the field, its enormous wicker basket floating about a foot off the ground. "It's beautiful," she sighed. "But how did you know? I never told you that a hot air balloon ride was a fantasy of mine."

"Your Mum mentioned it once, actually. She told me that as a little girl one landed behind your house and, since then, you've always dreamed of going up in one."

"I did. I do." She threw her arms around him and hugged him tightly. "I love it, Darcy. It's a lovely surprise."

He pulled her closer and kissed her softly. "I've

already checked with your doctor; she said it's fine, so, what do you think? Shall we soar through the heavens?"

"Are you kidding?" she laughed. "Let's go."

The pilot helped them into the basket and explained the safety precautions. Lizzie clung to Colin's arm and held her breath as the pilot released the tethers. He pulled the lever for the burner, sending a whoosh of flames up into the balloon. Within minutes they were airborne.

Colin curled his arms around her waist and nuzzled her ear. She snuggled more deeply into the warmth of his embrace as the exquisite panorama unfolded below them. It was a perfect autumn day as they floated through the crisp air. The only sound was the occasional whoosh as more hot air was released into the balloon to control their altitude. The sky was a clear, brilliant azure blue, unmarred by even the wispiest of clouds. A gentle breeze whispered through the vivid autumn leaves below, a cheerful patchwork of opulent golds, dazzling oranges, and intense reds against the cloudless sky. "It's spectacular."

The balloon descended a little, passing over her parents' stone rancher; Tori, Jim, and Bev gazed up at them from the backyard, waving madly.

"Thank goodness the wind was in our favor. I rather hoped we'd pass over," Colin said.

They crested a hill and coasted over a sun-dappled pond, so low they seemed to glide across the gold-gilded water. A surge of hot air and a favorable wind floated them higher, until they soared beside a flock of Canadian geese in tight 'V' formation as they headed south for the winter.

Lizzie smoothed a hand down Colin's arm and linked her fingers through his. "It's so peaceful up here. Thank you," she whispered.

"Happy Birthday, Lizzie," he murmured as he

lowered his mouth to hers. His lips brushed hers teasingly, a mere whisper of a kiss, then another, finally settling more firmly in an achingly sweet kiss that had her soaring miles above the hot air balloon.

"Thank you for making me walk on air, Darcy," she sighed as he lifted his lips from hers and smiled down at her. "You're making all my dreams come true." She grinned up at him and stood on tiptoe to kiss him again, blushing as she remembered that they weren't alone. "Er … sorry, Frank. We don't mean to subject you to all of our mushiness."

The pilot smiled at the pair. "It's okay, kids. I've gotten used to it in this job. Truth be told, I love it. Romance is good for the soul."

"You're a philosopher then, as well as a pilot?" Colin asked.

"I guess the solitude up here gives me time to think," he said. "And to appreciate what's important. From what I've seen, you two are pretty lucky."

Frank turned back to the radio, looking for a safe landing spot. Ten minutes later, the basket bounced along a grassy field where the chase team was waiting.

"Bit of a bumpy landing," Colin said hugging her. "You and Junior okay?" He ran his hands soothingly over her belly.

She grinned up at him and covered his hands with her own. "We're fine. I guess it's just a reminder that even the most perfect moments have their share of bumps along the way," she philosophized.

"And perhaps it's the bumps along the way that allow us to appreciate them," said Colin.

"Seems your trip to the heavens has made you both philosophers, too," Frank chuckled. "Must be the altitude."

One week later, Lizzie sat cross-legged on the

rumpled bedclothes gazing at her sleeping husband, smiling as she recalled exactly why the covers were so tangled. She suppressed the urge to trace his features, content to simply watch him sleep. Even now, she found it hard to believe that he was hers.

He mumbled incoherently in his sleep and rolled onto his back, causing the sheet to slip to his waist and giving her a delectable view of his broad shoulders and chest. His dark hair was a tangled mess of curls on the crisp white pillowcase. A dream-induced smile twitched at the corners of his mouth making his dimples dance playfully in his cheeks.

She sighed happily and inched cautiously across the bed, trying not to jostle it. When she reached the edge, she expelled a breath, but before her foot could touch the hardwood floor, a strong arm clamped around her waist and hauled her back, sprawling her unceremoniously atop Colin's body.

"And just where do you think you're creeping off to?" he asked with a wry grin.

"Humph. I was going to make you breakfast in bed. Now you've spoiled my surprise."

"I'd rather have something else in bed," he said wiggling his eyebrows suggestively.

She swatted him playfully. "Sex maniac," she teased. "Don't you ever get enough?"

"Enough of you? That's not possible, love. Besides, it is my birthday."

"Ah ... well in that case ... Happy Birthday, Darcy," she said as she wound her arms around his neck. "I love you."

They resurfaced slowly, content to hold each other until the rumbling in their bellies overwhelmed them. "C'mon," she said, slipping from under the covers. "I'm starving. For food."

They threw on sweats and headed downstairs to the

kitchen. Colin's leg was healing quickly; he'd progressed from crutches to an elegant cane just the day before. Lizzie was thankful for his progress, but the prospect of his going back to work made her a little sad. Lost in thought, she looked up to find him watching her intently.

"What's wrong, Lizzie?"

"Nothing really. It's just … you're going back to work next week. I'll miss having you around."

"Love, my office is ten feet down that hall." He pointed to the corridor connecting the addition to the main house.

"I know. I'm being silly and sentimental. Damned hormones!"

Colin laughed and tugged her into his arms for a long, cozy bear hug. He pulled back and laid his hand gently on her slightly rounded belly. "Don't let Junior hear you say that."

"Junior knows I'll happily put up with out of control hormones for his or her sake. Now, would the birthday boy like his present?"

"You've already given me something today, love."

"You really are a very bad man, you know."

"I know. You adore that about me," he teased.

"Yup. Back in a sec." Lizzie dashed into the dining room and grabbed a small, prettily wrapped package from its hiding place in the corner cupboard. She concealed it behind her back as she returned.

"What are you hiding there, Lizzie?"

"It's nothing really. Not as cool as a hot air balloon ride. Just a little something I made …" She laid her gift it on the table and pushed it toward him. "I hope you like it."

Colin tore into the silver wrapping paper as eagerly as a little boy on Christmas morning. Lizzie held her breath as he uncovered the CD she'd made for him, *Darcy and*

Lizzie's Greatest Hits. He grinned at the picture of them on the cover, taken at their engagement party at Snowhill. His smile broadened as his eyes scanned the list of songs, all of which had some special meaning for their life together. "What a lovely gift."

"There's a dedication on the back," she murmured.

Colin turned the case over and read it aloud. "I used to think that love songs were corny; now every one makes me think of you. I believed that romance and love were for others, but never for me. If I lived a thousand years, it wouldn't give me enough time to express all that I feel for you. You turned my life into a love song. Shall I sing it for you?" Colin's eyes glistened as they met hers. "I don't think you could give me a more perfect present. How did you manage this?"

Lizzie laughed softly. "My original idea was for me to sing a couple of songs with Tori playing the piano. But things kind of mushroomed along the way. While you were in physical therapy, I was rehearsing and recording."

"You sly girl. Shall we have a listen?"

"How bad could it be?" she laughed. "Don't forget, everyone's coming for dinner tonight."

"Are you certain you're up for that?" Colin knew how tired she'd been the last few weeks.

"I'll be okay."

"Ten dollars says you fall asleep on the sofa. Again."

Lizzie laughed, knowing he was right. "Now why would I take a bet like that? We both know you're right. I'll be out like a light by nine o'clock."

They spent the day together, enjoying the simple things. They picked apples from the tree in the side yard and ate them while they were still warm from the sun. They played like children in the crunchy autumn leaves, laughing and plucking them from each other's hair as they strolled back to the house for a nap. As they trudged up the stairs, Colin gently massaged Lizzie's neck and shoulders.

"Heaven," she sighed. "God, I'm beat."

"You are a little pale, love. Are you alright?"

"Just tired. Maybe I overdid it a little."

"How about a massage followed by a long nap?"

"Sounds blissful. I'll just be a minute," she said over her shoulder as she headed for the bathroom. She'd been nauseous and crampy all afternoon, but she hadn't wanted to worry Colin.

Two minutes later, she stumbled from the bathroom, tears streaming down her face as she clutched her belly. "D-darcy ..."

"Good God, Lizzie, what's the matter? You look dreadful." He rushed to her side, worry etched on his face as he helped her to the edge of the bed.

Lizzie clutched his hand tightly. "I'm spotting."

"A small amount of spotting is fairly normal," the obstetrician, Dr. Silver reassured as she examined Lizzie, who clung to Colin's hand, unwilling and unable to let go.

"Really? I thought ..." The word miscarriage weighed heavily on her mind. Colin gave her hand a gentle squeeze.

"Your body's going through a lot of changes, Mrs. Blake. But to be safe, we're going to do an ultrasound." There was a soft knock on the door and a young woman entered.

"Hi there, I'm Kit. Are you ready for baby's first picture?"

They nodded. Kit pulled the sheet down to expose Lizzie's stomach and smeared a liberal amount of gooey jelly on her bare skin; it was cool and sticky. "Suddenly I feel like a piece of toast," she quipped. "I never understood what the jelly's for."

"It eliminates the air between the probe and your skin and helps the sound waves pass through your body. That's what makes the picture." The technician smiled and began moving the probe over her belly. She paused from time to time to study the images on the screen. Her brow crinkled as she passed the wand over one spot, then another, then returned to the first. "Hmm."

Lizzie swallowed nervously and tightened her grip on Colin's hand. "Is something wrong?" he asked.

The technician glanced at the doctor, then beamed at them. "Not a thing. I'd say your babies are perfectly healthy."

It took a minute for what she'd said to register in Lizzie's mind. She glanced up at Colin, her eyes wide. "Did she say ... babies? As ... as in more than one ..."

Colin nodded slowly. "You mean our *baby* is perfectly healthy, don't you?"

The technician and the doctor both beamed at them. "No, Mr. Blake. I said your babies are perfectly healthy. Congratulations. You're having twins!"

"Oh. My. God," Lizzie said.

"Jesus," said Colin. "That's some birthday present. And you were afraid you'd never top my hot air balloon ride."

"I would recommend staying grounded for a while," said the doctor. "I'd like you to take it easy, Mrs. Blake. Bed rest for the next two weeks."

Two. Lizzie had repeated the small word like a mantra since they'd left the doctor's office. Her mind raced as scores of conflicting emotions struggled to the surface - fear, excitement, and overwhelming happiness. Happiness won out and spilled forth in an attack of the giggles and a flood of joyful tears. She sniffled loudly and stole a peek at Colin. "Two. Can you believe it?"

He caught her gaze and grinned back, tilting his head as he looked at her.

"What?"

"I've not decided if you're talking about two babies or two weeks of bed rest," he teased.

"Two babies," she sighed as she smoothed a hand over her stomach. "Funny how things work out."

"What do you mean, love?"

"You know how girls tend to fantasize about their future lives? Husbands, kids, all that stuff?"

"I have six sisters, remember?"

"Right. So you know. Okay, in my mind, when I pictured myself coming home after giving birth, I *always* had two babies. As if I knew that's how it would be. Strange, huh?"

"No stranger than having a couple of ghosts protecting us."

"No, I guess not. What do you think about all of this, Darcy?"

"I think it's bloody marvelous."

"There's only one thing that bugs me."

"Let me guess. Two weeks of bed rest?"

Lizzie nodded slowly. "I'm not good at sitting still."

"So I've noticed. Something we have in common."

"I'm also not too good at being taken care of, so go easy on me."

"Not a chance. I intend to make certain you get plenty of rest."

"In other words, paybacks are a bitch?"

Colin flashed her a wicked grin and wiggled his eyebrows. "Prepare to be coddled."

"I still think we should cancel," said Colin as he tucked Lizzie into their bed. "Last thing you need is a houseful of people."

"It's just our friends. And the doctor said it was okay

…"

"Yes. But she also said you're to stay put on the sofa and under no circumstances are you to lift a finger."

"Humph. Well, I can't very well order take-out if you won't even let my fingers do the walkin', now can I."

"Cute. Okay, I'll give you that."

"But you're not giving in, are you?"

"Not a chance, love."

"Please? I swear I'll behave myself. And I'll go to bed as soon as I start to feel tired."

"Is it really so important to you, Lizzie?"

"Yes," she nodded. "Besides … I'm dying to tell everyone!"

"Tell everyone what?" asked Tori from the open doorway of the bedroom. She waltzed into the room and planted gentle kisses on both their cheeks. "Happy Birthday, Daddy."

"Thank you, poppet."

"Mum, are you okay?" she frowned. "Why are you in bed?"

"I'm just a little tired, sweetie." Lizzie smiled, not wanting to cause her worry. "Being pregnant is harder than I imagined."

"Okay, as long as you're alright."

"Everyone's fine."

Colin's hand dropped to Lizzie's shoulder in a tender caress. She grinned up at him, eager to blurt out their very unexpected news and was rewarded with a glimpse of his heart-stopping dimpled grin.

"That's quite enough, you two!" Tori scolded. "Mind you, I'm quite used to the over-the-moon looks you give each other all the time, but suddenly … hmm. Alright, out with it. What is it you can't wait to tell everyone?"

Lizzie patted the bed beside her. "Maybe you ought to have a seat."

Tori rolled her eyes dramatically and shook her head,

her glossy dark curls bouncing on her shoulders. She eyed them quizzically and flopped onto the bed, sitting cross-legged and staring at them expectantly. "I'm waiting ..."

"Okay," Lizzie began. "First of all, everything is fine, but we had a little scare today."

"With the baby," Colin clarified. "So we went to the doctor's ..."

"And just to be sure, they did an ultrasound. Do you know what that is, Tori?" Lizzie asked.

"We talked about it in health class a couple of weeks ago." She smiled suddenly. "Is that what this is all about? Have you got a picture of our baby?"

Lizzie nodded. "Yep."

"But there's more," Colin said with a broad smile. He leaned down and planted a soft kiss on the top of Lizzie's head. "Your Mum here is a bit of an overachiever."

"Huh?" said Tori blankly. "Come again?"

"We're having two babies, Tori," she said.

"Twins," added Colin unnecessarily.

"No way!" blurted Tori. "Twins? Really?"

Lizzie wrapped her arms around her daughter and hugged her tightly. "Really."

CHAPTER 28

"I can't believe you're having twins," said Jess the next afternoon.

"It's one bombshell after another with you these days, darl," said Meg. "How do you feel about all this?"

"I love the way you cut to the chase, Megan Kay."

"No point in dancing 'round the issue," she said.

"True enough. Hmm … how am I feeling? Excited, terrified, happy, overwhelmed and pretty much everything in between. The twin thing I have time to adjust to. It's the two weeks of bed rest that's going to make me crazy!" she moaned.

"Two weeks in bed sounds deliciously decadent to me," Meg sighed. "Crikey, where's Lance when I need him!"

"Down girl!" Jess joked. "I think the operative term here is bed*rest*, Meg."

"That would be two weeks stuck in bed *without* sex," Lizzie reminded her. "Not to mention my doting husband. Is it possible to be coddled to death?" she whined.

"Surely he's not as bad as all that?" asked Meg.

"Oh, worse. Much, much worse."

"It's only been one day," Jess reminded Lizzie. "Don't you think he'll back off a little in a day or two?"

"Have you ever seen Colin Blake back off from anything?"

"Er … point taken," said Meg. "So what are you going to do with your time?"

"Well … I have been toying with an idea …"

"Ooh … do tell!" they said.

"When I learned that Colin was going to be okay, I had a little chat with Ruby." Lizzie was grateful that her two friends didn't bat an eyelash at the mention of her ghostly friend. "She asked me to write her a happy ending. And … well, you both know I've always wanted to be a writer, so I'm thinking I'll take Ruby and William's story and turn it into a novel. One with a very definite happily-ever-after."

"Oh, Lizzie, that's a marvelous idea," Meg gushed.

"You think?" They both nodded. "Good, because I'm counting on both of you for some brutally honest feedback."

The two weeks passed more pleasantly than Lizzie could have imagined. Colin coddled her, as she knew he would, but he also learned when to back off. Although she was restless, she was feeling less worn down by the day.

She was also feeling more creative. She'd explained her project to her sister-in-law, Nan, who offered to dig through the family archives for more information on Ruby Blake.

Nan came through in a huge way. She found letters written by Ruby's father, first angry, then remorseful, retelling the whole story with excruciating detail. She also searched Ruby's tower and unearthed Ruby's diaries and carefully preserved love letters from

William. Lizzie pored through the documents eagerly, feeling more in tune with her subjects with each sentence. By the time her two weeks was up, she had a solid outline for her novel and five carefully crafted chapters under her belt.

"Think you might ever let me read it, Lizzie?" Colin asked as she closed her brand new laptop.

She bit her lip and reopened the computer. "It's still a little raw …"

"Only if you're ready, love."

"It's fine. I just hope I've done them justice," she said nibbling her thumbnail. "After all, they're family." She handed the computer to Colin and held her breath as he scanned the screen. He smiled here, laughed there, and even blinked back tears once. "So?" she whispered.

He closed the laptop and reached across her to lay it on the nightstand, then gathered her into his strong arms and kissed her soundly. "It's wonderful, Lizzie."

"Really? You're not just saying that because you have to? I can take the truth, you know."

"The truth is that it's breathtaking. You've given them life, Lizzie. You've made me feel what they felt. You've even made me have a bit of sympathy for Ruby's father. I'd say you're well on your way to giving William and Ruby a much-deserved happy ending."

"I've had a lot of inspiration in that department," she grinned.

"I thought one or two scenes felt a bit familiar," he teased. "I'll wager you're grateful your two weeks in bed is up tomorrow all the same."

"You wager right. If that doctor doesn't give me a reprieve, I'll scream! I'm dying to take a walk."

The following morning was typically loud in the farmhouse. Tori blared music as she got ready for school, Colin yelled at her to keep it down, and Hershey added her two cents with her shrill puppy bark. Amid the din, Lizzie lay against the pillows, idly watching the morning news show and sipping her decaffeinated coffee. She was nervous about her doctor's appointment, praying that they'd be given a clean bill of health even as she felt the faint fluttering of butterflies in her belly.

Tori dashed in and gave Lizzie a quick kiss goodbye. "I don't want to miss the bus. Dad'll kill me if he has to take me to school. Again."

"You're right about that!" she agreed. "Have a good day, Tor."

"You too, Mum." She listened as Tori pounded down the stairs and the door slammed behind her. The butterflies fluttered again.

Meg and Jess peaked their heads in for a quick good morning. "We wanted to wish you luck this afternoon, darl," said Meg. They were gone as quickly as they'd breezed in, replaced by Colin. As he leaned down to kiss her goodbye, she felt the strange fluttering again. She smiled serenely.

"Thinking about the end of your sentence, love?"

"Something like that."

He kissed her again. "I've a conference call on my schedule this morning, but I'll be back to take you to the doctor after lunch."

"Can we please go somewhere after," she begged.

"Anxious for a bit of freedom?"

"More like salivating at the thought of fresh air and a little exercise," she sighed.

"Bye, love." Colin angled his face toward her belly. "Bye, kiddos."

As their father strode out the door, the twins kicked her. Hard. "Well," she cooed, stroking her belly. "Hello there."

Lizzie leaned back against the pillows, her hands resting lightly on her belly, waiting expectantly for the next tiny flutter. She closed her eyes, awed by the profoundness of this new connection with her babies.

"I can't wait to meet you," she whispered. She was rewarded with another gentle kick.

"Hey! That tickles," she giggled. "Still, it's nice to know you feel the same. There are so many things I want to teach you." Lizzie sighed, picturing all the firsts to come ... times two. First steps, first words, the first day of school. So many magical moments. She sighed again, knowing there would, inevitably, be less happy times too. There would be tears, skinned knees, and bruised feelings but she knew with Colin by her side, she could handle even the worst day their twins could throw at them. "Wait until you meet your Daddy," she told them. "You two definitely hit the jackpot."

She was so lost in her thoughts that she didn't hear Colin's uneven footsteps on the stairs. She didn't realize he'd come back until she heard his deep laugh and looked up to find him grinning at her from the doorway, his head tilted to one side. "You look like the proverbial cat that ate the proverbial canary, love."

She bit her lip, but it was impossible to hide her smile. "What are you doing back?"

"Forgot my briefcase. Now, come on, you're radiant ... and that's positively the biggest smile I've ever seen. Have you got a lover hiding under the bed?" he teased. He bent down, lifted the dust ruffle and peered beneath the bed. "Hmm ... nothing under here but a few stray dust bunnies. So, Mrs. Blake, what is it that has you glowing?"

Lizzie reached up, took his hand, and patted the bed beside her. Colin sat down, his eyes never leaving hers as she placed his hand on her stomach. She felt another fluttery kick from deep inside. "Did you feel that?" Colin's eyes widened, a look of profound joy on his face. "Now who's glowing?" she teased.

He laughed, his dimples dancing in his cheeks as he leaned forward to brush a soft kiss on her mouth. "Those are our babies," he said reverently. His fingers spread out over her abdomen as the kicks grew stronger. "I think they like me."

"I think they love you!" She curled her hand behind his neck, her fingers tangling in his dark curls as she pulled his lips to hers.

It was a kiss of sweet intensity - molten heat mingled with aching tenderness. "Wow," she said when they pulled apart.

"Lizzie, love, that's a major understatement." He smiled at her and leaned forward for another brief kiss. "This has been a very long two weeks."

"You're certain everything's fine?" Colin asked the doctor.

"Mrs. Blake is in excellent health and the twins' heartbeats are strong. I see no reason she can't resume normal activities as long as she gets plenty of rest and eats properly."

"Er …I'm right here," Lizzie reminded them. "You don't have to talk about me as if I'm not in the room, you know."

Colin smiled sheepishly. "Sorry, love."

"It's alright, Darcy, I forgive you. So … ah … Dr. Silver does normal activity include sex?" She laughed as a blush warmed her cheeks. Colin chuckled softly, but Lizzie merely shrugged her shoulders. "Well, it is a normal activity."

The doctor grinned at them. "At this point, sex should be fine. Just take it easy. I realize you're still newlyweds."

"I think she's saying no swinging from the chandeliers, love," Colin said with a suggestive wink.

"Damn," she said, snapping her fingers. "And after I

had that trapeze installed above the bed. Oh well, c'est la vie."

CHAPTER 29

For the first time since their return from Turkey, Lizzie and Colin could truly relax. With the pregnancy scare behind them and his broken leg on the mend, they began to settle in at last.

Life was beautiful, but not without its ups and downs. Lizzie was thrilled when her childhood friends, Kim and David Jameson moved into the house across the street. It felt right to have them so close, but her joy was tempered with concern when Dave's sister, Tessa, returned from Europe pale and lost. But time and love would heal her wounds.

It would heal Dare's wounds, too. Lizzie's brawny cousin had been shot in the line of duty, the bullet missing his heart by a fraction of an inch; his partner hadn't been so lucky. Colin had been her rock in the aftermath of the shooting and Lizzie felt incredibly blessed to share her life with him, for better or for worse.

Even when life wasn't perfect, with Colin by her side, life was beautiful.

As their December wedding grew closer, Lizzie's

belly grew larger. Unfortunately, the beautiful Regency gown no longer fit. When she began to panic about finding a pregnancy-friendly gown at the last minute, budding fashionista Tori and artistic Meg came to her rescue.

"It's gorgeous!" Lizzie gushed as the creamy satin of her new wedding gown slithered down her body. "Are you sure it's not too … slinky? Especially in this condition?" The dress was floor length ivory satin with a graceful draped neck, spaghetti straps and an empire waist that de-emphasized her rapidly growing tummy.

"What condition is that, darl?" Meg asked with a wry grin.

"This one," she said patting her belly. "I never pictured myself as a pregnant bride."

"No, I imagine not. But you are already married, right?" Jess countered.

"Yes."

"And you like the dress?" asked Tori.

"I *love* the dress. You two are absolute geniuses for designing it."

"We'll have to agree with you there," Tori grinned.

"Your kid may just take the fashion world by storm," Meg said proudly. "She's the mastermind behind the design."

"So what do you think?" Meg said, her eyes skittering critically up and down Lizzie's body.

"Honestly? It's perfect. And it makes me feel sexy, which is a major bonus."

"I do feel a *teensy* bit sorry for poor Colin, though," Meg said, feigning sadness.

"Why's that, Meg?"

"Because, darl, with you looking like that, the poor man won't know what hit him."

Colin's brand new Lear jet banked slowly and began

its descent into Manchester International Airport. Lizzie snuggled into the luxurious leather seat and fastened her seatbelt low around her ever-expanding waistline. Across the cabin, her mother clutched the armrest tightly. Lizzie flashed her a reassuring smile. Bev Kincaid had managed her first flight like a trooper. "You okay?"

Bev glanced up and loosened her grip on the armrest. "So far so good."

Meg, seated beside her, patted Bev's hand. "She'll be apples, darl. Almost back on terra firma."

"Thank God," Beverly whispered. "It wasn't as bad as I thought, though."

"Are you nervous, Lizzie," asked Jess.

"Nope, not at all. But we're already married, so it's a no-brainer. This one's for us to share with everyone else."

Meg and Jess shared an amused look. "Yeah right. You'll be shaking like a leaf and hyperventilating come Friday night," Meg teased.

"Damn it," Lizzie muttered. "I hate when you're right! You know, it's not nice for the bridesmaids to tease the bride."

"We just know you," Jess laughed. "And I have no doubt that you'll *happily* torture us when we get married so …"

"Call it a pre-emptive strike," Meg said blithely.

"Just remember, paybacks are … well, you know."

"What's paybacks?" asked Lizzie's niece Rachel.

"Nothing you need to worry about just yet, sweetie," Lizzie said. "All you need to think about is how gorgeous you're going to look in your flower girl dress. You too, Dani. I'm so glad you girls are with me!" She and her attendants were flying in the Sunday before the wedding so they could relax. Colin, Sam, Lance, and most of the rest of her family were flying over on

Wednesday night on a chartered Boeing 757.

"So Grandmom, are you excited to see Snowhill?" Tori asked.

Bev smiled at Tori. They'd formed a strong bond in the months since Tori had moved to America. "Of course I am, sweetheart. I'm sure it's every bit as beautiful as you've described."

"Okay, close your eyes, everyone, Snowhill is just around this bend." Tori giggled excitedly, eager to show off her family's home. "Wait until you see Ruby's Tower."

"Will she talk to us?" asked Dani.

"Perhaps. She's quite fond of Mum."

"It will be a big week for Ruby as well," Lizzie said. She'd been working feverishly on Ruby's happy ending, and she was thrilled to have finished it. She fingered the ruby cross around her neck, hoping her ghostly friend would like her gifts. In addition to the romantic story that Ruby had inspired, they had arranged another surprise for their protective ghost.

"Can we open our eyes yet?" Rachel asked impatiently.

"Almost there, sweetie pie," Lizzie assured her. Jenkins, the chauffeur, stopped the car at the exact spot where she'd caught her first glimpse of Snowhill. "Thank you, Jenkins." It had taken a while, and she was becoming accustomed to Colin's lifestyle. But having servants, even part time, still amazed her.

"You're quite welcome, Mrs. Colin," he replied.

"Open your eyes," she instructed her friends and family. When they did, the limousine was filled with a series of 'oohs' and 'ahs'.

"Jeeeesus!" Meg swore.

"It's like a fairy palace!" Rachel sighed.

"It's amazing!" Bev Kincaid agreed.

"It really is something, isn't it?" Lizzie mused.

Atop the snow-crusted knoll, Snowhill glimmered like a jewel. Her soaring towers shone like burnished gold against the brilliant white landscape and gray winter sky, warm and inviting, as if beckoning them to nestle in her arms. In the valley below, the ice-covered pond shone like mirrored silver.

"Can we go skating, Aunt Lizzie?" Dani asked.

"Please?" Rachel echoed.

"I don't see why not, as long as Tori goes along."

"It'll be brilliant!" Tori agreed. "We'll make a party of it. We can take a sleigh ride as well, if you like."

"Really?" Rachel asked, her eyes wide with excitement. "In a one-horse open sleigh, like in Jingle Bells?"

"Uh huh," said Tori. "Though we usually use a pair of horses. It's faster and more exciting!"

After a light brunch and a tour of the house, Bev went to her room to rest. The rest of the ladies traipsed up the stairs into Ruby's tower room. Lizzie was eager to give her the happy ending she'd requested.

She felt her presence as soon as she entered the room. "Hello, Ruby," she murmured. "I've brought some friends to meet you." She set the box she'd been carrying on the window seat.

"It feels weird in here," said Dani. "Kind of ... spooky."

"My scalp feels all prickly," added Rachel.

"Fear me not, little one," said a soft voice. "I would not harm you."

Despite her reassurance, Rachel gripped Lizzie's hand tightly. Slowly, Ruby's gowned form materialized by the window. "My dear friend!" she smiled. "You are happy as I promised?"

"I never dreamed I could be this happy," she said.

She walked over to where Ruby stood and pointed to her belly. "Twins!"

Tentatively, Ruby reached out a hand and placed it on Lizzie's belly. Her touch was barely perceptible, more a whisper than a tactile sensation. One of the babies kicked, followed quickly by the second, as if they, too, sensed Ruby's presence.

"'Tis most curious!" she murmured. "Like the flutter of a butterfly or a soft whisper in my ear. Does it feel so to you?"

"Exactly like that," Lizzie agreed. "May I introduce my friends?"

Ruby nodded. She glided across the room and knelt in front of Tori, Dani, and Rachel. Lizzie followed and laid a hand on Tori's shoulder. "My daughter, Victoria."

"Aye, we have met before though you would not recall, Miss Tori, for you were but a babe. You favor your handsome Papa, dear child."

"Thank you," Tori murmured; tears glistened on her lashes. "Thank you for everything ... for watching over Dad and for helping Mum find him."

"'Twas my privilege." Ruby turned to the younger girls. "Who might these two lovely young ladies be?"

"My nieces, Danielle and Rachel Kincaid."

"Are you a princess?" Rachel asked, "because you kind of look princessy in that dress."

Ruby smiled at her and plucked at her red brocade gown. "No, my pet, I am no princess. All young girls wore frocks like mine when I was a child."

"It's beautiful," said Dani. "Did you know it's the color of the dresses we're wearing for the wedding?"

"Aunt Lizzie said it was for you," Rachel informed her.

"Then I am truly flattered," said the ghost. "Might I share a secret?"

The girls leaned forward eagerly, no longer timid

with the ghost. Ruby smiled indulgently. "I wished to dress in breeches as you do," she whispered indicating their blue-jeaned legs. "Fancy gowns may be pretty, but they are *dreadfully* uncomfortable."

"Really?" asked Rachel.

Tori nodded knowingly. "I went to a costume party in a dress like that once. Ouch. And that was without all the petticoats and stays!"

"'Tis true … at times, it was difficult to even draw a breath." Ruby stood up and turned towards Lizzie's two friends. "Good afternoon, ladies."

"These are my dearest friends in the whole world," Lizzie told her. "Meg and Jess. Ladies, meet my ghost!"

"Hey," said Jess.

"G'day," said Meg.

"They're not normally this quiet!" Lizzie told Ruby.

"Crikey, Lizzie, give us a break. We're chatting with a ghost!" Meg protested.

"I'll admit it's not exactly your run of the mill conversation," Lizzie agreed. "But you're both attuned to the spiritual world."

"True … but I've never actually seen a ghost before," said Jess.

"I'm delighted to make your acquaintance," said Ruby with a curtsy. She stood back for a moment, head tilted as she scrutinized Lizzie's friends, then sighed as she looked down at her gown. "Perhaps I was born in the wrong century," she sighed. "Your hair," she said to Jess, "it is so loose and wild. This," she said as she touched a hand to her elaborate curls, "took an eternity to have arranged."

"Mine's wash and wear," Jess said gratefully.

"'Tis lovely," said Ruby. "And you, Mistress Meg … you wear a waistcoat which would make any man of my time quite envious." Meg's hand-painted waistcoat had a pattern of the moon and stars on navy blue silk.

"Thanks, darl," Meg said. "Did it myself."

"I painted as a girl," Ruby said sadly. "But ghosts do not have the luxury of such pursuits."

"I'm sorry, Ruby," Lizzie said. "I can't imagine how terrible it is to be caught between worlds."

"There are other rewards," she assured her. "For example, I know that Jess is soon to be betrothed to Mr. Colin's nephew and that Meg is from a place so far away I cannot even imagine it. Australia." Though she'd spoken with Ruby many times, details of her friends' lives had never been a topic of conversation.

"Bloody hell," sputtered Meg.

"How the ...?" said Jess.

"'Tis only a bit of ghostly intuition," Ruby said.

"Very cool!" said Jess.

"Is that good or bad?" Ruby asked, confused by their modern slang.

"Cool is good," Lizzie assured her.

"Cool," she repeated with a broad grin. "Very cool."

Jess laughed and shifted her weight onto one hip. Her ankle-length skirt fluttered, revealing the tattoo on her ankle.

"You bear a most striking birthmark upon your ankle, Mistress Jess," Ruby said with surprise.

"Er ... it's not actually a birthmark. It's a tattoo."

"A ... tat-too? What is that?" Ruby asked.

"A kind of art done with needles."

"It sounds most painful," Ruby said. "Yet you chose to have this done?"

"I guess it's part of the price of being cool."

"Ah," said Ruby. "Discomfort for the sake of beauty. *That* I am quite familiar with."

"Darl, I think that's universal to all women of all times," said Meg.

"'Tis as you say," Ruby agreed. "Dear Lizzie, thank you for bringing your friends to meet me. It has been so very long …"

"You're welcome, Ruby. I owe you so much! And … I have a gift for you." Lizzie opened up the box that she'd set down earlier. "You asked me to write a happy ending for you and your William. This is the final chapter of your story."

"Will you read it to me?" she asked softly.

Lizzie nodded and sat on the window seat. Ruby sat beside her, gazing sadly down at the flagstone below.

"Mistress Ruby, you have a letter from Master William," Hannah informed her in a hushed voice. "'Twas delivered just now!"

Ruby took the proffered letter and clutched it to her breast. "My father did not see?"

"No, mistress," Hannah assured her.

"Thank you, Hannah. You may go."

Hannah bobbed a curtsy and left Ruby alone with her letter. It was brief and to the point: My dearest love, meet me this eve beneath your tower room, and we shall elope, with deepest devotion, W. Travers.

"Oh, Will," Ruby murmured. "I wish that it did not have to be so! Why must Papa be so unreasonable?" She brushed the tears from her cheeks and hastily wrapped a few belongings in an old shawl - the silver hairbrush her mother had given her, her most recent diary, and an outgrown set of her brother's clothing. "In the event I must disguise myself," she murmured to herself.

She paced nervously around the small tower room that had always been her refuge. Her stomach fluttered, and she found herself unable to stay still.

As Ruby paced, Hannah scurried through the corridors of the house toward the sanctuary of the kitchen. She was uneasy about the note that she'd delivered to Mistress Ruby. Hannah knew, as all the servants did, that Master Blake did not approve of the match. She also knew, as Ruby's closest confidante, that her mistress loved William Travers desperately. She could only hope that her mistress would not do anything ill-advised.

"A word, Hannah," boomed the voice of John Blake.

Hannah quivered beneath his gaze. He was, after all, her employer. "M-master?"

"You accepted a letter from an unknown rider. To whom was it addressed?"

Hannah looked down, wringing her hands. "I ... I do not know, sir."

"You would not lie to me."

"N-no, sir."

"I thought not. I would not wish to see that young stable hand, Jem, lose his position."

"J-jem?" Hannah was shaking visibly now. Jem had promised to marry her when he was promoted to groom.

"Perhaps you recollect something about that letter now?"

Hannah felt ill. She hated to betray her mistress, but she wouldn't betray Jem. "P-perhaps."

"Was the letter for Mistress Ruby?" Blake demanded.

"Aye, sir," Hannah mumbled.

"You are a good girl, Hannah. You may go."

Hannah bit her lip, trying to hold back the tears as she ran to the tiny room she shared with another housemaid. She threw herself on the bed and let the tears flow. "What have I done?"

As dusk approached, Ruby gazed down from the tower room, watching for her beloved William's arrival. She saw him when he was still more than a mile away, recognizable by the distinctive red cloak he wore. Her heart leapt into her throat. It was time.

She gathered her bundled belongings and concealed them beneath her cloak. As she turned to leave, she found Hannah, her face stained with tears, standing in the doorway.

"Hannah?" she asked with a frown. "Has something happened?"

"Y-your ... your Papa ... he ... he made me tell."

"Dear God! Oh, my poor Hannah! I fear I have placed you in an impossible situation."

"Mistress, you must stop him ... Jem heard him ask to have his horse at the ready ... and ... he ... I fear he means to harm Master William."

Ruby tore down the stairs, her blue cloak billowing behind her. As she neared the Great Hall, she skittered to a stop as the ominous figure of her father loomed above her.

"'Tis late to be running about the countryside, Daughter," his voice boomed. "Into the library, now." He turned and strode purposefully into the library. Ruby followed more slowly.

"P-papa ... I wished only for some air ..."

"Perhaps you should stay indoors tonight," he said.

"No."

"Do you dare defy me?"

"I do not wish to do so, Papa." She squared her shoulders and looked her father bravely in the eyes. "I will not allow you to harm him."

"You cannot prevent it unless you agree to forget him."

"I can never forget him, Papa. I love him. As you loved Mama."

"Your future is decided. You will marry Lord Devlin."

"I shall never marry him!" she declared.

"You shall, or your precious William Travers will die." He was staring out the window, his back to Ruby, watching the figure on horseback draw near.

Ruby sucked in her breath, her eyes searching the

room for anything that would gain her some time. Her eyes lit on a small, jeweled dagger that her father used as a letter opener. She snatched it up quickly.

"I will die before I marry that lecherous old man," she vowed. She raised the dagger to her breast. "Look at me, Papa."

Blake turned slowly, the blood draining from his face. "Ruby!" he croaked.

"I swear I will do it." Her eyes locked with his in a fierce battle of wills. "I will do it, and you will be responsible for the death of your only daughter."

"No, please God, no!" he shouted.

A commotion in the hallway diverted their attention. Seconds later, Blake's bailiff shoved William Travers into the room, his hands bound behind his back.

"William!" Ruby breathed. She kept the knife pressed against the soft flesh of her breast.

"My love!" His eyes betrayed his panic at Ruby's precarious position.

"Papa intends for me to marry Lord Devlin, William. I have vowed that I will die first!"

"No, my love, you mustn't! I beg you, sir, please release Mistress Ruby from such an undesirable union."

"Undesirable? Pah! He has a title and a large estate."

"He is also reputed to be the worst sort of lecher and a drunkard. Would you wish such a miserable life on your child."

"You have no proof of these accusations. Devlin is well-respected and a favorite of the Queen."

"I do have proof, sir; my dear cousin was ruined by Devlin, in the Queen's own court. Her name was Isabel DeBurke."

Blake paled noticeably at the woman's name. Her death had been as scandalous as the debauchery that had preceded it and, although no names had ever been mentioned, rumors had circulated that a high-ranking member of Court had been a party to it. Surely William Travers would not mention such a painful episode if it were not true.

"Dear God," Blake breathed. "My dearest Ruby, I fear I have nearly delivered you into the hands of the devil himself."

Ruby eyed him suspiciously. "You will not force me to marry Lord Devlin?"

"Never."

"And I shall choose the man I wed?" she asked softly. Her eyes locked with William's. Her heart beat furiously in her chest as she gambled on her future.

Blake didn't answer. He turned to the young man who had won his daughter's heart. "William Travers, what is your situation in life?"

"I am not so wealthy as you, sir, but I shall inherit Oaklands one day. It is a prosperous estate with a comfortable living."

"My Ruby is the most precious jewel I possess," Blake said quietly. "But I see now that I have been unwise, for her heart belongs to someone else."

"Aye, Papa, so it does," she whispered.

"I cannot stand in the way of her happiness. Ruby, my sweet daughter, do you wish to marry this young man?"

"I do, Papa."

"William Travers!"

"Sir?"

"Can I trust you with my precious gem?"

"Aye, sir. I love her."

"Release him," Blake ordered the bailiff. The bailiff quickly untied the knots at his wrists. "Ruby, the dagger." Ruby carefully placed the dagger in her father's hand. He dropped it on the desk and took his daughter's small hand in his. "My dear child, forgive an *old man for attempting to organize your life." After kissing her on the cheek, he took Ruby's hand and placed it in William's. "Do you wish to marry my daughter?"*

"Aye, sir, I do." William gently squeezed Ruby's hand. "May we ask your blessing, sir?"

"You have it, my children."

"Truly, Papa?"

"Yes, my sweet girl. I wish only that you be happy."

"I am, Papa. I am happy at last!"

Muffled sniffles filled the room. Lizzie blinked back tears as she glanced at Ruby. Real tears flowed down her cheeks. She reached up to brush them away, mystified at their existence. "Ghosts can't weep," she murmured. She laid her hand on top of Lizzie's, the barest whisper of a touch. "Thank you," she sniffled. "That is how it should have been."

"I've made you sad."

"Perhaps a little. But it's lovely to imagine the life we should have had."

CHAPTER 30

Snowhill was a flurry of activity as Colin's sisters and their families began to arrive. Dani and Rachel were absorbed into the rambunctious gang of Tori's cousins and by midweek they'd both affected decent imitations of their accents. Bev was busy with Helen, attending to the small, last minute wedding details and enjoying her daily afternoon tea with Lady Frances; Lizzie was amused by the growing friendship between the unlikely pair.

She missed Colin, but not in a neurotic 'I can't live a second without him' way. She missed him because everything was sweeter when she shared it with him.

"Pardon me, Mrs. Colin, but you've a caller in the drawing room," Marston, the butler, informed Lizzie as she supervised the decoration of the ballroom. "A Millicent Fenwick."

"Doesn't ring any bells," she shrugged. "Oh well, probably someone Darcy knows. You girls feel like tagging along?"

"Why not?" said Jess.

"Yeah, it's not often I get to entertain guests in the

329

drawing room," drawled Meg.

"I could get used to this life," Jess sighed.

"I doubt that will be a problem, Jess," Lizzie teased. "I see a gigantic rock in your immediate future."

"There you have it, darl. The great Lizzini has spoken," Meg said with a cheeky grin.

"No worries, Meg. I've got a prediction or two up my sleeve for you," she said as they walked through the Great Hall to the formal drawing room.

"Oh, that's not nice. You can't say things like that and not tell," Meg protested.

"I'll tell. I promise. When the time is right."

"Witch," Meg muttered.

"I heard that," she shot over her shoulder as they entered the drawing room. "Mrs. Fenwick?"

Lizzie's mystery guest was an elderly tweed-clad lady with silver-blue hair. She stood when they came into the room and smiled warmly. "Mrs. Blake?"

Lizzie nodded.

"I do hope you'll forgive my dropping 'round unannounced."

"Of course," she murmured with a smile. "How do you know my husband?" Lizzie motioned for the older woman to sit back down and she and her friends did the same.

Mrs. Fenwick smiled mysteriously. "I don't, except by reputation."

"Oh, then … how can I help you, Mrs. Fenwick?" Lizzie asked, hoping her confusion wasn't too obvious.

"I have a gift for you," she said. "And please, call me Millicent."

"A gift? I'm sorry, now I'm really confused."

"You'll have to forgive her, Millicent," said Meg.

"She's getting married … again … on Friday, you know," said Jess.

"Not to mention she's up the duff," Meg said with a

laugh. Millicent looked at her blankly. Meg rolled her eyes and translated. "Preggers."

"Ah, I see." Millicent patted Lizzie's hand reassuringly. "Forgive an old lady for attempting a bit of mystery, dear. About thirty years ago a distant uncle passed on and left me a crumbling manor house. I wager you might see it from your grand towers on a clear day. My uncle hadn't kept the place up and I was forced to sell off a most of the furnishings to pay for repairs. I only kept a few items. This was one of them." She pointed to a large flat package wrapped in plain brown paper. "Perhaps I should mention the name of my home. It's Oaklands."

"Oaklands?" Lizzie breathed. "That house has an ancient connection to Snowhill."

"I know, my dear. Open the package."

Lizzie slipped off the sofa to kneel beside the package. Slowly, she ripped away the paper to reveal a portrait of a fair-haired young man in Elizabethan garb. She knew without asking that she was looking into William Travers gentle, haunted green eyes. A glance at the small, gold nameplate on the frame confirmed her suspicion. "How did you know?"

"My dear, Ruby and William's story is legend in this county. Our very own Romeo and Juliet. The entire neighborhood knows what you've planned. It seems only fitting that William's portrait should hang beside his beloved Ruby."

"Oh, Millicent, I don't know what to say," Lizzie sniffled.

"Say yes," she said with a gentle smile. She gazed fondly at the portrait. "I'll miss him, but he belongs with Ruby."

By evening, Snowhill was brimming with wedding guests. Wings that hadn't been used for years had been cleaned and refurbished and extra staff had been hired to keep the estate running smoothly. It felt incredible to have everyone that she loved together in one house.

Lizzie was overjoyed to have Colin back in her arms. No matter that it had only been a few days – she'd missed him terribly. So, while Helen and her sisters-in-law helped her family and friends settle in, Lizzie dragged Colin up to their suite for some alone time. Midway up the staircase, she stopped and looped her arms around his neck. "Was I too obvious?" she asked, wiggling her eyebrows.

He chuckled and brushed her lips with his. "Not at all, Lizzie my love, you were …" He kissed her again. "Perfectly subtle."

"Yeah, right," she giggled. "I'm surprised you don't have whiplash as fast as I dragged you out of there."

"Now you mention it, my neck is a bit sore," he said with a grin.

"Well then, I think I'd better get you into bed ASAP!"

"Brilliant idea, Mrs. Blake." He swept her into his arms and limped up the remaining stairs. Lizzie laughed and nuzzled her face into his shoulder as he carried her to their room. "Welcome home, Lord Colin," she whispered. "I missed you!"

"I missed you too, love," he said softly as he pushed the door open with his heel. Once inside, he kicked it shut again, strode across the room to the bed, and set her down gently. He stretched out facing her and played idly with the buttons on her blouse. Now that they were together, and alone, he seemed to be in no hurry. Neither was she.

He reached up a hand, his strong fingers softly caressing her cheek. "It's humbling, isn't it? Knowing you've found the one person you're meant to be with?"

She nodded, knowing exactly what he meant. "I

never let myself believe that life could be so sweet. But you ... Tori ... these little guys ..." She rubbed her hand over her belly. "I'm so blessed, Darcy. It makes me feel a little guilty."

"Guilty, why? Because of Ruby and William?"

"I know it's silly. I just wish ... They should have been together. They deserve so much more than a ghostly existence."

"Perhaps tomorrow night will free them."

"I hope so." She attempted a feeble smile.

"You can do better than that, Lizzie," Colin said gently. "C'mon ... where's that world-class smile of yours?" He grinned at her, his dimples dancing in his cheeks. "I know it's there ..." He leaned forward and nibbled on the corner of her mouth. She felt her lips curling into a smile. "Much better," he said with a self-satisfied smile. He pulled her forward, enfolding her snugly in his arms as his smiling mouth found hers again.

It began slowly, a languorous voyage of renewal and rediscovery. Kisses deepened, intensified as hot caresses seared her flesh. Buttons popped, scattering across the bed. Clothing was tossed carelessly, landing where it would, and Lizzie lay naked, quivering in Colin's strong arms.

In the afterglow, exhausted and content, she sighed happily and rested her head on his chest. "Life is damn near perfect."

"Damn near?" Colin croaked. "After that? I'm deeply hurt ..." he said with a mock pout.

"Poor baby," she teased.

"Seriously," he said. "How on earth could life be any more perfect?"

She angled her body up so she could look him in the eyes. "Well," she said with a laugh, "it would help if I didn't have a button poking me in the ass!"

"Arse," he corrected.

"You say 'aahss', I say 'ass', but I guarantee you one thing, Colin Darcy Blake."

"And what might that be, my Lizzie?"

"We're not calling anything off. Not ever!"

"You might think it odd to have a funeral four hundred years after the fact," Colin began.

"Or the day before a wedding for that matter," Lizzie continued.

"But William Travers and Ruby Blake have waited a very long time to be together," Colin said. "Their tragic tale is legend in the Blake family. Ruby's presence has been constant here over the years. She's been our self-appointed protector and her appearances are well-documented."

"William is more mysterious. He's been doomed to wander in the glade along the road for four centuries. He's protected the Blakes, too, though he's always been a little shyer than Ruby." She squeezed Colin's hand tightly as emotions threatened to overwhelm her. "By now I think everyone has heard of my friendship with Ruby. She helped me through the worst days of my life, as William did for Colin."

"William and Ruby never had the chance to be together. Our hope is that by honoring them tonight, they'll share some of our happiness."

Colin nodded at Tori, who moved forward and placed a single, deep red rose atop the new coffin that held William's remains.

"Thank you both," Colin said, his voice husky with emotion. "Rest well, William Travers."

"Together," Lizzie added. She walked to the gravesite and laid her own rose on the coffin. She closed her eyes and paused for a moment in a silent prayer of gratitude. As she walked back to Colin, a single tear slipped down her cheek and spilled its salt on her lips. Colin cupped her face tenderly in his hands and wiped the tear away with the pad of his thumb. He bent and placed a soft kiss on her lips. She smiled up at him. "It's remarkable, isn't it, how quickly the sweetness of a kiss can dissipate the sadness of a tear."

"It is indeed," said a quiet voice at her side. The guests let out an audible gasp.

"Good evening, Ruby."

"Good evening, my friend."

Lizzie glanced at their guests. "Er ... everyone ... this is Ruby."

They stared at her with open-mouthed awe. "I don't believe it," sputtered her sister-in-law Lisa.

"See Mom, we *told* you she was real!" said Dani.

Ruby smiled at Lizzie. "I've come to thank you," she murmured. She tilted her head toward the back of the crowd. "And to perform a long-awaited introduction." The handsome young man from the portrait stood there, beaming at the woman he'd loved for four hundred years. "William, my love ..."

He glided toward her, his cloak blowing in the icy breeze until he stood in front of her. "'Tis far too long since I've held you in my arms, Ruby Blake."

"Aye, William. Far too long." She stepped into his arms for a kiss that had been four centuries in the making. It was, understandably, a lengthy, intense kiss. When they finally parted, Ruby blushed prettily in his arms then turned to face Colin and Lizzie. "There are not words to express our gratitude to both of you. No longer are we doomed to wander alone for eternity." She smiled up at William and he tightened his arm around her. "William, I believe you have already met Colin Blake."

"Aye. 'Tis a pleasure to see you in good health," he said.

"Welcome to Snowhill, William. I'm in your debt."

Colin said. "You saved my life … more than once."

William blushed, clearly uneasy at being the center of attention. "And you've given me a bit of mine back."

Lizzie glanced at Ruby and rolled her eyes. "Men," she mouthed. Ruby laughed.

"William, may I present my dear friend Anna Elizabeth Blake?" she said.

William took Lizzie's hand with a flourish and lifted it to his lips. He pressed a kiss to her knuckles. "I'm delighted to make the acquaintance of so brave a lady," he said.

"It's nice to finally meet you." She turned her eyes to Ruby. "Damn girl, how could you not mention that he's a total babe?"

"What was the word you used to describe your Colin?" she asked.

"Hunk."

"Ah … yes. Hunk." She grinned up at William. "Come, my hunk, let me show you my home at last." She turned to go.

"Ruby," Lizzie said before she walked away. "Will we ever see you again?"

She turned back, smiling. "You shall."

"Good. Will you come to the wedding tomorrow?"

"Of course we shall come. It's been ages since I've danced!"

"Oh, sweetie, you look so beautiful." Bev Kincaid smoothed Lizzie's hair and choked back tears.

"Thanks, Mom."

"Hyperventilating yet?" asked Meg.

"Nope. Cool as the proverbial cucumber."

"So we see," sighed Jess.

"Calm, cool, and collected, eh, mate?" Meg asked with a grin. "You do look gorgeous, darl."

"You guys look pretty hot yourselves." They wore

ruby red silk dresses that had the same slinky, body-skimming style as Lizzie's. "It's a good thing you're all spoken for."

"I'm not," Tori piped up. "I wish some cute boys were coming."

"Sweetie, if there were, your Dad would never let you downstairs. You look beautiful Tor, very grown up."

Tori kissed Lizzie on the cheek. "Shall I check on Daddy?"

"Why don't we surprise him?" Lizzie grinned. "Don't want to risk him making you wear one of those ancient suits of armor over your beautiful dress."

"Good plan, Mum."

There was a soft knock on the door. "Come in."

"Just me, Lizzie," said Helen. "Bearing gifts."

"Ooh! I love presents, but you really shouldn't have."

"I didn't dear. It's from Colin." She handed her a large black velvet box.

"I'm almost afraid to open it."

"Come on, Mum, we're dying here," said Tori.

She held her breath as she flipped the box open. An exquisite antique ruby and diamond necklace nestled in the blue silk lining, along with a matching bracelet and earrings. "Oh." She covered her mouth in surprise.

"Crikey," exclaimed Meg. "More of the family jewels?" She directed her question to Helen.

"In a manner of speaking," Helen said. "These particular jewels should have belonged to Ruby, but she never had the chance to wear them. After her death, they disappeared … until last night. Lady Frances asked me to get her pearl choker from the safe in the library. As I was feeling around, I found a small brocade bag. These were inside."

"Wow. They must've been there all along," Lizzie said.

"Perhaps. But I've been in that safe hundreds of

times, and I've never seen that set before."

"Another gift from Ruby?" asked Jess.

"Seems that way. I'd planned to wear this," she said, fingering her ruby cross. She reached back, unhooked the clasp and removed the necklace. "Tor ... would you like to wear it?"

"I'd love to, Mum." She turned, and Lizzie fastened the cross around her. "Now you."

Lizzie held the ruby necklace up to her neck. "It's perfect."

"Let me help you with that," said Helen. Helen secured the clasp and let the necklace fall, the gems cool and heavy against Lizzie's skin. She added the earrings and bracelet and stole a peek in the mirror.

"Oh, Aunt Lizzie!" gushed Rachel. "You look like a princess!"

"You really do," Dani agreed.

"Really?" she breathed. They both nodded solemnly. "I guess I'm ready then."

"Breathe," Jess reminded her. "You've been holding your breath for quite a while now."

"I'm afraid if I breathe, I'll wake up and all of this will be some cruel, bizarre dream," she admitted, yelping as Meg pinched her, hard on the arm. "Hey!"

"Just making sure you're awake, darl," she said with a sly smile.

"Well ... thanks I guess."

"So ... everyone ready?" Bev asked. She was answered with a chorus of yups, uh huhs and rightos. "Lizzie-girl? Are you ready?"

"Yes, Mom. I've been ready for this for a very long time."

Colin swirled the amber Scotch in his glass as he paced the library. His leg was almost healed though he still had a slight limp.

"You alright, mate?" Court was leaning against the fireplace, his glass on the mantel. "Having second thoughts?"

"Not a chance," Colin grinned.

"Just as well since you've already married her once," Sam grinned.

"And got her up the duff," added Lance.

"With twins," Colin laughed. "If anyone had suggested last Christmas that I would be married ..." He caught Court's raised eyebrows and amended. "Happily married, living in the States, and about to become a father again twice over, I'd have called them mental."

"It's been an eventful year for all of us," Lance said with a contented grin.

"Most of us, at least." Sam shot Court a pitying look. "You don't know what you're missing, mate."

Court lifted his glass and took a long, slow sip of Scotch. "Bunch of lovesick idiots. Which is perfectly fine if that's what you want."

"But you don't?" Colin asked.

"I'm happy enough as I am," he said with a shrug. "Though I must compliment you all on your taste." He lifted his glass. "To sweet Jess, magnificent Meg, and lovely, lovely Lizzie."

Though Court's toast was heartfelt and genuine, Colin didn't miss the hint of sadness in his old friend's eyes. "And you, Court?"

"Content to nibble at the buffet, thank you very much."

"So many women, so little time?" Sam asked with a smirk. "I used to envy you, you know."

"Most men do," Court said with a twisted grin. "No expectations, no regrets."

"Frankly, it sounds lonely and depressing," Lance said with a sigh.

"Says the man who did his best to keep up with me

until a few short months ago," Court laughed and glanced at the Grandfather clock. "Almost time."

"Let me guess ... you've got a hot date later?" Colin asked shaking his head.

"For once, no. But I did notice the cutest little brunette running around, attempting to bring order to the chaos. Wouldn't mind getting to know her. Not sure I caught her name ... Amy, perhaps?"

"Abby," Colin breathed. "Sorry, mate, she's out-of-bounds."

"Why is that?"

"Hmm. Let's see ... she's barely twenty-one, she has a boyfriend, she's Matt Brody's little sister, and she's a very old friend of Lizzie's."

"Who the devil is Matt Brody?"

"The minister."

"Oh. Crikey. That does change things."

"Yeah, I thought it might." Colin laughed softly and clapped his friend on the back. "Alright, mate?"

"I reckon I'll survive," Court said with a sigh.

"Ah," Colin said. "You're my oldest friend, Court. I hope that one day you'll choose to do a bit more than merely survive."

"Bloody unlikely," Court said, downing the rest of his drink in one gulp. "Now then, we don't want to keep your beautiful bride waiting."

Lizzie descended the grand staircase slowly. Her father shook his head and winked at her. He looked handsome, if a little uncomfortable, in white tie and tails. "Oh, Daddy!"

"You're gorgeous, pumpkin," he said. "I guess you're not my little girl anymore," he whispered.

"Daddy, I'll always be your little girl. Remember? My heart belongs to daddy," she teased.

He smiled at her and kissed her on the cheek. "Thank

you for saying so, but I know that your heart belongs to Colin now."

"It's big enough for both of you," she insisted.

"Then I'm happy to share. So, what do you say? Ready to get this show on the road?"

She expelled a deep breath. "Yes, Daddy. Let's go."

Lizzie peeked into the ballroom. Colin stood at the end of the aisle, breathtakingly handsome in his tailcoat. He glanced up as the string quartet began playing and she caught his eye and winked.

Court, Sam, and Lance escorted Helen, Lady Frances and Bev to their seats, but not before Lance and Sam took a second to steal a quick kiss from their respective girls. "Cheeky devils, aren't they?" said Meg.

Meg and Jess helped Dani and Rachel start the procession, kneeling to whisper instructions before the two girls began their walk down the aisle. "I'm next," said Jess.

Lizzie nodded, took a deep breath and squeezed her hand as she made her way down the aisle. Meg followed, then her maid of honor, Tori.

Colin's eyes grew wide when he saw Tori in her bridesmaid's gown. She faltered a little, and he smiled at her, mouthing, 'you're beautiful' as she took her position beside Meg.

Finally, it was Lizzie's turn. She took her father's arm and stepped into the ballroom.

A thousand candles cast a golden glow over the ballroom, and the heady scent of roses teased her nose. There were flowers everywhere - roses, lilies, gardenias, stephanotis - all red and white. Christmas greens - holly, ivy, mistletoe - added a festive note.

Her eyes scanned the assembled guests. Everyone that they loved was there.

But Lizzie could only focus on one person.

Colin.

She took a deep breath as her father escorted her down the aisle. Her eyes locked with Colin's as she moved closer and closer to him.

Finally, she was at his side. Her father took her hand and placed it in Colin's. Jim Kincaid kissed his daughter softly on the cheek and took his place beside her mother.

And Lizzie lost herself in Colin's intense, loving eyes.

He leaned in to her and whispered in her ear, his warm breath a soft caress on her cheek. "You take my breath away."

"So do you," she whispered back.

"Shall we begin?" asked her childhood friend, Matt Brody.

"Er … sorry," Lizzie said, blushing.

He smiled at them. "No problem." He paused for a second and looked up at their guests. "These two have been through a lot in the short time they've known each other. Since most of you weren't able to share their first wedding with them, they've decided to renew their vows here today." He nodded at Colin.

Colin lifted her hand to his lips for a feather-light kiss and curled his hand behind her neck. She loved the feel of it, heavy and warm, gentle and reassuring. His thumb gently stroked her cheek as his coffee-brown eyes smiled down into hers.

"I spent a very long time convincing myself that I didn't need anyone. Needing someone meant risking heartache and I'd already suffered my share of that. I spent all my energy building my business and trying to be the best father I could be." He winked at Tori. "I thought it was enough. I never understood how completely wrong I was until the night I first heard your voice. There was something there, something that drew me to you. And unlike so many of the people in my life, you spoke your mind. Rather bluntly, I might add." He grinned down at her and she rolled her eyes. "Meeting you in person turned my world upside-down. The more time I spent with you, the more I *needed* to spend with you. And I found myself not minding in the least. That night at the airport, all I could think about was you. Leaving you … it simply felt wrong. And when I finally held you in my arms, everything felt right. Anna Elizabeth, you are the sweetest, funniest, sexiest, bravest woman I've ever known. How or why I'm lucky enough to spend my life with you, I'll never understand. But I will be eternally grateful. My Lizzie, having you to share the rest of my life with makes me happier than I dreamed possible. I promise to love you with all that I have and with all that I am, to be faithful and true, to work beside you as we share all of life's trials and joys, and to teach our children that love really *can* move mountains." He turned momentarily to his best man, Court, who handed him a ring. Lizzie looked at Colin questioningly as he slid the ruby and diamond eternity ring up her finger to nestle beside her engagement ring and the plain band of Turkish gold. He smiled sheepishly at her. "I realize we said we wouldn't, but I couldn't resist."

"You're spoiling me again, you know."

"Good. That's what I intend to spend the next sixty years doing."

"Sixty years? Oh, I love the sound of that." She looked down for a moment, collecting her thoughts, then raised her eyes back to his and cleared her throat. "Like you, I'd given up on love. It seemed to be for everyone else but never for me. Then late one Friday night I picked up the phone and nothing's been the same since. It didn't take long for me to see that despite your reserve, deep down you were incredibly sweet, adorably shy, and intensely passionate. Finding you on my doorstep in the pouring rain was the happiest moment of my life, but it pales to how it felt finding you alive, in a pile of rubble, when I was afraid I'd lost you. We've already survived so much. With you, I know I can handle anything. So, Colin Darcy, I promise to love and care for you for the rest of our lives, to always be honest and devoted to you, to stand together in life's sadness and to embrace its joys, to show our children that family and love are what make us truly wealthy and truly blessed." She reached up to cup his face in her hand, stroking the cleft in his chin with her thumb. "I love you, Darcy."

"I love you, too, Lizzie."

They stood still for a long time, completely lost in each other, until Matt Brody cleared his throat and smiled indulgently at them. "Anna Elizabeth and Colin Darcy have pledged themselves to each other for the second time this evening. I don't know two people who belong together more. So, it's my honor and my privilege to pronounce them husband and wife. Again. Colin, you may kiss your bride."

Colin grinned down at her, his dimples deeply etched in his cheeks. "You don't have to tell me twice, mate." He enfolded her tightly in his arms and his lips found hers, first barely grazing them, then, unsatisfied, seeking them again in a kiss that was at once sweetly reverent and blissfully intense.

"I love you so much," Lizzie whispered as they slowly drew apart amidst the applause of their friends and family. "You're the best surprise I ever got.

EPILOGUE

Four months later...

Sometimes Lizzie still half-expected to wake up and find out that the last, incredible year of her life had been a dream. But then she'd feel Colin's warm, hard body curved behind hers and she'd smile. Life was far better than any mere dream that her subconscious could concoct and it just kept getting sweeter.

It was a typical Friday night at Pemberley Farm. Sam and Jess and Lance and Meg had dropped by with spicy Indian take-out that they ate picnic style on the living room floor.

Jess was curled up beside Sam, her head on his shoulder as his fingers stroked up and down her left arm. His hand settled on top of hers, fingering the antique engagement ring he'd given her at Christmastime.

"Are you really going to make me tell this story again?" she moaned.

"Of course," Lizzie said blithely. "You know what a sucker I am for true love, and you wouldn't want to disappoint an extremely pregnant woman, would you?"

"I'd advise against it," Colin advised sagely. "I speak from experience."

"That you do," she grinned. "We'll call that a growth experience for you. So ... Jess ... go on."

Jess rolled her eyes and smiled at Sam. "After your wedding, we stayed at Snowhill through Christmas Eve. When I mentioned I'd never been to London, the next thing I knew we were on our way. It was wonderful, just the two of us at Sam's flat. We had so much fun exploring the city; Sam even pretended to be American once or twice ... he does a hell of a Midwest accent. Sorry ... I'm rambling ..."

"I love it when you ramble," Sam drawled in his best imitation of Jess. "It's very sexy."

"I ... oh ..." Jess blushed hotly. "So anyway ... Christmas night we took a walk along the Thames. It was so romantic; the air was cold and misty, but there were a few stars out. We were almost at the Tower Bridge when Sam dropped something. He bent to pick it up, and there he was in kneeling on one knee in front of me. So I laughed and said 'hey if I didn't know better I'd think you were about to propose.' and he got the goofiest grin on his face. That's when my heart skipped a beat."

"I looked up at her and said 'what if I was?'" Sam continued.

"At that point, I didn't know what to think. So I said 'if you were, I'd say yes.' Next thing I knew, he pulled a ring out of his pocket, slipped it on my finger and said 'I'll hold you to that, Jess.' So here we are."

"It's a beautiful story, Jess," Lizzie sighed. "Still, it feels weird that in six months you'll be what ... my niece-in-law?"

"Crikey. She'll be mine as well," said Meg who was blissfully curled on Lance's lap. "Fancy another trip to Vegas, darl?"

"Nothing could top the last one, love," he said.

"Thank God for unexpected layovers."

"Strewth," Meg chortled. "Shall I continue?"

"Yup," Lizzie nodded.

"Righto. I asked Lance to come home to Perth with me for the holidays. Meet the folks and all that. Had a lovely visit ... showed him off to all my friends ... took him to my favorite beach and out to the farm. Mum and Dad adored him, but then look at him." She winked at Lance. He grinned crookedly back at her. "Rowr."

"Right back atcha, love," he grinned. "I can't wait to go for a longer visit."

"Two weeks wasn't nearly enough," Meg agreed. "But we'd promised to be back by New Year. The flights were smooth until we got to Los Angeles, but our plane had mechanical problems, so we were forced to land in Las Vegas."

"At first, they said we'd only be on the ground for about an hour, but they later told us the flight wouldn't leave until the morning."

"So there we were, trapped in Las Vegas for the night. We started ringing hotels, trying to find a place to stay. I called what I *thought* was the Bellagio, but I must've misdialed. Instead of the front desk clerk, I was talking to a wedding planner at the Little White Wedding Chapel. Lance had gone to find us something to drink, and when he got back, I said, 'I've just been making wedding plans.' He just sort of chuckled and said, 'sounds like the perfect way to spend the evening ... what do you say, Meg? Shall we call back that wedding chapel?' After that, things happened pretty damn fast. The chapel sent a car to pick us up ... a pink Cadillac, no less. Within an hour, we were being married by an Elvis impersonator. He even serenaded us."

"Well I'm glad you decided to have it broadcast on the Internet, even if it was four in the morning here," Lizzie said.

"Yeah, at least we got to see it," Jess agreed. "Ladies, we have the three most amazing guys."

"We are incredibly lucky," Lizzie agreed, smiling gratefully at Colin.

"You've got it wrong, Lizzie," said Colin. "We're the lucky ones."

"We're *all* lucky," said Meg.

"Can't argue with that," Lizzie said as she massaged her lower back. "Whew."

"You okay, Lizzie?" Colin frowned.

"Yeah, just a little tired. My back's been killing me off and on all day."

"Er ... Lizzie, love? Has it been getting worse?"

"Now that you mention it, yes. Seems to come and go ... damn ... there it is again." She sucked in her breath as she felt another strong twinge in her lower back.

"Lizzie?"

"Yeah, Darcy?"

"Has it occurred to you that you're having contractions?"

"Wha? No. Can't be. I'm not due for two weeks."

"Darl, babies can't tell time," Meg teased.

"And twins have a habit of coming early," Jess reminded her.

"I ... oh my God! I'm having a baby!" She stood up and began to pace, not sure what to do next. "Christ! I'm having two babies!"

"Perhaps we should get to the hospital?" Colin suggested.

"Brilliant idea, Darcy. I knew there was a reason I married you." Lizzie turned to their friends. "Uh, sorry to run out ..."

"No worries, darl," Meg drawled. "Seems you've a more pressing engagement. Besides, we're coming with you."

Colin stood by the window, incredibly sexy in his green scrubs as he cradled their son in his arms. He walked over and sat beside Lizzie on the bed, gently stroking the dark curls on their daughter's head. "They're almost as gorgeous as their mum," he murmured.

"You're sweet to lie like that. I'm a mess."

"A beautiful mess, then," he insisted. "I love your mummy very much," he told the twins.

There was a soft knock on the door, and Tori pushed it open a crack. "Can we come in?" asked Tori. "I want to meet my brother and sister."

"They want to meet you too, Tor. Come on in."

Tori pushed the door open the rest of the way and came in, along with Sam, Lance, Meg and Jess. "Everyone, meet Sarah Ruby Blake. Would you like to hold her, Tori?"

Tori nodded, and Lizzie carefully handed her baby sister to her. "She's lovely, Mum, but so tiny!" She gently stroked the baby's little fingers. "Hallo, Sarah," she whispered. "I'm your big sister, Victoria, but everyone calls me Tori. We've a brother as well, but I suppose you already knew that."

"I reckon you're right about that, Tor," Colin said with a chuckle. "This big bruiser is your brother, Nicholas William."

"Hallo, Nicky," Tori cooed. "You're a handsome lad, aren't you?"

"They're so cute!" said Jess. "My little baby cousins-in-law! Well, almost."

"Near enough," said Colin.

"They're gorgeous," gushed Meg.

"Would you like to hold him?" Colin asked.

"Why not?" said Meg. She took the baby carefully from Colin and cradled him in her arms. Nicholas yawned contentedly and snuggled closer.

"Looks like he likes his Auntie Meg," Lizzie grinned.

"Lad shows good taste," Meg said.

"Good taste runs in the family," said Colin. He hugged Lizzie gently and brushed a soft kiss on her lips. "Do you realize what today is, Lizzie?"

"Last I checked it was our babies' birthday," she said dryly. "April twenty-fifth."

"And?"

"And, what? Wait ... why does that date seem familiar?"

"Because, love, the first time we spoke was *last* April twenty-fifth."

"Really? You were a real pain in the ass, you know," she reminded him.

"I know. But you fell in love with me all the same."

"I couldn't help myself. I still can't. I fall more in love with you every day."

"So do I."

"Darcy ... thanks for remembering." She looked around the room at their happily paired off friends, and at their children, realizing how many wonderful things had resulted from that single event. "Funny how it's all worked out."

"It's all worked out just as it was meant to," he sighed. "Have I told you lately how very much I love you?" He reached up to caress her cheek with the pad of his thumb.

She nuzzled her face into his touch and smiled at him. Her heart-stoppingly handsome lover. Her gently supportive partner. Her dearest friend. "Not in the last ten minutes," she sighed. "I'll never get tired of hearing it, or saying it back. I love you so much."

A loud pop echoed in the small room, startling Colin and Lizzie from their intimacy. She'd been so lost in him she'd nearly forgotten where she was and why, let alone the fact that they weren't alone.

"You two done being all mushy?" Meg asked with a wry grin. "Lance has popped open a bottle of bubbly …"

"I can't." Lizzie shook her head. "No alcohol for me."

"No worries, darl. It's sparkling cider," she assured her.

"Well okay then. What are we drinking to?" she asked as Lance handed her a plastic cup full of pseudo-champagne.

"To babies!" said Tori.

"To wonderful friends," said Jess.

"To true love," added Meg.

"And to surprises," Lizzie said, winking at Colin.

"To surprises," he echoed. "May there be *many* more."

Please keep reading for a sneak peek at
the next story in Lily Dobb's
Crossroads series

Tessa's Prince
Coming 2016

New Year's Eve

Simon Prince leaned against the polished oak bar staring intently across the dance floor. Absently, he swirled his drink, watching the amber scotch circle the glass. He took a sip and returned his gaze to the two women on the other side of the room.

His sister, Kimberly, looked radiantly happy, but then she had good reason. Just hours ago she had married her childhood sweetheart, David Jameson. It had touched Simon more than he cared to admit to witness the union of two people so obviously meant for each other - and so deeply in love. His sister had made a lovely bride, but it was the young woman beside her that had him captivated.

Tessa Jameson. David's sister and Kimberly's long-time best friend. Simon remembered the first time they'd met, the day that he, his sister, and their mother had moved in next door to the Jamesons. She was six; her long red hair was braided down her back, and a mischievous twinkle lit her turquoise blue eyes as she stuck out her tiny, grubby hand in greeting. "Hi there," she'd said. "I'm Tessa. I'm six." She was a charming child and in an instant, she'd claimed a small piece of his fifteen-year-old heart.

After their parents' messy divorce, he, Kimberly, and their American mother had moved from England to her small Pennsylvania hometown. He'd felt an instant and special kinship with the sweet, bright little girl.

But when had the little girl been replaced by this lovely, poised young woman? She was petite and slender, her long flame-red hair styled in an elegant French twist, exposing a tantalizing glimpse of the creamy skin of her neck. Simon expelled a heavy sigh and dragged a hand through his unruly black hair. 'At least I have an excuse to dance with her,' he thought. He knew she'd had a crush on him years ago. Now he found himself wondering ... hoping ... that maybe she still did.

"You okay, Simon?" The soft voice belonged to his good friend and second cousin, Lizzie Kincaid. "You look a little ... lost."

"Do I?" he said absently. "I ... I guess I can't believe my baby sister's a married woman."

"Liar," Lizzie laughed, smoothing a hand over the soft velvet of her bridesmaid's gown. "Can't take your eyes off her, can you?"

"Who? Kimmy?"

Lizzie expelled a snort of frustration and shook her head slowly. "Idiot."

"Wow, Lizzie. Not nice. Not nice at all."

"I call 'em as I see 'em, Simon. You've been staring at Tess since the moment she walked down the aisle tonight." She smiled up at him reassuringly. "It's okay, you know."

"She's just ... she's always been my little princess. Now ... now ..." He lifted his glass and took another sip of his drink.

"Now she's all grown up?"

"She's still just a kid," he protested.

"Face it, Simon. She's not a kid anymore. And judging by the look on your face, you're well aware of that fact. The question is, what are you going to do about it?"

"Do?" Simon asked with a frown. "What the hell

would I do, Lizzie?"

Lizzie took a sip of her champagne and patted her cousin's hand. "Let's see … for starters, you could figure out if that unbreakable bond the two of you have had forever might be more than a rather unique friendship."

"I … you … no," he said firmly.

"Positive about that?" she asked him. "After watching Kim and David's feelings grow and change over the years?"

"That's different."

"I'll give you that. But, Simon, you can't deny that you've always had a special place in your heart for Tessa."

"Well, no."

"Anymore than you can deny that you're completely blown away by the fact that your little princess is now a beautiful woman."

"I … she is beautiful," he muttered. "But, Jesus, Lizzie, don't you think it'd be bizarre?"

"Probably," Lizzie admitted. "But Simon?"

"Yeah, Lizzie?"

"Bizarre or not, somehow I think it might be inevitable. I guess it's up to you to decide." She stood on tiptoe to kiss him on the cheek. "Good luck."

Across the room, Tessa was helping Kimberly bustle up the full train of her satin wedding gown. She glanced up and noticed that Simon was watching her. Again. But every time she caught him, he looked away quickly. "What's up with Simon, Kim?"

"What do you mean, Tess?"

"Why's he keep staring at me like that?" Tessa found it unnerving that the object of all her adolescent fantasies was gazing at her, especially since she'd never quite gotten over the fantasies.

"Like what, sweetie?" She glanced across the room at her big brother and grinned at the naked longing on her brother's face. "Oh, you mean like you're Little Red Riding Hood, and he's the Big Bad Wolf?"

"Kim!" Tess exclaimed as a blush warmed her cheeks. "Jeez! I just meant … why is he staring at me like he's never seen me before?"

"Probably because he hasn't. Have you even looked in a mirror lately, Tess?"

"I'm just me. I haven't changed."

"Like hell you haven't. Last time Simon saw you, you were a flat-chested fourteen-year-old with a mouthful of braces and a bad haircut. Now look at you. Especially in that dress," she said referring to Tess's midnight blue velvet bridesmaid's dress. "I should be mad at you for stealing my thunder, you know."

"Still, don't you think it's weird?" Tessa asked with a frown.

"Sweetheart, what would be weird is if my brother wasn't staring at you. You're gorgeous, you know. And I suspect my poor big brother is trying to figure out exactly when his little princess went and grew up on him."

"I'll always just be the cute little girl with the big crush," she sighed. "I mean … I know your brother loves me, but … I'll always be a little girl to him. I … I think maybe it's time I accepted that."

"I think you're wrong," Kim said, glancing over at her brother. "That may have been true a few hours ago, but now? I wouldn't be so sure. Now … it's time for the wedding party to dance. Be kind to my brother, okay? Try to relieve some of poor Simon's misery."

'Perfect fit,' Simon thought as Tessa melted into his arms for their dance. He swallowed a sigh as his hand brushed the silky skin of her bare shoulder. "You look stunning, Tess."

Tessa looked up at him and smiled. "Thanks. You look pretty good yourself, Simon."

"I've been trying to figure out just when you went and grew up on me." He smiled as she blushed prettily in his arms. "How old are you now?"

"You can't not remember!" she said with a pout. "You never forget my birthday."

"I'm just teasing, Tess. I know very well that you'll be eighteen in … wow … in thirteen minutes. Will you save me your birthday dance?"

Tessa nodded happily. "Have you heard my big news?"

"Hmm. I know that you graduated a year early from high school and that you've just finished your first semester of college. Should I know something else?" He winked, teasing her again, enjoying the playful banter almost as much as the feel of her slender body in his arms.

"You're teasing me again!"

"Guilty. Of course I know that you've been accepted into the best art school in Paris. You're as profoundly talented as you are beautiful," he said proudly. "I always knew you'd make it, Princess."

"Thank you," she said, looking down shyly. "I'm so excited! Paris! Can you imagine?"

"For you? Yes. It's a magnificent city, Tess. Ancient. Luminous. Romantic. I can't imagine a more perfect setting for you."

"I … you … really?" she squeaked.

Simon smiled down at her and drew her body just the tiniest bit closer to his. "Really. You know …"

"What?" she breathed.

"Nothing," he mumbled.

"C'mon, Simon. It's just me. What were you going to say?"

"Only … I'm based in London …"

"Well, yes, I do know that," she interrupted.

"It's just … it'll be nice, you know? Having you nearby? I … I've missed you, Tess."

"You have? I …" her bright blue eyes searched his. "Me too."

Simon kept her by his side as midnight approached. He still felt a little strange about acknowledging his attraction to his baby sister's best friend, but he *was* attracted to her. And he needed to know if, maybe, she felt the same.

He grabbed two glasses of champagne from a passing waiter and pressed one into her hand.

"I'm not twenty-one," she protested.

"It's just one glass," he said, "and you're not driving. Besides, it's New Year's and it's your birthday."

"I guess it's okay then." She fanned her face, still flushed from their dance. "It's hot in here."

"Why don't we get some air?" he suggested. He placed a hand on her elbow and guided her through the French doors to the balcony. The cold air nipped at Tessa's bare shoulders, and she shivered. Simon removed his tuxedo jacket and helped her into it. The jacket still bore the heat of his body. Tessa snuggled into the warmth and sighed as she inhaled the scent of his spicy cologne. "Better?" he asked.

"Uh huh," Tessa said, taking a tiny sip of her champagne, She set the glass on the railing and grinned up at him. "I like it."

"I thought you might," he said with a chuckle. "Do you want to go back in for the big countdown?"

"No," Tessa whispered, shaking her head. "I'm happy here."

The revelry of the New Year's countdown echoed from inside. Simon smiled down at Tessa as cries of 'Happy New Year' rang out, and champagne corks popped.

"Happy New Year, Simon," she said as the crowd sang Auld Lang Syne.

"Happy New Year, Tessa," he said. He cupped her chin in his hand, his thumb softly stroking her cheek. "Happy Birthday," he whispered as he lowered his lips to hers.

She gasped as his lips brushed hers ever so softly. Her lips parted of their own accord and what Simon had intended as a simple, chaste kiss flared into something much more. His hands slipped beneath the jacket she wore - his jacket - his fingers digging into the soft velvet of her gown as her arms wound tightly around his neck, urging him ever closer. He groaned, and she pressed her lithe body to his as their mouths continued their discovery.

"Sweet Jesus, Tess." He fought to regain control over his emotions and his body before they both tread down a path of no return. His hands stroked soothingly down her back. "How can this be?"

"It just … is." She caressed his cheek, her fingers barely touching his skin. "It just is."

"We can't," he said softly, though he refused to release her.

"Why can't we?" Her eyes held a challenge.

Simon didn't have an answer. "We shouldn't."

"Why?"

"Jesus, Tess, I've known you since you were a child."

"I'm not a child anymore."

"I noticed. God, how I noticed. Tess … if we … get involved …"

"If? After that kiss, I'd say we already are. Simon … don't overthink this. Forget that you've known me since I was six. Pretend we've just met, two adults who … who have feelings for each other. Unless … unless you don't … " she looked down, tears welling up in her eyes.

Simon tilted her chin up with his hand, his green eyes searching hers. "God help me, but I do. Tessa ... I don't want to interfere with the plans you've made ..."

"Nothing's going to do that, Simon. I've dreamed of studying art in Paris forever, as you're well aware. But ... if we both feel ... whatever it is we feel ... then maybe we owe to ourselves ... and ... and to each other to figure out what this is ... or could be."

"How are you so wise?"

"I'm an old soul, Simon, remember?" Tessa shrugged and stood on tiptoes to kiss him softly. "So ... do we have a deal?"

"Are you certain, Tessa? I would never want to cause you pain."

"I'm sure, Simon."

"We'll have to take things slowly. And you aren't to give up your dreams."

"We will and I won't. Now ... you owe me another dance ..."

"I have a better idea," he murmured. "I ... what do you say we make our escape? Find someplace where we can ..." Simon took a deep breath. "Talk."

"Just talk?"

"Well ... maybe not just," he admitted. "God, Tess, this is all ..."

"A lot to wrap your head around?" she giggled. "I get it, Simon. I know it's ... strange and ... and ... unexpected but ..." she shrugged and stood on her tiptoes to kiss him softly. "It's good, isn't it?"

"Yes, Tess, it's good. And somehow it feels ..."

"Right?" she supplied.

"Yes. Right." He leaned in for one more sweet, slow kiss, shaking his head slowly as he lifted his lips from hers. "I don't pretend to understand it but, yes, Tessa, it feels so very right."

Tessa stared into the fireplace, watching the flames for a moment before turning her face back to Simon's. "So what happens now?"

'Honestly? I don't have a clue," he sighed. "I think we're in uncharted territory here." He tightened his arms around her, urging her body closer. "You've always held a piece of my heart, you know."

"I ... I guess I did, but ... I never thought we'd end up here. I ... I hoped it. Forever, it seems." She leaned her head back, smiling softly at him. "When I was little, I truly believed that you were my very own fairy tale prince. When I hit puberty, well, it all got tangled up in a crush that I knew was impossible, no matter how much I wished it wasn't."

"And yet here we are," Simon smiled. "Tess, I need to ask you ... is it still a teenage crush?"

Tessa shook her head firmly. "You were busy establishing yourself as a war correspondent. You stopped coming home. I ... I took everyone's advice and moved on, Simon. I went on dates, had a couple of boyfriends and ... let the idea of you go."

"What does that mean?"

"It was a fantasy, Simon. No matter how much I wanted it, I knew it could never be real. Not then." She reached up to run her fingers through his silky black hair. "But now? It's different, Simon. Yes, you're still my childhood hero and my adolescent crush, but it feels different. I feel ... more. I can't ... I can't quite put it into words." Instead, she reached out to trace his lips with one trembling finger. A moment later, she brushed her lips against his, once, twice, three times, before settling on them, teasing and tasting until they were both breathless.

"Jesus, Tess," he groaned. "Are you always this bold?"

"No. Only now, Simon. Only for you. I ... you ... we

..." She laughed softly, ducking her head against his chest for a few seconds before meeting his eyes again. "We've always had this connection and ... honestly, it never made sense, did it? But still, there it was. Now, finally, I think it makes sense. I ... please don't take this the wrong way, but I feel like maybe ... we're just ... meant to be but we just had to ... to ..."

"To wait until it made sense?" he murmured.

"Yes," she breathed. "Weird?"

"Special," he corrected. "But, Tess?"

"Yeah, Simon?"

"It doesn't feel weird anymore. I looked up tonight and saw you coming down the aisle, and you took my breath away. I ... I knew that you were still my Princess, but ... suddenly you were this stunning woman that made my heart pound."

"Do I?" she breathed. "Do I make your heart pound."

Simon took her hand and placed it over his wildly beating heart. "Wow."

"Yes, wow," he said with a soft laugh. "You're not a little girl anymore, Tessa. You're a beautiful woman and ... God help me, I am insanely attracted to you."

"You say that like it's a bad thing," she frowned.

"Definitely not bad," Simon assured her, "just unexpected in the most amazing way. I ... I adore you, Tess, you know that. I'm ... overwhelmed at the idea that my sweet little friend is now something so much more and ..."

Tessa silenced him with a kiss, slowly exploring his mouth until he groaned and rolled her onto her back, his body pressing hers into the floor as he took control of the kiss. "Mine," he murmured against her lips. "Mine."

"Yes, yours. All yours." Tessa opened her eyes slowly. "In case there was any doubt, I'm insanely attracted to you, too."

"Oddly enough, I worked that out for myself when

you had your tongue down my throat just now," he teased. "What am I going to do with you?"

"Anything you want?" she breathed.

"Jesus, Tess, you instinctively know how to tempt me."

"But you're going to resist, aren't you?"

"For now, Tess. What we have here … it feels like it could be something real. I don't want to screw it up by moving too fast. Besides, in case you've forgotten, we're in my mother's living room, which happens to be next door to your parents' living room and … that's a lot of explaining that I'm not sure we're ready for."

"Point taken. So, what now?"

Simon laughed and rolled off of her, sitting up and drawing her into his lap. "I'm not due back in London for a week. We could date like normal people."

"Huh, there's a thought," she laughed. "What about the whole family thing?"

"We'll figure it out, Tess, I promise. There's one other thing you should know before we go any farther."

"And what's that?"

"I love you."

"Well, yes, of course, we are friends first, after all."

"No, Tess. What I meant was, I'm in love with you."

"How can you know that already?"

He brushed a strand of burnished red hair back from her face. "I think I knew it the moment that midnight kiss … ignited."

"You mean it?"

"Have I ever lied to you, Tess?"

"Of course not. You're my prince," she joked. "Princes don't lie."

"No, they don't. I love you, Tess. I will always love you."

Simon squinted at the numbers on the bedside alarm

clock. It was just past eight in the morning and, though he and Tess had talked until well past three, he was wide-awake. He threw off the covers and rolled out of bed, eager to see where the day would lead them. Out of habit, he flipped his laptop open and, while he waited for three days worth of emails to load, he jumped in the shower.

All he could think about was Tessa. The sudden attraction had thrown him for a loop and the kiss ... the kiss had changed everything. Grinning broadly at the unexpected turn his life had taken, he turned off the water and stepped from the shower. After towel-drying his hair, he wrapped a towel around his hips, headed back to the bedroom and quickly dressed in jeans and a sweatshirt.

He grabbed his laptop, scanning quickly through his emails. Three from his producer discussing his next assignment - he'd have to call him eventually to discuss the future, a few from friends, a ton of junk mail and, at the very bottom of the list, a name he hadn't seen in over four years. Caitlin O'Mara.

Like Simon, Caitlin was a journalist. They'd met in the midst of a war zone, covering the horrific war crimes in Croatia and Bosnia, and when they realized they were working the same story, they'd joined forces. In the bitter brutality of the war zone, they'd become friends and, after narrowly escaping with their story and their lives, they'd become lovers. The affair had fizzled after less than a month and, though they had parted as friends, he hadn't heard from her since.

Until now. Puzzled, he clicked on the email, expecting nothing more than a quick update from an old friend.

But what he read changed everything ...

Dear Simon,

I don't know where to begin, so I suppose I'll be blunt. You always said you liked that about me.

Four years ago, I did a terrible thing. When we were together, I got pregnant, intentionally, without your knowledge. You have a daughter ... her name is Moira, and she's three. She has a baby sister (not yours, of course) named Michaela. After everything I saw in Bosnia and Croatia, I needed a fresh start, away from the horrors of war, away from journalism. I wanted a home, and I wanted children. I found a way to have them. They're beautiful girls, Simon. They fill my life with so much light and joy that I have no regrets.

But there's more. I'm dying. I have terminal cancer. It was discovered when I was pregnant with Michaela, and I put off treatment until after she was born. Unfortunately, it was too late for me. I'm weak, and I'm tired. It's almost time for me to go, but I need to see you, to beg your help. I need to know that Moira and her baby sister are cared for and safe. I don't expect you to raise them, only to help find someone who will care for them and love them.

We were friends once. And lovers. You're the only one I trust to help me. Please come to Ireland. I need you. My daughters need you. I have no right to ask for your help, except the right of a desperate, dying woman.

Caitlin

You have a daughter. Four simple words that changed his life, forever. Simon read the email three times before the stark reality of the situation finally sank in, filling him with an overwhelming sense of responsibility - to an old friend's dying wish and to the child he didn't know who, somehow, belonged to him. He thought about Tessa for a moment and imagined her, still sleeping, dreaming about a future with him, It had only taken a moment for him to fall in love with her and now, only hours later, he couldn't promise her anything.

He pinched the bridge of his nose as if he could somehow keep the pain at bay and hit the reply button. He didn't waste time on thoughtful words or condolences, typing only 'I'll be there tomorrow' before clicking send. A moment later, he shoved his feet into well-worn sneakers, grabbed his jacket and headed to the house next door.

Tessa beamed when she heard the door slam at the house next door. She rolled out of bed and pulled on her favorite purple velour robe, belting it tightly as she moved to the window and pulled the curtain aside. Simon's head was down, his hands shoved deeply in his pockets. Something about the set of his shoulders made her nervous, but with the glow of the previous night's kisses still fresh in her mind, she blithely decided that it was a result of the frigid temperatures.

With her parents still sound asleep, she didn't bother getting dressed. In spite of what had happened the night before, Simon was still Simon. He was still her best friend and dearest confidante. Besides, he'd seen her in her jammies so many times over the years that it seemed silly, childish even, to get dressed simply because their relationship had changed.

Simon loved her. He wanted a future with her. As a little girl, it had been her nightly wish-upon-a-star. As a teenager, it had been her desperate, impossible fantasy. But now, as a woman, the reality was even sweeter than she had imagined. One moment, one kiss, had transformed everything. She sighed again, quickly finger-combing her thick curls before bounding down the steps.

She pulled the door open before he had a chance to

knock, beaming at him before throwing herself into his arms. "Morning!"

Simon reached up a hand to smooth her hair and brushed a soft kiss against her forehead. "We need to talk."

"Such ominous words!" she laughed, ignoring his frown as she tugged him into the house. "Mom and Dad are still sleeping so shh!" She sank onto the sofa, smiling expectantly up at him, but instead of sitting beside her and gathering her into his arms, he sat on the edge of the armchair and buried his face in his hands. "Did I do something wrong?"

"No ... I ..." He lifted his face to hers, his green eyes filled with such desperation that she could feel his pain. "We need to talk."

"Yeah, you already said that." She scooted to the end of the sofa and laid her hand on his folded arms. "Tell me what's wrong, Simon. I'm your friend, first, remember. You've dried enough of my tears over the years that it's only fair that I return the favor."

"Fair?" he mumbled. "Nothing fair about it."

"Okay, now you're freaking me out. Talk to me. Please?"

He nodded slowly, squeezing his eyes shut for a moment to collect his thoughts. "What happened last night was the most ... astonishing, incredible, unexpected gift. I need you to know that."

"I do," she murmured. "It was the same for me. So why am I sensing a but here?"

"I got an email from an old friend."

"Old friend or old girlfriend?" she asked. "I may be young, Simon, but I do realize that you had a love life before last night." She watched his face and when he wouldn't meet her eyes she had her answer. "Girlfriend."

"Both, actually," he admitted. "Honestly, under normal circumstances, I think we'd have only ever been friends. But the ugliness of war can alter your perspective pretty quickly … the romance was short-lived, and we parted as friends, though we lost touch."

"Until today."

"Until today. I … she … Caitlin … her name's Caitlin. She has terminal cancer."

"Oh, Simon, I'm so sorry!" She lifted her hand to stroke his cheek, and he covered it with his own.

"There's more. She has children. Two little girls who are about to lose their mother. I …"

"You want to help?" she nodded. "Of course you do because it's who you are … but, well … they aren't your responsibility."

"Apparently at least one of them is," he said bleakly. "I … she never … I never knew …" He looked up at her, his green eyes bright with tears. "I have a daughter, Tess. I have a daughter who is about to lose her mother …"

"Hey," she crooned. "We can figure this out."

He shook his head firmly. "I already have. I have to go, Tess. I won't let my child or her sister be completely alone in the world. I … I have to make this right."

"And what about me, Simon? What about us?" She inhaled sharply in a futile attempt to stop the tears that burned her eyes.

"I'm sorry, Tess. I … I can't burden you with this. You're too …"

"What, Simon? Too young? Too immature? I thought … I thought, after last night we were a team. Guess I was wrong." She stood up then, needing to distance herself from him, pacing the room as she waited for him to say that she was wrong. "Just go, Simon. It's what you meant to do since the second you walked in the door, isn't it? You made your decisions before you ever came over here and it's obvious that I'm not included."

"Damn it, Tess … that's not … I don't … you're wrong."

"Am I?" she spat out. "I may be young, Simon, but I'm not stupid. If what we found was real, you would've asked my opinion. You didn't, so I'll just accept that last night was nothing but a hot make-out session and some pretty, meaningless words."

"You know that's not true."

She folded her arms across her chest and whirled around to face him. "You need to leave."

"Tess … please …"

"What? Please, what? Please stop acting like a child? Please tell me what you think about all of this? Or please, just let me live my life on my terms?"

"I don't want to hurt you, Tess." He stood up and took two steps towards her.

She took three steps backward. "Too late for that," she said bitterly. "It's done."

"Damn it, Tess, I just need to figure this out and then …"

"No, Simon. If you don't want me to be a part of this, then you don't want me to be a part of your life, not really. It's done. Over. Just … just go."

In the end, he'd simply nodded slowly, tears streaming down his cheeks. He lingered at the door, waiting for her to say something. "I'll be back, Tessa."

"It won't matter. I won't be here. Goodbye." She kept her chin up, her tear-filled eyes locked with his. "Goodbye."

He left then, and Tessa shut the door behind him, resting her forehead against the smooth, painted wood as she waited five long minutes to hear the sound of his footsteps on the stone walkway. "You promised you wouldn't," she murmured. "But you did. You didn't believe in me, in us."

In the house next door, Simon leaned against the door of his bedroom. He'd hated the look on her face and the accusation in her voice. He understood that she wasn't angry about Caitlin or the child. She was angry because he couldn't, wouldn't, allow her to be a part of his decision. He hated himself for it, but it was the right thing to do. She was a vibrant, talented eighteen-year-old on the verge of achieving her dream to become an artist. To allow her to delay that just to keep her by his side would've been the most selfish act of his life, but, even so, he knew he'd done the one thing he'd promised never to do.

He'd caused her pain.

PHOTO BY CLARA FANG

ABOUT THE AUTHOR

Lily Dobb is a lifelong book lover and has been an avid reader of romance novels since she discovered her first Barbara Cartland book as a teen. She has been telling stories for many years and loves journeying with her characters as they find romance and true love. Lizzie's Surprise is her first novel, but most definitely not her last.

She loves to travel and explore the world, but she is proud to be a small-town woman at heart. Lily has deep roots in her hometown and enjoys the sense of community, friendliness, and connection that small town life offers and infuses it into her stories.

Like her heroine, Lizzie, Lily spent many years as a corporate travel agent until leaving the business to focus on her writing.

She lives in the same Southeastern Pennsylvania town where she grew up and loves that she can't go anywhere without running into someone she knows. When she isn't writing or editing, she likes spending time with family and friends, delving into her genealogy, going to the movies, her handsome black cat Ninja, and all things Disney.

Please visit her website www.LilyDobb.com to learn more.